Louise Candlish studied English at University College London, and worked as an editor and copywriter before writing fiction. She is the author of six previous novels – including *I'll Be There For You*, *The Double Life of Anna Day*, *Since I Don't Have You*, *Before We Say Goodbye* and *Other People's Secrets*, which are all also published by Sphere. She lives in London with her partner and daughter.

Visit her website at *www.louisecandlish.co.uk*.

Also by Louise Candlish

I'll Be There For You
The Double Life of Anna Day
Since I Don't Have You
Before We Say Goodbye
Other People's Secrets

The Second Husband

Louise Candlish

SPHERE

First published in Great Britain as a paperback original in 2008 by Sphere
This edition published in 2009
Reprinted 2010

A CIP catalogue record for this book
is available from the British Library.

Typeset in Sabon by M Rules
Printed and bound in Great Britain by
Clays Ltd, St Ives plc

Papers used by Sphere are natural, renewable and
recyclable products sourced from well-managed forests and certified
in accordance with the rules of the Forest Stewardship Council.

Mixed Sources
Product group from well-managed
forests and other controlled sources
www.fsc.org Cert no. SGS-COC-004081
© 1996 Forest Stewardship Council

FSC

Sphere
An imprint of
Little, Brown Book Group
100 Victoria Embankment
London EC4Y 0DY

An Hachette UK Company
www.hachette.co.uk

www.littlebrown.co.uk

For Nips

Acknowledgements

For their friendship and creative collaboration and sheer hard work, my heartfelt thanks to Claire Paterson and Jo Dickinson. Thank you also to Rebecca Folland, Kirsty Gordon and all at Janklow & Nesbit in London, and to Cullen Stanley in New York. Also to the wonderful Little, Brown editorial team, including Caroline Hogg, Louise Davies, Emma Stonex, Nathalie Morse, and to the sales and marketing teams, especially my publicist Alex Richardson. And to Jenny Richards for another beautiful cover (and lots of patience!). I'm so lucky to have all of you as my champions.

Thank you to everyone involved in the Miss Write competition: Waterstone's, *Cosmopolitan*, and of course the many entrants. Other magazines have also been incredibly supportive of my writing, including *Elle* and *Red*.

Thank you to friends and family for support during the writing of this book, including my sister Jane, my soon-to-be brother-in-law Michael, my parents and brother, Heather, June, Mats 'n' Jo, Michael, Dawn and Oliver, Ha, Dorothy, Sharon, Mandy, Pat, Catherine, Sara-Jade and Maureen.

Thank you to Joanna for advice about advice-giving. And for keeping my website looking so good, Phil Carre at www.think-creative.co.uk.

The usual huge thank you to Nips and Greta for enduring another year of artistic ups and downs! And to everyone who has written to me about *Since I Don't Have You* – your response has been truly heart-warming.

Finally, readers will spot a debt of gratitude owed to *Lolita* by Vladimir Nabokov. *Roxana* by Daniel Defoe is also highly recommended.

The Second
Husband

'It is a pity so much Love . . . on both Sides,
shou'd ever separate'
Daniel Defoe, *Roxana*

Chapter 1

The day I met Davis Calder I was too distracted by Roxy to pay any close attention to him. Actually, distracted is probably the wrong word. Needled, unsettled, anxious – any of those might better describe the feeling a mother gets when she sees her teenage daughter stretched out virtually naked in the middle of communal gardens; gardens that by definition provide a view from every neighbour's window.

It was a Saturday, a rogue summer's day at Easter, and she was sunbathing with Marianne. That was a name I heard a lot these days, Marianne Suter. She was Roxy's new best friend from school, a precocious minx if ever there was one. Her ambition was to become an actress (or 'actor' as she preferred it) and she was already on the books of some casting agent in the West End. She was the kind of girl who would once have been known as a 'wild child' and was, in my view, at least partly responsible for the sudden metamorphosis of my daughter from Pollyanna into Playmate of the Month.

Well, I could only pray that the effects had been limited thus far to outward styling. Today Roxy wore a tiny blue-and-white striped top cropped just below the bra; denim shorts rolled up so high at the leg and slung so low at the hip as to be no bigger than a pair of knickers; oversized sunglasses; charm bracelets on both wrists; and, finally, one of her brother Matthew's cartoon Elastoplasts stuck horizontally across her right calf (whether this was purely decorative or there was actually a graze beneath, I had no idea). Marianne, meanwhile, modelled a bikini barely a tone or two darker than her own skin and a floppy-brimmed sunhat in a floral print inspired by more innocent times. Between them they had somehow contrived to make their arrangement on two bath towels look like a photo-shoot for a men's magazine. Roxy paints her toenails baby pink! Marianne sucks a lollipop! All the better that sample exam papers lay strewn – unsampled – by their feet.

'Is this it?' Davis Calder asked me. He stood in the living room of the rental flat and scanned from corner to corner as though calculating the precise square footage of the place. About our faces motes of dust still swirled from my final dust and polish this morning. 'I mean, kitchen and sitting room all in one?'

'That's right, it's open plan.'

'Open plan.' He repeated the phrase as though I'd asked him to break a code. His voice was low and grainy, his accent standard educated London, though a little scuffed around the edges, which made it confident and easy. I'd noticed at once that he was attractive, for that would have been impossible to miss. He was in his early forties, at a guess, with a hint of scholarly superiority about the lips. Dark curls silvered thickly over the ears and sprang into his eyes, a statement that he had better things to do than think about what his hair was doing. I wasn't close enough to gauge the exact colour of his eyes, but they were dark and, not watchful exactly, more observing. He was tall and broad-built at the shoulders, his blazer immaculately tailored. Not quite the type to be living alone in a rented flat at this time of his life. (For some reason this made me think of my younger sister Tash, never settled, always moving on.)

'It hasn't been rented before,' he said, suddenly. 'Has it?'

'How can you tell?' I asked him, curious.

'Oh, I've seen quite a few places this week, and this is the first one that doesn't make me want to throw myself under a bus on the way out.' He fixed me with an intense look. Brown, that was the colour of his eyes, not the brown that Roxy and I shared, the type that changed in the light like an autumn leaf, but that rich, nut brown, true and steadfast. 'There's something quite soulless about a rental flat that's just been vacated, isn't there? Like a motel room, when there are still stray hairs from the person before. When you can still feel their body heat.'

Body heat. Now I wanted to repeat *his* words, though I stopped myself just in time. 'You make it sound like a crime scene,' I said, chuckling. 'And it's not that, I assure you.' I realised that he was eyeing not me but the shelving space behind me, and in a peripheral nook somewhere inside I registered disappointment.

'I live next door,' I added, though he hadn't asked. 'With my two children. It used to be all one flat, but we sectioned this bit off and gave it its own front door.'

He just blinked at this, as if to say, We both have our bad-luck stories, let's spare each other the details. For a second I forgot myself and allowed my eyes to transmit the message that I didn't want to be spared the details, I wanted to know, but he was already out of range. It was probably just as well.

'Can I open a window?' He strolled across to one of the windows, reached for the brass lock and pulled up the lower sash. I assumed he wanted to check how much traffic noise we got up here – not much, for we were right at the top of the building on the fifth floor – and waited as he closed it again and refastened the lock.

He was the sixth person to come to view the front portion of my flat and consider renting it from me for £250 a week. Perhaps it was my distress at having had to bisect my home in this way – literally walling off three of the nine rooms to create a separate apartment – that had made me a less than exuberant guide to the previous five. Two couples and a single woman had already been and gone, all professionals in their twenties and thirties, all charmed by the sun-filled living room that used to be my study. And it *was* charming, with its parquet flooring and original sashes, the fat old radiators that took up so much space but felt so nice to pat. The woman, a solicitor, had pulled out chequebook and references there and then, but I had waved her off, waved all of them off, murmuring of last-minute details that had to be attended to before any final decision could be reached. There were no details, of course; I had done everything required of a new landlord. But as long as I could put off that final handshake I could stave off my fear that my sanctuary was to be invaded, that my life would never be the same again.

'Would you like to see the bedroom?' I led Calder through to our old spare (now guests would be on the living-room sofa) and then to the bathroom beyond. 'There's only a shower, I'm afraid.' It was my old cloakroom-cum-utility room and made a decent-sized bathroom for a one-bedroom rental. My nine-year-old son Matthew suffered most from the loss of the space; playing sports most days, he had used it almost as a locker room. Muddy wellies and trainers were accommodated in the kitchen now, or out on the fire escape. Roxy, of course, kept her footwear in her bedroom, the better to conceal illicit new acquisitions. I tried to remember what she'd worn on her feet this morning as she trotted off to meet Marianne at the garden gate. Her flip-flops, possibly, the ones with an oversized pink rubber flower sprouting between big toe and second.

'So what do you think?' I asked him, finally.

He nodded, more to himself than in response to my question. 'It's a nice place, but a little small, to be honest. I've got a lot of books. There's no way I'd get them all in here.'

'Well, have a think about it. Would you like a coffee before you go?'

4

He looked at his watch. 'Yes, why not.' I wondered where he was going next, where he had come from.

There was no coffee in the small galley kitchen, nor anything to drink it out of, for that matter, agents having advised that tenants liked to bring their own kitchenware, so I led him into the shared hallway, through my new front door and into the rear corner of the mansion block. Our kitchen was east facing, with windows on two sides and a glass door to the fire escape, which meant lots of warm sunlight early in the day. The previous owner had laid an extravagant chequerboard of marble and in weather like this you could almost spirit yourself to Italy, to the terrace of some palazzo in the hills. As I spooned coffee into two mugs I tasted the forbidden tang of a long-buried memory, my honeymoon with Alistair, Roxy's conception . . . though we didn't know that then. A lifetime ago – or at least a whole childhood. She was seventeen now.

'Here we go.' As I set the mug down in front of Calder I saw he was looking out of the window at Roxy and Marianne. Impossible not to, for they were plum in the centre of the lawn, long-wintered limbs gleaming porcelain white in the sun's dazzle. Kid, child, I still applied the words automatically to my daughter, but she was an adult now – or almost one. 'Cusp' was the word they used, wasn't it? She was on the cusp, though when exactly she had moved from childhood to this cusp, I didn't know. When she stopped kissing me goodnight on her way to bed, perhaps? When she stopped telling me who it was who had just been on the phone? Or when she stopped delighting in our physical likenesses – the dark hair that fell straight before curling under at its tips, the straight, serious brows that made us look so thoughtful – and sought instead to look as different from me as possible?

'My daughter,' I said to Calder, lightly. 'And her friend.' At that moment Roxy sprayed her stomach with sun lotion, recoiling from its coolness before rubbing at her skin in lazy circles.

Marianne, flat on her back, used both thumbs to send a text message on her phone and, as Roxy suddenly wiped her hands dry on her thighs and reached into her bag for *her* phone, I realised the two of them were actually texting each other.

'They're revising for exams,' I added.

Davis sipped his coffee, smiling at me with his eyes. 'You know, I've been teaching for twenty-five years, on and off, and I think I can safely say that's not a revision technique I'm familiar with.'

'Really? It must be a new one . . .' I surprised myself by laughing out loud. Lord, I was almost in a good mood! And there I'd been thinking today was going to be the worst day since – well, hard to say exactly; I usually chalked up the day Alistair left me as the official nadir, but there'd been a few other contenders over the years, it had to be said.

I watched as my guest wrapped both palms around the mug as though warming frostbitten fingers, a curiously vulnerable thing to do, and I felt newly intrigued. However I denied it, I knew he was the one I wanted to be our new tenant.

'Which one is yours?' he asked, gesturing to the girls.

Marianne stretched her arms long behind her head, tautening herself as though in anticipation of Valentino's kiss. I wondered, as I had several times since she'd entered our lives, what her mother must think.

'Not the nymphet,' I said, suddenly emotional. 'The other one.' The reason, I added, silently, my reason for everything.

Calder's eyeballs swivelled a fraction. 'Ah, I see.' Minutes later, he was on his feet. 'Well, thank you for the coffee. I guess I ought to be going.'

When Alistair and I split up, I made it my business to keep in touch with an old college friend of his, Shireen, whom I judged to be too kind-hearted to shun me, as others in his camp instinctively had. We'd meet for coffee, I going out of my way to make it convenient for her, crossing the city to seek her out at her office or suggesting a café at the end of her street – basically leaving her no choice but to see me. She knew I was there only for her link to Alistair, but she also knew I was the victim in this particular family drama, the one who had the right to act desperately. (It probably didn't hurt that I looked as bedraggled as any newly abandoned woman could be expected to, baby Matthew strapped to my chest in a sling or whimpering in the pushchair next to me.)

Shireen would answer my questions as diplomatically as she could, sometimes even dispensing a few unsolicited crumbs of her own. For instance, it was she who told me that Alistair had an agreement with Victoria that they would not be having children together.

'It was part of the deal.'

'What deal?' I asked, sharply. 'I thought they were in love.'

She eyed me with the blend of pity and fear I was becoming accustomed to as a single mother freshly adrift in the world. 'Just a figure of speech, Kate. It's more that they agree on what they want out of the relationship. She doesn't want children and he agrees with that.'

Victoria was younger than Alistair by over ten years and I could imagine his persuasiveness on the issue. 'This is about us,' he'd say, 'it's about sharing *our* lives. Let's not complicate it with kids, I've been through that and I know exactly what it does to a marriage.' He would shake his head, she would nod hers. She probably had colleagues who had young children, too, pitied them their surrendering of basic freedoms and their deteriorated physical shape. It would not seem too high a price to pay. I wondered if she would be allowed a pet.

'I read it's quite common among the Manhattan rich,' Shireen went on, 'in second and third marriages. They even write it into pre-nups.'

I gazed at her blankly. What did the Manhattan rich have to

7

do with me, with *my* hell? And who said anything about Alistair and Victoria marrying?

'Anyway,' she said, hastily, 'In a way, that might turn out to be a good thing. For you, I mean. People find it very difficult when a second family comes along. The whole half-sibling thing, you know? It creates a lot of tension.'

'Hmm.' I didn't believe in this deal or agreement for a moment. Victoria would change her mind because she was biologically hardwired to do so. The only question was when. Even so, it wasn't the first thing to spring to mind years later when Alistair phoned me one Saturday morning and asked if we could meet privately – he had some news to discuss. It was two or three weeks ago now, late March, and a weekend for him to take the kids. I usually dropped off Matthew after whatever sports practice he had, but on this occasion Alistair proposed that he come and pick him up from home instead. Victoria would take him for a treat while Alistair and I chatted.

'What's this about?' I asked. It was a long time since those shameful conferences with Shireen, when I would have picked up where we'd left off with barely a reproach, and these days my manner towards my ex-husband was honed, bright and professional, a variation on the one I used with clients. (Remain cheerful, yet impassive, my manager Ethan always advised new volunteers at the Neighbourhood Advice Office, This is not about saving the world; it's about giving the right information at the right time.)

I had a sense that Alistair's was not going to be the right information at the right time. He sat at the kitchen table with a take-out coffee he'd brought with him. This was the kind of detail that offended me, seeing in it as I did the implication that my coffee was not good enough for him, not any more. I lingered over the making of my own cup, opening and shutting jars, even stirring longer than necessary before joining him at the table.

'I'll get straight to the point.' His face settled into an

8

expression somewhere between coy and smug. 'Victoria is pregnant.'

I blinked, and with that downward sweep of the eyelids the wall came tumbling down once again, just as I had always known it would. Despair filled my lungs. It was finally happening. Now my children would have a blood connection with Victoria; now I would be linked for as long as I lived – and long into the future – to the woman who had replaced me. And that was just me; how would this affect Roxy and Matthew? Would Alistair alter towards them once the new baby arrived? Would he have less time for them? Less love?

'But I thought . . .' I tried to compose myself. 'Well, that's wonderful news, congratulations. For some reason I thought she wasn't able to.'

'She didn't *want* to,' he corrected me. 'But these things happen – as you know.'

With enormous effort I blocked memories of my breaking the news to him of my own first pregnancy, our young faces trying the read the thoughts behind one another's. 'When is it due?'

'October. It's still a bit early to tell people, but she hasn't been feeling great and I thought I'd tell the kids this weekend in case they were worried. That's if you think it's a good idea, of course.'

'Sure, that's fine. You will, you know, reassure them that—?'

He broke in. 'Of course I will. Leave it to me.'

Already I wanted exactly that, couldn't wait for him to go. I was glad for once that I'd be without Roxy and Matthew this weekend; I needed to deal with this news – to master it – on my own, before I saw them again.

But Alistair had more up his sleeve. 'The thing is, Kate, I'm afraid this is going to have ramifications for you.'

I looked up. 'Ramifications?' It was such an Alistair word. He'd told me once what it meant, not strictly a consequence, as it tended to be used, but actually a branch, a new branch to a complex situation. (He, naturally, took the role of the core, the trunk.) 'I'll be meeting with Roger on Tuesday so I'll know more then, but I just wanted to give you a bit of a heads up.' Roger was his financial advisor, one of an array of professionals who'd entered the picture in Victoria's wake.

'Heads up on what, exactly?'

'On the fact that I'll need to reduce my support payments a bit.'

Again I blinked, but this time with the upward sweep my defences were swiftly reassembled. '*What*?'

'Nothing major,' he added quickly, 'but you must see it has to happen. One more mouth to feed, only so much spare cash to go around.'

'Roxy and Matthew are not "mouths",' I said, stonily, 'they're children, people. They can't be uprooted at the drop of a hat.'

He looked surprised. 'Who's saying they'll be uprooted? You won't need to move, the mortgage on this place is tiny.'

Tiny to him, frighteningly large to me. I felt my control waver. 'We only just get by as it is, Alistair, you know how much I earn and what the service charges are like in these buildings ...' I hated the sound of my voice, weak and plaintive, appealing to him as the powerful authority, the parent figure.

He took a breath. 'Actually, that's partly what I wanted to talk about. I had an idea for you. How about getting a lodger in?'

I looked at him, appalled. 'A lodger? You can't be serious! Do you really want your children exposed to a stranger?'

He laughed. 'Must you be so dramatic, Kate? Think about it, this place is easily big enough to section some of it off with its own front door. The layout is perfect. A bit of refitting to make some kind of second kitchen, a few permissions. I can talk to the management committee if there's any resistance in that department.' He spoke as if this was all off the top of his head, but I knew him well enough to see that he'd clearly given it some thought. (There may even have been a spreadsheet on a computer screen somewhere.) How I hated the idea that my financial

10

position might have been discussed with Victoria, perhaps even in front of the children. 'There's a rental agent right across the street, so you wouldn't have to have any more contact with whoever it was than you do with the rest of the neighbours.' He was warming to his pitch now. 'And if you do get on, then that's a nice bonus. I'd say it was the ideal solution.'

I snorted. 'I'm sure you would. I'd prefer it if we didn't need a solution. Why don't *you* get a lodger to make up the shortfall?'

He didn't answer, just gave me a look that said, Well, I'll save you the humiliation of spelling *that* out, which was, of course, that he didn't need a lodger because he was supporting his family perfectly adequately already, thank you very much. I, meanwhile, earned a pittance as a charity worker and could never provide our children with a lifestyle like this on my own. I needed his contributions not only for luxuries – I needed them to survive.

He drained the last of his coffee and squeezed the paper cup in his fist so that the lid popped off. 'Just think about it, at least. This is a huge flat and you could give up a few rooms without even noticing.'

I scraped back my chair and stood. 'If you don't mind, I'd like some time on my own to think about it. It's all a bit of a shock.'

'Of course, no problem.' He knew better than to offer a gesture, or even a murmur, of sympathy, but rose straight away from his seat, hooking his car keys on his right index finger, just as he always had, twirling the ring up and down the finger with the rhythm of a majorette working her baton. 'Well, great to see you, Kate. I'll drop the kids back tomorrow, usual time.'

Roxy and Marianne reappeared not long after Calder had left. They clattered into the kitchen, sandals slapping on heels, phones beeping (those phones were squeezed to their ears with such frequency I was genuinely worried for the risk of carpal tunnel syndrome). Marianne had pulled on an expensive-looking patterned kaftan, sheer and low cut enough for me to see the edge of her bikini top, just where the nipples started. Though her complexion was apple fresh, her blue eyes were washed with a kind of weariness that disturbed me. She was far too knowing for a seventeen-year-old, it simply wasn't right. What experiences had she had to earn such adult jadedness? Next to her, Roxy looked as clean and untried as a new cygnet.

'How's studying going?' I asked, continuing my task of folding dry laundry into three piles. Odd what short work I'd made of it for once, what with my mind being so full of the morning's events.

'Yeah, fine,' Roxy said.

'Not fine,' Marianne corrected, amiably. 'I've got so much to do I can't even think about it or my head will explode.'

'Oh dear.'

'Mum?' Roxy turned to me with a faux-exasperated expression we both knew to conceal genuine displeasure. 'There's absolutely *nothing* in the fridge. Isn't it supposed to be your job to make sure students are well nourished?' They preferred to think of themselves as students, I'd noticed, rather than sixth-formers or, God forbid, schoolgirls. Marianne had recently been photographed by a magazine journalist on a trip to Oxford Street and appeared in a feature called 'Style Spy'; she'd given her age as eighteen (she was six months short of that) and her occupation as 'college student'.

The two of them stood peering in at the shelves of the fridge, the door obscuring their bodies so that my view was of the backs of four knees and four long, lean calves. I struggled to dismiss the image of my own body when last viewed naked in a full-length mirror, the way the flesh made garments of the different zones and limbs, like pads someone had inserted when I wasn't looking, everything a little lower than I'd imagined it to be, everything a little thicker. I would be the last person a fashion photographer would approach in the high street.

I adjusted one of Matthew's sweatshirts on the clothes rail, still damp at the collar and sleeves. 'There's some nice bread, I could make you a sandwich or cheese on toast?'

'No carbs after midday, I'm afraid,' Marianne said, over her shoulder. 'Have you got any avocados? Or yellow peppers, maybe?'

'Sorry, no. I was going to go to the supermarket tonight, Rox, when you're at Dad's. When are you heading over there? Shouldn't you be on your way by now?'

I could see just enough of them to sense the exchange of glances. Then Roxy's voice called out, 'Actually, I'm staying over at Marianne's tonight. Dad said it was OK.'

I knew that Alistair would in fact have approved it only if I had first. This was not an area where we were in disagreement. It would be unlikely to occur to him, however, that Roxy might report my permission by inference if not outright lie, standard practice for a teen shuttling between divorced parents. My first thought was that this might have something to do with Damien, her most recent boyfriend and the one with whose arrival week-end arrangements had begun to get complicated. But they were no longer together, or at least not as far as I could tell. (Such was the breakdown in communications between us, I had never actually discovered who had ended it or why. I couldn't help suspecting Marianne on both counts.)

After a brief pause I went on with the laundry. 'What are you doing? Anything exciting?'

Roxy emerged from behind the fridge door, shrugging. 'Just hanging out.' This, I knew, could mean anything from watching a DVD to dabbling in witchcraft. Most likely, post-Damien, it would entail a trip to some horrible pub in Camden; Marianne's boyfriend was a DJ and horrible pubs his natural habitat.

'Your dad will miss seeing you.'

Another shrug. 'He'll have Matt. Anyway, he said he'd pick me up in the morning and take me back to have lunch with them.'

'You're *so* lucky your dad is in London,' Marianne said, sighing. 'I have to schlep all the way to Norfolk to see mine.' She spoke as though it were an accepted fact that everyone's parents lived apart. How sad, I thought. If only ours was the family that proved her wrong.

'What happened with the viewings?' Roxy said, suddenly, leaving her friend at the fridge and approaching me with a friendlier air. She was willing to charm now that she didn't have the battle for Saturday-night leave she'd been expecting. She was so beautiful when she was happy, the good-natured smile of her infancy rising to the surface. It may have been a coincidence, but she had come to position herself directly next to the Metropolitan Police printout that was pinned to the kitchen corkboard. This was a schools' website document entitled 'What can I do at age . . .?'. The girls had one in their common room at school and Roxy had downloaded a copy for home. The top page read:

What can I do at age seventeen?
* You can hold a licence to drive cars and motorcycles
* You can go to war
* You can engage in street trading
* You can purchase an air rifle
* You can leave home without your parents' consent

The list for sixteen had been considerably longer and included such terrifying entries as 'You can leave school' and 'You can have heterosexual and homosexual sex', and I'd been relieved when it had been replaced with the seventeens. I tried not to anticipate the one for eighteen; by then, I imagined, she could do anything she liked and putting up notices to remind me of her rights would no longer be necessary.

'Earth to Mum? *Mum*? How did it go? Anyone good?'

'Possibly,' I said, focusing. 'I liked one guy, a teacher . . .' I realised I could picture Calder's face much more clearly than any of the others'. 'But he said it was too small. There was a trainee solicitor who seemed quite nice, as well. I may go for her. I'll talk to the agent on Monday.'

'You don't have to *like* them,' Roxy said. 'They're just tenants. We won't actually see them, will we?' I wondered if she were deliberately parroting Alistair's opinion to annoy me, and then I saw that she echoed it merely because it was the conclusion of any sensible person. In any case, giving up a portion of our home was not the wrench for her that it was for me. Once it had been established that her own quarters would not be touched by the upheaval, she'd been perfectly at ease with the prospect of change. And that was how it should be, I'd reminded myself repeatedly over the last few weeks. I didn't want her or Matthew to share my pain. It was my job to mop it up before it reached them.

'I could probably make us something with this,' Marianne said, finally emerging from the fridge with a carton of eggs and a potato. 'Tortilla or something basic.'

'You cook?' I asked, trying not to sound as amazed as I was. Somehow I had put her in the contingent of Roxy's schoolmates who had staff at home and a credit card for restaurants when they were not.

She pulled a face. 'Doesn't everyone?'

'Roxy hardly knows how to boil an . . .' I trailed off as I caught my daughter's glare. I wasn't allowed to do this, to point out her shortcomings in front of friends, or any third party for that matter, and even when we were alone criticism was seldom taken in the constructive spirit that it was given. Cooking in particular had an emotional history for us, for there'd been a few months in her life, after her father had left, when she *had* cooked, when she would not have eaten if she hadn't, when she had looked after me. Since then, I'd been just as keen as she was to re-establish who was the mother and who the mothered.

Marianne began cracking eggs into a bowl, placing the shell halves inside one another and expertly stopping any strings of egg white with her middle finger. The glamorous attire, the sunglasses pushed into her hair to free her face of the long strands honeyed with highlights, made her look like a TV chef preparing to talk to camera. 'My mother says that gaps in a child's knowledge are a reflection of their parents' failings, not their own,' she said, tone matter of fact.

Roxy giggled delightedly and watched for my reaction, eager to see if I'd take up the challenge.

'No offence, Mrs Easton,' Marianne added, getting to work with the whisk.

'None taken,' I said, weakly.

Chapter 2

Ours was one of several neighbourhoods in north London dubbed the 'toast rack' for their rows of identical and closely crammed terraces, and until I became pregnant with Matthew, Alistair, Roxy and I had lived in a maisonette in one just off the high street. Roxy occupied the tiny second bedroom at the back and with every year that she grew bigger the squeeze became more evident. But still we stayed. We told ourselves that moving was too expensive, but we both knew the real reason for our reluctance to upgrade. Getting more space, lining up extra bedrooms, factoring in a playroom, it all tempted an already likely fate: that we wouldn't be able to have the second child we dearly wanted. For years we tried, but every month it was the same: another period, another period of disappointment.

Then, when Roxy was seven, I finally got pregnant again, and with the first trimester safely negotiated, Alistair and I responded with a vengeance. He wanted a house, and as big as possible. He'd just been promoted to director and it was time for a demonstration of his rising status in the world. Other senior staff at his management consultancy lived in smart townhouses in west London or, if they'd yet to marry and breed, spectacular loft flats on the river. He'd been left behind in his modest maisonette.

The mansion flat was my idea. They were beautiful nineteenth-century buildings arranged in clusters by the green, almost a secret neighbourhood of their own, a separate community. I'd see people emerging from the vast double doors and wonder about their lives in a way I never did when I saw my own neighbours lock up their terraces and head for the Tube. And then there were those shared gardens, mysterious parklands forbidden to all but those in possession of the gate key. When we viewed Francombe Gardens, the agent took us out back right at the end of the tour – I sensed it was typically the clincher – and while he and Alistair talked about how gardeners' bills were split, Roxy and I explored. There was a ring of benches around a well-kept lawn, the wood weathered soft grey over the years; a tennis court, obviously recently resurfaced; climbing frames and swings; even a small walled garden planted with lupins and daisies and over-sized poppies that had purple-black innards and petals like crêpe paper.

Down by the playground Roxy found a length of hollow railing and called me over.

'Look, Mum, it's a speaking tube! We've got one of these at school.'

'What's a speaking tube?'

'You know, like on a submarine. Come on, you speak and I'll listen.'

I spoke into the hole at my end. 'Hello, Roxy Easton, do you think you'd like to live here?'

She giggled at the amplification as though the sound actually tickled her ear, and as I took my turn to listen I heard her say, 'Yes, please, Mum, it's *beautiful* here.' And then she blew me a kiss, its hot, exaggerated sound filling my head and flowing like liquid into my heart and lungs.

I whispered back, 'Then let's see if we can persuade Daddy.'

We launched our joint charm offensive that same afternoon ('Please, Daddy, I promise I'll be tidier in my new bedroom'), but

18

in the end, it came down to the figures. I presented Alistair with a list of the properties we'd viewed, complete with columns for price and square footage. A final column showed my calculation of the price per square foot. The mansion flats were better value than the houses, it was undeniable.

And so the offer was made, the conveyancing cranked into motion, but what with the various delays and an eleventh-hour hiccup with our own sale, we didn't move into Francombe Gardens until three weeks before Matthew was born.

Four months later, Alistair was gone.

The woman in the seat next to me was crying so discreetly it took me a few seconds to notice.

'Please,' I said, 'just take your time, Mrs Willis. Are you sure you wouldn't like a cup of tea?'

'I'm fine, thank you.' She sniffed, dabbing her nose with a tissue still folded from the packet. She used her own rather than helping herself from the box provided. Evidently she was used to keeping herself to herself, would have preferred not to impose herself on a stranger like this. For her, the Neighbourhood Advice Office was a last resort, as it was for many who came here. She was not our usual type, being about my mother's age, mid-sixties or so, and smartly dressed. Everything about her appearance suggested a well-taken-care-of woman with plenty of purpose – except for her face. There purpose had crumbled, the skin was chalky and puffed, her head bowed. Experience told me this was grief, fresh grief, and it quickly transpired that my instinct was right.

'They keep sending me letters, fines for hundreds of pounds, more every time, saying it's got to be moved, but it was my husband's car and I don't drive.'

'And your husband . . .?'

She dipped her eyes. 'He passed away.'

'I'm so sorry. When was that?'

'Four weeks ago now. The thing is, I don't even know where the keys are. I've looked everywhere.' She shook her head vigorously as if that might physically dislodge the keys from their hiding place. 'So, you see, I can't even get someone else to move it.' She was weeping now, and I cursed for possibly the thousandth time in my eight years here the policymakers of the local council's parking division. I could picture the scene quite clearly. Some of the local traffic wardens wouldn't even make eye contact with their victims; they said it increased their risk of assault. By a retired widow!

'I found the number for the insurance company, but they said they couldn't help, I have to sort it out with the council. I don't know what to do.'

I reached for the phone. 'Don't you worry, Mrs Willis, I'll ring the council and we'll get this sorted out here and now.'

I thought I saw a twitch of relief about the mouth, but it was gone as quickly as it came. My few minutes' help was a drop in the ocean, couldn't be anything more.

It was my mother who suggested I volunteer at the local Neighbourhood Advice Office. About a year after Alistair left, with Matthew settled and a new family routine of sorts in place, she told me it was time I got out.

'I'm worried you're spending too much time here in the flat.'

'I like it here.'

'I know, but you need to mix with other people. You used to be so sociable.'

It was true that I hardly left Francombe Gardens, or its environs, for long. With the park-sized gardens and the children's swings, I didn't even need to take my slippers off to take Matthew out to play. Roxy's school was a short walk away, and there was a bank, post office and supermarket on the local high street. Most of life could be accomplished without venturing too far beyond my own postcode.

'I don't want to socialise,' I said. 'I'm not ready.'

'I don't mean that, I mean work.' She told me of a newly divorced friend of hers who now volunteered at the Citizens Advice Bureau. 'Sometimes it's good to see that your situation is really not as bad as you think it is.'

I couldn't help smiling. 'Is that a nice way of telling me I need to count my blessings?'

'That, yes, but also just to fill your head with someone else's business for a few hours a day.'

'Someone else's problems, you mean?'

Mum pulled an expression, open and optimistic, that reminded me of Tash (though my sister's tended to accompany considerably less sensible proposals than this one). It still felt odd having Mum back in this role, rescuing me, supporting me, guiding me. Almost from the moment I'd left home for university to the moment Alistair left me for Victoria, I'd been in his care, and now, at the age of thirty-one, I felt like a teenager again.

'All I know is that Angela says it's the best thing she could have done. She's paid now, as well, and pretty much gets to pick her own hours.'

'Funny,' I said, 'I've never really seen myself as a do-gooder.'

'That's an out-of-date label. Anyway, if it does anyone any good it will be you,' Mum said, firmly.

At the end of my Monday shift I saw that my mobile had picked up four messages since I'd switched it off that morning, all from the agent handling the rental of the flat. Walking home, I called him back.

'Mrs Easton, finally! I have good news for you.'

'Oh yes?'

'Two of the clients who viewed the flat on Saturday would like to take it at the full rent.'

'That *is* good news,' I said, nervously. 'The lawyer? She seemed nice.'

'Yes, Miss Broadgate, she's very keen. And the other one is the teacher, Mr Calder.'

'Calder?' At once, my heart rate quickened. 'I thought he said it was too small for him?'

'Yes, that was his initial feedback on Saturday, but he seems to have changed his mind over the weekend. He called me first thing this morning. He's the better candidate, actually, if you want to get the rent coming in straight away. He could move in immediately, next weekend if possible, or even sooner. The other one doesn't leave her current place for another three weeks.'

A number of images floated across my eyes: figures – it would be nice to see four of them occasionally – in the credit column of my bank statement; Alistair's face as he mouthed, 'it's the perfect solution,' gently, helpfully, like a psychiatrist placating a patient only he knew how to handle; and the curious, enigmatic chuckle of a stranger sitting opposite me at my kitchen table. 'You can still feel their body heat . . .'

I cleared my throat, aware that I was dithering. I needed to make a decision. The woman, this Miss Broadgate, was a lawyer and that might remind me too much of Victoria, whereas a teacher, a man who cared about learning, whose career was dedicated to the education of children like my own . . . well, all the cards stacked up in his favour, anyone could see that. 'Fine,' I said, at last, 'you can tell Mr Calder the flat's his.'

'Good,' the agent said, pleased. 'I'll drop the paperwork over to you later today if that's all right, and I'll co-ordinate with your new tenant about keys and so on. I can't see any reason for anything to go wrong.'

'Thank you,' I said. 'You've done a great job.' And I spoke with a heart not nearly as heavy as I might have expected.

He moved in on the Saturday morning, exactly a week after his first and only viewing. It couldn't have been easier. Having supplied keys and instructions care of the agent, I was not even required to be there to welcome him but, with Matthew out at cricket and Roxy yet to emerge from her bedroom, it was hard to ignore all the bumps and shuffles taking place just a few feet beyond my own bedroom wall. A couple of removals guys, voices brutish in the calm of the main hallway, lugged box after box up the five flights of stairs, cursing the lack of a lift as though a shaft might materialise if they only complained hard enough. Calder himself seemed to be marshalling proceedings from the living room. I wondered how long it would be before I thought of it as his and not ours.

I waited until the coast was clear and then knocked on his front door. It still felt odd to see my old study door with a shiny Yale lock on it. There was a long pause before it opened and he appeared, expression impatient. Seeing me, however, he adjusted his features and nodded pleasantly. 'Ah, Mrs Easton, hello. Sorry, I thought it was those idiots back again.'

'Please, call me Kate.'

'Of course. And call me Davis. Come on in, I'm afraid you'll be appalled at the state of things, I've only just started unpacking.'

I followed him inside. It was a standard moving-in scene: boxes opened and abandoned, curls of packing paper everywhere, bubble-wrapped pictures propped against the fireplace, a huddle of coffee mugs dripping onto a folded newspaper. A laptop was already open on the desk under the window, its screen aglow, and all about, on desk and sofa and floor and kitchen worktop, were books, dozens of higgledy tower blocks of them.

'You have so many books!'

Davis nodded. 'This is just the tip of the iceberg. Most of them had to go into storage after . . .' He gave up on the thought, adding, 'Anyway, these are the ones I can't do without, the ones I need for my day-to-day teaching.'

'I never asked you what it is you teach?'

He plucked a scuffed old hardback from one of the towers and handed it to me. 'Take a wild guess.'

I read the words falteringly, unsure of their precise pronunciation: '*Jugend ohne Gott*. What does that mean?'

'"Godless Youth". Actually, you might know something about that, being the parent of a teenager in London.'

I didn't know what to say to that. Though he clearly joked, I tended instinctively to take every comment seriously, especially those from people I didn't know well. I put this down to my work (my friend Abi said it took at least half an hour for me to accept that the person I was talking to was not about to commit suicide). 'You teach German?'

'Literature, yes. A- and AS-level, mostly. I do quite a bit of French conversation, as well.'

'Do you work at a local school, then?' It occurred to me he might be at Willoughby Girls, Roxy's school, a coincidence that could well turn out to be a convenient one. There'd been murmurings lately of her not slacking exactly, but 'taking her eye off the ball', as her form tutor Mrs Harrison put it, though not far enough for it to have reached Alistair's ears. Still, it was a potentially damaging turn with university applications just a term away. Calder could be a useful spy. I felt instantly ashamed. What was I thinking? This was my daughter! If there was anything to be discovered, then *I* should be the one to discover it.

'I do private tutoring,' Calder said, 'Prepping for exams and university interviews. Revision courses, that sort of thing. And it's seasonal, as well, which suits me. I've got other projects on the go, too.'

He didn't say what these were and I didn't have time to ask before something new seemed to strike him and he added, more urgently, 'That's a point, actually, Kate. I sometimes go to my pupils' homes for sessions, but generally they come to me. That way I can fit more in. That's not going to be a problem, is it?'

I felt my eyes widen in surprise as I realised he was asking my

24

permission. Yes, it was going to take a while for me to get used to this landlady–lodger dynamic. 'Of course not, it's your flat now. And I'm sure it must be inspiring for them to come here and work surrounded by books.'

He grinned. 'Oh, they've all got plenty of books at home, don't worry about that. Their parents have read that a book-lined home produces A-grade students, even if they haven't read any of them themselves.'

I smiled, recognising the theory as one subscribed to by Alistair. I placed the book on the desk by the laptop. 'German,' I said, 'I didn't think that was very popular any more. Roxy is taking French and Spanish.'

'It's not so fashionable, you're right. But then I'm not a par-ticularly fashionable man.' His face broke into a very attractive smile and an unexpected thrill filled my stomach. I began to imagine how it would feel for a pupil to arrive here for a lesson, to settle on that low olive-green sofa (or did they sit together at the desk? It wasn't a therapy session, after all) and have an hour or so of his attention, his opinion, but then I stopped myself, told myself not to be so silly.

'Well, I won't keep you. I just wanted to say that if there's any-thing you need . . .'

'I should ask the agent, yep, that's understood.'

'No, the agents aren't managing the property, they just found you. I'll take care of anything that goes wrong now you're here.'

He grinned. 'Within reason, I assume?'

'Hmm, yes.' Tongue-tied once more, I began to retreat, but he called out after me, 'Oh, Kate?'

'Yes?'

As he followed me into the hallway it seemed to me that he looked at me with new interest for a second or two. 'The hot water and all that, do I need to know anything? Any switches or knobs needing special Victorian wizardry?'

'No, nothing like that.' I was relieved by his question (though what I'd been expecting that might have been more troublesome, I didn't know). 'The water is constant, you don't need to turn anything on or off. There's central plumbing, so it's all included in the rent.'

'Hot water on tap? What will they think of next?' And he turned away, lips curling, eyes already back to his unpacking.

Back in the main flat, looking in the hall mirror, I was horrified to find that my cheeks were aflame. 'I won't keep you': I'd sounded so prim, like something from a different century! He'd only been teasing me, looking for some harmless neighbourly banter, not guessing quite how out of practice I was.

'Mum, is that you?' Roxy padded towards me from the kitchen, a mug of black coffee in one hand, and squinted at me through her long reeds of dark hair. I thought I caught a trace of stale cigarette smoke and ignored it. That was one battle I could never win. (It had appeared on the 'What can I do at age sixteen?' page, in fact: 'You can buy cigarettes or tobacco'.) 'What was all that noise earlier?'

'Just our new neighbour moving in. He's called Davis.'

But the information obviously fell some way short of interesting and, though I was unusually eager to discuss our new arrival, Roxy didn't even bother to respond, just turned off into her bedroom and closed the door.

Chapter 3

The link between Matthew's arrival and Alistair's departure was obvious enough for me to dismiss any notions that Roxy might not have noticed it for herself. She'd just turned eight when her father left – her birthday was one of the last days he spent with us – and until her brother came along, life had been relatively constant. One comfortable home, ten minutes' walk from the only school she'd attended; two parents, happy enough together and certainly undivided in their attention to her. Now, though, in six short months there was a new house, a new baby brother, and a missing parent. Whatever misfortunes were to overtake her in adulthood, I felt sure she would look back on that period as the one that ended her innocence. How on earth could she not?

Though Matthew had been an easy pregnancy, he was not an easy baby. For months he was tormented by colic, and while he wailed and wailed, Alistair worked and worked. I knew the psychology – hunter-gatherer intensifies efforts with the birth of a son and heir – but that didn't seem quite so compelling at six o'clock in the morning when I'd endured another sleepless night, only to face another rest-free day alone. I'd drop Roxy at school and walk slowly back to the flat, all the time staring at Matt in his pram and thinking, 'How am I going to get through today?

How?' I'd never thought that way when Roxy was a baby, I was sure of it.

Alistair and I began to row. He had always been easy to inflame and traditionally I'd been the one to talk him down from whatever contretemps had flared with a colleague or friend, but now I found myself supplying the provocation and not the after-care. It was a rare morning when the breakfast/packed-lunch drill was not accompanied by some vicious exchange, ending with Alistair leaving for work without saying goodbye.

Roxy became understandably subdued. Her class teacher called me in to ask if everything was all right. She agreed that it was a sensitive time, with a new baby in the house, even for a child of Roxy's age, and they would make sure she got plenty of attention there to offset any shortfall at home. I was grateful for the support, and not a little guilty. Too often I waved my daughter away saying, 'Not now, Matthew's not well,' or 'Stop asking me questions! You can see I'm busy!' taking out my frustration with Alistair – and with the baby – on her. I kept meaning to find a moment when it was just the two of us and I could try to explain that this was just a temporary madness, that soon things would be back to normal, they'd be *better* than normal. Then, one morning, the sound of the slammed door reverberating around the flat and Alistair's stomp on the stairs still audible, Roxy sat at the breakfast table with her fingers in her ears and I had the most awful suspicion that I'd left it too late.

'Darling, I'm sorry I'm always so cross at the moment. I'm just really, really tired.' It was too simplistic for her, she was eight now, but it seemed I'd lost that sensitivity I'd always had for her growing awareness of other people's emotions. 'I don't expect you to understand. It's an adult problem.'

Hurt welled in her eyes; she hadn't yet learned how to hide her feelings. 'I *do* understand. You and Dad hate each other.'

'No, that's not true . . .' But my protest wasn't convincing even to me.

'When I'm grown-up I'm *never* getting married or having a baby. I'm going to live on my own!'

That was when I knew for certain I'd left it too late. The last time we'd talked about her being grown-up she'd still wanted to be a princess or a pop star. She should never have had to make that leap so violently.

When Alistair left I blamed myself. Roxy blamed me, too, at first, so at least we were in agreement on that. We didn't know about Victoria yet, and when we did, well, that was the one good thing that came of her, the relocation of the target board from my head to hers.

Matthew, finally finding his sleep stride, missed the whole thing.

'So,' Abi said, thumping down a cafetière between us on her coffee table. 'Spill.'

I grinned. 'I wouldn't want to ruin your new rug.'

'Come on, you know what I'm talking about. The sexy new lodger.'

'He's not a lodger, he's a tenant.'

She pressed down the plunger and began pouring. 'I notice you don't deny the "sexy". Well, well, well, I never thought I'd see the day . . .'

With my neighbour Abigail Thorpe I liked to think I had a flavour of what the rest of the city's female population consumed every day: company, kinship, sorority. Women were endlessly entertained and sustained by one another's lives, analysing and interpreting the smallest events, conjuring drama out of nowhere and thriving on it. I'd not had that since university and the year that followed, when I'd worked full time in an office with several other new graduates. Every day we'd gone for lunch together, eating our rolls and salads in five minutes flat and then spending the rest of the hour discussing our colleagues. And laughing, always laughing. That was presumably how it was for Abi, too, in her office building by the Thames, where she and a team of others worked for the headquarters of a chain of pizza restaurants. But at the Advice Office there was no time for gossip – there was hardly time to nod hello before the doors opened and the day's needy began their advance.

'So, name?' Abi demanded.

'He's called Davis, Davis Calder.'

'Hmm, yep, I like it. Sounds very upstanding. He's English, I assume?'

'Yes, I think he's from London. His previous addresses were here, anyway.'

'And what does your Mr Calder do for a living?'

I ignored the 'your'. 'He teaches German literature.'

'German?' She frowned at me. 'Not exactly the language of love, is it?'

I raised my eyebrows. 'I don't necessarily *want* the language of love, thank you very much.'

She mirrored my expression and then smirked naughtily. 'Well, I suppose that explains the very geeky boy I saw him with on the stairs the other day. I thought it might be his son.'

'No, one of his pupils, probably. They come to the flat for their sessions.'

'So he hasn't got kids of his own?'

I shrugged. 'I assume not, if he's living alone in a one-bedroomed flat. Divorced fathers tend to keep an extra bedroom for any visiting kids.'

There was a silence as the figure of Alistair rose between us. Abi's face was flat and broad, her conker-brown bobbed hair hooked behind her ears, and I could almost see the awning of caution roll down over her eyes. 'How are things in that department? Any news on the baby?'

I shook my head. 'All going as expected. No word of any complications – not that I would wish that on Victoria. Alistair and I hardly speak except about arrangements, and Roxy never breathes a word.'

'Bloody annoying teens, they're so secretive. I bet she knows every detail, as well.'

I wasn't sure about that. Since the advent of sixth form and boyfriends – not to mention her fascination with Marianne – Roxy had become the very picture of a preoccupied teenager. Armed robbery could take place in front of her nose and she'd swear nothing had happened. 'Matthew has started asking me questions. I think he's getting excited at the idea of a younger brother or sister.'

Abi watched me, weighing caution against her natural outspokenness. 'You're not worried they'll . . .' she paused. 'You know, switch allegiance or anything?'

'To be honest I don't think I *have* Roxy's allegiance any more.'

'Oh, I'm sure that's not true.' But she didn't mean it, and she knew I knew she didn't mean it, for Abi took great pleasure in not understanding children. She and her boyfriend Seb had made the decision not to have a family early in their relationship and I suspected that this was partly why I had gravitated towards them in the first place. We'd met at a bonfire party in the gardens several years ago. Through my work I'd come to spot the beleaguered a mile off (and whatever we all knew about its joys, parenthood was a form of a beleaguerment). Abi and Seb, however, were carefree. They spoke differently, looked at each other differently, they even moved differently. I'd walked straight over to them that evening, as though towards a window with a view I couldn't afford to miss.

I sighed. 'Maybe you're right. Maybe it's all just another phase.'

'Yeah, teenage girls and moons, who'd have thought there'd be a parallel. Werewolves, yes.'

As I laughed I thought once more of the person my daughter had become, or at least chose to present herself to be. Not independent yet, more resentfully dependent. The final stage before independence, perhaps, and if she weren't my eldest child I'd doubtless recognise it more easily. Certainly my own mother thought nothing remarkable in her granddaughter's behaviour. 'You were just the same,' she said repeatedly, and I wondered if I might simply have forgotten how it felt to be seventeen; perhaps the intensity, once survived, was self-erasing. 'Anyway, I'm more worried that Alistair will have less time for them. That's the classic consequence, isn't it?' The ramification.

Abi nodded. 'I saw in the paper that soon over half the kids in Britain will be living in a stepfamily. That means living with a man who isn't their own father while theirs lives with someone else's children. Crazy!'

'Tell me about it.'

But there was nothing more to tell, her interest was already elsewhere. 'Hey, look at the sun, Kate! Shall we sit outside?'

I followed her through the French windows that led to her garden. She and Seb had a square of private terrace to themselves, separated by a flowerbed from the communal parkland beyond. They didn't have the natural light of my flat, but they had this, the green rolling away from their feet as far as the eye could see, or at least as far as the line of trees that obscured the row of garages. The magnolia blossom had already darkened and dropped, though we were barely into May. The daffodils were long gone, but there were tulips and Michaelmas daisies and, in the meadowy corner at this end, buttercups galore. It was beautiful. It was why I fought to stay here every time finances threatened to overwhelm me, and ignored the doubts that surfaced when I thought about a future without Alistair's child support. It was unlikely Davis would still be about by then. Would there be more lodgers? Would this really work out as I hoped?

As we settled on the two little wrought-iron chairs, I wondered instinctively if Abi and Seb kept a third in a store cupboard somewhere. For as long as I could remember I had thought in threes: first Alistair, Roxy and me; then, after the briefest of interludes as a four, Matthew, Roxy and me. But everything in Abi's flat was in pairs. So simple.

'You don't seem to know very much about him,' she remarked, rotating her pale face to the sky. 'This Davis Calder bloke.'

'The agent checked his references and they were fine.'

'Anyone can fake a reference.'

'Abi, stop looking for drama! I have enough of that from Roxy, thank you very much.'

Again, she smirked. 'Not drama, romance . . .'

I gave her a warning look. 'Romance is a word for little girls and old ladies. Anyway, you know my golden rule about no more relationships.'

'"Golden rule"! Now who sounds like a little girl?'

Despite myself, I could feel adrenaline lashing away at my insides. I needed to stop right now; this was dangerous talk, dangerous thinking. My early-warning systems may not have been operating at full capacity with Davis Calder, but they had not completely failed.

'I just think it's worth checking him out,' Abi said, more casually. 'I mean, considering you're sharing the same flat.'

I pinched the end of my nose, cold despite the sun. 'I can't think of it like that now.' I looked across to the corner of my building, to the exoskeleton of the fire escape as it zigzagged to the ground from our kitchen door. Beyond it was the exterior wall we now shared with Davis. 'His bit isn't ours any more.'

I next saw Davis in the ground-floor lobby. He was checking our pigeonhole for mail – that we did share, for there was no spare to allocate to the newcomer – and extracting a letter or two of his own from the thick wedge I knew to contain my own monthly bills.

'How are you settling in?' I asked.

'Fine, good.' He looked fresh and groomed in the warm, airless space, making me conscious of the sweat on my T-shirt.

Victorian mansion blocks had not been built with twenty-first-century climate change in mind.

'You must be busy with all the last-minute cramming. I've seen the kids around the area – they look so stressed.'

'Oh yes, you can say that again. Generation Stress, I call them.' He shot me a waggish look. 'I blame the parents.'

I was improving; it only took me a split second to see the funny side. 'Oh, me too.'

Together we made for the stairs and began the long climb up. I felt pleased to have been arriving and not leaving, to have the chance to extend our conversation.

'It's such a long time ago now,' I went on, 'but I still remember the nerves of exams, the feeling that how you performed was going to determine *everything*.' And so it had. I'd gained the grades I'd needed to get to Warwick and there, six weeks into my first term, I'd met Alistair.

'Your daughter,' Davis asked, 'she's not doing A-levels this term, then?'

'Roxy, no, not till next year.'

'She's seventeen, is she?'

'Yes, just. You've probably seen her going for her driving lessons on Thursdays after school.'

'No, no, I haven't. How are they going?'

'Fine, I think. She seems to find it easy. She seems to find everything easy.'

'How very fortunate.'

I grinned. I was getting used to his drawled speech, mocking but inviting at the same time. 'Not that she's inherited that from me. She's like her father. He's a very successful management consultant.'

'Hmm. Not a profession I've had any dealings with.'

'Think yourself lucky,' I said.

We'd reached the landing outside our outer front door and he lingered behind me a step or two, deferring to my prior claim to the lock. 'Do you have time for a cup of tea?' I asked, careful to keep my voice casual while at the same time wondering why I felt I had to take such care in the first place.

'Sorry,' he said, 'I can't. I've got a stack of papers to mark . . .'

'OK, no problem.' As we moved into the shared hallway I decided to leave it at that but, watching him ease his key into the lock, I heard myself add, 'Well, perhaps you'd like to come over for dinner one night next week?'

He turned back, it seemed to me a little wearily.

'Nothing special, we'd just like to welcome you properly. You could meet the kids.'

Only after I'd spoken did I realise how presumptuous this sounded, not to mention potentially terrifying to the single male neighbour of a divorcée. He probably suspected me of lying in wait for just this sort of 'chance' encounter. He was so very good looking, too, it must happen to him all the time. The thought made me feel unexpectedly deflated.

'I mean, if they're in, that is. Well, Matthew is usually, but Roxy's out a lot.'

Even worse, the idea that he would prefer to see me alone in some sort of grisly forced date! Now I imagined Abi sniggering and I cursed myself for being so out of practice with all of this. All of what? With the initiation of friendship, I told myself firmly. For that was what I sought from this man, attractive or otherwise, a friendship, that 'bonus' Alistair had spoken of.

Looking up again I saw to my surprise that the expression in Davis's eyes had altered to one of genuine interest. 'Thank you,' he said, with gentle formality. 'That would be very nice. I have sessions booked for Monday, Tuesday and Wednesday evenings, but I could keep Thursday free?'

'Perfect.' And I put the flood of relief I felt down to inexperience in my new duties as a landlady.

Chapter 4

It was only when my husband dusted down his morning suit and actually married another woman that I finally gave up hope of reconciliation between us. Roxy needed no encouragement in boycotting the event.

'I hate Victoria,' she said.

'Oh, Roxy, you mustn't say that!' But I protested much too weakly. Though I knew it was wrong of me, I relished the childish venom in her voice.

Matthew, three by then and recently potty-trained, was taken along to the register office by my mother-in-law (former mother-in-law) and, I later discovered, represented me beautifully by agitating loudly for the loo before wetting himself on her lap.

Someone, Shireen perhaps, told me that Alistair had quoted Johnson in his speech, that famous line about a second marriage being the triumph of hope over experience. I found that very hurtful.

When it was over and the newlyweds were in their business-class seats bound for the Maldives, I made myself a promise: I would never marry again. Not only that, but I would never have a relationship again. I would never subject my children to this maelstrom again and I would never subject myself to it. I simply didn't think I could survive a second time.

And I didn't once waver. On the few occasions that men appeared to be steering conversation into the danger zone, I would cut off their suggestion of a drink or dinner before it could even be aired. Once, another volunteer at work persisted and I had to explain myself more clearly: 'I'm sorry, but I really can't. It's not personal; I would say the same to anyone.' He gave me a look that said, 'I know a line when I hear one,' and I gave one back that I hoped said, 'It's not a line, it's the truth'.

'You can't shut down completely,' Abi told me. 'It's unnatural. Even nuns struggle with that one. You must still have urges. Fantasies.'

'I suppose.' I was far too ashamed to admit to her that after everything Alistair had done to me, he was still the one who appeared in those fantasies, fantasies in which life rewound ten years to the times when we'd wake up together and steal a minute or two on our own before Roxy came bounding through the door. I thought of that man as Old Alistair or My Alistair, as though his body had been snatched and returned with someone else inside it. In a way, that *was* what had happened.

It was remarkable how focused one could be without the distraction of romantic love. I devoted myself to the children, making their home as peaceful and stable as I could, my mood towards them unaffected by relationships beyond our own. And I applied myself to my new job with a dedication that drew praise and appreciation from all sides. Though I continued to torture myself with those memories of my marriage at its best, and to contend with regular teasing by Abi and others, I was never attracted to another man, never came close to breaking my rule.

Everything was in place for the dinner for Davis Calder. I had changed hours ago, choosing a striped shirt-dress and switching my usual moccasin slippers for the sequinned flip-flops my sister had given me for Christmas (Tash's gifts couldn't always be counted on to be seasonally appropriate). I wore as much make-up as I thought I could risk without stirring Roxy's new instinct for mockery. She was just back from her driving lesson and taking a bath – impossible yet to assess her mood. With Roxy, it was like praying for sun.

The food had been prepared in advance, the table laid and wine glasses polished, so now I had only to get Matthew indoors and into the bath before I could see to a final tidy of the living room (hopefully, Roxy would be out by the time I came back – I didn't want to get into a row about it). I slipped out of the kitchen door and down the fire escape into the gardens. Whereas Roxy's circle was exclusively drawn from her sixth form, her friends living in a fan shape of neighbourhoods either side of our own north London spot, Matthew had a coterie of pals within Francombe Gardens itself: Ruben, Jack and Evert from families across the way, and occasionally a pair of brothers from the building next to ours, David and Gary. The group would play together most evenings, making use of every corner of the park and usually ending up in the sandpit in a violent game of their own devising.

'Matt!' I called, skipping up the playground steps towards the epicentre of their war cries. 'Time to come in now!'

No one heard me and I stood back for a moment, watching the action. Just as people saw instantly Roxy's likeness to me, you would know Matthew was his father's son the moment you laid eyes on him: the same height advantage over his peers, the same direct gaze beneath arched brows, the thicket of sandy hair I'd always hoped he would inherit. I kept it long over his ears, much to Alistair's disapproval, and every time he returned from a stay at his father's I expected a different boy to walk back in. But Alistair never did it, never took his son for the shearing I feared. The hair had become a symbol of my casting vote. Besides, Alistair knew as well as I did that if Matthew went to one of the academic secondary schools we had in mind for him, a sober time awaited. He'd probably need his hair cut for the interviews, which meant he had approximately eighteen months remaining of this lovely floppy-haired boyhood. Only Evert had the same long, loose style. His parents were Swedish and his father Jan had told me once, 'In Sweden we have the word *slitvargar*. It means wear and tear wolves, let children be wolves.'

It wasn't a bad analogy when you saw them playing as they were now. The game was Machete Hell, the aim of which – as with most others – was to wrestle the others to the ground and break their necks.

'Missed!' Evert yelled, shoving at Gary's chest and falling down on top of him. I winced; the sand was only inches deep.

'Stay down, stay down!' Ruben shouted to Matthew. 'You're dead, I just macheted your head off!'

'No,' Matthew protested through a mouthful of sand, 'I moved. I'm in Heaven now.'

Ruben dismissed this. 'There *is* no Heaven.'

'Oh.' Matthew deferred, as he always did, to Ruben's leadership. Ruben was the oldest of the gang and a stern dictator. He did, however, manage up as effortlessly as he did down, and was scrupulously courteous to adults. Now he acknowledged me with an easy smile and nodded at once to Matt. 'Your mum's here.'

Seeing me, Matthew climbed out quite willingly (the degree of reluctance tended to vary according to how well he was doing in the game).

'The sandman comes,' I said, brushing the grains off his bare arms. It was a joke of ours whenever I picked him up from the pit. It had been one of his favourite lullabies when he was little.

He smiled, Alistair's smile. 'I'm staying up, though, aren't I? For dinner?'

'Sure you are.' I linked my arm through his as we walked back and he didn't object, his chums being now safely out of sight. 'I need you to help me entertain our new neighbour.'

When Davis knocked at our door at eight o'clock, I felt nerves I knew to be entirely unconnected with the two of us and certainly nothing to do with Matthew. It was Roxy, of course. She'd emerged from her bath in a dark mood and I feared the sabotage she might effect on my efforts to present the three of us as a happy, regular meal-sharing family, getting on perfectly well, thank you very much – even if the man of the house did sit on a considerably more expensive sofa a few miles away, fondly rubbing the pregnant belly of his second wife.

As I settled Davis into an armchair with a glass of red wine, Roxy made her appearance, feet bare and hair dripping. She'd at least dressed, choosing a short, floral-print dress in cornflower blue and yellow – it was another warm, humid evening – and I felt a lurch of pride in her sheer style, the simple radiance of her youth.

Davis rose to his feet and she turned, eyes expectant, inviting his appraisal.

'Davis, this is my daughter, Roxy,' I said, brightly. 'Roxy, this is our new neighbour, Davis.'

'Hi.' She looked beyond him, probably in search of the remote control for the TV, while he regarded her with immaculate politeness. 'Roxy, a pleasure. Is your name short for Roxanne?'

'No, Roxana.' And she added, as I knew she would, 'My parents named me after an eighteenth-century prostitute. Nice, eh?'

'That's not true,' I said, smiling. 'Neither your father nor I had read the book when we chose it.'

Davis nodded. 'Ah, of course, Defoe's *Roxana*. A fascinating character, though I can see why you might object. Still, better than going all the way and naming you Nell, eh?'

'Nell Gwynn? True.' Roxy narrowed her eyes as if in grave concession. (Could no one overawe these girls?)

40

'We just loved the name, that was all,' I said, but neither seemed to hear me.

'And your mother tells me you're at Willoughby Girls. What are your A-levels?'

'English, French, Spanish and History.'

'Ah, a linguist. A woman after my own heart.'

Roxy smiled quickly at the 'woman' (she and Marianne found 'girl' patronising). Personally I thought it extraordinary that, girl or woman, she could cope with four A-levels at all. I seemed to remember struggling with three.

'Roxy's thinking about reading law at university,' I told Davis. 'Even when she was little she wanted to be a lawyer.'

'Maybe,' she shrugged. 'I haven't decided yet.'

'She has a placement with a City law firm this summer,' I added. 'She did brilliantly to get it, it's an amazing opportunity.'

Roxy smiled, but with the cold vacant eyes that told me I was committing the double sin of speaking for her *and* embarrassing her with my show of pride.

'You're not attracted to the sciences, then?' Davis asked, sipping his wine. The fingers of his free hand tapped his thigh like a keyboard.

She regarded him with a playfulness I hadn't seen before in her, but only in Marianne. 'To be perfectly honest I'm not "attracted" to anything school has to offer. It's all so incredibly safe.'

'I see. Well, fine, if it were down to me, I happen to agree. But will the universities, I wonder?'

She giggled, then, and I felt myself relax. This was going to be OK. Clearly Davis knew exactly how to handle this age group; he delivered that intentness that they liked, as though whatever they had to say was of particular interest to him. No wonder he was so busy with his private tuition; it was a competitive business around here and he must get results.

I wondered what was keeping Matthew, in his bedroom dressing after his bath. Dinner guests were rare enough for him to relish the opportunity to display his various talents. More than once Abi and Seb had been called upon to enjoy his magic tricks and impersonations. 'Do you have any children?' I asked Davis.

He drank again, this time taking a deep swallow. 'No, no. My wife and I did not have that pleasure.' I looked for clues, but he'd turned his face so that it was in profile to me. It was a very fine profile, I saw, the nose a clean, straight line, slightly downturned at the nostrils, the jawline square and strong.

'So you're divorced, then?' Roxy asked, bluntly.

'I am. We've been apart for a few years now.'

'That's what we thought.'

'We?' I said, laughing, quick to dispel any notion that the two of us had been speculating together. Roxy just shot me a pitying look before returning her attention to Davis.

'Marianne and me. We saw you the other day reading in the garden. We said straight away you looked like a bachelor.'

Davis chuckled. 'Very observant, I'm impressed. What are the clues, I wonder? An attitude of extreme misery, perhaps, or is it extreme relief?'

Roxy just giggled again, blushing slightly. I thought of that comment of Abi's: I bet she knows every detail. Was that self-absorption of hers just an act, then? For a student urged constantly to expand her list of extracurricular accomplishments (think of your personal statement on the UCAS application, girls!), she certainly seemed to do an awful lot of 'observing'.

As if sensing that he wasn't quite home and dry yet, Davis continued to charm her. 'Well, it's very kind of you to invite me for dinner and, indeed, to give up some of your home for me.'

Roxy shrugged. 'Oh, you mean the flat? It's no big deal. We need the money, don't we, Mum?'

'Roxy!' I exclaimed, embarrassed. Among the myriad other adjustments to her manner of late, she had developed a way of speaking with jaded sarcasm of anything that suggested financial struggle. It was a disappointing development, for I'd always believed that, private education or not, she had been raised to appreciate her privileges for what they were and – one of those clichés parents like to cling to – to know the value of money. Though I'd tried to hide my anxieties from her in the past, especially before the paid position had come up at work, she'd always been sensitive to the situation, occasionally not pushing for a costly school extra I knew she wanted expressly to save face for me. I'd been grateful to her, and proud, too. Well, no more. Now she made regular demands, coming to me with an attitude that suggested I was merely being given first refusal and that the goods could always be procured elsewhere if I chose to demur. Easy, as usual, to blame Marianne and her expensive wardrobe, but the fact was there were several people who might influence Roxy on this score, who might skew her attitude and expectations. Alistair and Victoria were the obvious culprits; they lived a considerably more lavish lifestyle than we did and when Roxy was with them it was hers to share. Though Alistair and I had an agreement that the children be given expensive presents only at birthdays, Christmas or occasions of special achievement, that didn't solve the fundamental problem of him actively encouraging a sense of entitlement in them. How else were they going to win those university places and traineeships if they didn't believe they were the crème de la crème?

'It's all right,' Davis said, smiling from Roxy to me. 'We all need to earn money one way or another. I'm only glad mine goes to such a happy cause.'

'Yeah,' Roxy grinned, 'it makes me laugh to think that the parents of the kids getting private tutoring are helping pay my school fees.'

I didn't point out that this was not strictly true, for it was Alistair's clients who paid her school fees, not Davis's. I couldn't have afforded Willoughby Girls with or without the new rental income. But, no matter, Davis was doing perfectly well on his own. He didn't need my protection.

'Well, that *is* how the economy works,' he said to her. His fingers had stopped tapping and now curled the hair at the back of his neck. It was such a mesmerising blend, the wry tone of voice and the easy physical manner. 'We have to keep the money circulating. But then, you already said, your interest is purely in the humanities.'

Roxy raised her eyebrows at that, reminding me once again of Marianne, who had a habit of perceiving entendre when none was intended and yet invariably played the innocent at the first sign of sarcasm. Playing games with adults, that was what it was, the two of them were like kittens practising their pouncing on toy mice. (And it was impossible not to notice how much more willing a toy grown men made than women, teacher or otherwise.)

In the kitchen the oven timer pinged and I motioned to the door. 'Shall we move to the kitchen? Dinner's ready. Let me just grab Matt . . .'

At the table Roxy helped herself to red wine and I decided against making a fuss about drinking on a school night. I asked her to light the candles while I served the food and she took a large mouthful from her glass before obliging. The candles flickered prettily and I noticed, as I had before, how much fuller the atmosphere felt, how right, with an extra person in the room.

As we ate, Davis turned his beam on Matthew, quickly learning of his recent passion for the guitar and telling him of a school in west London that taught electric guitar to would-be rock stars. Matt brimmed with eagerness, detailing the plot of a short story he'd written at school about a guitarist-cum-explorer who was trapped in an underground jail. 'Dad's taking us to South Africa in the summer. We're going to Robben Island and Table Mountain and then on safari. We're going to live in tents and have ostrich eggs for breakfast.'

'That sounds wonderful,' Davis said. 'Quite an adventure.'

I smiled through clenched teeth. Alistair always delivered

44

some grandstanding summer holiday and though I'd suggested he take the kids this year to France to help improve Roxy's spoken French – it was reportedly her weakest area – he'd come up instead with something that required jabs and a bucketful of worry on my part. Roxy was one thing, more than capable of looking after herself, but surely he knew I wouldn't rest knowing Matthew was out in the middle of the plains with just a sheet of canvas separating his sweet face from a herd of beasts?

'Even Roxy's coming,' Matthew said to Davis, as though the trip would have to be pretty damn special for her to deign to participate. She merely rolled her eyes at his comment and reached for her wine. The age gap between them had never been wider; they had so little in common these days. Perhaps I should be more grateful to Alistair for his family holidays, after all, for all his activities. If it weren't for those regular weekends with their father, they'd probably do nothing together at all.

After the meal I sent Matthew off to bed and Roxy removed herself of her own accord, leaving Davis and me to face each other across the table. I opened more wine, looking up as he sighed, exhaling the air like cigarette smoke.

'Well, you have very nice children. They're a credit to you.' I sensed that he meant it, too, wasn't simply fulfilling the guest's obligation.

'Thank you. It's hard, sometimes, though.' I regretted saying it at once; I'd warned myself not to stray into any of the territory that might lead him to fear he was being sized up romantically.

He nodded dutifully, bracing himself no doubt for the standard parental rant. Lord only knew what kind of family tensions he was privy to in his everyday work. He patted his trouser pocket. 'Do you mind if I smoke?'

I did, primarily for the message it sent Roxy – on the one occasion she'd found me smoking, literally a drag or two with Abi, she'd crowed about it for weeks – but I got the feeling that if I said no I would ruin this lovely, easy atmosphere between us;

he'd only be edgy to get back to his own quarters. 'No, not at all. Just let me open the window a bit more . . .'

I stretched to reach the frame and, as I did, spotted the wide gape between buttons across my bust. Seated once more, I straightened the fabric, fingers out of sight under the table, but thankfully Davis was too busy lighting a cigarette to have noticed. With the window pushed right up, we automatically turned to look out of it, the view obscured by nightfall but still revealing a lovely shadowy landscape of black-green, lit by the interior lights of the flats beyond. Our block was about halfway down the street, the two shorter sides that squared off the rectangle only in peripheral sight, so it was like looking across a river. Opposite me Davis wouldn't have looked out of place in a Left Bank café in the 1950s, narrowing his eyes as he blew smoke into the night.

'Roxy smokes,' I said, watching the stream of grey leave his lips. 'And probably more than I think, as well.'

He nodded. 'They all do. They think it makes them look grown up, but what they don't realise is that they're the only ones doing it. All the grown-ups have given up. Except for the occasional hopeless case like me, of course.'

I smiled. 'She hid it at first, of course, but I told her there was no point. I'd rather know.'

He blinked heavily, almost sleepily, another of his slightly distracted mannerisms, like the winding of his hair around his finger, and the effect was curiously lulling, like a hushed voice. 'Parents say that to me a lot, you know. They'd "rather know". I wonder sometimes if that's the right approach.'

'How do you mean?'

He held my gaze. In the candlelight the irises of his eyes looked quite black. 'Well, I'm obviously not qualified to say, but I seem to remember that the whole idea of adolescence was the secrecy. An enlightened parental attitude doesn't present nearly the same challenge, does it?'

I thought about Roxy. Though guarded in her own comments towards me, there was a particular way she looked at me whenever anyone else said something she thought I might find insulting; she'd get watchful, even gleeful, enjoying my discomfort while knowing she wouldn't get the blame. 'Maybe. I think they want their subversiveness noted, though. They want to have their cake and eat it. They want to break the rules *and* get credit for it.'

He looked at me with interest. 'You think it's all a form of innocence, then? Even when they're sinning they're doing it for effect? Deep down they simply yearn for the correct moral line to be reinforced?'

I stared, uncertain how to respond. I couldn't think of anyone else I knew who used words like 'yearn' and 'sinning'. It reminded me of tutorials at university, times when I'd invariably struggled to hold my own. 'I don't suppose I really think about it, not intellectually like that. I just try to cope with all the moods and changes without being too much of a dragon. Appreciate what I've got while I've got it.'

I was disappointed with my own answer; it sounded sentimental and distinctly lacking in wit, but Davis's face softened with sympathy. 'And all the time you have your own moods and changes, too, of course.'

'Not that they would care.' I smiled. 'I say "they", but I don't mean Matthew. He's still young.' He's still mine. I surprised myself with the thought, for it was the first time I'd acknowledged to myself that Roxy may no longer be. Whose was she then? Her father's? Her friends'? Her own?

There was a sudden silence as the whirr of the extractor fan in the bathroom puttered out – Roxy off to bed – just as the music from the CD player faded. I thought about getting up to put on a new disc but the silence made me bolder and I stayed where I was. 'I was wondering,' I said, but seeing his raised eyebrows changed my mind and muttered, 'no, sorry, it's rude to ask.'

'Go on, please.' He smiled encouragingly. 'Your daughter certainly would.'

'Well, it's just, someone like you, how do you come to be renting on your own around here . . .?'

He looked at me with an arch expression. 'At my time of life, you mean? How am I not a man of property? Isn't that the sole aim and ambition of every inhabitant of this city?'

'Your divorce, I suppose?' I said, suddenly realising.

'Actually, my wife and I never did buy a house together. We lived in a flat owned by her father, which gave her the illusion of renting she wanted so much.'

'How do you mean?'

'You could say she was slumming it with me. She saw me as the penniless artist and cast herself in the role of muse.'

'Artist? You mean you paint?' I didn't remember seeing any art materials when he'd moved in, but then he had hardly started unpacking when I'd dropped by and I hadn't been into the flat since. I thought with concern of dripping canvases stacked against my furniture and was immediately ashamed of my lack of bohemian spirit. 'What kind of thing do you do?'

He ground out his cigarette. 'Not paint, write.'

'Oh! You're working on a novel? How exciting!'

He shook his head. 'I think of it more as fragments.'

'Fragments? Like poetry?'

'In part.' He paused. 'I hope you don't mind, but I don't like to give too much away. That's when it starts to become something it's not, if you see what I mean.'

'Of course, I understand totally.' Now that I knew my parquet wasn't to be destroyed by turps I found I was ridiculously impressed by the idea of some mysterious masterwork being brought to life on the premises. I imagined a new figure appearing in these 'fragments', an unlikely new muse. (Only afterwards did I notice the parallel with his ex-wife, that I was simply replicating the very fantasy of hers that he had just mocked.)

48

'Why did you split up?' I asked before I could stop myself. And nor could I stop myself leaning forward, the better to absorb his answer.

'Why do we all split up?' he said, and blinked that mesmerising heavy blink again.

'I don't know.' I waited, enthralled, the wine making me feel a sense of significance that wasn't really there. I was the pilgrim who'd travelled for days through hostile terrain for that once-in-a-lifetime five minutes with the sage in the mountain cave.

'There was someone else,' he said, finally, and looked away. Then he tucked his lighter into his cigarette packet as if to indicate that the subject was closed.

'Oh.' It didn't feel appropriate to ask whether the 'someone else' in question had been hers or his.

Chapter 5

He left me a note a day or two later, a beautifully phrased thank you on a postcard of a Viennese street scene. I pinned it on the corkboard in the kitchen next to Roxy's police printout and admired his taste in photography. I couldn't help feeling disappointed that he'd not found the time to come by in person, however. The nature of our jobs meant that we both spent more time at home than the average London worker; there had to be idle moments in his day when he might consider strolling the dozen or so steps from his desk to my front door. As the days slipped by I wondered if he might, in fact, be avoiding me.

I knew I was denying my attraction to Davis, but in acknowledging the denial I only acknowledged the attraction. It was a classic case of protesting too much. A couple of times at work when I was typing up case notes between clients, I would allow my mind to wander to him and then I would remind myself of a golden rule that had suddenly lost its shine. Was this happening because I was ready to consider a relationship again – as Abi said, I couldn't realistically shut down forever – or was I responding to something in Davis that hadn't existed in anyone else I'd met since Alistair? Whether this was an accident of timing or a genuinely worthwhile connection seemed to me to be a crucial distinction.

I re-read the line on the screen in front of me: 'Mr Bicknell has been issued with a final warning from the finance company with which he last year refinanced a personal loan, and has asked for advice about filing for bankruptcy . . .' Continue with the burden of a loan he could never hope to repay or cripple himself with a label that would send alarm bells ringing in the head of any prospective employer or landlord? Now *that* was a proper dilemma. My own was just self-indulgent nonsense. I'd keep my anxieties to myself, I decided, I wouldn't even voice them to Abi. Just imagining how I'd phrase it to her made me understand how girlish it was, like confessing to a crush. So naïve, so teenage.

'Kate, it's me. Is now a good time?'

Alistair's barked tone immediately put my back up. All those years of exorcising him from the flat and he could still invade it afresh with a single phone call. I could always sense when it was him, the phone seemed to ring with greater potency, and no matter how closely I held it to my ear his energy would leak into the atmosphere around me. This morning he was on the offensive, that much was clear; more budget cuts, no doubt. As for that arrogant 'It's me' – how I resented his assumption that still, after all this time, there was no one else who might be my 'me'.

'What's up?' I started to ask, but he interrupted at once, impatient even to allow those two words from me. 'What the fuck is going on with Roxy?'

'With Roxy?' She'd been quite sunny that morning, I remembered, at least sunny on the Roxy Easton barometer.

'Yes, Roxy. Our darling daughter. She's just rung to say she's pulling out of her summer placement. Are you *mad*? I thought we agreed it's an incredible opportunity for her?'

'We did and it is.' I ignored the personal accusation he'd flung in there for the hell of it and automatically adopted my calm, level work voice. 'Alistair, I don't know anything about this, I promise you. What do you mean she's just called? She's supposed to be in class.'

He gave an exasperated growl, as if to say he'd been expecting this, it had only been a matter of time before I finally lost all control over my daughter (for, when in trouble, Roxy was inevitably mine and not ours). I could hear traffic noise in the background, he was obviously driving and phoning simultaneously. I imagined him scowling at other drivers, spoiling for a fight, daring someone to take him on.

'This is a top five law firm, for God's sake! And I don't need to add that it won't reflect well on Victoria. She had to put a lot of pressure on HR to get Roxy in, and now she's pregnant, well, they're playing silly buggers, of course, exactly as we predicted.'

'*I* didn't predict anything,' I said, sharply. There it was, under two minutes and I was already bristling. Victoria remained, and perhaps always would, my Achilles heel. It had taken every ounce of my dignity – already a much-depleted resource – to celebrate her arrangement of a coveted work-experience position for Roxy with one of her partners. 'I'm afraid you'll have to forgive me if I'm not weeping over her treatment.'

Alistair snorted. 'Well, you should be. Isn't sexual discrimination the kind of thing you deal with every day? You're supposed to look out for the little guy, aren't you? Sorry, little "woman".'

I regretted my sarcasm. Alistair found this sort of exchange irresistible, confident from the outset of his victory. He fired up quickly, was always the first to allow a discussion to escalate into a row, ready to draw in every possible tangential issue. I forced myself to pause and regroup. I of all people knew that his sudden flames needed extinguishing, not fanning. It was also, and had generally been to date, the only way I could keep our co-parenting amicable (if your definition of amicable was reasonably flexible). 'It tends to be more housing issues we deal with, Alistair, or debt problems, but that's not the point. Shall we get back to the Roxy situation? Are you sure she's pulling out?'

'That's what she said. She wants to get paid work and is applying for a job in a deli. A *deli*!' He said the word with disgust, as he might 'sewer'.

'A deli?' I repeated. 'That's odd.'

'It's fucking *insane*. You know what? If she wants the money she'd earn skivvying, then I'll give it to her up front!'

I frowned. 'I'm not sure that's the best idea. We shouldn't reward her for messing people around.'

He growled again. 'Well, what exactly do you suggest, then?'

'I'll talk to her as soon as she comes back and try to persuade her to change her mind. In the meantime, Victoria shouldn't say anything at work.'

'Well, I know that.' There was a silence. Evidently he was on a quieter part of the route now and I could hear him calming as he weighed up the advantages still in his favour. 'It doesn't start for a few weeks, I suppose. We've got time.'

'And I'm sure Roxy is still very grateful to Victoria for offering her this opportunity . . .'

'She bloody should be, there's a reserve list as long as your arm. Last year's two both got Oxbridge offers, you know?'

I did know, for it had been discussed at length, and I felt my stomach twist with anxiety for Roxy and the competitiveness of her generation, a competitiveness foisted upon her and every child by their schools, by parents, by society. Generation Stressed, Davis had called it, though its members seemed to me remarkably absorbent of it all. At the age of seventeen every last one of them had credentials and experience to fill a dozen supplementary pages on their UCAS applications. Though I didn't know anything about this deli alternative, whatever it was, I could guarantee that it would be being contested by girls who at some time in the near future would be sitting four A-levels and expecting top grades. And, come the college interview, it would have been rebranded as some sort of triumphant revitalisation of an ailing local business, complete with Fairtrade beans and a new village school in Guatemala. It was exhausting just thinking about it.

'Let me call you later,' I said with finality. 'We want the same thing here, Alistair, OK?'

I hung up and began loading the dishwasher with Matthew's and my breakfast things (Roxy had been meeting friends for a cappuccino before class – I wondered if that was where she'd called her father from; the idea may have struck just minutes before she phoned him). *Did* we want the same thing, Alistair and I, for our daughter? All I had ever thought I wanted was for her to be happy (another cliché clung to!), and yet lately she seemed happy only when following Marianne Suter to some gig or party or music festival, obviously drinking and smoking and God knew what else while she was at it, and that was *not* what I wanted. Alistair at least had tangible ambitions for his children: an excellent education, the best his money could buy; a top university, preferably Oxford or Cambridge, but, if not, then certainly one of the remaining top five (he could quote the top five of everything, it was an obsession; sixth place was not negotiable); a starting salary three times the national average; and, finally, a prominent career. Only when the Easton offspring had been quoted in *The Times* on the subject of his or her particular genius would their father dust his hands and be done.

Personal lives he left to the gods.

I had to wait until ten in the evening for an audience with Roxy. Rehearsals had begun for the summer play, a musical this year, *Bugsy Malone*. Another notch on the sixth-form CV. Marianne starred as Tallulah and Roxy had been cast as the detective Captain Smolsky. She had hoped to be one of Tallulah's showgirls, which would mean spending all rehearsals with Marianne, but girls like her (i.e. those who were tall with small breasts and narrow hips) were in demand at a girls' school for the male roles, and Captain Smolsky it was.

Her bedroom door was ajar and I knocked before pushing it open any further. I decided it was best not to skirt around the issue. 'Roxy, your father tells me you've decided not to go ahead with the placement at Clifton Merchant.'

She turned from her desk, laptop open in front of her. 'News travels fast.'

'It's true, then?'

'Yeah.'

'But why?'

She pouted, as if 'Why not?' was as good an answer as any, and then said, 'I just thought I'll be way too busy to do that on top of everything else.'

'Everything else?'

'Yeah, theatre summer school, if I get in, all my voluntary stuff, catching up on French. Mrs Richardson says I need extra conversation practice. She's going to recommend a summer course.' She went on to list, quite passionlessly, further, lesser commitments and I felt my concern rising even before she reached the last. 'And maybe working at Eli's . . .'

I pounced. 'As in Eli's, the deli on the high street?'

'Yep, I've got an interview there on Saturday.'

'But if you're too busy to do the law thing then aren't you too busy for that, as well? It doesn't make sense, darling.'

She visibly prickled at the 'darling'. I did it automatically; still permitted my endearments with Matthew, I'd forget that they were to be dropped for her. It was a horrible feeling, having to stifle an expression of love, but for now that was what was required of me. 'It makes perfect sense. They've got extra wait-ressing shifts going and it's just down the road. If I have to make coffee for a bunch of yuppies I'd rather earn tips doing it.' She paused. 'Marianne's going to the Edinburgh Festival, you know, and I'm not doing *that*.'

I knew a red herring when I heard one. This was hardly the first time that the subject of Marianne's greater freedoms had been introduced as a useful diversion. 'But the placement is such a rare opportunity, Roxy. You seemed so pleased when you heard you'd got it.'

She shrugged. 'That's because I still thought I might want to do law at university. Now I know I don't.'

I gasped at the casualness of her tone. For as long as I could remember it had been her (and Alistair's) plan to apply for law at Cambridge. I must have been wrong about her changing her mind on a whim; this was a serious about-turn. 'Well, why not do the placement and then decide? You can't possibly know for sure without seeing what it's really like.'

Another shrug. 'Why not? Loads of girls at school want to do law and they're sure. Maybe I should give the Clifton Merchant place to one of them? Everyone knows I only got it through nepotism, anyway.'

I knew better than to start arguing the pros and cons of nepotism. Another red herring. How adept she was at these sorts of exchanges, she was all guile. Where Alistair exploded, she entrapped. I wasn't present at the arguments they had together (one benefit of our divorce, at least), but I could only assume that she was much the cooler-headed. As for how I matched up . . . well, I didn't, it was as simple as that. I couldn't pinpoint exactly when it was that her skills had begun to exceed mine, but they had. Sometimes, it hardly seemed a moment since she was three or four, sweetly transparent in her challenges, delighted just to get a rise out of an adult. I remembered being amazed at how eager she was to get the power struggle underway, even before she had the words to present her case. No, as with Alistair, all I could do was manage the personality – the only problem was that with Roxy I was never quite sure that what I was managing was the same as it had been the day before.

'OK,' I said brightly. 'Well, even if you don't want to study law, it will still be fantastic experience. It might give you ideas for other careers.'

She grimaced. 'For other ways to make a shed load of cash, you mean? That may be important to you and Dad, Mum, but I don't care about money.'

That wasn't fair, and nor did it gel with her argument about choosing the paid work over the unpaid, but again I resisted the bait. 'OK, so if you've changed your mind about the law, what is it you think you'd like to do at university?' I remembered that exchange with Davis. Nothing attracts me, she'd said, and though it had sounded like affectation, I'd had a feeling she meant it. I had sympathy for her, really I did. She was expected to choose so early, to plot her course before she'd even learned how to sail.

She shuffled the mouse on its mat and clicked open her email, tossing the words over her shoulder as she scanned her new messages: 'I thought modern languages, possibly. French.'

'*French*? But that's . . .' I stopped myself from remarking that this was by all accounts her weakest subject. It was relative, after all, a B as opposed to an A. I thought again of the trip to South Africa in place of the French one I'd hoped for, and that gave me an idea.

'You know, if you pull out of the law placement, Dad will be very disappointed. He might decide to cancel the safari.'

Now I had her full attention. She turned from her email to meet my eye with a look that said, Is that *really* the best you can come up with?, and then wheeled back around and began tapping at the keyboard. 'Whatever.' (Whatever. I'd tried to institute a ban on that word, but it kept slipping through, just like my own 'darling's and 'love's.)

'It's late,' I said, fairly sure she was bluffing. 'Let's talk again in the morning, OK?'

'If you like.'

'Yes, Roxy, I *do* like.'

As she resumed her typing, apparently still brimming with energy, I had no choice but to give up and go to bed. Not for the first time I wished both Alistair and her to some faraway place where I could no longer be their go-between. Keeping the peace, putting the fires out – it was a full-time job.

She left the next morning before breakfast, another new habit, and as I walked back from dropping Matthew at school, Alistair was already on the phone. I related the previous night's conversation and waited for the explosion. For once it didn't come.

'You'd better let me try,' he said, wearily, as though dismissing a junior he'd never believed up to the job in the first place. 'Put her on the phone, will you.'

'It's nine-thirty on a Wednesday, Alistair. She's at school, and her phone will be switched off. I'll ask her to call you as soon as I see her.' I paused. 'I was thinking, when you do speak to her, if you threaten not to take her to South Africa she might be more likely to come around.'

He gave a short, mirthless bark of laughter. 'Oh, *I* get it.'

'You get what?'

'You want me to be the bad cop. You haven't tried at all, have you? You've just buttered her up and now you want to leave the nasty bit to me.'

'Oh, don't be ridiculous! Of course I've tried. I just don't have the same leverage you do at this moment in time. What can I say to her? Do the placement or I won't wash your bed linen? I don't think that would work somehow, do you?'

'There's her driving lessons.'

'She pays for those herself out of her allowance.' Topped up constantly by you, I added, silently. There were times when it seemed to me that Roxy and her friends were practically salaried. 'And anyway, that's hardly withdrawing a treat, is it?'

'Right. So I'm supposed to lose my holiday with her, the only quality time I get with my daughter the whole year. Come on, Kate, that's fucking crap and you know it!'

Again my throat buzzed with unspoken protest. It's not my

choice you don't get any time with her, you selfish bastard, not my choice you left her, left *me* . . . And what kind of quality time did he think *I* got with her, exactly? Certainly not the luxury of a two-week trip to South Africa! 'That's not the idea, Alistair, and *you* know it. The idea is that you threaten to pull the trip, she goes through with the placement and gets the holiday after all. Everybody wins. It's a negotiation.'

He gave a contemptuous huff. 'Well, thanks for your negotiation tips, but I think you might be overestimating the allure of the big cat. Matthew, maybe, but not Roxy. Perhaps if I withhold her pass to the spa tent?'

I smiled at that, despite myself. 'Look, I'll have another go, and if that doesn't work, then you try. But we might just have to accept that she isn't going to do it. Ultimately, her career is her own choice.'

'I'm sure the admissions panel at Tin Pan Poly will be delighted to hear it.'

There was a second huff and the line went dead. I'd reached the steps of the building and slotted my key into the lock. The door closed heavily behind me and I leaned against it to deaden the slam, allowing its weight to guide me forward into the silence. I seriously considered screaming. Perhaps if I pressed my face into my pigeonhole it would muffle the sound so well no one would hear it. I resisted (I always resisted), but as I reached the fifth floor and unlocked the outer door, I realised I was exhaling too noisily, almost groaning, a reaction that was way out of proportion to the effects of the climb.

'Is everything all right?'

I looked up. It was Davis Calder, cool and amiable. 'I'm fine, yes, thank you.'

'Are you sure? You seem a little distressed.'

'Oh . . .' I broke off, sighing. 'Just family stuff. Roxy.'

'Ah. Stuff but not nonsense.' Drawn to him though I was, I was in no mood for his literary wordplays, so I just smiled briefly at him and made for my front door. As I passed his, however, he opened it wide and beckoned me in. 'Come on, I owe you a coffee. Let me see if I can help, eh?'

Behind him I could see the twin windows sparkling with sunlight, a framed picture over the mantelpiece, some sort of spiral design, like the shell of a snail. There was a Persian rug, too, a large one that covered much of the floor, all faded and frayed, which only enhanced the beauty of the patterning. Once, this had been my favourite room in the apartment, but already I couldn't remember it without the picture and the rug.

'All right.' Obediently, I followed him in. It smelled different now, of old books and coffee beans and the faint musk of tobacco. As he fiddled with the kettle I studied the picture above the fireplace. *Phare des Baleines*, the caption said.

'It's the inside of a lighthouse,' Davis said, 'the spiral staircase photographed from below. If you look closely, you can see a hand gripping on to the railing . . .'

I searched the picture. 'Oh, yes, how clever to show the scale like that. It must be very tall.'

'Yep, two-hundred-and-fifty steps, something like that. I've got a friend who lives right next to it.' He handed me a mug and continued on to the bookshelves, where he located and pulled down a slim paperback. Joining me by the fireplace he handed it to me. 'Have you read any Mishima?'

'I don't think so, no.' I took the book with care – its yellowed innards were coming unstuck from the spine – and read the title: *The Sound of Waves*.

'There's a very nice scene where the two lovers undress in front of the fire,' he said, almost in a murmur.

I continued to stare at the book, feeling colour spread in a slow ripple from the tip of my nose. I couldn't tell if Davis was still looking at me or not, but I heard him laugh. 'It's set in a lighthouse. That's what made me think of it.'

'Oh, OK.' I pretended to study the text on the back cover. 'An exquisite story of first love . . .' What on earth had I thought he'd meant (*hoped* he'd meant)? For a stupid moment I considered dashing from the room, getting out of his sight before my blushes could give me away, but what would that achieve? It would only draw attention to my foolishness.

Meanwhile, Davis settled himself on the sofa and finished stirring sugar into his coffee. Then he rapped the spoon on the rim of the cup like a judge calling for order. 'Now, tell me what's going on with your daughter.'

Emerging an hour later, I felt less like screaming than singing. The world had not stopped turning, after all. Davis had given me exactly what I needed from Alistair but so rarely got: sympathy for my daily frontline battering, constructive suggestions for a ceasefire, a peace treaty for the future, or at least the foreseeable future. He would talk to Roxy himself. He had a student who had an offer from Oxford to read modern languages and he would introduce Roxy to her the very next day. Together they would explain why the forthcoming summer break could be the most important of her life.

When I told Roxy the plan, she merely shrugged her agreement. Bombarded with advice from morning till night, she saw nothing peculiar about being hustled into a neighbour's flat between breakfast and the school run to hear a complete stranger's view on her career options.

'Promise me you'll listen to him, Rox. He knows what he's talking about.'

'Yeah, yeah.' But she was interested, I could tell; she'd liked Davis that night over dinner. With his glamorous looks and that flow of wry, easy banter, he'd made it onto the Roxy radar.

I was due at work and didn't see her again until we met in the kitchen that evening, but whatever Davis had said, it had clearly done the trick.

'You'll be pleased to hear I'm doing the placement,' she

announced, cracking open a Diet Coke and eyeing me over the top of the can.

'You are?' I felt my lips stretch sideways into a grin. It was so long since I'd smiled like this I actually felt muscular strain in my cheeks. 'That's wonderful news, darling!'

'Davis says Clifton Merchant have a Paris office and I should ask if I can visit while I'm there. Even if it's just for a day, it will look good on my application if I do go for modern languages.'

That was a smart idea, I thought, impressed. 'You met one of his students, the one going to Oxford?'

'Yeah, Lucy something. She was cool. Her French was way better than mine, though, it was embarrassing.'

'Don't forget she's a year ahead of you.'

'Hmm, obviously. But anyway Davis says he'll give me extra coaching over the summer to catch up.'

'He will?' I frowned. 'Will you have time?'

'I will if I pass my driving test next month.' Her test was scheduled for the last day of term and appeared to hold none of the terror for her that I remembered from my own. 'We said Thursday nights, maybe weekends as well. And don't worry, he's going to waive his fees in the interests of neighbourly goodwill.'

'That's very kind of him.' I felt my whole body go warm with pleasure, with the idea that Davis had done this for *me*, to make *my* life easier. 'Well, your father will be pleased,' I added.

'It's not about Dad,' Roxy said, airily. 'It's about me.'

I suppressed a smile. 'OK. Well, I'm glad you found your chat with Davis useful. He's a nice guy, isn't he?'

It seemed to me that the look she gave me then was full of knowing, knowing that I was fishing for her recognition that Davis had gone out of his way to help, that his offer might have some greater significance than simple kindness. 'By the way,' she said, finally, 'Auntie Tash rang. She spoke to Matt and said she's coming down soon. She said she'd take him on the London Eye again. I hope they remember to get off this time.'

'"Soon"? Didn't she say exactly when?'

'She wasn't "exactly" sure.' Roxy grinned, enjoying the shared joke of Tash's unreliability. It was the same grin Matthew and I had begun to use recently for Roxy herself, though in her case it was less about unreliability than unpredictability. Diva, that's what Matthew called her, Roxy the diva.

'Are you in for dinner?' I asked, expecting the usual negative.

She gulped the Coke. 'Yeah, sure. I haven't seen Matt properly for ages.'

Turning to the cupboard for pasta, I found my eyes full of tears. Crisis over, we could be, for now, for one evening, a happy family again. I'd call Alistair tomorrow with the good news. Let him stew in his own juice for a night.

Chapter 6

When I first began working at the Advice Centre I was distressed by some of the cases presented to me, often finishing my shift in tears. It was perfectly natural, Ethan said. I had fallen into the trap of overempathising, imagining behind-the-scenes horrors that had not taken place: children neglected and wives abused, slum deprivations that belonged to another century. There was an episode when a man trailed in at eleven in the morning, can of Special Brew in one hand, three infants and a puppy in the other, and though his problem had been a straightforward one involving disability benefits, I slipped into the supervisor's office afterwards to ask Ethan if I shouldn't probe other areas of his domestic situation as well.

'Think about it,' Ethan said. He had a calm, methodical manner that really did make everything seem like it was going to be all right. 'Did the children look tired or unwell?'

'No, not really.'

'Was the puppy clean?'

'Yes, and it was wagging its tail.' I flushed, realising that I sounded about five years old.

To Ethan's credit he continued to regard me with perfect seriousness. 'Right, well, that's all you need to know. So what if the guy wants a drink in the middle of the day, it's a free country and maybe he's having a bad day. You're no one's buddy, Kate. People come here because something about the administrative system has stumped them. Just sort it out as best you can.'

'Of course.'

There was always the fear, especially in the early years after my divorce, that I might be presented with a situation that echoed my own and allow the two to get tangled up together in my head. In fact, this did happen, though more in the form of a glimpse of a worst-case scenario than any real parallel. A woman needed advice about getting a family lawyer through legal aid, her ex-husband having announced that he wanted custody of their eight-year-old daughter. An older child, a boy of eleven, had already chosen to live with his father.

'I suppose if it's what they want,' she kept saying in a small, wobbly voice.

'It's not what they *want*, it's what is best for their welfare,' I said, trying to emulate Ethan's peaceful tones, but already sounding overemotional. Welfare: the word never failed to remind me of the day that my mother had intervened in my own crisis. It was about a week after I'd found out that the 'friend' Alistair had been staying with was in fact his new lover, her flat no longer just somewhere to receive redirected mail but a permanent change of address. The Francombe Gardens flat was a pigsty, Roxy was virtually looking after herself – and her infant brother, while I lay in bed inert with grief, hardly eating, and sobbing at the drop of a hat.

'My God, I had no idea!' Mum took in the general disarray and looked thoroughly appalled. 'This is affecting their welfare, Kate.'

'They're fine,' I snuffled. 'They've got me.'

'Well, they need you in better shape than this.'

Later I heard her on the phone to my father. 'It's not a break-down, Chris, don't say that. She just needs sorting out a bit.' She moved in the next day – it was either that or send the children temporarily to Alistair's, which meant around-the-clock child-care, since both Alistair and Victoria worked twelve-hour days – and reinstituted all the normal family routines I'd let slip. Slowly, step by step, I re-emerged from my hell and, once free of it, vowed never to return.

'He's got more money,' the woman said, the fight dribbling from her with every sentence. 'And his new wife has some posh job as well. They'll have more opportunities with him. Better prospects.' The way she said it made me think she was repeating someone else's lines.

'Money isn't the issue,' I said, briskly, 'and, anyway, it's very rare for a father to be awarded a residence order. He'd have to prove that you're unfit.'

She looked uncertain.

'Which you're not, of course.'

I told myself I'd only reinforced her own instincts, instincts that were spot-on – every mother should have her children with her, surely! Afterwards, though, looking at her file and reading the long history of complaints against her, I wondered if all I'd done was fill her with false hope, and condemn the children to future agonies they didn't deserve.

At Abi's insistence I invited Davis to come out with us for a drink at the bar on the high street overlooking the green. Ostensibly, the occasion was to be a thank you for his having helped with the Roxy situation, but in reality it was an opportunity for Abi to appraise him. Seb, a pianist turned accountant who could be relied on to mix well with most people, was drafted in as a reserve juror. It was only with a certain dragging of feet that Roxy agreed to mind Matt – hardly a chore, as he would be asleep in bed for the most part and she had already arranged for Marianne to come over to learn their lines for the school play. Personally, I didn't think Marianne would need much rehearsal, she was a born Tallulah. Even now, in casual wide-legged workout trousers and ribbed vest, she exuded a kind of starlet glamour.

'Hi, Mrs Easton, you look very nice. Roxy says you're going out with Davis tonight.'

Instantly I was alert to the subtext: 'Mrs Easton' for me but 'Davis' for him, as though Marianne knew him considerably better than she did me. Had she even met Davis? And, if so, when? Either way, she would seem to be suggesting that while my seniority was beyond dispute, his was somehow more flexible. I blinked, alarmed at my own neuroses – it was only a simple pleasantry, for goodness sake! – and smiled back at her. 'That's right, Marianne, we're just going for a quick drink with friends.'

That was when Roxy waded in: 'I know, it's *so* tacky, isn't it? Going after the lodger.' She had adopted an unmistakably proprietorial air around Davis since his coup over the work experience and the promise of coaching. As usual, though, she had waited for Marianne's presence before commencing her sniping. (I told myself this was a good thing: if she needed the moral support then she couldn't yet be wholly evil.)

'I'm not *going after* anyone,' I objected. 'Unless a large glass of red wine counts?'

Marianne pulled a face. I'd have to do better than that to amuse her. 'Could be worse, I suppose. My mum's shagging her personal trainer. Now *that*'s a cliché.'

Roxy laughed. 'Oh, but he's seriously hot.'

'I know, who wouldn't?'

Abi, who had just arrived to pick me up on the way, was taken aback by this sort of talk. She looked at me as if to say, 'Aren't you going to do something about this?'

I tried to take control, re-establish the facts. 'Look, there is nothing between Davis and me.' I sent Roxy a warning look but it was far too late in the conversation for me to expect it to have any effect. 'He is simply one of three friends with whom I'm having a casual drink.'

'As adults do,' Abi added. It was the worst possible approach – insinuating that Roxy and Marianne were *not* adults – and they both glared unpleasantly at her as though she had brought in a particularly nasty smell. The sight of Roxy's sneer made me unhappy. When we'd first got to know Abi, she had admired her, but these days my friend seemed to fall short of the requisite glamour in both appearance and job. Like me, she lacked cool.

'Well,' Marianne said, ignoring Abi and directing her next comment at me, 'I can think of worse guys to have a "casual drink" with.' Her Mae West drawl made it sound as rude as if she'd openly said 'have sex with', but before I could protest I noticed Roxy frown at her friend, drawing a quizzical look in return. My heart lifted a little. Was that it, then, the cause of her hostility, simple fear that I might one day have a new relationship and be taken away from her, just as Alistair had? I tried to catch her eye again, this time to reassure her that nothing was going to change, but she was already turning impatiently away. I realised she'd only been gesturing to Marianne to wrap this up and get rid of us.

'Have fun,' they called as we left, openly insincere, minds already on other things.

'Bloody hell,' said Abi, on the stairs. 'Talk about mean girls! What happened to sweet little Roxy?'

I chuckled. 'She's been taken by aliens and replaced with some kind of London Valley Girl.'

'I had no idea! I mean, you said she'd changed recently, but God Almighty. Poor you! How do you cope with all that bitchiness? It must be awful.'

I knew better than to answer with my immediate emotional response, something along the lines of, 'Because I love her more than life itself, because one minute of her sunshine is worth a hundred of her thunder,' as that would sound melodramatic (or plain wet – one of the two). Instead, I said, 'Oh, I just try to put it down to what it is: someone who has the attitude but not the experience. They know not what they say, kind of thing.'

Abi wasn't having any of it. 'You mean it's all talk and no action? They're still virgins? Didn't Roxy sleep with that dark-haired one, then? Damien?'

I took a sharp intake of breath. Over the last year or so, and especially when she'd been seeing Damien, I had tried many approaches to gain Roxy's confidence about sex – direct questioning, one-to-ones about birth control and HIV, casual little anecdotes about clients' dilemmas intended to draw related confessions of her own – and had emphasised with varying degrees of passion that I could be trusted implicitly not to judge or to pry. Not a single night had been spent, officially, with Damien, though there'd been plenty at girlfriends' houses and I had been very strict with myself about never phoning to check up on her. But, without exception, I'd been kept at arm's length. All of which meant that I'd spent far too many hours inside my own head pondering exactly Abi's question. If only I could go into work and look up the answer on our database, then get a helpline number to call if I wanted to appeal it. 'I don't know,' I said, truthfully. 'She never really told me. But I haven't heard much about Damien recently. Marianne has someone, though, a DJ she met in a club. Rob, he's called. He's twenty-two, five years older than her.'

'Is that the trendy thing, then, an older man?'

'I think whatever Marianne does is the trendy thing.' I thought of Alistair. Though married to a woman ten years younger than he was, he would erupt at the mere suggestion of Roxy with someone of Rob's age. 'She has a double bed in her bedroom, apparently.'

Abi looked aghast. 'No way? That's like suggesting to your daughter that she goes ahead and has sex with everyone she meets!'

'Or that it's no big deal and therefore not worth using as an

69

act of rebellion.' I remembered what Davis had said about parents flattering themselves to think that their opinions figured in their teenagers' decisions in the first place. He was right: girls like Roxy didn't do what we said *or* did; they did whatever their friends were doing.

Abi still looked scandalised. 'She's like a model or something, that Marianne. But even Roxy, I used to think of her as a late developer, y'know, flat-chested and a bit gawky, but she looks completely grown-up now.'

I nodded. 'They are, physically. If you think about it, there are plenty of girls out there their age with a couple of babies already. It could be a lot worse.'

'Yes, they could have the vote.' We both laughed. 'Right, forget about Roxy now. You never get out, this will be fun.'

It was true that a night out was rare for me. Even my regular free nights, when the children were with Alistair, were spent in my own kitchen or in Abi's, or occasionally at the table of a parent friend from Matt's school for overcooked pasta and exhausted conversation. I didn't have the budget for extensive socialising, nor even for babysitting. This *was* a treat, whether Davis was involved or not.

We had reached the green. The bar was already full, most of the outside tables crowded with groups of office workers. It was June, the trees were full and green, screening the sky on every side. The air seemed to hold an uneasy blend of traffic fumes and pollen.

Abi nudged me. 'There he is, look, the handsome devil. Ooh, he's getting to his feet, as well, *very* gallant.'

Having spent the days since I'd last seen Davis stifling any but the most neighbourly instincts, I now allowed myself to tingle slightly at the kisses that he administered to my cheeks before he took Abi's hand. 'Well, another Francombe Gardens neighbour. Very pleased to meet you, Abigail. It strikes me that we could do with our own bar.'

I watched Abi take in the loose, silver-black curls and patrician bone structure, the rich timbre of his voice that made every comment sound so incredibly intimate. 'I vote we go the whole hog and get a swimming pool,' she said, rather throatily, 'and then we can have a swim-up bar.'

'What a good idea. I'll get my landlady to propose it at the next residents' committee meeting.'

We all laughed. He had already begun a bottle of red wine and poured a glass for each us. It was a nice one, smoother than the discounted supermarket stuff I bought for myself, and I gulped enthusiastically.

'So you're our new resident Germanist,' Abi said, angling her face flirtatiously to his.

'Was there ever an old one?' he asked.

'There was Mrs Weiss,' I said, 'She was very sweet. She used to give us Viennese truffles at Christmas.'

'She's dead now,' Abi said. 'Most inconvenient for those of us with a sweet tooth. So I hope you'll be looking up her supplier and continuing the tradition, Davis?'

'Consider it an *homage*, Abi – and may she rest in peace . . .'

As Abi and Davis settled into the kind of banter that was second nature to them, I couldn't help thinking of the widow who'd come into the Advice Centre with the problem of the car. Was this what we left behind when we went? Our loved ones forced to deal with parking iniquities, while our neighbours remembered us only for our chocolates? Oh dear, running a light heart was so much harder than running a heavy one. How serious my days were, what with the advice work and the wrangles with Alistair and the tiptoeing around Roxy. Always I was so cautious, so mindful of the feelings of others. If I ever let rip it was with Matthew, the only innocent one among them, poor thing, scolding him for his muddy footprints or forgotten homework. Abi was right, I deserved some fun.

'How's your week been?' I asked Davis, brightly.

He grimaced. 'Oh, another A grade, another dollar. But it's all last-minute fine-tuning at this stage, just a slap on the back in the trenches before they go up over the top, nothing like as crazy as the Easter revision frenzy. I just want to slit my own throat when that's going on.'

'I'm not surprised,' Abi said, rolling her eyes. 'Teenagers are appalling creatures if you ask me. No offence, Kate, but please let's not talk about them all night. They pay themselves so much attention, do they really need all of ours as well?'

'Couldn't put it better myself,' Davis smiled. I caught his eye and knew he'd got the measure of Abi at once, recognised her good heart beneath the wisecracking exterior. He was a decent person, I thought, more than decent, a thoughtful neighbour and, it had to be said, a godsend of a tenant. The rent arrived in my bank account on precisely the agreed day; there'd not been a single problem with the flat, or if there had been, he hadn't bothered me with it. As Alistair had said, it was the perfect solution. It was as though he'd been there for ever.

Seb arrived just then, and soon he and Davis were engaged in a discussion of some avant-garde production of an opera I'd not seen (nor any other in the last ten years) and I sat back and enjoyed the spectacle. My friends liked Davis, I could tell; like me, they were impressed, everyone was, even those two young madams, Roxy and Marianne.

Roxy. Despite myself my mind drifted again to that question of Abi's that had caught me off guard. You mean they're still virgins? Can that be possible? Years ago, when I must have been doing some preparatory worrying, I'd asked the mother of a friend of Matt's, who also had a daughter at university, at what age girls began having sex. 'It's not so much an age thing,' she said, 'it's if they have a boyfriend. If they do, then assume yes.' Assume yes. And yet instinct told me Roxy had not taken that step with Damien. Wouldn't a mother recognise the transformation? But so much had been obscured lately, couldn't that have been, too?

When I was her age it was obvious what was happening in my life from the calls made to the one phone line in the house. The phone was hung on the wall in the hallway and the cord didn't stretch beyond the foot of the stairs, which meant I was forced to conduct coded conversation a couple of feet from where my mother worked in the kitchen. Whether she let on or not, she knew my every move. Roxy, meanwhile, with her password-protected email and texts she deleted as soon as she'd read them, not to mention the crammed schedule that made comings and goings impossible to monitor, could be leading a double life and I'd be none the wiser.

'More wine, Kate?'

'What? Oh, yes please.' Again, I realised I had withdrawn from the main conversation. I couldn't allow myself to waste the evening thinking about my family. I drained my glass and held it out for Seb to pour more. He'd already supplied a second bottle and was now asking Davis about the novels he was currently teaching. Which were the favourites among 'the youth', as he called them?

'It helps if there's some kind of hook to the main character,' Davis said, lighting himself a cigarette, 'like Effi Briest. Her parents marry her off at seventeen, which is exactly the age of the students, so they're automatically interested in what happens to her.'

'Who's Effi Briest?' I asked.

'The heroine of a novel by Theodor Fontane; a very famous German novel, possibly the most famous. It's always on the syllabus.'

Abi laughed. 'Don't you hate it when people do that? Say something's incredibly famous when you've already admitted you've never heard of it.'

I smiled distantly, hoping Davis didn't take me for a Philistine. Seeing Abi's puzzled face, I scolded myself: the last thing I needed was to start pretending I was something I was not (Lord, if I had even half of Marianne's self-possession!). And Davis was, after all, a teacher; he was used to unformed minds.

73

I caught his eye. 'Tell us about *Effi* . . . what was it again?'

'*Briest*. It's a kind of German *Anna Karenina* or *Madame Bovary*. Well worth a look.'

'Roxy's reading *Madame Bovary* for French. She loves it.'

I was vaguely aware of Abi rolling her eyes at another reference to Roxy, but Davis kept his eyes locked on mine. 'They all love it. They enjoy a tale of doomed love.' He dragged on the cigarette. 'But I'm not sure they always understand.'

'Understand what?' Seb asked.

We all waited for Davis's answer and I felt that same sense of breathlessness I'd had that evening in my kitchen, the conviction that he was someone with something to say, something more profound than the usual.

He tilted his head back slightly to blow smoke away from our faces. 'Sometimes I get the feeling they think the disastrous endings are just a product of the time, not of human nature. As though it's not something that could ever happen to them.'

Abi frowned. 'I take it Effi doesn't enjoy a happy ever after, then?'

'Not really. She's back where she started, actually, living with her parents.'

'How nicely symmetrical,' Seb said.

'How depressing,' Abi said, pulling a face.

Personally, I could think of worse fates.

We left Abi and Seb at the main doors – the entrance to their block was around the corner in the next street – and walked up the stairs together. It was a cliché, but I had a spring in my step that hadn't been there when I'd left the building earlier. I felt almost young, what with all that cerebral talk of opera and literature; I hadn't talked like that since university. Not to mention the déjà vu of halls-of-residence goodbyes as Davis and I fiddled with our keys to our adjoining front doors.

'Thank you for coming,' I said. 'They were intrigued by a new neighbour. I was never going to hear the end of it if I didn't ask you.'

He smiled. 'My pleasure. They're an interesting couple.'

'Yes, Abi's great. She's been a good friend over the years.' I wondered who *his* friends were. Other teachers and academics? Survivors of his former marital circle? I'd not been aware of there having been any entertaining in the flat, just the arrival or departure of his students. 'Well, see you, then. I ought to go in and see what the kids have been up to.'

'Yes, I hope for all our sakes the Bugsy rehearsals are over. The last thing we need is a full-volume reconstruction of Fat Sam's as the head hits the pillow.'

'I'm surprised you're so familiar with it,' I laughed, my voice loud and bright in the enclosed space. 'Isn't it a bit lowbrow for you?'

'I think perhaps you've got the wrong idea about me, Mrs Easton.' He held my gaze, smirking quite wolfishly, and I smiled delightedly back. Much too tipsy to make sense of the clues his last remark might hold, I rushed on, 'Anyway, I don't think they were actually *singing* tonight. At least I hope not or Matthew won't have slept and he's impossible to get up in the morning if that happens.' I paused. 'So . . . goodnight.'

'Goodnight.' After a lingering silence, he turned to go in, and I did the same. Roxy's light was on and her door open. Her bedroom was the nearest to the front door and it occurred to me that she may have overheard our conversation. I knocked, waited for her reluctant 'Come in', and put my head around the door. She was lying on top of the duvet in pyjama shorts and vest, hair back in a pony tail, the pages of her script open in front of her. 'Hi darling. Marianne gone? Has Matt been OK?'

She cast me an irritated look. 'It's twelve-thirty at night, what d'you think? I was just falling asleep myself when you woke me up with your awful cackling.'

'*Cackling*?'

She huffed impatiently. 'Yes. You're embarrassing yourself, you know.'

'What?' Her comment winded me like a physical blow and it took a moment to get enough breath back to retaliate. 'Roxy! How *dare* you speak to me like that?'

She wriggled sideways onto her elbow to look at me. 'What? It's true.'

'What on earth is wrong with two people laughing together?' She didn't answer and I raged on. 'Do I pass judgment on your friends? No, I respect your choices. Do I make any comment on how you spend your time with those friends? No, I respect your privacy.'

Roxy rolled her eyes. 'Oh, get over it, Mum, it's not the debating society. You're drunk.'

'I am not.'

'Anyway, you *do* pass judgment. You just don't always share it.'

'That's not true!'

She swept her papers to the floor and yawned. 'Look, I need to sleep. OK?' And she stretched out a long bare leg and kicked the door closed, causing me to back out of the room, just like that. Next thing the light on her side had been snapped off. I stood blinking outside her door, feeling quite ambushed by the scene and not at all satisfied with its conclusion. I couldn't bear to storm back in and force her up to explain herself in some odd perversion of domestic conflict, but not doing anything felt wrong, too, like some sort of admission of guilt.

She was right about one thing, though: I *was* drunk. I contented myself with an inaudible mutter, 'Just be grateful I don't marry you off, young lady, like Effi Briest!' and headed to bed.

76

Chapter 7

It was unfortunate for my sister Tash that I had married so young and had a baby almost at once, for it meant she would forever be closer in age to my daughter than she was to me. And I couldn't help making comparisons between Roxy and her, no one could. Even now my mother gave the two of them the same gifts, the same 'little something' handouts, apparently quite forgetting that one of them was in her late twenties and should by now be perfectly capable of looking after herself.

We were twelve years apart; surely that made closeness between us an impossibility? What had my parents been thinking? But then I had gone and done exactly the same myself, left an age gap between children that placed them out of sync with the other's development – no sooner would one depart the mire of puberty and adolescence than the other would enter it. And what older sibling wanted to revisit an experience she'd only just left behind? These days, if Roxy paid attention to Matthew at all, it was only to find him more irritating, more embarrassing. I liked to think that the two of them would become close again once they were both adults, but I had to admit that that had hardly been the case with Tash and me, and we were now twenty-seven and thirty-nine respectively. No, no matter how I tried, I could not alter the fact that we were completely different people. More specifically, I was responsible, she irresponsible, I the victim of relationship break-up, she perpetually the cause of it. I was the realist, while she had her head in the clouds – or at least that was how I saw it.

When you considered her childhood, though, you could hardly blame her. Unlike Matthew, she had not been a planned baby. ('We wanted to put all our resources into you,' my mother told me – she was not one to be unduly sentimental.) Tash liked to call herself the big mistake, but there was no doubt that she had benefited from the error. As the bonus baby, the extra gift, she was indulged by Mum and Dad almost as though by an extra set of grandparents. Before my parents knew it, they had on their hands a daughter who was spoiled. Not that she was brattish or unpleasant; she was simply a creature of the moment, incapable of acknowledging any possibility of a future, of ramifications.

'Life is a long game, Tash,' Alistair said to her once, a little pompously, and I had listened out for her response, wondering if he would succeed where others had failed in getting her to 'get it'.

'Where's the fun in that?' she replied, genuinely mystified.

And so she had dropped out of university, travelled without aim, had at least two business ideas that I knew of, both of which she persuaded others to finance before abandoning them, she left flat after flat, boyfriend after boyfriend, job after job. Mostly, her activities were based around my parents' home in Leicestershire, which meant she did not often appear in London. For this I was guiltily grateful. I didn't need any more dependants.

Whenever she did visit, though, I had to hand it to her: the sun shone. Matthew would get excited in the same way he did when a holiday was coming up; the younger Roxy begged that Tash be allowed to share her room and they'd disappear off together to do the girl things I never seemed to have time for. Even the new

Roxy perked up at news of an imminent arrival. I heard her describing her aunt to Marianne as 'a real laugh, more like us' (and couldn't help putting the words in her mouth that might follow, 'unlike *Mum*').

I wondered if Tash would notice a difference in her niece, spot some key development that had been obscured to me by familiarity. More likely she'd introduce her to some new and crazy – and possibly illegal – activity. I chided myself for the thought. What was Ethan always saying to us at work? Don't invent complications where there are none. There are already enough to go around.

Bring the weather with her she might, but Tash also had a habit of arriving at exactly the wrong time. It was early July, the last – and busiest – week of term and though exams were done and dusted and most of the coursework out of the way, Roxy still had her performances of *Bugsy Malone* to come, followed by her driving test at the end of the week. Though it was a three-night run, she had naturally organised tickets for me to attend the play the same night as Alistair and Victoria. I would never know whether this was deliberate and, if so, whether the idea was an extremely tardy attempt at reconciliation or simply an opportunity to watch me squirm.

As usual Tash entered into the spirit of family life as though a permanent member of the household. She just appeared, overnight bag in hand (history had taught me hers would be at least a ten-day stay, however), and joined in every conversation that followed as though fully briefed on its back story. It was really quite a gift, I thought, no dipping of toes, just a huge leap and then full immersion.

'Don't worry, I'll be there to keep the side up,' she said to me, when Roxy broke the news of the tickets. 'I promise I'll clap extra loudly to drown beastly Victoria out.'

'Beastly?' Matt said, looking puzzled.

'She's only joking,' I said swiftly. 'And it's no problem about the tickets.' I frowned faintly in my sister's direction. Fail though I sometimes might, I did at least try not to talk politically – or critically – of the children's stepmother in front of them.

Tash looked vacantly back. She had our mother's chestnut hair and creamy complexion and the summer sun had brought out freckles across her nose. She looked younger every time I saw her. 'Hey, I take it there *is* a ticket for me?' she said. 'I mean, I *loved* that movie, especially Tallulah . . .' She caught Matt's eye and began singing, moving her upper body to the melody in an exaggerated Charleston. The effect was, however, more cobra than showgirl, and he burst out laughing. 'Tash! What are you doing?'

'Just getting into the spirit of it, Munch.' (Short for 'Munchkin': Tash was allowed all sorts of liberties with both children that had long been denied me.) 'So are you playing Tallulah, Rox?'

'No,' Roxy said. 'Marianne is.'

'Her best friend,' I put in, partly to test if this were true.

Rox nodded. 'I'm Captain Smolsky.'

'Which one is that?'

'The detective. He's got a sidekick called Knuckles.'

'Oh yeah,' Tash said, 'I remember. He's really funny, isn't he? I can see you as a comedienne, Roxy, you've got that touch.'

'Thanks, Tash. People don't always realise comedy is much harder to do than tragedy.'

My sister nodded wisely. 'That's 'cos everyone thinks they're funny, have you noticed that? But no one ever thinks they're *tragic*.'

I followed this exchange with amusement. The only 'touch' of Roxy's I'd seen lately was that of her thumbs on the keypad of her mobile phone. As for Tash and her pearls of wisdom, I remembered how Alistair used to refer to her as our *idiot savant*, adding, a little meanly, 'But the jury's still out on the "*savant*".' It hardly mattered, in any case, for by the time any fault could be found with her logic, she had already alighted on some wonderful new idea. And so it was now.

'Hey, I know, Mum!' – it was her affectation to call me 'Mum' when in the presence of her niece and nephew, a habit I found both absurd and inevitable – 'Why don't we ask your neighbour to come with us? I'm *dying* to meet him.'

'Oh, Davis you mean?' I wasn't expecting the suggestion and was disconcerted to feel my eyes move shiftily from hers. I hadn't mentioned Davis to her at all so far, except to explain how the revised layout of the flat would affect her own sleeping arrangements. Roxy must have said something to her, then, perhaps about the night of our drink. Our argument had not been properly debriefed, of course; there was not the precedent for that, nor, frankly, the time in the day. In the end I had settled for cornering her as she came out of the bathroom and making the comment that I'd found her attitude unacceptable (even then I'd managed to get the tone wrong, as though I were quoting code-of-conduct policy to a client), after which she had made an apology that we both knew was not felt, and we'd left it at that.

'That's not a bad idea,' I continued, brightly. 'You get on really well with him, don't you, Rox?' I decided not to add the rather shameful thought that it would be more than a little satisfying to see Alistair's face if I turned up with an attractive, intellectual companion, and more satisfying still were Davis to take it upon himself to charm Victoria under her husband's nose. I allowed myself to picture a costumed Roxy greeting us backstage, making automatically for Davis and me in clear preference to her father and stepmother, perhaps shooting the two of them with a splurge gun for good measure.

My reverie was broken by the sight of a fierce scowl. 'No,' she said, stonily. 'We've only got two tickets and Matt's already coming, aren't you, Matt?'

'Yes,' Matt said, pleased to be included by his sister, even if it were only as a pawn in a game he wasn't aware of.

'What about me?' Tash wailed. 'I want to come!'

Again Matt laughed, imagining perhaps that his aunt play-acted this petulance.

'Look, I'm sure we could get more,' I said. 'It's not sold out yet, is it, Roxy? And if we're getting an extra one for Tash then we could get a fourth for Davis while we're at it. I'm sure he'd like to join us.'

'I said *no*!' We all started as Roxy ground her chair into the marble and sprang up. 'Doesn't *anyone* listen? It's *my* show and I decide who to invite, OK?'

She flounced off and we heard the sound of her bedroom door smacking shut.

'How hilarious!' Tash said, hooting. Though it was not remotely funny to me, she at least kept the atmosphere light for Matt. 'Well, I take it Madam doesn't like the idea of you having a new relationship, Mum?'

I glanced at my son. He'd been strapping on his trainers but had stopped abruptly, rapt by the sudden turn in the conversation. 'It is *not* a new relationship, Tash, Davis is our tenant. How many times do I have to say it?'

My sister put her hands up. 'OK, OK, calm down. God, Kate, talk about a sore point!' She made a grab for Matt, as I should have done, to give him a bear hug. 'These women! Look what you have to put up with, Munch!' As he wriggled out of her grasp with a happy little growl, she added, 'You need another man about the house, if you ask me . . .'

Victoria Mitchell (I still found it impossible to call her Easton) was precisely the specimen of urban womanhood I might have become myself had I not got pregnant at twenty-one and opted out of a serious career before I'd even settled on what it might actually be. She was both hard- and snub-nosed, pretty and lethal in one, a lawyer for a City firm where only the prettiest and most lethal survived into their thirties. Alistair was delighted

82

by her textbook ascent. He'd told me a few times – though I'd certainly never enquired – that a partnership was a year away, 'tops' (such an Alistair word), which would make her the youngest partner in the firm, man or woman.

Then, just as she was about to turn thirty, she got pregnant, and her mission extended to making sure she was treated exactly as any expectant male parent might: i.e. the same as before. She began keeping a work diary in case of any future injustices. I didn't fancy her chances, but I had to admit a grudging respect for her foresight, not to mention her principles. It sent Roxy the right message, too. If she was going to be a lawyer (albeit one who preferred to be based in Paris), she'd need that kind of single-mindedness.

I spotted her straight away, the only pregnant figure at a gathering of parents who had children of sixth-form age. Though I steadfastly disliked her – for all his faults, Alistair was not the classic predatory womaniser and the original play had to have been made by her – I felt instant sympathy when I saw the exhaustion on her face. An airless school theatre in July, the hormonal buzz of an all-girl cast, not to mention the rows of younger girls in the audience hissing with overexcitement, it had to be the last place she wanted to be after twelve hours in the office.

'Hello Alistair, Victoria.' As our parties squared up, I tried to bring some warmth to my smile, if only for Matthew's benefit.

'Hi Kate.' The usual chaste kisses were exchanged.

'You remember my sister, Tash?' I asked Victoria, pleasantly.

'Yes, of course, how are you, Tash?' Victoria and Tash were only three years apart in age, but the contrast couldn't have been more starkly drawn if a fashion stylist had been responsible for it, Tash all boho mismatching and long hair somewhere between unbrushed and dreadlocked, and Victoria, despite the six-month bump, in tailored charcoal suit and newsreader blow-dry.

'So what are you up to these days? Alistair asked Tash, 'Come on, what's the latest wheeze?'

As Tash replied, oblivious to his sarcasm, I thought I saw Victoria look a little more closely at me than she usually did. Finally feeling guilty, perhaps, for having stolen a pregnant woman's husband, for having bedded him when his wife was exactly the shape she was now. I caught her eye. Not a very nice thought, is it, dear? For the first time since Alistair had left me, I felt as though I might, to the outside world at least, appear to be in the more enviable position. My job did not carry high status, but it was helpful and, what was more, the help I gave came free of charge, which was more than you could say for hers. I was well rested and healthy, my child-bearing in the past. Yes, my daughter might rejoice to see me walk under a bus, but she was still my daughter, a beautiful seventeen-year-old about to display the fruits of my genes on stage for all to see. A gorgeous rumpled blond boy stood at my side, my own loyal sister at the other. And me, in the middle, feeling more relaxed than I had since I could remember, allowing my mind to be picked up on the breeze of expectancy around the theatre. Yes, Roxy and Marianne and their friends had all of life ahead of them, but there were possibilities ahead for me, too, weren't there? And Davis Calder, not invited tonight after all, might he play a part in that future?

'We ought to get to our seats,' Alistair said, arm around Victoria. As I watched them move towards spots considerably better placed than my own, I had to laugh at my own pride. Don't get carried away, I told myself, life is not suddenly going to get miraculously easy. The most you can hope for is a good summer.

'Come on Matt, let's sit down and open the sweets.'

He nodded, adorably intent. 'I want all the black ones. *And* the green ones.'

'Red for me, Mum,' Tash said in a baby voice.

'OK,' I played along. 'I'll have the orange ones.'

We'd watched the DVD a dozen times, but Matt was

enthralled by the performance, as I'd known he would be, by all the live slapstick and wisecracking. Roxy was hilarious, Marianne preternaturally sexy, the music and singing of an extraordinary standard compared with the school plays I'd taken part in.

'Why don't we do a *Bugsy Malone* theme for your tenth birthday party?' I whispered to him during a scene break. 'We could have custard pie fights in the gardens?'

'Can we? That would be *amazing*. Can I dress as a gangster?'

'You can dress as anything you like.'

'Great, I'll be Fat Sam. Ruben can be Dandy Dan.' He stuffed a couple of sweets into his left cheek and sat back, satisfied.

Success for Roxy continued. Three days later she passed her driving test, and soon after that we heard that she and Marianne had won places at the youth theatre summer school they'd tried out for at the Central School of Speech and Drama. The dates were compatible with the law placement, so Alistair was happy; he even forwarded software to her for a digital diary they used in his office; he thought it might help her organise her time more efficiently. Personally I thought this was taking things a step too far, but Roxy claimed to be delighted with seeing her schedule laid out like that of a corporate professional and so I feigned admiration of my own.

It was a shock, therefore, when she appeared one morning the following week with bloodshot eyes and puffy lids.

'Are you all right?' I asked, careful not to fuss.

'Hmm, fine.'

'Fallen out with Marianne?' I remembered the flurry around the little star the night of the play after the applause had died down and the cast began to trickle through to join their parents in the hall. It couldn't be easy having a best friend who got all of the limelight. Reflected glory went only so far.

'God, Mum!' Roxy turned on me, but dispiritedly, lacking her usual bite. 'You say that with such hope! Well, I'm sorry to disappoint you, but no, we haven't fallen out, and we're not going to. We're *friends*.'

I paused. Her eyes really were terribly swollen. 'You're not upset about Tash leaving? I know you two—'

She interrupted me: 'For God's sake, I'm not three years old! Why would I be upset by anyone leaving? Anyway, she said I can go and see her in her new place whenever I like.' This last comment I recognised at once to be a false lead, intended to get me to question the appropriateness of the two of them making arrangements without consulting me – or, indeed, the existence of this 'new' place of Tash's – and thus forget the original point of the conversation.

'OK, I'm sorry. It's just, well, your eyes are very red. You look as though you've been crying, or maybe you've got an infection or something.'

She touched her face with her fingers, squinting into the window pane to catch her own reflection. 'Oh, sure. Just got something in my eye in the night.'

In both eyes, I thought, sadly. But I knew any further sympathy would only infuriate her more. 'There's a bottle of saline in the bathroom cabinet, and some drops if you . . .'

She cut me off again. 'Yeah, sure, Mum.'

Tash appeared just then and, noticing Roxy's face, met my look with a querying one of her own. Already I was getting used to her being around to trade glances like this, proper grown-up glances that could not be shared with Matt. And that way she had of making everything seem less critical than it was, it had rubbed off on me a little this last week. Frustrating though she could be, she was a good foil to my excessive worrying.

'All right?' she said to Roxy, and reached across her for the Rice Krispies packet on the table.

Roxy shrugged.

'God, I can't believe I'm going back today. And tomorrow I'll be working as a waitress in Leicester town centre. Not exactly a dream job, is it?'

'I think it's cool,' Roxy said and I thought of her plan to swap the law placement for a stint making cappuccinos at Eli's. Was that what was upsetting her, the crushing realisation of all the pressures to come? The theatre course would look great on her UCAS form, certainly, but might it also be the straw that broke the sixth former's back? This was supposed to be a school vacation, after all, a break from hard work. For the hundredth time I felt guilty for my part in coaxing her to go along with the Clifton Merchant placement. Why on earth shouldn't she spend her summer waitressing or whatever else she preferred? At her age I'd just hung out in friends' bedrooms playing music and gossiping; we'd had scarcely a Saturday job between us.

A little later I was hanging up the phone after a conversation with Abi, when I overheard a snatch of conversation from Roxy's room. Tash was in there with her, evidently probing for more detail than had been shared at the breakfast table.

'So what happened with Damien, then? I never did meet him, did I?'

'Hmm. We weren't together that long.'

'Do you still see him?'

'Now and then.'

'Thank God you're at an all-girls' school, eh? Don't have to run into any inconvenient exes. That was a big problem for me. I almost gave up my A-levels because of that. This one guy was like, God, some kind of wounded beagle. I thought it was supposed to be girls who don't know how to let go.'

There was the sound of a reluctant laugh from Roxy; I suppressed one of my own.

'So who *are* you seeing at the moment?'

'I told you before, Tash, no one.'

'Seriously no one, or I'm-not-going-to-tell-an-oldie-like-you no one?'

87

Another laugh. '*Seriously* no one.'

'I don't believe you. You're way too pretty to not have someone on the scene.'

Bless Tash, I thought, she was a natural at this; better than I was. 'Isn't there *anyone* you like? Just a teeny bit?'

I held my breath for several seconds, but there was no evidence of an answer. Roxy must be shaking her head, or doing that half-shrug thing with her left shoulder.

What Tash said next surprised me almost as much as it evidently threw Roxy. 'Rox, it's OK to like girls, as well, you know . . .'

'I know.' Then, 'What d'you mean?'

'I mean instead of blokes. Being gay.'

'*Gay?*'

There was a short silence and then Tash giggled. 'OK, so maybe I've misread this . . .'

The next thing they were both laughing like children, in lovely rise-and-fall waves, one first and then the other, as though taking it in turns to tickle each other. I hadn't heard Roxy laugh like that in a long time.

Walking Tash down to her taxi, I said, 'I heard you two earlier, you know. When she said she wasn't seeing anyone.'

Tash pulled a face. 'I think she might have realised you were listening in.'

'Oh God, really?'

'You were sort of shuffling.'

'I didn't mean to, I was just there and I couldn't help it. She tells me so little.' I hesitated. 'You think she was deliberately holding back, then, in case I heard?'

'Of course she was. I mean, there's got to be a boy, hasn't there? As soon as I saw she'd been crying . . . We're not stupid.' She twisted her mouth to the side, another mannerism that reminded me of our mother. 'Maybe Damien is still on the go, after all. Or maybe he was, and then he ditched her.'

'It's possible. What else has she said to you this last week?' I asked. 'That I haven't heard?'

'Nothing, she won't say anything. The only person who knows what's really going on is our Tallulah.'

'Marianne?'

'And there'll be no chance of getting anything out of her. If you ask me, she's a right sphinx. Ah, here's the cab.'

As I watched her slide her holdall into the back seat, her last remark gave me an idea. Roxy let slip titbits about Marianne's relationship with Rob all the time, and that was in spite of the code-red secrecy she applied to all communications with me, so surely Marianne, who by all accounts had a much closer relationship with her mother, did the same about Roxy? If so, the two of us could trade our secrets to the other's advantage. I had never met Marianne's mother, but I had the Willoughby School directory, which listed all the pupils' home phone numbers. It was certainly a strategy worth saving for a rainy day.

Tash and I hugged goodbye. 'I'd just keep your distance if I were you,' she said, uncannily reading my mind. 'The worst thing you can do is interfere.' With that, she was in the taxi and waving goodbye. For the first time in our family history I wanted to run after her and call out for her to stay.

How often Alistair and I had criticised her for her attachment to her gut feeling, her refusal to learn from experience while remaining in perpetual readiness to dispense advice to those in need of it. But I had to admit that on this occasion she seemed to be talking sense. It was agony not to be able to comfort Roxy when she was upset, just as it was agony to be excluded from her joy, but it was at least something to know that I was not the problem. Lord knew I would prefer to be the cause of neither than of both.

Chapter 8

Roxy left for her first morning at Clifton Merchant with the same bloodshot eyes and down-turned mouth. And then the second, and then the third. I couldn't imagine what her new employers must be thinking at the sight of such obvious distress and felt guiltier than ever for colluding in the campaign to get her there in the first place. If it weren't for her parents' machinations she could cry off her crisis in the privacy of her own bedroom and come out again only when she felt better. I could only hope that Victoria wouldn't alert Alistair to the problem and bring more heavy-handed intervention Roxy's way.

Though I continued to follow Tash's advice about keeping my distance, still I worried privately. I felt more keenly than ever my sheer aloneness in my concerns for my daughter. Alistair and I were never going to be a happy team, I had to accept that once and for all. Constantly I had to compromise to accommodate his parenting philosophies and I could only assume that he felt the same about mine. Abi's opinion, on the other hand, was always a breath of fresh air. The only problem was that she was by her own admission not the best sounding-board on the subject of teenage girls (if she wasn't dismissing them as she-devils then she was telling me of her own transgressions at that age: Soho clubs, binge drinking, pills, the lifestyle of a woman ten years older. And, typically, each anecdote ended with some expression of regret: 'I wish I'd studied harder, I'd be earning a damn sight more now if I had').

As for the natural advisors, other mothers, well, I hardly knew any of those these days, at least none related to Roxy's school year. The circle I'd been part of when she was small had gradually broken down as the children went off to different schools and the mothers returned to work. My network was now the parents of Matthew's friends, but most had only one child or siblings close in age, and so there were no other seventeen-year-olds about whom I could compare notes. There were, of course, my workmates at the Advice Centre, but by definition our own problems paled into insignificance next to those of our clients. None of us faced eviction or deportation or the seizure of our worldly goods by bailiffs, least of all me. A little brooding about standard teenage behaviour was so far under the radar as to be laughable.

Which left me with . . . Davis. On the fourth morning, as I returned from dropping Matthew at swimming camp and before I even realised what I was doing, I found myself knocking on his door. He answered with an expression that contained both pleasure and resignation. 'I know that face. Roxy again?'

I nodded. 'She's really upset about something. It's been going on for days. I'm worried she's overcommitted herself this summer, or been dumped by a boyfriend or something.'

He stepped aside to usher me in. 'A boyfriend? I didn't realise she had one.'

'Well, she hasn't exactly confirmed that she has,' I admitted, following him to the sofa. 'But Tash thought she might be back with her ex.'

'Tash?'

'My sister, I don't think you've met her.'

'Ah, yes. Roxy mentioned her when we met on the stairs the

other day.' Though I'd left space next to me on the sofa, he by-passed it in favour of the armchair.

'But it might not be a boy at all,' I rushed on. 'I can't help worrying about drugs, as well. It said in the paper that fifty per cent of seventeen-year-olds have taken cocaine.'

Davis looked at me with raised eyebrows. 'I find that highly unlikely.'

'I know how it sounds, I'm just spilling out clichés, aren't I? It's pathetic, I know that. It's just, well, you're so good at getting inside their heads. I thought you might be able to point me in the right direction before I go completely mad.'

He brought his palms together in front of his chin and the fingertips began tapping. 'OK, you'd better tell me the full story.'

To my embarrassment, it took little more than five minutes to do so, at least in terms of actual facts. Eyes that were red from crying, that was all I had, and denials of a relationship I'd learned only by means of illicit snooping. As for drug use, in truth, I'd hardly considered the issue, having generally assumed that someone as busy as Roxy wouldn't have the time, not if she wanted to get up in the morning for her hundred-and-one appointments. Searching for other evidence of her recent over-loading, I cited Alistair's new digital diary.

'That doesn't sound so different from a normal school timetable, to be honest,' Davis said. He must have been working when I arrived, for there was a stack of papers on the coffee table, a chewed pencil atop. Sitting as we did, sofa and armchair angled towards one another just so, I felt a little like his patient, here to receive my weekly soothing.

'It just seems so clinical and businesslike,' I said. 'I mean, this is supposed to be her summer holiday. Remember how we spent ours at that age? I don't think I did any studying at all, let alone career work experience.'

'It's different now,' he said simply. He was kind enough not to point out that the last time I'd appealed to him for help it had been to get him to help persuade her *into* work experience.

'But shouldn't her diary be somewhere she writes about her feelings? Not just a list of appointments. You know, a secret thing with a padlock . . .'

At this, his lips twitched at the corners. 'A secret thing you can break open and read, you mean?'

'I would never do that!' I exclaimed. But I wasn't sure, I honestly wasn't sure. I decided not to tell him about the other newspaper story I'd read recently, the one about the surveillance equipment that some parents now used to monitor their children's web-chat and texts, or the fact that I'd dismissed such measures only with reluctance. 'Oh, Davis, I just feel so guilty, and yet so completely powerless. If I try to show I care she makes me feel like I'm harassing her.'

He looked at me with deeply furrowed brow, lips pressed thoughtfully together, just the kind of openly judging stance we were taught to avoid with our clients at work. Then, noticing the newspaper on the corner of his desk, he reached for it and began flicking through the pages.

'Talking of stories in the papers, have you heard of the Parkbridge estate?'

'Of course.'

He handed me the report. It was about a shooting on an estate in north-west London well known for its crime. Though located in a different borough from my office, which made its residents ineligible for our services, I was familiar with Parkbridge and its stories, everyone was. There were the parents who used their eight-year-old children as drugs couriers, the old folk robbed on their doorstep for loose change, the gun culture that had spawned a whole new generation of criminals – and victims. Police raids were followed by murders, which were followed in turn by anti-firearms rallies and pictures of bereaved single mothers in the press. Only last year a double shooting involving twelve-year-olds had led to open warfare and the temporary evacuation of the police shop there. The photograph now in front of me showed a disused road bridge above a wide street of low housing, some of it boarded up, with a cluster of tower blocks at its end.

'It's not as bad as it looks,' Davis said. 'There are a lot of regeneration projects going on now, architectural stuff that's worked on other estates, and some youth programmes, as well.'

The earnestness of his voice made me look up, just as the sun streamed through the windows and brightened the lines of his profile, separating him from me almost as if spotlit in an art museum. I, then, was the spectator, the art lover.

'That's good.' I placed the newspaper back on the table and he leaned forward to take another look. He was genuinely fascinated; he might almost have pulled out a magnifying glass. I supposed he must be tired of my Roxy neuroses and was looking for something to change the subject. I didn't blame him. 'So how do you know so much about this place?' But the answer, I saw, was in his last remark. 'Oh, you teach there?'

He nodded. 'Just one student, a girl called Jasmina. She lives in that block right there in the picture, on the left.'

I gaped. 'I can't imagine you going in there.'

'I don't. Her mother and brothers don't even know we meet. From what she says, they're a pretty formidable clan.'

'She comes to the flat, then?'

'No, it's not practical for her to come here . . .' Something in the way he said it, a trace of irritation, made me see at once that what he really meant was that some of the grander residents of Francombe Gardens might object to the sight of someone like this Jasmina on the doorstep. 'I meet her in a library up in Stonebridge Park. They let us use a quiet corner there.'

'But . . . I mean, how does she come to need a languages tutor?'

'She came to me through another teacher, someone involved in

94

a new forum up here. Actually, the thing was designed for male kids, computer skills, communications, that kind of thing, but someone mentioned this girl and the committee approached me to get involved. She's very talented, extraordinarily talented. She picks up new languages totally naturally.'

I watched as he began winding the hair at his neck around his fingers. It was long; he had not had it cut since we'd met. 'How old is she?'

'Fifteen. It's enough of an achievement that she's still in school, to be honest. There are people who hope she'll make it to university, but I have my doubts. For one thing she doesn't want to go somewhere she so obviously wouldn't fit in. Languages are not the same as sport or music, they don't equalise in the same way.'

I thought of Roxy and her friends heading off to university next year, driving themselves in cars given as birthday presents or chauffeured by their parents, back seats and boots full of luxury gadgets and brand-new books, wardrobes stuffed with the proceeds of years of generous allowances. And, worst of all, heads full of their own entitlement – no equalising required for them. The idea that they might be joined by a girl from a Parkbridge tower block was improbable, to say the least.

'Why are you showing me this?' I asked. 'To show me that life isn't all Francombe Gardens? That it's all relative? I think I know that already, you know, from my work.' It was just fighting talk, though; for all my perceived worthiness, my job took place in an office on the leafy high street of a middle-class neighbourhood. There was the deli and the organic butchers and, right next door, the florist's that specialised in hand-tied 'vintage' bouquets.

'I was thinking more of your worries about Roxy,' Davis said, quietly.

I went still. 'Oh?'

'I suppose I'm just trying to show you that she is already a winner, whatever she does. She's a winner by birth. It may not seem like it, but your job is pretty much done. From now on, whatever she does, wherever she goes, it's her call. And if something's upsetting her, as it obviously is now, then she's old enough to sort it out herself.'

I was as startled by the sudden passion in his voice as I was by the message. 'Well, that's . . . kind of not what I was expecting you to say, I must admit.'

He smiled. 'I'm not saying she's not lucky to have you, Kate, just that she needs you less than you think.'

Our eyes met, his still glowing with the sunlight, mine cool and shaded. 'Yes, I think she still needs me a little.' Though I made it sound like I was agreeing with him, we both knew I was actually protesting.

He nodded, accepting the stalemate. He was not one to press for victory as Alistair most certainly would have done, for his was a different kind of confidence, one I was less experienced in handling. I reminded myself that he would not have made his point if I had not knocked on his door and asked for it. 'Anyway,' he said, standing. 'We begin our French conversation sessions next week, so I'll try to find out more for you then.'

I got to my feet. 'Thank you.'

Returning to my flat I felt suddenly ashamed of myself. Davis was a hardworking man, noble, even; he had clients like this Jasmina girl. And yet here I was whining about my privileged daughter and asking him to spy on her for me! For all my belief that I kept a balanced view of the world, that I helped make a difference to it, the truth was I would sweat into my clothes simply by setting foot in a neighbourhood like Parkbridge. I was hardly more enlightened than Roxy herself.

He was right again, of course. She did sort it out herself, whatever it was, and just days later, too. The cried-out eyes were mercifully clear once more and the laughter returned – at least when she was on the phone. 'It's just so great not having exams,' was all she said when I casually enquired if she was fitting it all in OK. She had begun to combine her full-time placement at Clifton Merchant with Saturday theatre school and, it seemed to me, non-stop nightly socialising. Her energy was breathtaking.

With the long summer holidays upon us, the household settled into a routine. As I always did at this time of year, I took time off work and shuttled Matt to his various sports camps and play dates, and we spent most of the remaining time in the garden. And just as Davis had promised, the family soon had another regular fixture: every Thursday evening he would arrive with his books and he and Roxy would work at the kitchen table while I watched television with Matthew or, if he was playing out, went to coax him indoors for his bath (an ever-lengthier process on these long, light evenings). On particularly hot evenings, they'd go out to the garden and work in the open air, partly, I suspected, so that one – or both – of them could have a cigarette. Without fail, Roxy would reappear in an excellent mood.

'Whatever you're doing, carry on doing it,' I joked, seeing Davis to the door one evening. 'I haven't seen her this happy in a long time.'

Though I meant it wholeheartedly, I had to admit that I would have liked to have seen a little more of Davis myself and, judging by the way he lingered over farewells, I couldn't help sensing that he felt the same. By the third week of the holiday and with Sunday evenings added to the programme, I asked him to stay for dinner. It was the least I could do in return for his efforts. Soon it became habit for him to stay for dinner every time, which made him a twice-weekly dinner guest, the most frequent in family history. Roxy was delighted, it was obvious, and would dominate the conversation, focusing her attention squarely on our guest and talking mostly about books. She treated any contribution I might make with a kind of humouring detachment that I would have found infuriating if I hadn't

97

been so pleased simply to be spending time with her. I learned more in those dinner conversations with Davis about her work experience, her excitement about the forthcoming trip to South Africa, even her feelings about the future, than I ever would have gleaned on my own. Matthew, meanwhile, was just thrilled to be allowed to stay up so late so often (still so beautifully easy to please!).

One evening Davis noticed the printout from the police site on the corkboard, and stood up to take a closer look. Roxy didn't like him reading it, I could tell; she didn't want any reminders that she was not yet eighteen and an adult, our equal (though the fact that Davis was here in order to coach her for A-levels made any deception about her age a little pointless).

'So, Roxana, you can go to war, can you?' I liked the way he called her by her full name sometimes; it sounded so elegant.

Roxy snorted. 'I would *never* "go to war". I'm not a blood-thirsty Imperialist.' Like most of her generation, she was fervently opposed to military intervention of any sort and loathed our own prime minister, preferring instead the gentler methods of Hollywood-based peace ambassadors. (Davis had told me that Marianne had proposed the motion in the school debating society: 'Angelina Jolie for US President' and was said to have argued most convincingly for it.)

'What about you, Matt?' he asked. He always remembered to include him, listening with genuine interest to the replies. 'What can you do? There's no list for age nine, I suppose?'

Matt pulled a face. 'Nothing for *ages*. Not till I'm twelve.'

'And even then he can only buy a pet without Mum's permission,' Roxy said, giggling. 'That will be his symbol of independence, a gerbil!'

'Shut up!' Matt protested. 'There's other stuff, as well.'

'Yeah, like rabbits and guinea pigs. Oh, I know! Goldfish!'

Davis chuckled. 'Yes, I'm afraid that for now it would seem that your hands are tied, little man.'

'Enjoy it while you can,' I told Matt. 'With independence comes responsibility.'

'Hey, that's what Spider-Man says!' Matt exclaimed. Next to him, Roxy scoffed.

'Is it?' I tried to hide my embarrassment by beaming indulgently at him.

'Yeah, but he doesn't say *that*. He says, "With great power comes great responsibility." It's a *very* famous line.'

'OK, my mistake,' I said, playing along.

'Trust Mum to misquote,' Roxy said, adding for Davis's benefit, 'She always does, it's one of her things.'

I started to wonder what these other 'things' might be, but was distracted by something in her manner, an unmistakable echo of the way I tended to dismiss Tash, a kind of easy superiority, as though the other's lesser intelligence was somehow a given. Well, I didn't think Roxy was being at all fair towards me when she did it, so did that mean Tash thought I was unfair towards her? I made a mental note to phone her and thank her for spending so much time with the children during her last visit. She hadn't had to do it, after all.

Davis was looking with amusement from Roxy to me. 'Misquotations often make more sense than the original. Rather in the same way misdeeds can be more fun than the good ones.'

Roxy laughed out loud. 'I'm not sure that's the sort of thing a teacher should be saying.' She paused. 'Mr Calder.'

As they smirked at one another, she began playing with the bracelet on her left wrist, a delicate silver chain with a butterfly charm. I hadn't seen it before. 'Is that a new bracelet, Roxy? Let's have a look.' On closer inspection I saw that it was from Tiffany's, which made it a very costly new trinket indeed. 'When did you get this?'

'Marianne gave me it for passing my driving test. Nice, isn't it?'

The response was a little too immediate, a little too co-operative (not to mention the fact that the driving-test triumph was by now several weeks in the past), and I thought at once of that last conversation with Tash. Surely this was clear evidence that there was a boy in the picture? And if not Damien, then who? But I couldn't possibly know, not when she insisted on living so secretively. It was like guessing Rumpelstiltskin's name, I'd never get it right.

I tried to catch Davis's eye, to communicate my suspicions, but he was too busy talking about cricket with Matt to notice.

'That's very generous of Marianne,' I said, carefully. 'It must have been very expensive.'

Roxy looked impatient. 'I wouldn't know. I'm not in the habit of asking how much gifts cost.'

I smiled, not wanting such a dispute to ruin the evening. I looked again at the charm, twinkling silver-white against her tanned wrist. Would Marianne choose a butterfly? It seemed too young for her, too cute (her own charm bracelet featured, if I remembered rightly, a series of spiky stilettos that looked as if they might do someone an injury if he or she got too close). Certainly she could afford it – that much was not in doubt. From what I could gather the girl had pots of cash. Besides her mother, an HR director for a software firm, there was the father, some sort of entrepreneur whose exact productivity remained unspecified, as well as Rob (from the clues Roxy had dropped, I'd gathered he was a 'starving' musician with a trust fund), not to mention her own occasional modelling work.

I told myself to put the bracelet out of my mind, at least for the time being. So what if Roxy had a new boyfriend and he was thoughtful enough to want to celebrate her success with a piece of jewellery? Shouldn't it be a relief that she was with someone who treated her so well and not someone who caused her to cry her eyes out? (Though, realistically, the culprit was likely to be one and the same.) I thought of Davis's charge Jasmina, as I had often since our uncomfortable conversation that time. Who did *she* go out with? What gifts did *she* get given? *Her* mother

100

probably had more pressing – maybe even life-threatening – things to worry about than the day-to-day acquisitions of a teenager.

Once again, I was taking it all much too seriously. Davis had been absolutely right and so, too, had Tash: whether I liked it or not, Roxy was almost grown-up now. She could go to war and there was nothing I could do to stop her.

Chapter 9

The man in the chair next to me was beginning to make me uneasy. Mr Newman, he was called, Grant Newman. The feeling had crept up on me, for I'd been less focused than usual, allowing my thoughts to wander to the children, now three nights into their holiday with Alistair, but it was clear that he was seething. Like many of the people who dropped in, he was angry at an injustice, in this case an argument with a neighbour that had escalated into a charge of harassment, a finding by the local council against him, and a court appearance scheduled for later in the week.

I scanned his case notes. 'What exactly is the issue? Is there a problem with your solicitor?'

'Nah, it's not that. I want to complain to the people at the council. The bloke they sent round was the racist, racist against *me*.'

'I see.' I looked impassively at him. I knew from his details that he was thirty-eight, but he looked at least ten years older. The trials of his life were stamped on his face as visibly as any physical disfigurement. 'Well, I can explain the procedure for complaining about a council employee, yes, but for this week I advise you to put that out of your mind and concentrate on your court appearance. Listen very carefully to your solicitor and do exactly what he says.'

He nodded, momentarily quietened, and then, remembering something new, scowled furiously. 'I told you about the smell from up there, didn't I? It's a weird chemical smell. There's something going on, crack, I reckon. I've seen the boyfriend, he's obviously dealing. Scum. They're the ones that should be in court, not me.' He snorted, an almost feral sound. I feared for the impression he would make in court.

I tried again. 'Just focus on this court appearance and hold on about your other concerns until afterwards. If you give the idea that you're involved in a feud with the council, you'll only complicate things and make it look as though you're the type of person who might inflame a situation.'

'Hmm. What about *them* inflaming the situation?' He looked torn. He could see I was helping, talking sense, but each time I pointed out how others might view his position, it merely stoked his original fury.

'I bet your life is just perfect, isn't it?'

'What?' I was taken aback as much by the loathing in his voice as the inappropriateness of the comment. He watched, seeming to relish my lack of retaliatory wit. 'Bet you don't have a fucking Pole bitch living above *you*, do you?'

The line had been crossed on so many counts I hardly knew where to begin: the swearing, the racist slur, the enquiry into my personal life – all strictly against the code of conduct demanded of those who used our service. By rights I should remind him of this and proceed with the interview. If it recurred, I should bring the interview to a close and seek the assistance of Ethan or his most senior advisor and second-in-command, Jocelyn. Both were on duty today.

Newman waited, eyes daring me to meet his challenge. Somehow he had transferred his domestic power-struggle to a third enemy: me. I pictured him lying in wait and following me home, forcing his way into the flat. Instinctively I thought of Roxy; whatever my new resolution to let her go a little, I knew I would do anything in my power to stop her from falling into the path of a character like this.

But I was letting my imagination run away with me again. Nothing was going to happen. The client was just a bit jittery about his court appearance. 'I live on the top floor,' I said, quietly, 'so there is no one living above me, but I'm sorry for your situation. Neighbours can be difficult, disputes occur all the time, so you're certainly not alone. But in this case it is a question of your word against hers, which is always problematic. You need to present yourself as calmly as you possibly can, Mr Newman, OK? Try not to lose your temper. Now, there's not really anything else I can say.'

Mercifully he'd stopped staring me out as he muttered his parting shot: 'It'll all come crashing down. You wait.'

It was not a threat, he seemed hardly even to be addressing me any longer, thinking probably of the circumstances that had brought him to this crisis, but I felt nonetheless warned.

It always felt strange at first when the children were on holiday with their father. It was quite different from the weekend visits, which went by in a flash and which I'd come to view as a welcome respite from the rush of the school week. Thirty-six hours off every two weeks meant a chance to catch up on chores, to meet Abi or other friends, or, my favourite indulgence, to read a novel from cover to cover, living someone else's life and returning to my own just minutes before Roxy and Matthew walked back through the door.

Just as I took the early part of the school holidays off, I always arranged extra shifts to fill my time when the children were away, and at this time of year, with all of society bar our clients away for their summer break, a daily commitment was gratefully welcomed. Even so, the days now stretched ahead of me in a bland, regular line, stalled, like cars stuck bumper to bumper on the motorway. There was nothing in particular to look forward to, nothing specifically to dread. Admittedly, in previous years I would have considered bland regularity the height of my ambitions, but this time something had changed. What? Why was the silence more than just the absence of the children?

I was ironing in the kitchen, noting, as I often did, how few items of my own made the cut compared to what looked like the entire contents of both children's wardrobes, when it struck me that I hadn't put the radio on as I normally would. Nor had I closed the kitchen door to keep the breakfast smells from permeating every corner of the flat – another rule generally observed. The reason was obvious: I wasn't fooling anyone, least of all myself. Davis. I was listening out for him. He'd been out of the city for several days and was due back today. I hadn't seen him since his final French session with Roxy almost a week ago. I missed his part in our routine almost as much as I did the kids, the way he'd slotted so comfortably into our world, so amiably, playing devil's advocate to Roxy on every subject under the sun, turning her teasing of Matt into encouragement, entertaining us all with endless witticisms. Yes, as much as I missed my children, I was unsettled – excited – by the idea that the next time Davis and I met we would be on our own.

Whatever I thought I was going to do when I did hear him, I was not prepared, for when the sound came first of his key in the lock and then the firm bang of the door, I was still in the towelling robe I'd put on after my shower hours ago. I decided I would pop around and say hello, but not before I'd distributed the fresh laundry to the three bedrooms and made myself presentable. Matthew's room first. It was a typical young boy's retreat, the release schedule of the last few years' Hollywood blockbusters evident in the superheroes around the room, in the posters and duvet cover and packaging of computer games. Piled in one corner were his school bags: one for books, one for sports, one for swimming, one for lunch. Sometimes he set off for school as though about to tackle the Inca Trail.

105

Next door, in Roxy's room, her presence lingered like a security guard among the student's paraphernalia: the laptop, the piles and piles of coursework, the magazines and novels, the 'Way Out' sign on the wall, pinched from some public place by pre-Marianne friends (as I thought of them) and given to Roxy as a Christmas present. It was tidy, though, and determinedly devoid of all but the most obvious clues, almost a stage set designed by someone with no actual experience of teenage girls. Clearly she had locked away – or taken with her – anything of emotional significance. I caught a trace of sweet lemon from the fragrance Tash had given her when she was here. It sprayed glitter with the scent and shimmered on her skin. I imagined Alistair remarking on it around the campfire and felt a twist of sorrow that I was not there to laugh along, still a part of his life, the four of us, not the three of them.

It was not my habit to go into Roxy's wardrobe or drawers, but to leave her clothes in a pile on her bed or another clear surface, sometimes hanging dresses up on the door of the wardrobe. I slipped a hanger into the shoulders of her blue-and-yellow floral dress (a vintage print, she called it, though it had probably been stitched together in China just weeks before appearing on the high street), wondering, idly, how I would look in such a skimpy design, cut for the young and slender. Fascinated, I untied my gown and stepped into the dress, slipping my arms into the fluttery capped sleeves. In the wardrobe mirror it looked surprisingly pretty, a little shorter in length than on Roxy, my curvier dimensions causing it to cling and gather at the hip. In the mirror my face peered back, a little flushed, scrubbed fresh from the shower. I looked younger, far younger than I was, and I felt wistful, both for myself and for Roxy. Her final year at school would be her final year at home and when I lost her to university the page would turn on a finite calendar of parenthood, another chunk of time between me and the girl I'd once been. But everyone felt like that, I guessed, every empty-nester.

I jumped at the sound of a rap of knuckles at the front door. It could only be Davis, for all other visitors would ring the intercom or, if a resident of the block, at least ring the bell at the outer front door. I didn't want to miss him – he might be on his way back out again – but the zip didn't do up at the back of the dress and I stood stranded in front of the mirror for a second before gripping the fabric behind me with one hand and answering the door with the other.

'Davis, I thought it might be you . . .' Though he must have been travelling, he looked as dapper as ever in pale shirt and pressed trousers, his face freshly shaved.

'Hello, just wondering how you're getting on without . . .'

He broke off, noticing the dress. He must recognise it as Roxy's, of course, I thought. Would it sound odd to explain what I'd been up to?

'I see you're dressed for the heatwave. It's hotter than ever out there – have you been outside yet? It's got to be well over thirty degrees.'

So he didn't recognise it. I felt relieved, though also a little concerned that he would think I would choose something so revealing for myself. And what if he saw Roxy in it in the future and made some comment about her borrowing my clothes? It didn't bear thinking about.

'Actually it's not mine,' I said, hurriedly. 'The dress, I was just . . . Listen, Davis, can I—' I started to ask him if I could catch up with him later, or at least be given a couple of minutes to sort myself out, but he was already strolling past me towards the kitchen, familiar by now with the lay of the land, even with the contents of our cupboards. I followed, grabbing a cardigan from the hook in the hallway and pulling it over my bare back. It was pink and snug, also Roxy's. Damn. 'How was your job in the country? Where did you go again?'

He lounged against the doorframe, watching me fuss over the coffee mugs. 'The Cotswolds, one of my pupils' parents has got

107

a house there. They're cracking the whip over some retakes. Five hours a day we were at it, but the rest of the time I had to myself. Oh, except when the mother decided she needed to brush up on her French conversation, as well.'

Irrationally, I felt a bolt of jealousy. 'Still, nice to get out of London.'

'Yes and no. It's beautiful down there, of course, but it's a little too groomed for me. Even the sheep look like they've been hand-picked by the tourist board.'

'How funny . . .'

Though the small talk was easy enough, there was definitely something heightened in his manner towards me, something alert, and I could only think that the dress was the problem. How high was the hemline at the back? The cardigan was itchy and I longed to get rid of it; the weather had risen into the thirties earlier in the week and looked set to stay there.

We sat on the sofa in the living room and I folded my bare legs beneath me.

'Have you heard from Roxy and Matt?' he asked. 'They arrived OK in Cape Town?'

'Yes, though there was quite a bit of turbulence on the flight, apparently, and Matt gets nervous. It's a long journey on your own with children.'

'Alistair's wife isn't with them, then?'

I felt sure he'd asked this before – the trip had been much discussed during those dinners together – but I repeated the information. 'No, she's too pregnant to fly and she definitely wouldn't be allowed to do anything like a jeep safari. Anyway, I understand she's notching up the extra work time so she can take as long as possible when the baby comes. It's not unusual for Alistair to take them away on his own, he's very good like that.'

'They're close, are they? It's hard to tell from what Roxy says.'

'Pretty close, considering. I can't say I think Roxy's pouring her heart out to him at this very moment, but they get on, definitely. He's their father. And they like Victoria a lot, which helps.'

It occurred to me that it was only with Davis that I talked of Alistair and Victoria as I should, reporting their comings and goings with the same matter-of-factness one might use for news of any friend of relative; without bitterness or envy or – much worse for any listener – straightforward sorrow. It seemed that Roxy wasn't the only family member he'd helped me to learn to regard with more patience, more of a sense of proportion.

'Yes, so I've got a bit of time on my own, I suppose . . .'

'Hmm.' He kept looking down at the dress. I was not wearing a bra, or any underwear at all, and I wondered if that was as obvious to him as it was to me. The fabric was so thin it looked almost sheer where the pattern was pale yellow. I couldn't have felt more selfconscious if I was completely nude, and it didn't help that I wore no make-up to cover my blushes, which were deepening by the minute. I squeezed my thighs together, making culottes of the skirt. Still Davis stared. I was starting to feel a combination of fear and arousal; the moment had finally arrived when I knew I couldn't trust myself. I was intensely attracted to him, I was clear about that to myself, if not anyone else, but I could never, ever act on it. Not only was there my long-term dis-avowal of relationships (it's not just your life, Kate, it's the children's, too!), but also the more immediate risk of rejection. That in itself would be impossible to survive.

He stretched forward to put his mug on the coffee table and settled back again. Was it my imagination or was he just a little closer to me this time? I was conscious of the rise and fall of his chest, as though I were the one breathing through his lungs.

'Thank you again for helping out Roxy with her French this summer,' I said, smiling. 'I'm sure it will really make all the dif-ference. And I really appreciate all your other advice, as well.' Too many 'really's; again I felt childish, especially when he didn't say a word in reply. 'I enjoyed our drink that time,' I rushed on. 'We should do it again.'

'Yes, we should.' Then, without a word, he took my coffee from my hands and placed it deliberately on the coffee table next to his own, and, as he turned back to face me, he didn't stop moving until he had pressed himself flat against me and begun kissing me. I gasped. In a single manoeuvre, in a matter of a second, we'd gone from complete separation to full body contact, as though squeezed together in a press. I could feel my left nipple tauten as it came into contact with a shirt button of his and the shock I felt as I responded to him only electrified the rush already running through me. I could hear myself groaning.

He kissed my neck, his fingers moving all over my bare thighs and inside the dress, and he murmured, 'My God,' as he realised there was nothing else. Then he was on top of me in a motion that felt almost violent and I breathed in sharply at the thrill of it. Moments later he'd pulled me on to his lap astride him and began fumbling in his pockets for his wallet, tearing at the wrapper of a condom.

I began to pull the dress over my head, but his hands stopped me, ordering, 'No, keep it on,' and turning me once more onto my back as I helped him push himself inside me. Now he had one hand gripping mine, pinning them above my head and the other inside the dress once more, flattening my breasts. I peered at his face, hardly believing that this was him, *Davis*, that this was really happening. His eyes were firmly closed, and I closed mine again, drenched by the smell of him and the memories that flooded of Alistair, *his* smell, *his* expressions of arousal. I felt weighed down by his body and by my own pleasure. Feeling it build, he pressed harder, to the brink of pain and held me there. I was shocked by his expertise, the way he read my body as though we'd been lovers for years. Soon he relaxed on top of me, his face buried in my neck.

I heard myself speak. 'That was amazing.'

He pulled himself up, his face was hot with exertion, and when he looked at me his eyes were disappointingly unreadable. I'd expected what? Adoration, admiration, a reflection of my own delight? Out of practice I may have been, but I felt certain he had not knocked on my door with the purpose of seducing me. This had happened by accident, it had happened of itself. 'Amazing': I regretted the adjective now, it was unimaginative, childish.

'You . . .' he began, breathless still. 'You took me by surprise.'

The eyes allowed me in a fraction now and it was only as I felt my chest deflate that I realised I had been holding my breath.

I smiled. 'I kind of thought it was *you* who took *me* by surprise.'

'So I did.' He pulled down the fabric over my thighs, using the flat of his palm to press it against me and I felt my body stir again. He zipped himself up and fiddled with the buttons of his shirt.

Following his lead, I edged back into a sitting position and smoothed down my hair. I felt like I was in a school play, having just simulated intimacy with a classmate. What now? Resume our coffee, still a perfectly drinkable temperature in the mugs on the table in front of us? Hunt down some biscuits? I wanted to giggle. Through the window I had a direct view into my neighbours' flat opposite; the two flats were mirror images of one another, which meant that the room I was looking into was their living room, too. The sash was pulled up and the blind only half drawn, but the room was empty, thank God.

Davis sighed. 'I'm sorry, this sounds terrible, but I have to go, really. I have a student arriving at twelve-thirty and I have to go and pick something up first. I just came to see how you were.'

He kissed me on the corner of the lips and stood watching me for a moment, scratching his left eyelid with his thumbnail and frowning slightly, the most awkward I'd seen him since we'd met.

'I'm fine,' I said, smiling. 'Never better.'

I waited for the invitation to meet him later, but it didn't come.

Chapter 10

Listening to the succession of doors opening and closing between us, Davis's footsteps fading on the first flight of stairs, I sat dumbstruck for a few minutes before reaching for the phone and dialling Abi's office number. I had to report this to a third party at once or I might come to distrust my own memory.

'Hello, Abigail Thorpe.'

'Abi, something unbelievable has just happened.' I got breathless again just recounting the events, but somehow managed to blurt out the news that already sounded too extraordinary to be true.

'Unbelievable to you, Kate. Entirely predictable to the rest of the world. Seb and I said straight away you two would get together.'

'Really?' I was exhilarated by the suggestion that there'd been an attraction between us so tangible it had been picked up by others. 'But what am I going to do when I see him again? Do I pretend it never happened?'

She chuckled. 'You are funny. We're not sixteen, you know!'

'Please, Abi, I know I sound ridiculous, but I really need your advice.'

She sighed indulgently. 'Well, I suppose what you do depends on whether you want a repeat performance or not. Do you?'

'I don't know.' I was partly embarrassed by the intimacy of this conversation and partly glorying in it. It was a strange feeling.

'Come on, be completely honest with yourself for once.'

I hesitated, found myself whispering my answer: 'Yes, I do want . . .' I broke off. 'You know.' I could hear the sound of voices in her office; she often called her colleagues her brothers and sisters, said they had the same love–hate relationships as family. Such a busy, sociable existence she had, no wonder she regarded my attachment to privacy as a foible, an eccentricity. All the affairs and flings she must routinely discuss and yet I made such a big deal of mine. Then my other ear caught the grating of a lawn mower out back and I felt comforted by its sound, grounded once again in the safety of Francombe Gardens. 'So what do I say?'

'Well,' she said, 'it's been a while for me, obviously, since this "dating" phase, if I can use that euphemism, but if I remember rightly you don't need to say anything in particular. Just do whatever you did this time.'

'OK.' I looked down at the tiny blue dress. And wear whatever I did this time, as well, perhaps.

Davis came back at about nightfall and led me straight from the door into my bedroom. My headboard was under the window facing the hallway and with the door open I could see into Roxy's room, her desk against the wall with the laptop shut, her wardrobe door on which the dress I was wearing should be hanging. I tried to move to kick the door closed, but Davis had me in such a firm grip I couldn't stretch my leg far enough. All I could do was adjust my position so that it was he and not me who was propped against the pillows.

The dress stayed on all night.

Routine and structure were extremely important to me, so it came as no surprise that a pattern should develop to my affair with Davis. After that first time (I referred to it in my head in teenage fashion as 'the day it happened'), I would spend each morning at work and then, returning home mid-afternoon, get straight in the shower. It was sweaty work, righting wrongs, and the office was not air-conditioned. What was more, it was a lucky day when we didn't have a man or woman shuffle forward with a smell so overwhelming it caused an immediate gag reflex in the throats of all within range. Ethan called it the smell of life gone bad and we all noticed how it permeated our clothes and stayed on our skin until we physically rinsed it off.

After opening my post and doing the chores, I'd eat, perhaps prepare some food for later, and wait. At about nine, Davis would knock. I'd open the door and fall at once into his arms, or allow myself to be thrust back against the wall or pulled straight into my bedroom. After several hours together, he would return next door to his own flat to sleep, waiting until I was sleepy before slipping away.

'You never suggest I stay,' he said once, in a tone that implied the omission to be highly irregular in his experience.

I nodded. 'I think it's better you go back.' In case of what, I wondered? The possibility that the children might land a week early and burst through the doors at six in the morning clutching stuffed giraffes? Partly, though the likelihood was next to non-existent. No, the truth was less straightforward and certainly not something I was going to share with Davis. It was so clear to me that I was behaving completely out of character that I simply couldn't believe that those I saw regularly – like my colleagues – wouldn't notice it too. But with Davis safely back in his own quarters I could wake up every morning just the same as I always did – alone. I could get dressed, have breakfast, shake off this extraordinary new nocturnal version of me and recover my real self. I even used a different perfume. That way, by the time I pushed open the Advice Centre doors I was as I should be: beyond reproach – or at least trying to be.

I watched his face, uncertain of his reasons for bringing the subject up. Was he saying that he wanted us to wake up together? 'You know what might work?' I said, finally. 'If I came and stayed next door with you.'

He shook his head. 'No. I prefer it here.'

'Why? What have you got hidden back there?' I regarded him with open desire, for when we were together I was nothing but excited by this smouldering persona of mine. 'Some other lover tucked away? Or are you just worried I'll see how you've wrecked the place? You know, I haven't seen the bedroom once since you moved in.'

He didn't answer, just ran his palms over my back and bottom, down to my thighs, quickly lost in private thought.

I wasn't surprised by his resistance. Structured though this little adventure was, there were odd conflicts between us that had quickly become part of the game. (Not that game was the right word at all – obsessive grip, thrall. Yes, that was it, I was in his thrall.) For instance, I had hoped for more of the daytime encounters like our first – it still took my breath away to remember the erotic turn that neighbourly coffee had taken – but he preferred to confine our meetings to the night; I wanted to stay sober, to feel every last sensation of this in the real, he liked to have plenty of alcohol involved, as well as his beloved cigarettes; I wanted to be naked, he liked me to keep at least some clothes on. He'd asked repeatedly for the blue dress and though I had put it away after the first night, I did deduce from his attachment to it that my own clothes were not quite right. How practical and matronly those shirt dresses seemed now, the choice of a woman who did not have sex. I picked up a few little dresses and skirts and vest tops from the cheap boutiques Roxy went to on the high street and made sure I was wearing those. Once I switched to more traditional garb of seduction – black underwear, stockings, a plunging neckline – and he immediately objected. 'Is that the kind of thing Alistair liked?' His words were coated with contempt and I felt flattered that he might view Alistair as some sort of rival.

Otherwise, however, this was not an arrangement that in any way brought to mind my early relationship with Alistair. Nor did it feel much like the beginning of any kind of relationship, for that matter. The way Davis looked at me and handled me in private felt completely removed from any public encounters we had, an unexpected meeting in the street or in the gardens. Then, he would revert to his old amiable gallantry and I to my garrulous friendliness – or so I now judged my previous manner to have been.

Our conversation during those evenings together was mostly impersonal. He'd tell me something from a text he was teaching or I'd mention a case at work. There were no exchanged admissions of our growing fondness or coy second-guessing of the other's feelings, no confidences about the horrors of the failed relationships in our pasts, including our respective marriages.

Now I thought about it, Davis had never been especially curious about Alistair. He referred to him usually only in relation to the children and even then in dispassionate tones, as though collecting data for a controlled experiment of some sort. Had Alistair always been so ambitious for his children, he would ask. He didn't sense any drive from within them, at least not from Roxy. And did I think it a blessing or a curse that Matthew resembled his father so strikingly?

Only once did I ask him about his ex-wife. Camilla, she was called, I'd gathered as much from occasional remarks he had made in the past.

'How did you meet?'

Though the question was out of the blue, his face did not flicker. He was lying on his back and continued to look at the ceiling as he answered. 'She was my student. I was recommended to her family by a friend of her older brother's who I'd been coaching for his retakes.'

As he turned to meet my eye, I felt my forehead furrow. 'I didn't know that. What was the age difference?'

'Ten years.' The same as Alistair and Victoria; that was a coincidence. 'We married when she was too young.'

Well, I could hardly criticise that. 'Us, too. I was only twenty when I got engaged, still at college. Crazy, now I look back, it was completely against the trend. All our friends were saying they would never get married, there was no point.'

But Davis didn't appear to have heard any of this, involved now in his own memories. 'There was always an imbalance, I suppose, with her family being so wealthy. A sense that I was on the payroll and belonged to them.' He pulled himself onto his elbows and looked about for his cigarettes, but they were in the kitchen where we'd been drinking wine earlier and instead he reached across and began playing with my hair. 'I trundled along for a few years, though. Well, more than a few, over a decade in the end.'

'Until she was unfaithful?' I prompted, delicately.

'Yes, she began seeing an artist friend of hers. Well, I use the term "artist" in the loosest sense, as he didn't have any particular talent, but that didn't stop her putting on a show for him.'

'She worked in an art gallery?'

'Yes, quite a well-known one in Chelsea. He did very poor sculptures, this guy, with an acorn theme, as I remember. Giant clay acorns in various states of repose.' He raised an eyebrow at me. 'I know what you're going to ask: repose from what, exactly? They're acorns!'

I laughed, flattered by the inference that I shared his superior aesthetic judgment.

'I suppose I should have been grateful she wasn't posing nude for him.'

That reminded me of the comment he'd once made about Camilla seeing herself as his muse, but those 'fragments' of his had not been mentioned since that same conversation and I

117

sensed it might be a mistake to bring them up now. I suspected Davis had abandoned his writing for the moment, what with being so busy with teaching, and now, I hardly dared add, even to myself, all the time he was spending with me.

'It must have been a pretty bitter divorce, then?' I said.

'What makes you say that?'

'Just that it usually is when someone's been unfaithful.'

Davis gave me his sleepy, heavy-lidded look. 'Well, let's just say we haven't spoken since the day I left. The divorce was all done through the lawyers; we never even talked on the phone.'

I waited, watching him. It was a while before he spoke again. 'So you see, my dear, your own situation is highly civilised compared to mine, however desperate you may once have felt.'

I flushed. 'You thought I was desperate when we met?'

Again, he didn't flicker. I supposed that after his expert seduction of me I shouldn't have been at all surprised by his coolness; he clearly understood women perfectly, right down to the booby traps of our interrogations. 'Not at all, of course not. But I did think you might be in need of a little . . . rescuing.'

I thought of how he'd grabbed me on the sofa, moving in a single, unstoppable lunge. I was so addicted to the memory of it – really, there was no other way to say it than that he had *ravished* me – that I even fantasised about it when we made love. (What would Abi say about that? A sexual attraction so perfect even my secret fantasies were about him!)

'Well, everyone needs rescuing occasionally,' I conceded, finally, and in the kind of drawl I'd last heard from the mouth of seventeen-year-old Marianne Suter.

I didn't ask if things would end when Roxy and Matthew came back, and nor did I instruct him that they would. It was inconceivable that I could continue to be this new character when I was required to be a mother again. The two simply weren't compatible, were they?

*

On the sixth day Tash phoned, sounding unusually disillusioned. She'd been sacked from her waitressing job and had somehow become embroiled in a falling-out between the couple who ran the café. She made it seem as though she'd crossed some sort of Reggie Kray character and needed to go into hiding.

'I wondered if I could come and stay with you again for a few days? Just lie low for a bit. Mum's driving me nuts with the career advice and I know you're on your own. I thought I might keep you company, maybe look for a job in London.'

There were so many issues to address here that I hardly knew where to begin, not least the satisfaction that she was finally tiring of life at home (when I considered how eager Roxy was to fly the nest, it astounded me that Tash could live with our parents in her late twenties), but the one that overrode all others was the need to put her off, to preserve my space for Davis and me. The idea of the three of us sitting at the kitchen table, locked in small talk, filled me with panic. I would be eaten up with frustration at not being able to touch him, I would never be able to hide it. A frightening thought flared – would I be able to see him at all after this, in the company of any third party? – but I quickly snuffed it out.

'I'm so sorry, Tash, but I'm gong to have to say no, just this once. It's not a great time.'

'Why?'

Excuses whirled: it was no good saying I was busy at work because that only underlined the fact that the flat was empty and available for guests. Building or decoration work going on? Well, everyone knew I had no money for that, especially after the conversion of the front rooms. Illness, perhaps? But she'd only offer to look after me and in any case I sounded as fit as a fiddle. What then?

'I just need some time on my own,' I said, finally.

There was a pause and a scuffling sound, as though she'd

staggered from the phone with surprise. 'On your own? I thought you'd be really lonely without the kids.'

I sighed. 'I do exist in my own right, you know, Tash, I'm not just a parent. I may have things on my mind . . .'

'What things?' This was not going well, not least because it would shortly be relayed to our mother and undoubtedly interpreted as my concealment of terminal illness.

'Is it a bloke?' Tash lowered her voice to a whisper. 'Oh my God, it is, isn't it? Is he there now?'

I wouldn't be answering the phone if he was, I thought, which only brought to mind another uncomfortable realisation, the fact that I'd taken to ignoring the phone whenever Davis and I were together. That, in turn, added another essential task to my morning rehabilitation routine, checking all forms of communication for news from the kids.

'Who is he? Not the guy next door, the one we wanted to take—'

I interrupted, my patience exhausted. 'Look, this is none of your business, Tash. Please just respect my privacy. Is that too much to ask?'

She gave a half-offended 'hmmph'. 'All right, all right. There's no need to speak to me like I'm Roxy.'

'I wasn't,' I said, surprised. What did she mean? How did I speak to Roxy?

We said goodbye and hung up. The conversation had been just short enough for me to be able to seal it up and push it into the outer reaches of my mind where I could no longer hear it.

The day before the children were due back from holiday I finally came to my senses. I went into the kitchen in the morning to put the kettle on and for the first time felt sickened by the mess about the place. It felt sordid, like the paraphernalia of something illegal: wine glasses, sediment so gluey it stuck to the glass even when turned upside down for the dishwasher; ashtrays loaded with butts, stray bits of clothes, condom packets, even hairs. I remembered something Davis had said when we first met, about finding human hairs in a motel room from the person who'd stayed the night before, and my response: You make it sound like a crime scene. Now my whole flat was a crime scene and I would need to obliterate all evidence of this strange erotic twilight world I'd created before I was found out.

First, I texted Davis – 'Can't meet tonight, kids back tomorrow' – and then I began cleaning. I scrubbed and sprayed and polished until all was sanitised and chaste, the parquet gleaming, the sheets as fresh and tightly tucked as those of a hospital ward. Roxy's blue dress was re-laundered and hooked with her others on the door of her wardrobe. A spring clean in the sultriest part of August; Roxy and Matthew would think it was especially for them (if they noticed at all), but if it was for anyone's benefit, it was Alistair's, in case I couldn't stop him from coming into the flat and noticing, just sensing something residually carnal about the place. He wasn't just anyone, after all, but the last one I'd slept with, the one who, though he'd abandoned me years ago, liked to believe he still knew what was best for me.

The established form on such returns was that Victoria would pick up the three of them from the airport, drive them back to Francombe Gardens and wait in the car while Alistair helped the children upstairs with their luggage. Determined to prevent him from coming up today, I began watching out for the car at least an hour before they could reasonably have arrived, and by the time they pulled up I was sitting on the steps by the main doors. Alistair rolled down the window and called out, 'What're you doing out here, Kate?'

I sprang to my feet. 'Waiting for you guys, of course, what do you think?' I peered over his shoulder into the back seat. 'Hi guys, I've missed you!'

Matthew leapt out first and I cuddled him hard and close, for a second or two forgetting everything else in the world but him.

He smelled of stale aeroplane air and sweet spearmint. I held him at arm's length to get a better look at him. His eyes glittered, his hair was almost to his shoulders, and there was the scab of a graze on his chin. A little savage back from living with the animals. 'Darling, did you have a fantastic time?'

He beamed and I saw that the sun had brought out freckles on his nose, a slightly stretched nose, if I wasn't mistaken. Two weeks apart and he'd grown! 'The best, it was awesome. There's so much to tell you!' Long-haul or not, he was full of beans. 'Dad's going to email the pictures later, we took millions. We saw all of the big five, you know. Elephants, leopards, lions . . .' He checked them off with his fingers. 'Did you get my post-card?'

'Not yet, what a shame. But maybe it will come tomorrow.'

'It's got lions on it, exactly like the ones we saw. Weren't they, Dad?'

Alistair was out of the car now, ruffling Matt's hair before kissing me emptily on my cheek. The door was open and behind him Victoria leaned across to wave hello. She was enormously pregnant, appeared almost to have doubled in size since I'd last seen her. I tried not to speculate as to whether this meant Alistair was more or less likely to come up to the flat (or both of them – she might need the loo!).

'Hi Mum.'

'Roxy! Did you enjoy it, too?'

She stepped around the car from the road side and onto the pavement, a yellow patterned bag I didn't recognise swinging from her shoulder. Her bare arms were deeply tanned, her lips shiny with balm. She'd put her hair in pigtails, but still looked several years older than she was, every inch the world traveller. She glanced straight up at the front windows of our flat – Davis's now, of course – as if to say, 'I thought I'd outgrown this, but no, here I am, back again.'

'God, that was the flight from hell. The plane was completely packed and there were two brats in the seats in front who didn't sleep the whole time . . .'

'Darling!' I grabbed her to me and as she relaxed into my grasp I felt that same initial arrow of pure love I'd felt for Matt a moment ago, except this was diluted almost at once with gratitude, gratitude for her co-operating with my hug at all, and in that second it all rushed back: the rows and suspicions, the yo-yo moods, my own wariness of her attitude towards me in front of people like Victoria, people like . . . I banished the figure of Davis before it could be fully fleshed out. Not allowed, no arguments. I had made my mind up in good time for this doorstep reunion, got my priorities right. Yes, being with him had helped me free my mind of my worries while the children were away, but now they were back I needed to free it of him. Every time I thought of him as my lover I would replace the image instantly with an old one of him, cycling off for one of his sessions, perhaps, or frowning over a book in the garden. Surely if I did it often enough I'd be able to trick myself; surely if I could just ignore Abi's voice in my ear: *Be honest with yourself for once, Kate . . .*

'Kate? We're going to head straight back,' Alistair was saying, 'Victoria's bushed. Can you manage with the luggage?'

'Of course, no problem.'

'I can carry my own,' Matt protested, though Roxy happily let me play porter for her.

'And thank you again for the lovely present, guys,' Victoria called after them. My usual instinct was to bristle at any thought of my children buying gifts for their stepmother, but today that was notably absent – presumably because I was so pleased to be getting rid of her and Alistair so easily.

As we made our way up and passed Davis's door, my stomach lurched suddenly with lust and yearning. Clearly I was going to have to strengthen my resolve if this was going to work. I *had* to get everything back to normal, there was simply no choice in the matter. Thank God he had given no indication that he intended to make it any harder than it need be, responding to that last text of mine with the simple agreement: 'OK.'

Opening the door, I squeezed Matt's hand, but he humoured me for only a second or two before slithering from my grasp and making for his room. Roxy was already in hers. 'I've missed you,' I said into the empty hallway between their doors. 'I'm not going to let you go away for that long ever again.'

And I stood for a moment with my back to the front door, as if I could barricade us in, barricade the world out.

Chapter 11

The first thing I discovered was that the holiday had not improved Roxy's mood, at least not where I was concerned. Over the next few weeks she talked more and more openly of looking forward to leaving for university (she hadn't even applied yet!), and for no other reason than for the unsupervised living. 'Just to be able to choose the colour of my own loo roll,' she said, as though this were an issue of gravest artistic expression. I wondered if she had considered that she'd be shopping for her loo roll herself, too, and paying for it.

I should have let her be, I knew that. But it was no good; jittery from my separation from Davis, I couldn't seem to stop myself from seeking an opening between her and me, a renewal of friendship, as if it were somehow up to me and me alone to win her back. (If this echoed my behaviour after Alistair left, the discarded lover holding out for a second chance, then I chose not to acknowledge it.)

'Hi, Rox! Everything all right?'

'Hmm, fine.' She was reading in the living room, an elongated shape under a throw on the sofa, the inevitable mug of black coffee on the table beside her. The picture on the book cover was of a pale-faced girl in high-necked black dress, her misfortunes painfully visible in her face. By contrast, Roxy's was perfectly blank.

'It's good to see you in the "common parts",' I said, using her own ironic term for the living room and kitchen. She spent at least ninety per cent of her time at home in her bedroom.

She didn't reply and I perched on the armchair by the door as though just passing on my way to the kitchen. I looked again at the book cover. 'You're reading *Effi Briest*?'

'Yeah, Davis lent me it. It's good, actually.'

'He said it was a bit like *Madame Bovary*.'

'Maybe.' She seemed about to say something else and then changed her mind. She didn't like to waste her literary criticisms on me. I was much too ill-read.

I searched her face for clues of secret knowledge. Though the French sessions had officially ended with her holiday, and a new school term now begun, her association with Davis had continued. I often heard them talking in the hallway and she liked to pop over to chat about books. I'd hear their laughter, hers ringing, his gruff, like some kind of duet in merriment. There couldn't possibly have been any meaningful correlation and yet I couldn't help observing that the more I avoided him, the more Roxy seemed to seek him out. Once or twice I'd even dared wonder if it were he who kept the alliance between them alive – deliberately, as a way of connecting with me.

'Roxy, don't take this the wrong way, but do you think you might be seeing a bit too much of him?'

She looked up, eyes sharp. 'Who?'

'Davis, of course. You know, you must remember he's got dozens of students on his books, he may not have the time to see so much of you now that term has started.'

She laid the novel flat on her chest and reached behind her head to twist her ponytail into a tight coil, all the while regarding me with intense irritation. 'Did he say that?'

'No, no, I'm just . . . well, I'm just worried you might be getting some sort of crush on him.' I regretted this even as the words

126

left my lips, even before I saw her contract her facial muscles in a horrible expression of contempt.

'Unbelievable,' she muttered. 'A *crush*? You really still think I'm twelve or something, don't you?'

'I just . . .' I tailed off, trapped by my own folly. What was I doing, looking for trouble like this? I gazed at her, not knowing whether to apologise or to plough on. Inches below her sneer, the smaller face of Effi Briest looked beseechingly up at me and I had the urge to pull the throw over the book as one might cover the face of a corpse. 'He was just helping you with your French, Roxy.'

'Yes, which you and Dad have gone on and on about since God knows when. Have you forgotten that he's meant to be preparing me for Cambridge?'

'You've finished your sessions, though, I thought? And, anyway, I'm not sure that was ever his brief, was it?'

She laughed out loud at that. 'Of course it was. You're *so* out of the loop. What other brief could there possibly be?' With this she adopted the robotic Dalek monotone Matt and his friends used for their *Doctor Who* games: '"Roxy must go to Oxbridge. If mission fails, exterminate." That's all you care about.'

I blinked, startled. 'Roxy, that's not true. I want you to go to whichever university you'd be happiest at. I mean it.'

She shrugged. 'Well, Dad, anyway. You know, you should be pleased I want to spend time with a teacher. Or would you prefer I hung out with crack addicts? I'm sure it could be arranged.'

'Don't be ridiculous.' I stared down at her, bewildered. 'Look, he's a teacher, yes, but he's also our tenant and we need to respect his privacy.' This sounded disingenuous even to me – would I really be saying this to her if I wasn't haunted by my own recent history with him, recent enough for my body still to ache for him? Was a part of this approach of mine simply the desire to discuss him with someone, to find out if he'd dropped any hints about how he felt about me? If so, I'd chosen the wrong person to indulge me and was quite unprepared for what she said next.

'You're jealous.' She spoke with viper calm. 'Jealous that he wants to spend time with me. You're jealous because he prefers me, because I'm young and you're dried up and old!'

I gasped, feeling the trauma of her words with such abrupt force I couldn't keep pace. To be spoken to in this way by anyone was shocking enough, but to be asked to accept that my daughter and I might be rivals, rivals in any situation, much less for Davis's affection, that was terrifying. Terrifying and unnatural. The worst of it was that there was a grain of truth in there: I *was* jealous, though not in the way she thought. I was jealous of the easy companionship she had with him that I had had so recently, too, and could never hope to reclaim; the passing of the time of day without worrying about what was being left unsaid. That was the price I had paid for that heady ten-day fling. I had flung out our friendship.

'You know what? I won't even dignify that with a response.' I tried to configure my face into its unemotional work expression, but found I couldn't do it. My breath was coming in hot, shallow gulps. It would be quite obvious to her that she'd hit a nerve. 'I suggest you apologise right now, or else . . .'

'Or else what?' She cocked her head, taunting me. 'You'll go running to Dad to grass me up for insubordination? Like he gives a shit.'

'Roxy, stop this! You're really upsetting me.' But her last remark brought me up short. What on earth was this idea that Alistair didn't care? She'd said that twice, in effect, in an exchange that couldn't have lasted five minutes. Why, though, why now, when she'd just spent two weeks alone with him? Hadn't that been quality father–daughter time, by anyone's standards?

Because his new baby was just a month from being born, that was why; because she feared with all her heart that she was going to be pushed out. I remembered my own misgivings about the arrival of Tash and she had been a full sister, my parents' marriage indubitably intact. Had Alistair spoken to Roxy about it while on holiday? He talked a lot about 'key memories' and 'once-in-a-lifetime experiences', as though these self-contained chunks of childhood were equal to the considerably longer periods that made up the rest of life. He liked to play the dream-maker (leaving me to the packed lunches and laundry). Yes, it was entirely possible that he might deliberately have avoided all talk of the new baby in order to stop anything from spoiling their last great adventure. In that context the link with Davis was hardly difficult to fathom; he had become some kind of temporary father figure to Roxy – while her real one prepared to spend the rest of his life with a different family.

'What, Mum?' Roxy demanded, impatient of my silence. 'Eh?' And she pulled herself up a little more upright, roused enough to give me her full attention.

But I was backing off, had already risen from the chair and taken a side step towards the door. 'Look, I don't want to argue with you, Roxy, I just want to make sure everything's OK with you. This is such an important time for you . . .'

'Blah, blah, blah.' She slumped down again, rearranged her limbs exhaustedly. 'You're the one who started it. I was just reading.'

Disturbing though the incident was, it at least told me that she didn't know about Davis and me; she couldn't possibly have a clue, to come out with something as personal as that. Even so, I had to bring an end to this. It was bad enough that I had to deal with my own feelings for Davis without having to watch my daughter flaunt her growing friendship with him in front of me.

Frustratingly, it was several days before I actually saw him again with neither Roxy nor Matthew about, by which time my emotions were so feverish I could no longer sit still, spending hours moving restlessly about the flat in a state of suspense that was all the more agonising for my having created it for myself. Then, at last, the moment presented itself. It was mid-afternoon and he was in the garden. I could see him from the kitchen window, settled on one of the park benches not far from Abi's patio, absorbed in his reading. Even that incensed me: was I the only one around here who didn't have time to sit lazing with a book?

I marched down the fire escape, hardly watching my footing and began striding across the grass. I hated him for looking so innocent, the mild-mannered professor with his head in his book, noting his insights in an exercise book for the benefit of the local youth. And I hated him for his magnetism, evident even in his solitude: twice in the time it took me to reach him he'd responded to a wave or a greeting from someone outside my vision. How popular he'd become here at Francombe Gardens, people were as naturally attracted to him as I was, and he now appeared to know more residents than I did! I imagined Abi bringing him cappuccino and biscotti, someone else inviting him in for dinner, trips to the theatre being arranged without anyone thinking to invite me.

At the sound of my footsteps (or perhaps my huffing and puffing), he looked up and smiled. Then he stretched his right arm across the top of the seat in a gesture of invitation. 'Kate! How nice. Long time no see . . .'

'Oh, don't give me that!' I sat down right at the far end of the seat, beyond the reach of his hand and ludicrously sidelong, like a spy trained to pass on information without appearing actually to make contact. I had never behaved like this before and he was understandably perplexed.

'What on earth is the matter?' He pulled his arm away and leaned forward. 'Has something happened?'

'What is the matter,' I hissed, no longer able to resist looking at him directly, 'is that I don't want you to say anything to Roxy. About us.'

He drew his eyebrows together in concern. 'Why would I want to do that?' By contrast with mine, his tone was reasonable, his body language open and natural. I dreaded he might reach out his arm again and touch my hand or my hair and cause me to crumble completely.

'Well, she's always popping round, isn't she?' I said. 'You might say something to her without realising . . .'

He sighed. 'Oh, give me a little credit, please.'

I pinched my lips together to the point of pain, as if denying them the memory that they'd once touched his. 'No, Davis, I can't take the risk. Can't you tell her you don't have time to chat? Just gently discourage her until she loses interest.'

Davis lowered his voice (a technique, I wondered, for getting me to move closer to him?). 'Well, I could, I suppose. But I have to say I think it will seem very strange to her if I cut off all contact. She still needs support for this Cambridge application. And what will her father say if I break our agreement without any explanation?'

I stared. 'What agreement? Alistair knows the tutoring was just a summer thing.'

Davis frowned again. 'I thought you knew? He phoned me last week and asked me to continue with her until the Cambridge interview – if she gets one, of course, though I have no doubt they'll want . . .'

I cried out, interrupting him. 'I don't believe this! How did he even get your number?'

'I assumed you'd given him it.'

'Oh, God.' All at once I felt hot and dizzy. Alistair must know. He must have found out about Davis and me and stepped in because he wanted to investigate the situation, get Davis under his control. Then I relaxed a little. That was nonsense and I should be thankful I hadn't said it out loud. Any belief I had that Alistair continued to follow my emotional life in any way was, and always had been, wishful thinking. Even so, I didn't like this,

I didn't like this sensation that the small authority I did have in my family was being removed from me, that decisions were being made without me, discussions taking place.

'It must have slipped his mind,' I said, finally. 'We can't always remember to tell each other everything.'

'Of course not.'

'Roxy should have let me know, though.' But once more I had to admit defeat, for it made perfect sense that she had not. After all, she'd announced the arrangement of the summer sessions as casually as could be. 'Oh, by the way, Davis says he'll give me extra coaching . . .' If I thought about it, I had not been consulted about that either, not exactly.

Davis went on: 'If I refuse to see her now then she really will know something has happened. She's no fool.'

'I know.' And nor was her father. Davis was right, Alistair would certainly want to know why his daughter's miracle-working tutor was suddenly unavailable. I imagined him phoning Davis a second time, persuading him to get back 'on board', offering new financial incentives to hold Roxy's hand over the final hurdle.

Davis leaned towards me, sensing my capitulation. 'I'm sorry if you feel this has been sprung on you, Kate, but you can rest assured I have no intention of saying anything to Roxy about us.'

'You, maybe.' Suddenly I thought of Abi and my calls to her for advice, my boasts about my new sexual adventures. I'd asked her to be discreet, but naturally she would have shared the gossip with Seb. Who else in the building might either of them have told? A conversation overheard in the gardens – Matthew spent half his life in the playground; a bit of gossip in the lobby – Roxy was in and out several times a day. Yes, they were in their own worlds, but that did not mean they were deaf. And, in any case, if anyone had been watching for the next instalment, here I was delivering it by acting like a madwoman in the communal gardens. I couldn't look more like a spurned lover if I tried.

132

'I don't like us not speaking,' I blurted out. 'It feels weird.'

Davis shook his head helplessly. 'Kate, may I remind you that you were the one to end our . . .' – he paused to find the word – '. . . liaison.'

Ridiculously, I felt my body respond in arousal to the word, the way he drew out the second syllable a little longer than was necessary, as though tasting it on his tongue, tasting me . . . I couldn't be sure that had he grabbed me there and then, in full view of a hundred neighbours, I wouldn't have submitted in an instant.

'I didn't *end* it,' I said, looking down, but when I met his eye again I found the caring frown of a friend, not a lover. I could have wailed with disappointment.

'Well, that was what I thought you were doing,' he said. 'We haven't exchanged two words since, and every time I see you, you seem to vanish into thin air. I just assumed you were avoiding me.'

'Of course I'm avoiding you!' I cried, irrationally. 'You know I can't have some kind of sordid affair with my children sitting in the next room. It's sick!'

He looked a little hurt at that. 'It's hardly "sick", is it? Two consenting adults . . .'

'But if Matthew heard any of what we—' I broke off, covering my face to block the image of a little boy chancing upon his mother and her lover, the man he thought was a neighbour, a family friend.

'Fine,' Davis said, changing tack and adopting the soothing tones of a therapist. 'I understand completely, of course I do. It's exactly what I thought.'

'Fine,' I repeated. How fast an acquiescence on his part, it was almost cruel in its easiness. All that assuming! Hadn't he considered seeking anything more solid, more real? How about asking me? But I wanted it all my way, I saw that now. I wanted him to be injured by my withdrawal, to beg me to continue, to still want

133

me. Whichever way this concluded now, whether he continued to coach Roxy or not, I knew I would not be happy. I had lost control. And this was exactly why I'd forbidden myself from starting a new relationship all these years, to protect myself from being reduced once more to this position of confusion and powerlessness.

Davis wrinkled his brow again. 'Look, Kate, of course let's speak. We're grown-ups, we can be amicable. But I'll keep my distance, if that's what you still want. Besides, Roxy's got into the habit of coming round to my place for her sessions, so you won't have to see me as much.' As he fixed me with an emphatic look, a look of honest disavowal, I felt like screaming, 'The last thing I want is never to see you! Can't you see that?'

I had to get away from here before I broke down completely. The truth was oozing through with every new word of protest, a truth too shocking to admit to anyone but myself. What I wanted was to have that twilight life back again, to be that person again, to forget there was a daughter to fight with and a son to protect and an ex-husband to mourn. To act unconsciously, for no other end than my own body's pleasure, to be his lover again. *That* was what I wanted and I had no idea how to stop myself from feeling this way.

I looked imploringly at him, willing him to understand. Now, at last, he made physical contact, taking my hand gently in his, his fingers on the flat of my hand, a fatherly squeeze. 'Perhaps you ought to go back upstairs and calm down a bit. You've got this out of proportion. There's really nothing to worry about.'

Back in the flat I went straight to the kitchen drawer that I had been using for personal papers since losing my study to Davis. There it was, exactly where I'd expected, in a blue plastic folder labelled 'Flat rental': a copy of the tenancy agreement drawn up by the agent and signed first by Davis and then by me. My eyes scanned expertly after years of practice with documents pressed on me by clients. (They couldn't make head or tail of them themselves and yet expected me to home in on the crucial loophole in a couple of seconds.) I found the clause I was looking for on the third page. I had thought so, there was a six-month break clause. Either one of us could now give a month's notice to end the tenancy at six months. He had moved in in April, just after Easter; we were now in September. I counted the months on my fingers: April, May, June . . .

Then, not allowing myself time to change my mind, I found some stationery and began writing:

Dear Davis,
I am very sorry to have to do this, but after much thought
I think that the best thing would be for you to move out.
Please consider this notice that you should vacate 8a
Francombe Gardens by Saturday the 13th of October.
I very much hope the matter can be concluded
amicably. I will, of course, be happy to provide a
landlord's reference should one be required.
Yours, Kate

I folded the note in two and slipped it under his door. It was brutal, more than unfair, but I was in an impossible situation. Doing this gave me no satisfaction, it was merely the lesser of two evils. And when he did go I knew I would be devastated, crying into my pillow exactly as I had when Alistair left, that ghastly silent sobbing that could not be fully vented in case the children heard and grew distressed. For the thousandth time I cursed myself for falling into this trap, for surrendering to all this desire. It was exactly as I had feared; I'd lost myself, and in doing so risked hurting the children. Well, at least this time I could assume it would be an agony relatively short-lived. Davis would disappear, Roxy wouldn't care either way, Alistair could be placated somehow; and tomorrow I'd ask at the school for recommendations for a new French tutor.

I was out at the supermarket when he came back up from the garden, but when I walked past his door to mine I heard the familiar sounds of pottering, the kettle and the radio, the flush of the loo. I let myself in and began unpacking the shopping, handling in turn each packet and tin and bottle, wondering which item would be in my fingers when he finally read the note and came knocking.

Smoothies, that was my answer, the ones I bought for Roxy. A kilo of berries crushed into a thimbleful of liquid, something like that. Brainfood. I went to answer the door, turning off the hall light as I went; I didn't want to see his face spot-lit in front of me, his justifiable anger at my betrayal.

He held the letter in his fingers, while his feet and eyes moved about with agitation. 'What is this, Kate? Have you gone completely mad?'

I wrapped my arms protectively around myself, working hard to keep the emotion from my voice. 'Davis, I have to ask you to go. It's the only way out of this.'

'Out of what? I thought we just agreed we'd forget about the summer?' He looked genuinely bewildered, but weary, too, terribly weary, as though all too familiar with the delicate mysteries of life's dealings with women. He was thinking perhaps of his ex-wife and I felt new distress at being filed in the same compartment as her, being reshuffled from the present to the past.

'I can't forget,' I said, calmly, 'that's the problem, not while you're still here. And even when you go, I don't want you to make any contact, not with any of us. I'm going to find Roxy another tutor.'

'This is madness!' he cried out.

'I know it's unfair of me, but I have to be selfish, just once I have to do what's best for me.'

'But why, Kate? Why is this best for you?' His voice was desperate now. 'I don't want to move out, you know that. I'm very happy here. Please, can't we talk about this? I thought we got on so well, you and I.'

I closed my eyes, stomach sick, throat dry. Even in the dim light, I didn't know if I could bear to experience his reaction to what I was about to say, to have his rejection of me spelled out once and for all. But he was going, he was going, I repeated to myself, I would say it and he would be gone and I would never be able to blame myself for being a coward. For someone like me who tortured herself after the event, it had to be better to be truthful. 'The thing is, Davis, you call it "getting on", that's what it is to you, and that's fine, of course it is. But I . . . I think I've fallen in love with you.' My voice dropped away. *Fallen*, as though love were a descent, and it was as far as I could see, a descent into misery.

The fingers gripping the letter slackened and his mouth gaped. 'In love?'

I nodded, all at once able to hold my head up and make eye contact. My distress had left me, at least for the moment. There was a kind of power in honesty, however uncomfortably it was received. 'Yes, it's pathetic, I know, you don't have to tell me. We just had sex a few times, I should be able to accept it for what it was. But I can't, and it makes it impossible for me to go on with things as they are. The Roxy issue is incidental. I can't have you next door, you have to see that.'

There was a silence. I waited for him to turn and withdraw. It's just a few weeks, I told myself, a matter of days really, to count down on the kitchen calendar before he goes and I can start to forget that he ever arrived. Someone else will move in, someone like the female solicitor I should have chosen in the first place. Life will go back to normal, it will.

'There is one other way, you know.' Davis's voice was completely different now, sweet, intimate, demanding my full attention in exactly the same way it had when we'd been in bed together. Wrong-footed, my body leaned towards his.

'What?' Still, I didn't dare hope for anything more than a discreet withdrawal, a promise that he'd do as I asked and never come back and remind me of my fall.

He cleared his throat and tested a small smile on his lips. 'You could agree to marry me.'

'*Marry* you?' Now it was I who gaped. 'That's crazy!'

I thought I saw him swallow, then, lose control of the muscles his throat. He must be nervous, I thought. This was extraordinary, extraordinary.

'Will you?' he asked, urgently, and took a small step towards me. 'You've just said you love me.' His arm dropped to his side and as the letter fell from his hand I watched it in wonder, as though waiting for a butterfly to land on outstretched fingers.

And then I heard myself say yes.

Chapter 12

It seemed perfectly fitting that, having taken my original marriage from me, Victoria should steal my thunder over the announcement of my second – by giving birth three weeks early to a baby girl.

Over the last few months I'd speculated constantly as to whether there could be any preference for a boy or girl from my own children's point of view and had, in the end, settled on a girl. Matthew, so much younger than Roxy, was surely more likely to be unsettled by the arrival of another boy, whereas she, already an adult (I was at last beginning to fall into line about that technicality, at least) could hardly view a newborn as a direct rival. With an age advantage of almost eighteen years, she would inevitably come to feel more like an aunt than a sister.

Then had come that awful conversation about Davis and her remarks about Alistair not caring, and I'd made a last-minute reversal: a boy, please, Victoria. That would be much better. Matthew and I were still close enough for me to be able to reassure him that he was still number one, but Roxy and I were demonstrably not, and any reassurance I offered might just be interpreted as interference.

And so, naturally, Victoria failed to comply and delivered a girl, after all. She was named Elizabeth, Elizabeth Susan Easton.

I imagined Alistair saying, 'I've given one daughter an "artistic" name, this time I'm playing it straight'.

The children heard the news before I did. It was the Tuesday evening after Davis had proposed to me and the first time I'd been able to get the two of them together for any longer than half a minute. Now I had the perfect opportunity before me. I had picked Matthew up from school and we had arrived back a little ahead of Roxy, who intended spending the whole evening at home writing an essay. Then, just as I announced I had something important to tell them, the phone rang – Ethan from work, wanting to confirm my schedule for the following week – and I sent the two of them to get themselves a drink in the kitchen and wait for me there. Co-operative for once, they were now sitting at the kitchen table stirring hot chocolate and chatting.

I took a very deep breath. It had been agony waiting to share my news, but it had felt crucial that I tell them together. If one (Roxy) were to hear from the other (Matthew) or, indeed, from anyone at all but me, it would be judged at best discourteous on my part, at worst catastrophic. Davis had offered to break the news with me, of course, in case of any difficulties, but I had declined. Odd the confidence this engagement had given me. Unexpected it may have been, but I would have defended its rightness to the highest court in the land. Not only did I love Davis, but I knew both Roxy and Matthew liked him enormously (I would never have considered marrying him otherwise, would I?). Even so, it had been only a matter of months since he'd come into our lives and this development could only take them by surprise. This was the most important year in Roxy's life – as everyone in the Western hemisphere was surely now aware – and timing and other logistics needed to be hammered out. I could be in for a lengthy discussion.

'Guys, I wanted to tell you something—' I began, but Roxy interrupted at once, noticeably livelier than she'd been when I'd left them fifteen minutes ago.

'It's all right, Mum, we already know.' She held up her mobile phone and my heart contracted – surely Davis had not gone against my wishes and let something slip? – and then relaxed again. They were obviously both fine about it, whatever he'd said, just sitting there, blowing on their hot drinks, pulling 'Wow!' faces when they caught the other's eye.

'You do?' I asked, cautiously.

'Yeah, Dad literally just texted me while you were on the phone. He said to tell Matt. We were just talking about it now.'

I stared, confused, as Matt nodded his confirmation. '*Dad* told you?'

Roxy smiled. 'Well, who else? The midwife's not going to call us, is she?'

'Her hands would be covered in blood,' Matt added and Roxy screwed up her face and flicked her bare foot against his leg under the table. 'Urgh, shut up, you, that's gross!'

Now the penny dropped. 'Oh, I see, the baby's been born. Well, that's early.'

I sat down at the table, quickly dismissing all thoughts of my own prepared script and applying myself instead to assessing their reactions to this other, equally dangerous, bombshell. Roxy was playing it cool, but she was excited, I could tell. There was high colour across her cheekbones and chest, an outward clue that what was on her mind was too big to be contained. This was drama, this was something profound in anyone's experience; even she could not deny a primal response to new life. Looking more closely, however, Matthew seemed a little off-balance, per-haps knocked by the fact of the premature arrival, or, more likely, by Alistair not sending word to him directly. He did not yet have a mobile phone of his own.

'Have you spoken to Dad?' I asked him, gently.

'No.'

'Perhaps he was trying to get through just now, when I was on the phone to work.'

Matt wrinkled his brow. 'Will he want to take us to see Elizabeth tonight, then?'

I reached for his hand, longing to take Roxy's with my other, but hers were gripped tightly around her mug and in any case I wouldn't have dared.

'It may be a bit too soon, sweetie, if she's just been born. Do we know what kind of birth it was?'

'A Caesarean,' Roxy said, not quite hiding a squeamish twist of the mouth. I suppressed a smile: she was not so different from her brother when it came to the grisly details. 'Six pounds exactly. Pretty tiny. But Dad's message said they were both doing well.'

I nodded. 'OK, well, why don't I ring him now and arrange when we can go and meet your new sister. Tomorrow evening, maybe, after school?'

'We?' Roxy asked, sharply. 'You mean *you're* coming?'

'There's no reason why I can't take you to the hospital and wait in reception or something. Now, we need to think about getting the baby a present. Any ideas?'

The two of them exchanged a disbelieving look. This was not the approach they had expected of me and I felt ashamed that they might have anticipated instead some sort of breakdown or, at the very least, the choking back of a fresh attack of bitterness. For the first time it occurred to me that I must be a complicating factor in their working out of their own emotions about the baby. They felt excitement, pleasure, the natural beginnings of new love, but they didn't want to hurt my feelings by showing any of it. I needed to let them know I was not about to stand in their way.

'This is fantastic, guys, you've got a new sister! Come on, let's get Dad on the phone now.' Throwing caution to the wind I reached for Roxy's hand, after all, and she let me take it. The smile that came with it was genuine and I felt absurdly elated by the sight of it.

142

'Careful,' Matt said, 'he might be with the baby and we don't want to wake her up if she's sleeping.'

'You're right, or he may have his phone switched off. We'll leave a message. Why don't *you* speak, darling? Just say you'd like to come and visit as soon as it's allowed.'

Matt grinned, leaning close, head bowed over the screen of my mobile as I located the number. It occurred to me that this cheerful display of mine was actually less of a performance than it might have been. Still buoyed to the point of ecstasy by the secret knowledge of my engagement to Davis, I was able genuinely to share Matt's excitement, not to mention recognise Roxy's more cautious joy for what it was. I slipped my arm around Matt's back. He deserved nothing less – and nor did she. Perhaps Victoria's timing had been spot on, after all.

'What were you going to tell us?' Roxy asked, suddenly. 'When you came in? You didn't know about the baby until we told you, did you?'

I hit 'Call' and handed the phone to Matthew. 'Oh, don't worry about that. It can wait for now.'

The hospital lobby was an interior-designed triumph of plush leaf-green furnishings and spa fragrances – only a few discreet security fittings belied that this was any kind of medical unit at all – and I decided I was perfectly happy to spend an hour alone here while the children went up to meet their new sister.

'Wow, this is like a hotel. I feel like I should be ordering a cocktail,' Roxy joked. 'Where's the waitress?'

'Get one for me too,' I agreed and savoured the treat of her laughter. Since the breaking of the baby news yesterday, the three of us had been experiencing a period of togetherness that I could hardly bear to end – though, teenagers being teenagers, I had to assume it would.

We'd yet to sit down when Alistair emerged from a silent lift to the left of reception and called, 'Hello.' I almost buckled at the sight of him. He was familiar in a way I had seen only twice before: the day after the birth of a child, exhaustion and joy plaited tightly together, never again to be parted. He couldn't stop smiling and when he hugged the kids his eyes filled with tears.

'Congratulations,' I said, and handed over the gift box of bath things we'd chosen for the baby. 'We didn't bring flowers because Roxy read that some patients are allergic to them and hospitals discourage it.'

'Elizabeth might have hayfever, we thought,' Matt agreed. 'But you might not know yet.'

Alistair ruffled his hair. 'Very sensible, mate.' He turned to me and hesitated. 'Thank you for giving them a lift.' He knew, of course, that Roxy was now qualified to borrow the car and drive herself. 'Are you . . . did you want to come up as well?'

I smiled. I could just imagine Victoria's face if I did. 'No, thank you, I'll just wait here. You guys should be on your own. Maybe next time, though.'

He looked at me for a long moment, as though witnessing a miracle, and then blinked, remembering possibly that the real miracle had occurred yesterday in the operating theatre.

'Come on then, gang, what are we waiting for?'

They walked off together towards the lift, Roxy slim and smart in red skinny jeans and a black jacket, a long silk scarf trailing over her shoulder, Matt in new chinos, tall and clean cut. Was it my imagination, or were those shoulders of his already broadening? The receptionist looked up as they passed, couldn't help but follow their progress, thinking no doubt what a handsome family they were. If she'd noticed me and spared any thought at all, she would probably take me for a spinster aunt. Well, I thought, she'd be wrong. I have my life, too.

I flipped through a travel magazine and mused a little on honeymoons. Thanks to the delay in breaking the news, my wedding was fast becoming a private dreamworld, like a fantasy

144

from my own adolescence that could be developed in instalments, like a soap opera. I thought over and over of Davis's proposal, his nervous eyes and gulping throat, his sudden surrender to the feelings that must have tormented him just as mine had me. What with Alistair's news and our own busy schedules, we'd barely seen each other since then, though I longed to be with him more than anything in the world. We'd managed an hour or two together earlier today and he'd feigned amusement at my eagerness to leap straight into bed.

'Perhaps we should catch up in other ways? I'll make some coffee.'

'Don't tell me you've changed your mind,' I said, joking, for his proposal had come so out of the blue it could only have been propelled by a rocket-force of real love. It felt wonderful to be so open and playful after the weeks of tension.

'Not at all.' He came back to kiss my forehead. 'It's just that, until I know everyone's happy with the news, I don't want to allow myself to completely believe it.'

'Everyone' meant the children, of course. I was as touched by the admission of insecurity as I was pleased by his thoughtfulness. 'Don't worry, it will be fine,' I said, taking the mug he offered. 'Oh, could I have some milk, please?'

'Of course.' He chuckled. 'I need to start remembering this sort of thing, don't I?'

I wallowed in his words for a second, glimpsed an image of us as an old man and woman sitting together with our crosswords and slippers, and added, 'Anyway, it's not as if they don't like you. Quite the opposite, in fact – they think you're great.'

'Even so, is now really the best time to break the news, do you think? With this new baby arriving? It's a lot for them to take in. I wonder if it might be an idea to slow things down a bit?'

I was quick to dismiss this idea. 'There'll never be a time when there isn't something big happening. We could wait till after Roxy's university interviews, or after exams, or after she leaves home, but by then it will be time for Matt's entrance exams and the whole thing will start all over again. Honestly, now is as good a time as any.' I didn't add that there was a part of me that thrilled to the drama of this whirlwind of ours, a part that revelled in the sensation of the headlong. The fact was I didn't want to slow things down.

'Kate?'

I blinked, confused, my secret reverie disturbed. Alistair was standing in front of me, hands in trouser pockets, legs planted solidly apart. For a couple of seconds he was all I could see. 'Hello. Is everything all right? Where are the kids?'

'Up with Victoria. I just wanted to . . .' He settled beside me, right in the corner of the sofa, orange velvet cushions framing him on either side like a pair of stiff petals. I raised my eyebrows expectantly and he sighed. 'So what's this really in aid of, Kate? I mean, don't get me wrong, I'm delighted you're being so great about it, but you can't blame me for expecting a bit more . . .'

'Resistance?' I supplied.

'Exactly. To be honest I thought Roxy would drive her and Matt over tonight and you'd stay well clear of the whole thing.'

'I thought you might give her champagne,' I said, reasonably. 'And anyway, the last thing I want is to spoil things for them. It's important they feel like they're a part of this and not left out. Elizabeth is their sister and they shouldn't worry about the "half" bit.'

He nodded. 'Of course, I couldn't agree more.'

We each took a moment to marvel at that last sentence, Alistair and I in ready agreement, not sarcastic, not grudging, not personal.

He peered at me. 'There is something, though, isn't there? You seem different. Happier than usual, if that doesn't sound rude.' He glanced at the magazine on my lap, open on a spread about the world's most exclusive hideaways. 'You haven't won the lottery, have you?'

I laughed. 'Are you kidding? I don't even buy tickets. I've seen the people who get hooked. They lose everything, their home, their family. It's a horrible addiction. We had one woman come in who was spending all her child benefit on scratchcards . . .'

He waited for me to finish, obviously battling to conceal his distaste at the subject. He'd never quite got used to my 'gritty' choice of job. Satisfied though he was that the hours and location facilitated an always available mother for his children, he was genuinely baffled as to how anyone could voluntarily spend time with the 'underclass' – his term. (Impossible not to compare his attitude with that of Davis, who thought nothing of cycling up to one of the roughest estates in London to teach a crack dealer's sister for free.) 'OK, what then?'

I hesitated. I couldn't help enjoying holding his attention like this. He was utterly rapt and I knew didn't have the first inkling of what my news might be. 'There *is* something, but I can't tell you. I haven't even told Matt and Rox yet.'

He edged a little further forward, ready to meet the challenge. 'Well, I told *you* about the baby first, didn't I, before I told them? Way back when we'd just found out.'

The same day he'd first suggested his scheme for me to take in a lodger, the lodger who would become my second husband. How funny that I had the same person to thank for this reversal of fortune as I had to blame for the last. And that call he'd made to Davis behind my back, retaining him as Roxy's tutor – that, too, had played a part in bringing us to this happy point. In that respect, Alistair's ego was justified. 'All right,' I said, 'but you must swear not to say anything, because it needs to be handled sensitively.'

'OK.'

'I'm getting married.'

He drew in breath, shocked. '*What*? Who on earth to?'

I laughed, far too happy to take offence. 'To Davis. We've been seeing each other for a little while now.'

147

'Davis? You mean your tenant? Roxy's tutor?'

'That's him.'

'My God, Kate, that's very fast.' He stared at me, flabbergasted. 'You can't have known him six months. Do you even know what kind of a person he is?'

Though I felt myself prickle with irritation I kept my voice perfectly pleasant. 'Of course I do. He's a good person. Good enough for us to allow him to spend time with our daughter.'

'True.'

'Besides, how long did it take you to know what kind of a person Victoria was?' I paused. 'Or me? We knew each other for how long before we got together?'

'We were just kids,' he said, dismissively. 'Hardly older than Roxy.'

'Old enough, though, eh?'

He held my eye and I was surprised to see real apprehension in his gaze. 'This is incredible. I mean, do they have any idea this is happening?'

'I don't think so. I was going to tell them yesterday, but then Elizabeth arrived and I thought it best to wait. This is more important.' That was big of me, I thought, but he seemed not to have heard me, just continued shaking his head.

'God, this is going to rock their world.'

'*This* has rocked their world,' I said, gesturing to the space around us. 'Their father having a new baby with someone who isn't their mother.'

Having moments earlier insisted that the 'half' bit was irrelevant, I might have expected Alistair to seize on the inconsistency and throw it back at me, but for once he refused to be sidetracked. 'Yes, but they had a while to get used to the idea, didn't they? It's six months since we told them.'

'A lot can happen in six months.'

'Evidently.'

I decided not to correct his assumption that Davis and I had struck up a romance immediately he'd moved in. The truth – a ten-day sexual marathon preceded by a couple of drinks and a dozen family meals – was the briefest of courtships by anyone's standards and understandably questionable to those who had yet to witness first hand how natural a fit we were. As for Victoria, any further parallels with her were not worth drawing, for Alistair had never admitted that their relationship began with opportunistic sex while I was pregnant with Matthew.

'Well, aren't you going to congratulate me?' I asked, cheerfully.

He pulled a face. 'Did you congratulate me when I got engaged to Victoria?'

So further parallels *were* worth drawing, then. I decided that this obliging new line of mine had its limits, after all, and when I next spoke my tone was rather colder. 'You were lucky anyone congratulated you, Alistair, considering we were only just separated then.'

He looked at his watch and rose. 'We have two children, Kate. We're never going to be completely separated, are we?' He threw me a look that was obviously supposed to signal that he'd just said something immensely profound about human relationships. The last word was always his, always. Nevertheless, as he strode back to the lift, towards his newly expanded family, I decided that the encounter had gone well, certainly as well as I could ever have expected.

And it may have been my imagination, but the receptionist seemed to regard me with new interest now.

Chapter 13

In the end, I talked to the children separately. Matthew was first. I picked him up from school on the Friday and suggested going to the shop for ice cream. I didn't like to count my chickens before they hatched, but in the September sunshine, a cold treat in hand and a whole weekend's play ahead, the conditions couldn't have been more favourable.

'Matt, I wanted to talk to you about something, to get your advice.'

'Uh-huh?'

'You know how I've become really good friends with Davis?'

'Yep.'

'Well, I have some exciting news. We want to get married.'

He tore the paper in a circle from the top of his ice cream and grinned up at me. I wondered for a second if he'd misunderstood and thought I'd told some sort of joke. I saw he was holding out the paper, looking half-heartedly about for a bin, and I reached out and took it from him, an old habit. I'd be taking my children's litter from them till my dying day.

'But only if you think it's a good idea,' I added, hastily. 'I want you and Roxy to be happy about it or I won't do it.'

He took a mouthful of chocolate and nuts. 'Will you still live with us?'

'Of course I will, darling. I'll always be where you are, right until the moment you're grown up and decide you want to leave. You're my number-one priority, always.'

'And Roxy.'

'And Roxy. You're my joint number ones. But she'll be going to university next year, remember? We'll be going to visit her in her halls of residence, or wherever she lives. Hopefully she'll want to come home for holidays, though.' I closed the lid on the beginnings of an unpleasant new anxiety: would Roxy want to come back home in college holidays? Would we ever spend any real time together again or was this it for us, as for some other mammals, I'd just wave her off, job done, and recognise her in the future only by her scent? Then I remembered the new counter-claim I'd created for myself, the positive thinking: we would have an online relationship by then, I would be emailing her regularly during term time, sending texts, keeping in touch the way she and her friends seemed to prefer.

'Will Davis come and live with us then?' Matthew asked. He had a smear of white ice cream on his cheek, still such a baby.

'Oh, I should think so. Married couples do usually live together.'

'Will we join up the flats again? I could help smash the walls down.'

I smiled. 'Thank you, that's very kind. We need to work all of that out. But the important thing is that nothing will change for you, I promise. Life will go on in exactly the same way.'

'Cool.'

'Are you sure, darling?'

'Yeah.' I waited for him to lick some more. 'Did I tell you I showed Davis my tongue thing? You know, how I can curl it like Dad?'

'Oh yes, was he impressed?'

'Very impressed. *He* can't do it.'

'Good. It's a good trick. Only special people can do it.'

'That's what I told him.'

And that was that. We walked back in companiable silence, he concentrating on his ice cream, I resisting the urge every few steps to grab him and squeeze him so tight he might break.

Thank God we met Ruben at the garden gate and I agreed to Matt's going straight out back to play, because I didn't know how I would have explained to him Roxy's distress if we'd gone up together. Her cries were audible from outside the front door, an animal rhythm of heaves and moans, the proper sobbing of someone who knows there is no one in earshot. (Davis must have been out or he surely would have heard it from inside his flat and rushed to her rescue.) I stood for a moment with my key in my hand, Matt's blazer over my arm and his schoolbags heavy on my shoulder, unsure what to do. The tactful thing would be to retreat, to give her her privacy, come back in an hour and never mention the incident again. The natural thing, however, was to race in, discover who had upset my darling, and race back out again to rip that person's skin off with my nails.

As soon as I turned the key in the lock the wails stopped abruptly and I sensed her listening behind her closed door. I put the bags down and knocked quietly. 'Roxy, it's me. Is something wrong?'

Silence, and then the sound of her blowing her nose a few feet away. 'No, I'm fine.'

'I'm sorry, I didn't mean to surprise you. We just came back from school. Matt's in the garden.' Though she couldn't see me, I went to hang up her brother's blazer on the hook by the front door as if to demonstrate how normal the world outside her door was. Then the sobbing resumed at volume and I dashed back to her door. 'What is it, my love? *Please* let me in.'

'No. Go away.'

I paused, close to tears myself. What could possibly have happened? It had to be some sort of a delayed outpouring over the baby. I should have known that the brief family harmony was too good to be true. Damn Alistair and Victoria, tearing these children apart – couldn't they have stuck to their original decision not to have a family? 'Is it about the baby? Why don't we talk about it?'

'No.'

'Just let me come in . . .'

'No!'

Despite repeated requests, she'd never been allowed to have a lock or a bolt on her door, but the understanding was that if she was in her room with the door closed, then I (or Matt) had to knock and wait to be invited in. So far, even in anger or concern, I had honoured my side of the agreement, but this felt different. 'Please Roxy, or I *will* come in.'

I decided to take her silence for acquiescence and pushed open the door. She was sitting on the edge of the bed, her hands at her sides, head bowed. Her face was a large oval blotch of red and when she looked up the yellow-brown of her irises was vivid against the rawness of the pink. I sat down next to her and tried to take her hand but she whipped it away immediately.

'Please, sweetie, you can tell me. Has something happened at school today?'

She shook her head.

'It is about the baby, then?'

She just squeezed her eyes shut and groaned, as if the sound of the word alone was unbearable.

I took a deep breath. 'Listen, I know this is going to be a weird time, but it will settle down and you'll grow to love her. Remember how amazing you were when Matt was tiny. You were like a second mother to him, you were wonderful, such a natural.' Saying the words, I realised how little I'd praised her recently; not at all, in fact, since the school play and the driving test, both months ago now. 'You used to do his bottles in the microwave, do you remember? And sing songs to him for hours. "The Sandman Comes", and "Rockabye Baby".'

She sniffed.

'He liked "Three Blind Mice", as well, didn't he? And Elizabeth will have her favourites too. Victoria will love it if you're involved, you mustn't worry about that. If anything, this is going to bring everyone closer together, a new start all round.'

This was not working. I stared at her flushed, swollen profile, completely at a loss. I badly wanted to cheer her up with some good news, something unrelated to the baby. And then the thought struck: what better than the only news I had, the news that I should ideally break before she next saw her brother? She adored Davis: the idea that he might fill any gap left by a distracted father, well, it could only help. And how often had I seen the prospect of a big party transform her mood?

'Rox, I have some other news I need to tell you, something that might make you feel a bit better.'

She stiffened. 'What?'

'Well, it might be a bit of a surprise, but Davis and I have decided to get married.'

She stared, the misery in her eyes quite unchanged. 'Why?' she asked in a little-girl whisper. '*Why?*' Then the sobs began again. To my horror I saw that I had only made things worse.

'Oh, Roxy, please don't worry, nothing will change for you, nothing. We'll work the wedding dates around your schedule so you're not distracted from your schoolwork. You're still my number-one priority, I promise.' But the words that had won over Matthew with the help of sunshine and ice cream were powerless here, no more than glib clichés. I needed to do better than this, much better.

'Look, I know it feels like everything is happening at once. That's how life seems to work. Just tell me exactly what's worrying you and I'll—'

She interrupted: 'Please, Mum, I just want you to leave me alone.'

'But I can't leave you like this. You're upset, I want to help.'

'You can't help.'

We just sat there side by side, as helpless as each other. Once again, as I did several times daily, I tried to understand what was going on with her by dredging memories of myself at this age and hunting for parallels. 'You were just the same yourself,' Mum said; what, then, had caused me to collapse in this way over two decades ago? There'd been several incidents when I'd cried my heart out and refused to leave my bedroom. (Mum had responded by delivering food to the door, sandwiches and a drink on a tray, sometimes one of Tash's treats, a chocolate coin or a child's biscuit, a sweet reminder that I was as much her child as my little sister was.) Always it had been about love, or what I thought was love; love and its humiliations, all those disappointments and rejections that served as dress rehearsals for the real business of adult partnerships. A bolt of inspiration shot suddenly through me. Of course! How ridiculous to have imagined that a new half-sister could have been the cause of this; it was no more devastating than my own news. No, this was about an affair of her own, it had to be, perhaps something to do with the boy who had given her the charm bracelet. Sneaking a glance, I saw that it was no longer on her wrist; I was sure it had been there the night of the hospital visit.

'Is this about a relationship, Rox? Are you back with Damien? You can talk to me about him, you know. I'll understand.'

'No!' She crossed her wrists over her stomach and I was struck at once by the most horrific thought.

'Oh my God, Roxy, you're not . . . you're not pregnant, are you?'

She laughed at that, loudly and with a scorn that was comfortingly familiar. I was off the mark, then, thank God. But no sooner had she stopped laughing than the look of desolation returned to her face, almost as though she were suddenly thinking that an unplanned pregnancy would be preferable to what she *was* experiencing.

'At least tell me his name?' I cast about, trying to recall her recent schedule. 'Maybe the one from theatre club? What's his name, Jacob or something?'

She crushed her hands to her ears. 'No, please, stop! I don't want to talk about it.'

I waited until she took the hands away and said, 'OK, I understand. You don't want to talk about it and that's fine. Look, let's have a night in on our own, watch a DVD? Or were you supposed to be going out with Marianne tonight?'

Again, that wretched, broken shake of the head. 'I'm not going.'

'Shall I make us some dinner then?'

'I'm not hungry.'

I thought again of my mother and her trays. 'Can I at least bring you something to drink? A hot chocolate or a Coke?'

'No.'

'Do you want to call Marianne and ask her to come over? I promise I'll leave you alone. Maybe I could take Matt to the cinema and give you some space?'

'No, I'm fine, honestly.'

I had to give up, there was nothing else I could say. When Matt came up for tea I told him his sister wasn't feeling well and had gone to bed early. Every so often I walked down the corridor and hovered at her door. Finally, I went in and found she'd crashed into sleep still wearing her clothes, so I pulled the blanket over her, lowered the blind, and tiptoed away.

She stayed in her room all weekend and my trays were collected untouched. I had run out of ideas.

'You have no idea how many conversations begin with you saying, "I don't know what to do about Roxy,"' Abi told me, when I popped over to say hello. I was trying to distract myself, but it soon transpired that I couldn't free my mind of my daughter's inexplicable collapse.

'Really? Oh God. Is it really boring for you?'

'Not boring. But I worry you empathise too much. Girls her age are pretty resilient, and hearts do need toughening up a bit. The earlier the better, if you ask me. By the time she gets to college she'll have had plenty of experience.'

'That's true.' It was sound advice, a variation on the theme offered both by Tash and Davis. But when I thought of the way I'd felt and the way I'd behaved over Davis at the age of thirty-nine, well, I wondered if some hearts simply couldn't be toughened, but remained instead callus-free all their lives. Roxy must have inherited that defect from me, which meant not only that I was to blame for her pain, but also the only one who could understand it.

'What does Alistair say?' Abi asked. 'He's the great solutions man, isn't he?'

'I haven't spoken to him about it,' I said, pulling a face. I couldn't involve him, and not just because I disliked admitting defeat, something I seemed to be doing rather a lot these days where Roxy was concerned. No, the man had a new baby to worry about, and Elizabeth had only recently been taken home from hospital. With Victoria's mother in residence and a maternity nurse on the payroll, too, Alistair's house – and head – would be full by anyone's standards. Besides, since he'd begun making arrangements without consulting me, I didn't feel the need to report every last skirmish to him, either.

I decided to phone my mother. Understandably too dazzled by my own news to worry too much about the romantic tussles of the next generation, she simply echoed everybody else by advocating trust. 'Trust her to work this out herself. She'll come to you if she really needs you.'

'OK.' I asked to speak to Tash, still a little ashamed of my treatment of her during our last phone conversation, but Mum reported that she was in Ibiza for a week, having won the price of the flight from our father in a game of poker. 'I kid you not,' Mum said, though I hadn't for a moment imagined she did.

After several more abortive attempts to comfort Roxy, I could see that my nerves were even starting to infect Davis, too. 'She feels crowded by everything that's going on,' he said, 'I think we should wait a few months before going ahead with the wedding.'

I shook my head. 'I don't think us getting married has anything to do with it, I really don't. She's desperate to leave home, she considers herself independent. There's no way that the idea of sharing me can be causing this.'

'But you did say you thought you made it worse when you tried to talk about us?'

'I guess it must be in some way connected.'

'What are you thinking?' He listened intently for my answer, his eyes unblinking.

'Well, the only thing I can think is that the contrast is upsetting.'

'The contrast?'

'You know, my fairytale situation . . .' – I raised my eyebrows to show this was meant semi-ironically, though the truth was that when I was with him I did feel as if I'd wandered into some sort of a fairytale – '. . . compared with whatever break-up she's going through herself. I mean, there *must* be some relationship we don't know anything about. Everyone thinks so.'

He nodded, slowly. 'I think you're right. But who?'

Again I could only shake my head. 'Well, that's the point. She doesn't mention these things, she's totally secretive. But someone gave her that bracelet a few weeks ago – it must have cost hundreds of pounds – and I can't believe it was Marianne. Do you think I should talk to her? She might be able to give me some idea what's going on.'

'Marianne? I wouldn't do that,' Davis said, quickly. 'If Roxy found out you'd gone behind her back she'd see it as a heinous invasion of privacy.' And she'd be right, too, though Davis was much too tactful to say so outright.

He repositioned himself behind me and began kneading my shoulders with his fingertips. 'You mustn't feel guilty, you know. You haven't done anything wrong.'

'I know. It's just so hard . . .' As he worked on my knots I sensed him searching for a solution. How sweet he was to share my agonies so keenly, to care so much about my children, all the while presenting so uncomplicated a proposition himself. He had no children of his own, his parents had died when he was in his twenties, and his living family consisted of one brother long settled in Canada and an elderly aunt and uncle in Bristol. 'Perhaps you could have a word with her, Davis? You did so brilliantly over that business of the work placement. And she seems to respect you in a different way.'

He dipped to plant a kiss on the top of my head. 'Well, my darling, if it will make you feel better I can certainly have a try.'

Truly, he was some sort of magician, the 'whisperer', Abi called him when I reported this, his latest triumph of persuasion. 'Maybe parents aren't hiring him to teach their kids languages at all, maybe it's to get them to tidy their bedrooms and do what they're told.' I wouldn't have been at all surprised.

I hadn't even been aware that the assignation had been arranged when I saw them outside together, walking towards the walled garden, Davis's hand cupping Roxy's elbow like some nineteenth-century consort. How clever to take her away from the flat, but not too far, to a beautiful, peaceful spot where they could talk unobserved. They were out for about an hour and when they returned she was happy as Larry. She even came to apologise to me, hanging her head sheepishly as she spoke.

'I didn't want to tell you, but I've been sort of seeing Damien again . . .'

'I thought you must be!' I exclaimed.

'*Was*.' Her eyes narrowed. 'He binned me last week.'

'Oh Roxy.' I stepped forward and pulled her to me. 'Why didn't you say something?'

'I didn't want to cause a fuss . . .'

'But darling, don't you see it's much more of a fuss if I have to try to read your mind? I was frantic to see you so upset.'

'Sorry,' she muttered into my shoulder.

I closed my eyes. Her hair on my cheek was warm and smelled of sunshine and the outdoors. It was exactly the softness of my own. 'You don't have to be sorry, don't be silly.'

'OK.' And she pulled away from me, the hug over, and drifted off to her room.

I went to find Davis. 'Did she tell you about the boy?' he asked at once.

'Yes. What did you say to her to get her to open up?'

One corner of his mouth twitched upwards in a smile. 'I just told her to stop being so damn selfish.'

'Selfish?' I was taken aback.

'Yes. I said that whatever her own situation, she needs to remember that you're entitled to a private life as well.'

'Wow.' I couldn't imagine saying that to her myself, not if I expected us to speak again in this life. 'Do you believe it?' I asked, abruptly. 'I mean about getting back together with Damien? Why would she have kept it a secret when I've met him in the past and we all got along perfectly well?'

Davis rubbed his right eyelid and sighed. 'Lord only knows. Don't worry, though, my love. Whatever their little contretemps, she's over it now.'

He made it sound so easy, like a line from a movie when the scene needs to be tied up as quickly as possible for the main plot to proceed. It was almost too simple. And although the last thing I wanted was to press the point with her and scare her off once more, I still needed to hear from her, just once before I confirmed the date with the registrar, that we had her blessing for the marriage.

'I need to be absolutely sure this is OK with you, Rox. It's not too late for us to cancel. The last thing I want is to make you unhappy, in any way.'

It was so hard to read that face, the ever-changing flecks of her eyes were like camouflage. Was that a glimmer of sadness or merely a twinge of ennui? 'It's OK, really.'

'Good. And I'm sure there's room in the budget for a new outfit for you. Anything you like.'

She looked pleased. 'And can I invite Marianne to the party?'

'Of course you can. You can invite whoever you like.' It was on the tip of my tongue to add, 'A boy, as well, if you like,' but I realised just in time that now was hardly the moment.

Chapter 14

Davis and I got married on the very day I had cited for his eviction from the flat, Saturday 13 October. Fitting, in the end, for he soon would be moving out – and into the main flat with the children and me. We had decided to leave the partitions in place and restore his living room and bedroom to the study and spare bedroom they had originally been. We would take his bathroom for ourselves, leaving the main one for Roxy and Matt to share (that would please her, at least). Locks would come off the doors just as soon as we returned from our honeymoon.

The wedding date was fortuitous on several counts: a last-minute cancellation at the register office when the waiting list for a Saturday was usually several months' long; the first weekend of half term and therefore a natural time for Alistair to take Matthew while Davis and I went on honeymoon (Roxy, it was agreed, would be free to move between home, her father's house and Marianne's as she pleased); and it was just early enough in the autumn to risk holding the reception in the walled garden, my preference from the start. Neither Davis nor I had money to spare and so our celebration was to consist of champagne for family and friends, with canapés supplied by the local deli. Numbers were small enough for the event to be comfortably relocated to the flat if the weather let us down.

Modest though our plans were, Davis was soon exhausted by the flurry of preparations. I found him one day sitting on his sofa with his head in his hands. He seemed to be almost on the verge of tears.

'What is it, darling?'

'Oh, just all this . . . this absolute madness!' He made an effort to compose himself, even managing a smile, but I'd seen him troubled rarely enough to know to take this seriously. He had the air of someone who'd woken from a long sleep and found himself in the middle of a crisis of someone else's devising.

'This is about as casual as it gets, you know,' I said, snuggling against him.

'Oh, I realise that.' His first wedding, planned and paid for by Camilla's parents, had been a considerably more sumptuous affair, with hundreds of guests and a photographer from the society pages of a well-known magazine. I could tell it made him quite ill to remember.

I ran my fingers through his hair, marvelling at the fact that I – and no one else – was allowed to do this. 'Don't worry, this will be easy. And there's really nothing for you to do.'

I'd already sent out invitations – if you could call my quick handwritten notes invitations – to those I hoped might come. I prayed that the low-key presentation and general lack of trappings might counteract reaction to the sensational suddenness of the event (for most guests the announcement and the invitation were one and the same). Davis had surprisingly few guests of his own to invite, just a handful of locals, most of whom I'd now met and found perfectly friendly. Others, he explained, had sided with Camilla after their divorce. As for his brother, it was much too short notice for him to bring his family from Canada or even to come by himself.

A couple of weekends before the wedding, Davis went up to York to visit an old university friend with the idea of inviting him to be best man. But this also turned out to be too little too late.

The friend, who had children of school age, already had a half-term holiday booked, and though the two enjoyed a pleasant enough reunion, Davis returned to London empty handed.

'Actually, I'm relieved in a way,' he said. 'Graham was my best man first time around, so it would have been awkward for him. It was a stupid idea.'

The night away had done him good, though, I noticed. He looked refreshed, renewed. He'd gone away full of tension and returned looser, readier, like a man who'd suddenly found his nerve. Only now did I realise how worried he must have been about contributing his share to all of this, holding up his end. And all the fuss about Roxy, too! I needed to be careful not to swallow him up into my world, just as I had once been swallowed by Alistair's.

I leaned forward to kiss him, letting my nose linger in his hair. His smell was still new enough to have an immediate physical effect on me. 'Honestly, Davis, it doesn't matter. The smaller the better, as far as I'm concerned. We don't need a best man or maid of honour of any of that stuff, even speeches. What is there to say that people can't already see for themselves? I like the idea of everyone just getting up, exactly like any other day, and walking down here for a few drinks, then going home again.'

He chuckled. 'Oh, Kate, I do love your idealism.'

There were papers at his feet, he was supposed to be marking essays, but I couldn't help pressing my mouth hungrily to his, heart suspended for that split second before his lips moved in response.

After all the tumultuous emotion that had surrounded her acquisition of a new baby sister – not to mention a stepfather – Roxy appeared to be enjoying a purple patch. Her Cambridge application was now complete (what with input from Alistair, Davis and her school, the process had been relatively painless for me) and she had months before she needed to worry either about

164

interviews or exams. Her mobile hardly stopped ringing and I often heard her laughter trilling through the open doors. I imagined there'd been an increase in attention; if Marianne was anything to go by, then theirs was a circle in which personal drama trumped all else and there'd been no shortage of that for Roxy these last months. She'd recently spent a weekend at Marianne's, in between two at Alistair's, a series of absences that had done us both good. Now, when she was home, I made a point of suggesting we set time aside for fun activities: shopping for a dress for her for the wedding, getting pizza or coffee, having a pedicure together. I wondered if this was anything like what Marianne reportedly enjoyed with her mother. ('They're more like sisters,' Roxy would say; personally I'd always been suspicious of such an idea as though being sisters somehow bettered the more prosaic mother–daughter dynamic.) But whatever we were experiencing now, if not as peaceful as those brief couple of days immediately after Elizabeth's birth, it was certainly an improvement on the hostilities of the summer.

'Are you nervous about hearing back from Cambridge?' I asked, one time, a coffee together at Eli's.

She smiled, though not before narrowing her eyes fractionally. I could tell that she'd come to find my questions on the subject irritating, but was at least making a conscious effort to hide it. 'No, not at all. Actually, I've been thinking I'd prefer to stay in London, so I don't mind if I don't get in.'

My mouth dropped open. 'London? After all that, you'd rather not go for it?'

'I have "gone for it", Mum. But that doesn't mean I'll get in. Do you have any idea how many applications they get per place?'

My feelings, as with all matters concerning Roxy's future education, were mixed. I was secretly delighted by the new information that she might stay in London for college, perhaps even choosing to continue to live at home (though I thought that a hope too far, given her constant gripes about lack of privacy. Somehow, a bathroom-share with a nine-year-old was not going to swing it). I also wondered if Cambridge might prove too demanding, even for her; mightn't a low-key alternative allow for a more balanced three years, for a little more fun? There was something to be said for being a big fish in a small pond, surely. But a part of me continued to think for Alistair, to feel the need to advocate on his behalf, and there was no question of pond life as far as he was concerned; only the biggest, deepest ocean would do for his offspring. The Cambridge application – whether it were for law, French or the meaning of life – was as much for him as it was for her. He may not yet have realised that, but I certainly had.

'Well,' I said, 'I think the best thing is just to see who makes an offer and then decide.'

'Oh, sure, exactly.' For once she didn't mock me for stating the obvious, just stirred her latte with a contented look on her face. The charm bracelet was back on her wrist, I noticed, but I didn't remark on it. 'Maybe none of them will want me,' she added, licking foam off her spoon.

'I don't think that's likely,' I said. Not after a small fortune in school fees; Willoughby Girls all but guaranteed a decent university, and if they didn't deliver, then I wouldn't put it past Alistair to demand a refund for the full seven years. No, only an act of God would prevent Roxy's future from unfolding just as we all predicted. 'And you know Davis is committed to coaching you for the interviews, so you'll be in the best possible position.'

'Hmm.'

I hesitated. 'I'm glad you get on so well with him, Rox, it makes a difference, especially to Matt.' I was not being entirely straightforward in my observation, however, for there had been a definite downturn in relations between the two of them of late. The chats about books seemed to have all but fizzled out, and though she dutifully attended her tutoring sessions and remained perfectly polite to him when we were all together, something had shifted. It was almost as if a more formal distance had been introduced just as he was about to join the family. Typical teenage contrariness, I supposed, but I wondered if it might also be explained partly by that talk they'd had in the garden. 'I told her to stop being so damn selfish . . .' He'd got his point across, of course, saved the day, in fact, but no one liked criticism, however skilfully it was delivered. I told myself to stop fussing, that it wasn't so long ago that I'd begged him to institute this very separation between them.

No, a little resentment on Roxy's part was natural, nothing more than any other mother had to deal with when mixing her new partner with her teenage children. All the books and newspapers said how rich and loving and varied stepfamily life could be, but none suggested it was easy.

The walled garden at Francombe Gardens in October lacked the glorious palette of spring and summer but it was still the most beautiful place in the world to me.

The loss of the flowers that came with autumn only made blooms of the female guests as they drifted among the beds in their petal-coloured dresses. Davis wore a bold, chalk-coloured suit, I a pale blue tea dress, and as we greeted our guests at the gate, it was obvious that everyone thought we made a striking couple. We were certainly a happy one.

It had been important to me that Alistair and Victoria should come to the reception. I wanted the children, particularly Matthew, to see that this new union of mine marked a progression in wider family relations, not a setback.

'You look wonderful, Kate,' Alistair said and Victoria could only nod in agreement. She looked a little down and, once more, just as I had that night at the school play, I felt my seniority for what it was: an advantage. I tried not to allow the words 'tables' and 'turned' to enter my head, especially as I was genuinely indebted to her for having helped with Roxy's work experience, but even so, this was my day, and I was allowed my thoughts.

'No Elizabeth?' I asked. I still hadn't met the baby, who by all accounts reached her weekly milestones satisfyingly ahead of target.

'We left her with Judy.'

'Ah, good.' It no longer rankled that Alistair used Victoria's relatives' names, including his mother-in-law Judy's, as though I were intimately familiar with their full family tree.

'So, what do you think of Davis?' I asked them, eager for praise on my new husband's behalf.

'I really like him,' Victoria said, perking up. 'He's so dapper, isn't he? And kind of old-fashioned, like something out of an old movie.'

A ghost of a grimace appeared on Alistair's face. 'Yes, he seems perfectly all right.'

Perfectly, I agreed with that.

'The important thing is the kids get on with him,' Victoria added, dutifully.

'He's done wonders with Roxy's French,' Alistair conceded. 'Shame she's not doing German for A-level, he could have helped with that as well.'

Automatically the three of us turned to look for Roxy. She was the nearest this small gathering had to a loose cannon, but had so far proved herself an impeccable guest. She and Marianne seemed even to be acting as impromptu waitresses, topping up wine glasses and beaming at everyone as they did it (I had yet to point out the irony to Alistair, for the catering had been done by the very deli where Roxy had almost worked over the summer). Both girls wore strapless, full-skirted dresses and lots of black eyeliner, from which I gathered that a fifties revival was afoot. They looked incredibly sophisticated and glamorous. Also in tow today was a new friend, Jacob, whom the two of them had met at theatre club. (Now I'd been introduced to him, I thought him an unlikely heartbreaker, at least where the girls were concerned. He was delicate and a little effete, very likely gay.) Earlier, I'd overheard him and Marianne chatting together, drawn in a moment's lull by their droll, confident tones on other side of the lily pond.

'I just don't understand the appeal,' Jacob said. He had the demeanour, just as Roxy often did when she was alone with Marianne, of being the chosen confidante of Marie Antoinette, proud and deferential in one. 'Though I seem to be the only one . . .'

'He's just so immensely intelligent, J,' Marianne drawled. 'It's the ultimate aphrodisiac. God, he makes Rob seem so . . .'

She broke off to search for the right word and, eager to help, Jacob put in, 'Infantile?'

The two of them cackled at that, then Marianne said, 'No, not that, more kind of *unformed*. Do you know what I mean?'

I wondered idly who might have supplanted Rob in madam's affections. I wished him luck, whoever he was. Seeing me looking, she gave me a radiant smile, which I immediately returned. It was an awful thing to think, but I really couldn't help feeling grateful that she was not my daughter. The way I had come to see it, Roxy gave the impression of being uncaring when in reality she had a good heart, while Marianne gave the impression of having a good heart when she was in fact as cold as a fish. I couldn't imagine her crying her eyes out for anyone.

'Kate!' My mother approached, resplendent in apple-coloured linen. 'I came to tell you what a wonderful man your new husband is.' She turned to Alistair, who was still in earshot, and they exchanged wary smiles. 'No offence, Alistair.'

He looked tempted to object, but settled for a tight little nod.

'Oh, thank you, Mum!' I beamed with delight, refusing to allow the overlaps of past lives to cast the slightest shadow on my happiness. 'I'm so glad you approve. Everyone seems to, actually . . .'

Even as we talked, I couldn't help stealing glances at Davis across the shrubbery. He was fascinating to watch, for he had that ability to adapt to the personality of the person he was with, even adjusting his body language to fall into line with theirs. With Ethan he stood in earnest conversation, leaning in with lots of comradely nodding, even a little plucking at the chin; with Abi he was more upright, braced for their customary rapid-fire banter, until such a moment when they'd reached their mutual punchlines and could tilt back their heads in laughter; with Tash he engaged rather as he did with Roxy and Marianne, with a kind of amused curiosity, only half-conscious of their flirtations; and with those of my parents' generation there was a heightening of that natural gallantry of his, the old-fashioned manners and language Victoria had picked up on. For most guests it was the first time they'd met him, including my parents, who had postponed a longstanding trip to New Zealand to come and celebrate. I couldn't help comparing my mother's breezy acceptance of this whirlwind marriage of mine with my own boundless fears for Roxy.

'You don't seem very surprised by all of this,' I said to her, knowing full well that it wouldn't have made a jot of difference if she had advised caution.

'Oh, you're a big girl now, you know what you're doing. Now Tash, she's a different story. You know she's determined to come to London and find a job here?'

'Oh yes?' I'd forgotten that detail. 'She might have mentioned it a while ago.'

'We've tried to talk her out of it, of course. London's not the place for someone like her. She's not equipped.'

I stopped just short of rolling my eyes. She made Tash sound like Dick Whittington, arriving shoeless in a city overrun with rats. So London was too dangerous for her, but not for me and my children? And yet it seemed to me that if anyone could dodge the capital's predators it was Tash, who had reached the age of

170

twenty-seven physically and emotionally scot-free. But then I had, too, hadn't I, in my own way? Ignorance had been *my* bliss, as well, at her age. I'd been a happily married young mother with no idea of the traumas to come. My defeats occurred in my thirties. Perhaps I should be a bit more generous in allowing Tash the last of her decade of freedom.

'I think she'd be OK,' I said to my mother, seriously, 'if she ever actually comes.'

'You would keep an eye on her, wouldn't you?'

'Of course I would. Though I do have a few other things on my plate.' Like a new husband and two children, not to mention the demands at work of people who were genuinely adrift in the world and not merely irresolute. But there I went again, too quick to judge. (I hated to think I was one of those charity workers so busy with helping strangers they overlooked their own.) I needed to start giving my sister the benefit of the doubt. I would make it a new resolution of my marriage, I decided, to treat both Roxy and Tash as the adults they were.

Mum nodded. 'You're a natural, though. That's why I knew you'd enjoy the advice job so much. You know how the world works. But Tash – she only *thinks* she knows.'

I wasn't sure who was getting the benefit of the doubt this time, Tash or me. In any case, moments later my sister sidled up to resume her London campaign in person. She was dressed in some sort of sequinned djellaba, which looked a little unusual among the twin-sets and suits. (I wondered if she pleased or displeased Roxy's and Marianne's stern fashion eye.) 'So,' she said, 'now Davis is moving in, I don't suppose you need a new tenant for his flat, do you?'

'Thank you, no. We're going to use those rooms for ourselves for now, give Roxy and Matt a bit of space, though we may have to take another tenant next year, depending on finances.'

She pouted and I felt my expression hover between amusement and exasperation. We both knew that she had not been proposing to pay market-rate rent, or anything at all, for that matter. 'What about a cat sitter, then, just while you're away?'

'We don't have a cat, Tash, you know that.'

'Then I'll buy you one as a wedding present!'

I laughed. 'I don't think the fifth floor of a block of flats is the best home for a cat, do you?'

'I hate cats,' she agreed. 'They're so pouncy!'

I shook my head, laughing. Peas in a pod we were not, but I couldn't imagine not having Tash in my life. It was impossible to deny her charm. Perhaps I should just cave in straight away and offer her the spare room. But no, I realised with a tingle, I would need to consult Davis before making such an important decision. Perhaps when Roxy had left home ... 'Listen, I'll phone you when I get back and we'll put our heads together about a new career for you.'

'Thanks, Kate. I guess I'll just hang out at Mum and Dad's for a bit longer then.'

As she moved away I saw with a little lurch of pleasure that Davis was headed through the gathering to join me.

'Isn't this perfect?' I said. 'I can't believe how well it's going.'

He squeezed my hand. 'Yes, but it will be nice to leave it all behind, won't it?'

Tomorrow we were going to France, to the seaport city of La Rochelle, a place I'd never been to before but that Davis knew well. He talked of us eating oysters and drinking good wine and taking long walks along the coast. It appealed to me enormously that he would be my guide. Yesterday I had borrowed Roxy's laptop to look at the website of the guesthouse he'd booked and found a picture of a loft suite with windows on three sides. '*Cette chambre est celle qu'on préfère pour les escapades amoureuses ...*' Well, you didn't need Roxy's Oxbridge French to understand *that*. I imagined something like the time we'd spent together over the summer, a routine dictated by physical desire. Yes, I liked the idea that he would take

172

charge of us, and not just for the honeymoon, for our life together.

'Come on,' he said, pulling me forward and motioning for our guests to gather around. 'I think it's time for a toast.'

And he set about charming them all all over again, quoting the line from Balzac's *Physiologie du mariage*: '*Un mari, comme un gouvernement, ne doit jamais avouer de faute*'.

In English: a husband, like a government, should never admit fault.

Chapter 15

When Alistair and I got married, we were barely out of college, and impoverished enough for our parents to insist on treating us to our honeymoon. They put their heads together and chose the kind of place they liked themselves: a smart hotel in the Tuscan hills. We were the youngest guests by at least twenty years and soon learned to enjoy being petted by the older couples, who inevitably reminded us of our own parents, and generally indulged by the staff. During the day we'd go off on walks, eat picnics of bread and cheese and tomatoes, drink lots of cheap wine and sometimes make love out of sight in the grass. Not once did anyone suggest we were too young to be married. Nonetheless, it did feel a little like playing at being grown-ups.

'Where d'you think we'll be in twenty years' time?' I asked Alistair, one evening, Prosecco cocktails on the terrace, another perfect dusk.

He grinned. 'Probably back here, but paying the bill ourselves, if I have anything to do with it.'

I was excited by how ambitious Alistair had become since entering the working world. He was about to move from the small consultancy he'd joined after college to a much bigger one. It was one of the top five, he said, a launch pad *par excellence*. We talked a lot about his career during that holiday.

'Tell you what, let's come back on our twentieth wedding anniversary,' he said, 'See what we've achieved.'

'It's a date.' As far as we were concerned, the only thing that could part us between that moment and a date in twenty years' time was a tragedy, nothing less than one of us falling down dead.

When we discovered I was pregnant, there was a period of uncertainty while we considered our options. I was only twenty-one, Alistair twenty-two. Now we wouldn't be playing at being grown-ups, we'd be signing up for the real thing.

'Shouldn't I get my own career established a bit first?' I said, worried. It seemed to me I'd be moving from childhood to parenthood with very little in between. I'd been ready for marriage, but not necessarily motherhood.

Alistair nodded. To my amusement, he tended to do this even when he disagreed; it was probably one of his new consultants' techniques. 'I'd say yes if you knew what you wanted your career to be. I don't know, Kate . . .' – he tended to say this even when he *did* know, another technique – 'This way, you get a break to think about it some more.'

It was true that I was totally at a loss as to my career. It was simply a hole waiting to be filled. I hadn't won any of the graduate traineeships I'd gone for, partly because I hadn't been convinced I wanted them myself. The faceless insurance company I'd wound up in when I'd moved to London to join Alistair full time was clearly not right for me. Within weeks I was clock-watching and going stir crazy at my desk. My latest idea was to look into teacher training.

'We can't get rid of a honeymoon baby,' Alistair said. 'That would be like putting a curse on the marriage.'

'You can't say that!' I protested.

'But you know what I mean, don't you?'

We kept the baby, of course, baby Roxana, and she did fill the hole. She filled it to overflowing.

On the evening of our arrival in La Rochelle, Davis took me for a stroll around the harbour. I was surprised by how familiar it all was: bottle-green water rippling in the breeze, wide stretches of cobbled quayside, café terraces with their green-and-white cane chairs, bowls heaped with *moules* and crisp yellow *frites*. It was the face of first French holidays and old school trips.

'I used to spend a lot of time on this coast,' Davis said, when I asked him why he'd chosen it for us, 'though I haven't been here for years.'

'How did you discover it?'

'Oh, just through friends.'

I made a series of connections in my head. 'Oh, is this where that lovely old lighthouse is, the one in your picture? Was *that* the friend?'

He looked at me quizzically before remembering. 'Oh, no, that's at Baleines.'

'Where's that? Near here?'

He gestured vaguely. 'Over the bridge. But if you like lighthouses, my dear, let me show you the famous Tour de la Lanterne . . .'

This, it was revealed, was a tall lantern-shaped tower by the castle that had once been a prison as well as a lighthouse and contained graffiti in the various languages of those who'd been wretched enough to be thrown into it over the centuries. There was plenty of other *Boys' Own* imagery in La Rochelle, too: the old stone keep with its labyrinth of steps and corridors ('Built to keep the English out,' Davis said, as if he weren't for a moment quite certain which side he was on); a gargantuan anchor laid to rest on the cobbles, a maritime museum, grand naval statuary on every corner. Everywhere boats and flags and ropes and bells. I kept thinking how much Matthew would enjoy exploring the

176

place, working out whether that huge rusting chain really was long enough to stretch between the two towers as the information claimed; counting the boats; aiming his fingers like a gun at the seagulls.

It was not quite what I had expected for a honeymoon, I had to admit. Not that I had any intention of comparing it to my fairytale first – I'd been virtually a student then, still an innocent – but, even so, it was all just a little too educational, Davis so extremely thorough in his historical commentary. I reminded myself that our guesthouse more than matched my expectations, with its huge windows and overstuffed sofas where you could sit and watch the ocean change colour with the light. In any case, places were sometimes special not for what they were, but for the people who took you there.

'It's beautiful,' I said to him, slipping my fingers into the crook of his elbow as we walked by the water, wrapped up warm in gloves and scarves. 'I love the wind and salty air. London was just a bit too hot this summer, wasn't it?'

He kissed the top of my head through my woollen hat. 'I thought tomorrow we could hire bikes and cycle though the park.'

'OK. God, I haven't been on a bike for years.' But my imagination was running riot now as I made mental snapshots of the two of us spinning around together on a tandem, me beaming over my shoulder at him, hair flying; we both wore trench-coats belted tightly at the waist, though I didn't own one and nor, to my knowledge, did Davis. I imagined showing friends and family footage of our joy, drawing cries of how utterly perfect it all looked.

As we walked, the sun finally escaped the cloud cover and turned everything golden-white. Davis put on sunglasses and looked extremely glamorous. It was October, the season was at its end, but it felt no different from a season just beginning.

*

'Tell me more about your first honeymoon,' I said to him later. First honeymoon – the words made me feel so very wise, as though having taken this second vow all the emotional detritus from the first could be deleted without trace, all my mistakes expunged.

'Must we?' Davis pulled on his cigarette and gave me that wry look of his that I found particularly attractive. He was delighting in the opportunity to smoke indoors, recently prohibited in all London venues. We were in a bistro, seafood dinner over, and lingering over wine. It was a quaint little place, with a low, timbered ceiling, nautical items nailed to every wall and a bar shaped like the hull of a boat. After years of little travel, I'd forgotten how civilised France was; even in the simplest of cafés the cutlery had been polished till it gleamed, the napkins folded just so. 'Surely ex-spouses are the last thing we want to discuss at this moment in time?'

I smiled. 'I just feel as though I know so little about your life with Camilla. I mean, considering my ex came to our wedding, there's a bit of an information gap, isn't there?'

'An information gap,' he repeated, as though using foreign vocabulary he couldn't fathom. I was learning that Davis didn't like phrasing that sounded too corporate, he thought words should be used expressively, with humanity – not stripped down so they sounded like something a computer had programmed. 'OK, well, if you insist, I'll share some information about my first honeymoon. You know, what I remember most about it was Camilla being attacked by a macaw.'

'A *macaw*?'

He grinned. 'Well, pecked really. And it spoke to her, as well, kept saying this one thing over and over, though we couldn't make out what it was. She insisted it was some kind of curse. It all got very hysterical.'

I couldn't help giggling. 'How bizarre. Where were you? The Caribbean or somewhere?'

'No, here in France, believe it or not, in some kind of tropical bird park. There were hundreds of macaws, as I remember. Kind of Hitchcock with a twist.'

I felt myself stiffen. 'You came to France for your first honeymoon, as well?'

'Yes, Camilla's family had a place in Paris and another down here. That's how I came to improve my French so dramatically. My degree was in German, as you know.'

'"Down here"? You mean *she* was the friend who brought you here, to La Rochelle?'

There was a pause. Unusually, uncertainty crossed Davis's face. 'One of them, yes. Does that matter, darling?'

I took a moment to decide how to react. While it was disappointing to have been brought by my new husband somewhere he clearly associated with a previous love, it was also perfectly obvious that this was nothing but an insignificant coincidence to him. He had simply wanted to share with me a favourite city. And he knew it well, very well. The conversation that swirled around us was French, and not tourist English, for Davis knew where the locals liked to dine. He also knew the best place for morning coffee, the hidden bar with Art Deco fittings that had eluded the guidebook listings, the bookshop crammed with old paperbacks where you could find 'almost anything' you could name. Yes, he fitted right in here. When it rained he wore an old mustard-yellow waxed jacket that made him look French (especially with that slightly Gallic profile of his), and it was clear that the staff in the restaurants took him for a native.

'You didn't spend your first honeymoon *here*, though, I assume?' I asked, pointedly. I thought he should at least demonstrate sensitivity to my position even if I didn't specifically demand it of him. 'I mean, not the same hotel?'

'Oh, no, of course not, not in La Rochelle at all, a little place up the coast.' He glanced towards the door. 'Nothing as glamorous as your own Tuscan adventure, of course.'

I smiled, pleased that he'd remembered the detail. My own honeymoon account, shared before we'd even become a couple, had been studded with asides that disparaged Alistair ('If I'd had any idea how he was going to change . . .') and it struck me now that I might do better to emulate Davis's diplomacy rather than try to break it down. Looking at his youthful face, lips tipped up at the corners and eyes always alert with interest, I had all the evidence I needed that he had weathered his romantic tragedies better than I had mine. How experienced we were, sitting here with four honeymoons between us. I corrected myself: three, for this one was shared.

'Did you travel a lot together, you and Camilla?' It seemed I was unable to stop myself from probing.

He refilled our wine glasses, suppressed a sigh. 'A fair bit. We were both quite attached to France, nothing unusual there. Actually, you know, we got on best when we were away from home. Funny, I haven't thought of that before.'

'Away from home temptations, I suppose,' I said, referring to his wife's infidelities, but thinking immediately of the one holiday Alistair and I had taken between Matthew's birth and our separation, a weekend away that contained the only harmonious forty-eight-hour period I could remember from that time. He'd been seeing Victoria for a while by then, though I was of course completely unaware of it. I marvelled once more at the anaesthetic effect my new marriage had had on the memory of the old. Only a matter of months ago the thought of Alistair and Victoria sneaking about while he was still married to me, while Matthew was a helpless newborn, was my very definition of human misery, and yet now the two of them might have been actors I remembered seeing in a movie long ago.

I watched as Davis took a deep gulp of wine, wondering if he would say any more about Camilla. I wanted very much for him to lean across the table now and kiss me, rekindle exactly that primal connection between us that had begun all of this, but he did not, merely gestured for the waiter to bring more wine. In truth, I was a little disappointed with the lack of ravishing generally on this trip. There'd been one night when he'd already fallen asleep by the time I presented myself to him, another when he was absorbed in a novel he'd found in a second-hand bookshop the same afternoon – 'I've been looking for this for years,' he'd said, and quite fervently, too, as though any allure of mine could not begin to compete with long-term desire of that sort. (The book even had its own smell, dry and slightly sour, as if giving off pheromones.)

Looking up, I saw that he was regarding me with a peculiar expression in his eyes. 'What are you thinking?' I asked, and then laughed at my own words. 'Sorry, I sound like a teenager.'

He smiled. 'Funny you should say that, because I was just thinking how like your daughter you looked just now. I know she takes after you *physically*, of course, but when you're puzzling over something there's a *true* likeness, as if you're *morally* the same.'

'Really?' For the first time I was a little irritated by that profound way he emphasised certain words. I didn't want to think about Roxy at that moment, or for him to think of her, either. We were on our honeymoon. Perhaps sensing my resistance, he finally shifted gear, reaching across the table to grip my hand in his. Then he began working his fingers into my palm, stroking my wrist, stirring me up with his touch. The room shrank around us.

'So are you going to tell your new husband what you were puzzling over?'

I sighed. 'Oh, nothing. Just the nature of honeymoons.'

'The nature of honeymoons has been fairly well documented, I believe. And I see no reason why we should stray from the received wisdom . . .' He beckoned once more for the waiter, this time for the bill, still playing with my hand. 'Let's go.'

'But we just ordered wine.'

181

'We'll take it with us.'

The guesthouse was just a few streets away and we hurried into the warmth together, waving *bonsoir* to the receptionist on our way to the stairs. As soon as we were through the door Davis pushed me onto the bed and tore away my coat and blouse. The same fingers that had teased me in the restaurant now touched me more brusquely and I pressed my face greedily to his. He made me feel very soft and female as he roved and squeezed, utterly confident that there'd be no opposition. My low mood forgotten, I was once more flooded with happiness.

'Oh, Davis, I want it to be like this forever, I don't want us ever to be separated . . .'

In an instant he froze, his body motionless as it hovered over mine.

'What?' I said, wriggling my arms out of my underwear while keeping my face close to his. I nibbled his lower lip. 'What's wrong?'

'Nothing, just . . .'

Someone else must have said that to him before, I thought, or something similar. Camilla, presumably, his child bride from long ago.

'Forget her,' I said, confident now of my strength. 'You were right, we don't want to think of old lovers now.'

I pulled impatiently at his waistband and moved downwards. Next time I looked, his eyes were tightly closed.

Towards the end of our stay we got up earlier than usual one morning, early enough to be the first down for breakfast. We had plans to cycle out into the country and wanted to get an early start. As Davis chatted to the receptionist about restaurants for the evening, I noticed her ledger on the desk between us, with its grid of dates and fluorescent squares that marked the various reservations. The place had been booked solid from April to September and even into the early part of October. This week was still half full, but from the next Monday the weekday squares were blank, the season would be over and trade would be limited mainly to weekend breaks. One tourist season, that was precisely how long Davis and I had known each other – Easter to October. In the school calendar, that was just a term and a half. I looked at his face, turned three-quarters towards me, and traced the outline of his nose and jaw as though seeing him for the first time. What on earth could you learn about someone in a term and a half? Surely a full academic year was needed before you were ready to marry?

For a wild moment I had an impulse to bolt, to rush out the door and get away from this windswept place, back to Francombe Gardens, to the walled garden within the private parkland out back, a sanctuary within a sanctuary. For so long my flat had been the only place I could trust myself, and yet with Davis's arrival I'd begun to behave quite differently even there. And my children, left at home, what was I thinking? We'd been apart many times, of course, what with their weekend stays with Alistair and their holidays with him twice a year, but this was the first time *I* had left *them*. What message did that send to them? How could this *not* have an impact on their well-being?

'Kate, are you all right?' Davis slipped his arm around my waist. 'You look a bit strange.' To his left I saw the receptionist's indulgent smile. 'Good news, darling, Annette is going to try to get us a table at Jardin de Mer tonight. It's supposed to be the best restaurant in town.'

'That's great. Davis. Listen, can we just . . .' I took his wrist and pulled him over to the banquette by the window. From our room the view was of the castle and the sea, but at ground level all you could see were rows and rows of parked cars.

'What is it?' he asked, solicitously. 'Are you feeling unwell?'

I looked at him, wild-eyed. 'No, it's just . . . I know this sounds mad, but I need to know.'

'Need to know what?'

'Do you *really* love me?'

He stared, taken aback. 'Do I . . .?'

'I mean, do you *really* think we've done the right thing?' Hysteria rose in my throat, making my voice weak and breathy. 'Are you a hundred per cent certain we haven't just rushed into something completely insane?'

He looked for a fraction of a second so acutely embarrassed by this display of neediness I felt angry, wanted to push him away and shout at him to get away from me. He didn't go so far as to glance to see if Annette had been following our conversation, but I could tell that was what he was thinking (he needn't have worried – at the first whisper of a lovers' tiff she'd discreetly withdrawn).

'Davis? I'm serious!'

'Yes,' he said at once, 'I can see you are. Yes, I *really* do love you, of course I do. And I'm a hundred per cent certain this isn't insane.'

'OK.'

He smiled a soothing, compliant smile. 'Is that all, my darling? You had me worried for a minute.'

At last I exhaled. 'That's all.'

Chapter 16

'Kate,' Ethan cried, springing up from the office chair to greet me. 'Great to see you. How was the honeymoon?'

He had left a message on my voicemail asking me get in touch as soon as I was back and I'd decided to stroll down to the office and get some air. After the high, racing clouds and ocean horizons of La Rochelle, London felt oppressive, the streets close and crowding, as though my home city were demanding I scale down my emotions now that I was back. I wasn't sure I could comply. After that little wobble in La Rochelle, the remainder of our honeymoon had been idyllic, and I'd embraced my new happiness with a vengeance. Just one doubt remained, and as doubts went it was a happy one: the question of whether I would take Davis's surname. On the one hand, I didn't like the idea of having a different name from the children, which was why I'd never reverted to my maiden name after my divorce from Alistair; on the other, now that I had remarried, it might feel odd to bear the name of a different man. Davis, conciliatory as ever, said he didn't mind either way, whatever I thought best (now that was something you'd never have heard Alistair say).

Ethan made us peppermint tea in the staff office. There was no budget for tea and coffee, so he replenished the supplies at his own expense. I had never known him to forget and, as he squeezed the teabags over the mugs, I felt a pang of gratitude for his constancy.

'Is everything all right?' I asked, taking my mug and sipping. There was always a distant fear that some piece of advice might have backfired and led to a disastrous outcome.

He nodded. 'Yes, absolutely, I just wanted to tell you before anyone else that Jocelyn is leaving. Moving, actually. She'll be transferring to a branch in Kent when she moves house at Christmas.' Jocelyn was Ethan's senior advisor, his second in command and the only other paid full-time position in the office. The rest of us were a mixture of paid part-timers and volunteers. 'Obviously there's a procedure we have to follow, but I wondered if you would be interested in going for the job?'

This was a surprise. I was flattered that he'd thought of me at all, for there were at least two others on the roster who were more experienced than I was and who I went to routinely for a second opinion. 'I'm not sure. I mean, yes, ideally, but as you know, I've always tried to work around Matthew's school hours.'

Ethan fingered his beard. His instincts were purely constructive and already he was engaged in figuring out a way to solve this. 'I'm not sure about that. It's always been a full-time position. But you could maybe start a bit later than Jocelyn does, after you drop Matthew at school, and we could probably be flexible about days, get you out of Saturdays.'

'That would definitely help.'

'It would be excellent if we could do this, Kate. You must realise how indispensable you are to us now. You're great with the clients, everyone agrees.'

'Let me have a think.' It occurred to me that things were different at home now. Davis would be there at least some of the time and, with a modicum of forward planning, we could juggle things so that Matthew would hardly notice the increase in my working hours. In any case, once he started secondary school there'd probably be a bus to take him, or he might want to travel on the Tube on his own. Previously, the idea of this might have worried me, but once again I felt that new swell of confidence, the feeling that from now on anything was possible. It was such a gift, that feeling, and it was Davis, my new husband, who had given it to me. My new husband. I liked saying the words to myself. Considering how resolved I'd been never again to share my life with a man, I had turned out to be no different from any other newlywed. Impossible now to understand why I'd kept the lid so tightly shut for so long, imagining that the only joy I needed was from watching my children grow ever-more independent of me. Well, by definition, that had to run out eventually, didn't it?

The supervisor's office had internal windows to the corridor behind reception and I saw that just one of our four interview rooms was occupied. It was strangely quiet. 'I was going to say I'd help you out if you were busy, but it doesn't look as if you need me.'

Ethan chuckled. 'Yes, bizarrely, it's been like this for most of the day.'

'You mean everyone's happy for once?'

'Looks that way. Must be something in the air.'

That sense of lull extended to the children. Roxy in particular had a subdued quality about her, a cautiousness that at first made me suspect the illicit hosting of parties in our absence. But there were no missing alcohol stocks or telltale cigarette ends on the fire escape and I quickly realised that what I was sensing was anti-climax, plain and simple. The bombshells had been dropped, the excitement had evaporated, and now we all had to return to real life, in Roxy's case exams in December and the prospect of university interviews in the New Year. I made a mental note to talk to Davis about taking the children away over the Christmas holidays, a cottage on the south coast, perhaps; it would give everyone something nice to look forward to.

Of all of us Davis was the busiest this first week back, holed up with students in the front flat well into the late evening of Monday and Tuesday and by midweek out catching up with those he taught elsewhere. Sometimes I couldn't even reach him by phone. It was helpful, though, in a way, for it meant that his move into the main flat could be phased in. I decided I would do a little reorganisation every day and by the weekend he would be fully resident. I hoped Roxy would agree to stay in on Saturday night so that I could cook a special dinner for the four of us.

First I cleaned the galley kitchen, transferring Davis's few utensils and provisions to the main kitchen; then the bedroom, a question of vacuuming the carpet and stripping the bed. After a moment's guilt, remembering Tash and her hopes to relocate to London, I made it up again with fresh sheets, arranging a throw and plumping the pillows as though I expected her that very day. Next I moved Davis's clothes from his wardrobe to mine (ours!). He proved scrupulously organised in that department, with rows of suits and blazers and shirts kept on pristine padded hangers, many items tailored at obvious expense (the legacy of a marriage to a much wealthier woman, I supposed). It was a relief that he was so impeccable; it seemed to me that I'd already spent enough days of my life pairing other people's socks.

By Thursday morning I was ready to reconfigure his living room into the much-missed family office space. Gathering up my own papers and books, stored since Davis's arrival in boxes in my bedroom or stuffed in no particular order in kitchen drawers, I realised why I had left it till last. That great wall of books, already crammed to capacity, and yet somehow I needed to find space for more! How on earth was I going to tackle this? Davis had promised to clear the lower two shelves for me, but had obviously been too busy with work to make a start. Looking once more at all my own piles of material, I didn't think two would be enough, anyhow. No, the only way to do this was to take everything down and start again with an empty wall.

I pulled up a stool and set about bringing Davis's books down, topmost first. They'd barely been up there long enough to gather dust. Three shelves in and I was already beginning to think my plan a little rash; this was hard work, my arms were already aching, and the ceilings were so high I had to balance on tiptoe to reach the top shelves. Well, I couldn't just leave it half done. I reached up for a line of Middle English textbooks – he didn't need those for teaching, surely? – and as I pulled them down I noticed a green patterned notebook that had been wedged tightly behind them in the narrow gap between wood and wall. Curious, I put Chaucer to one side and prised the notebook out. It was slim and covered in floral fabric of an incongruously feminine design, the sort you simply had to stroke, and I ran my fingers back and forth over the raised shapes of the petals. Once I'd done that, it felt quite natural that I should follow the length of silky green ribbon and open the book at the marked page.

I guessed as soon as I saw the dense blocks of handwriting that these were Davis's 'Fragments', or something similar in concept, for they were a collection of passages laid out rather like a journal, but without any dates. I climbed down from the stool and settled on the sofa, not allowing myself to question whether or not I should be doing this. Leaving the marker in place I leafed to the front. The first page was headed 'The River' and a dozen pages were taken up with a short story set on a Thames houseboat. The language was dry; I found it hard to follow what was happening in the story, skipped a page or two. The next was entitled 'Suspended Sentence', this double the length of the first, and again I lost patience with the complicated sentences. After that was some sort of verse in French, and a succession of others in German, but I didn't understand enough even to pick up the gist. I couldn't help feeling disappointed. Even the ink colour was dull watery blue (faded with age, presumably; he had, after all, begun this project when he was still with Camilla).

189

Turning the page, I came to a fresh passage in brighter ink and, more to the point, in English:

Finally, it begins. Before, you were a dream, vapour, alive only in my imagination. Now that dream is made flesh. Come into my life, my darling, for I have been waiting.

I gasped, instantly moved by this ardent new voice. It was so flowing, so completely different from the tangled sentences of the first section. It might have been written by a different person. I read on:

I have taken the flat. Reason protested, just as it should, but my heart insisted. I must have you near, even if nothing can come of this. You would never consider me, I understand that, you would never notice me. But just discovering your existence is enough.

I can't help myself watching for you, listening for you. You come and go with your strange, loud friend, she always very knowing and you so perfectly unknowing. I am mesmerised by your innocence, your beautiful silence.

Tears welled in my eyes and goosepimples rose on my skin at the realisation that this was about me. More than that, it was as if Davis were speaking directly to me, intending me to read it. All the endearments I'd longed for in France but never quite received were here, in his hand, in this beautiful secret wooing. I loved the courtly language, the admissions of vulnerability (as for the 'strange, loud' friend, I could only assume that he referred to Abi! I would need to be careful not to repeat the phrase in future conversation and betray myself).

I turned the page:

I am overjoyed to report a permission beyond my dreams: I have held you and kissed you.

I stopped reading and closed my eyes for a moment. My brain was flooded with pleasure and, quite overcome with sentimentality, it was all I could do not to press the page to my heart. I wanted to memorise every word or, better still, transcribe it in a secret book of my own that I could bring out and reread whenever I felt low. I'd find my own hiding place for it, perhaps here in the same room. How lucky I was, so lucky that I could no longer bear to remember myself as the woman I was a year ago, six months ago, even. She seemed now like some spinster neighbour who neither offended nor intrigued, someone you might say hello to on the stairs without bothering to make eye contact, someone not fully alive.

> I have never in my whole life known such anxiety. I thought it would break me in two with its agony. But we have made love, and what love! And it was your decision, not mine, it was you who took the chance, my younger in years and yet my wiser in heart . . .

I gasped with delight. Well, that was certainly an interesting take on our first time together!

> You say you want us to be like this forever. I cannot improve on your words, simple and true.

It seemed we'd moved on a few weeks already and reached La Rochelle. What a shame, I'd been hoping for more from that first, most erotic phase of our relationship – how much better than I Davis was at expressing that extraordinary passion that had materialised out of nowhere. *I want it to be like this forever:* I remembered quite clearly the moment I'd said that to him, on the bed in our attic room in La Rochelle, and how he'd paused mid-kiss as though he'd heard the words before. It hadn't occurred to me that he'd been committing the endearment to memory, that he'd want to cherish it on paper. Had he taken this little book with him on the trip? There *had* been a few hours here and there when he'd slipped off to be alone.

I read on, faster now, gobbling up the words, greedy to feed my vanity with further compliments:

> Later, amidst the fury of complications (my fault, all of it!), you say you have a quotation for me: 'It is a pity so much Love . . . on both Sides, shou'd ever separate.' I recognise it straight away, of course: your own Mr Defoe. Even the words you borrow from others are the perfect ones.

I frowned. *It is a pity so much love . . .* Did I say that? I didn't recognise the quotation at all and, in any case, tended not to quote great literature if I could help it. As Roxy had rather rudely pointed out that time at dinner, I was apt to misquote. And what, I wondered, did he mean by 'complications'? If these outpourings were chronological, then by this stage we were married and mercifully free of any of those, weren't we? Perhaps he meant the return to work and the prospect of his move into the main flat. No matter. I reminded myself that this was not strictly a diary, there was poetic licence at work here, and an author was free to play with time and place as he pleased. This may even have been his recollection of those dark days after the children had come back from South Africa, when, fool that I was, I had avoided him, given him that awful letter asking him to leave. He'd told me afterwards how wretched that had made him feel. *Wretched*, such an old-fashioned, Davis sort of word.

Even the words you borrow from others are the perfect ones . . . The sound of the phone ringing in the main flat suddenly jolted me back to reality. For the first time I admitted to myself that it might be wrong to read this, that I shouldn't be doing it, however lovely. Some feelings should remain private. I closed the cover, but my fingers still marked the page, refusing to let go. Next door the ringing stopped. I got to my feet. But the muscles in my legs wouldn't allow me to walk back over to the shelves and put the book back where I'd found it, or to slip it discreetly into one of the piles. It was just as Davis said himself, reason protested but the heart insisted! How could it be wrong to discover from my new husband exactly how much I meant to him? Better, surely, to read it? This way, my last insecurities could be dismissed and I need never again pester him for reassurances. He need never know why.

One more page, I told myself, though there was little more beyond that, anyway. Davis was apparently not a prolific writer (but, then, he *had* been rather busy lately). I reopened the book and found my place:

> To touch you again after time apart is to re-enter paradise. Impossible not to shudder when I remember her body, always too soft, too yielding. That neediness! Doesn't she see it only repulses? But you are mysterious and playful, you resist and evade before you invite me in, you move always out of my reach and then into it once more, your skin under my fingers like cool silk after her warm dough. Oh, Roxana, to be home.

I stopped. I blinked several times, my eyelids moving in odd, uncontrolled twitches. Then came an abrupt, painful surge of adrenaline that made the words swim in front of me. I blinked again, and as they resurfaced so did my common sense: of course, stupid me, my intellectual inferiority had prevented me from understanding the correct meaning of this passage. Read it again, I told myself, and it will all make sense. 'The other woman's body', 'that neediness!', these referred, of course, to Camilla. She must have been on his mind after my incessant probing in France. As for that last phrase, 'Oh, Roxana, to be home', a simple slip of the pen, perhaps? He'd meant to write 'Oh, Kate', of course, but, mindful of an appointment with Roxy, had made the error. Perhaps she had even been knocking at his door as he wrote, calling out to see if he was at home; she did that sometimes. Matthew, too.

But I knew already that this was not how it had happened, even before I scanned the page that followed and saw her name repeated over and over, the tall 'R's standing out like a pulse through the handwriting:

> Roxana, I know I have made a mistake and betrayed you. I thought this the best way, the only way to avoid banishment from you for ever, for that was what she threatened! My mouth opened and a coward spoke. But I see now I have hurt you too roughly. I swear I will dedicate my life to recompense. She is nothing, you are everything. Roxana, you are everything.
> L'amour est injustice, mais la justice ne suffit pas.
> (Camus)

I closed the book, looked once more at the cover, remembering how I had felt ten minutes ago before it had been opened. I was nauseous with the knowledge that I could never go back. It was one of those times that came rarely in life, when you can pinpoint exactly the moment that you have been forced off course or, worse, when the vessel carrying you has exploded into the air and you no longer exist in the form you know as your own. There was one last brief flare of hope as I asked myself, 'Can I bury this, can I pretend I never found it, never read it? Can I perform on myself the ultimate trick?' But I couldn't, of course. For myself, perhaps I could have done, but not for Roxy.

On legs that no longer worked properly I felt my way to the bathroom as though moving through pitch blackness, and vomited into the toilet bowl. Above the basin on a thick glass shelf stood the toiletries I'd arranged just a day or two before, his to the right, mine to the left. I'd carried mine through from the main bathroom in armfuls, looking forward to creating a little his and hers display. If I'd had the strength I would have swept them to the floor and stamped on them. I stumbled back into the living room and sat again on the sofa, holding the book, touching its cover for the last time. It was like stroking an animal that was dying in front of my eyes.

Chapter 17

Time passed, probably only minutes. My hands shook badly as I spoke into the phone. 'Davis, this is Kate. I've read your notes. Those fragments. I know about you and Roxy. Don't come back, don't come near us or I will call the police. I'm changing the locks. Stay away, stay away . . .' My voice rose maniacally and I fumbled for the end button mid-cry. As soon as I'd pressed it I realised my mistake: I should have waited until I'd got to Roxy before I phoned him; now all I'd done was given him the gift of advance warning.

Panic set in. I raced out of the flat and down the stairs, pushed open the door and into the street. How gentle the air felt compared to the bracing winds of the French coast – what had Ethan said? Everyone's happy, it must be something in the air. And I'd been innocent enough – arrogant enough! – to believe that I was one of the happy ones, maybe even the one so happy that all the calmness was for my benefit.

Not seeing, not hearing, I hit Roxy's number, willing the connection. But all I got was the message from the network that her phone was switched off. Classroom rules, otherwise they'd all just sit there sending texts to each other. Sometimes when she came home from school she'd forget to turn her phone on again for hours and when she did the beeps would go on for several minutes as the messages were delivered.

I gripped the phone, mind turning furiously. I had to get to her first, to return her to safety, to protect her. There was a chance that those words of Davis's were some ghastly fantasy of his, that nothing whatsoever had happened between them; either way, I had to reach her before he did. I'd phone her school, get them to fetch her from class and hold her in the office until I could get there. I hoped it would be Mrs Prentice who answered; I'd spoken to her often in the past. I'd say there was an emergency and that I'd explain when I got there. Don't let her leave, whatever you do . . . I searched for the number as my legs carried me on – 'Willoughby', right at the end of the alphabet – my fingers stumbling over the quick keys as my feet found the kerb.

'Good afternoon, Willoughby School for Girls?'

I could hardly breathe with relief. 'Hi, is that Mrs Pr—'

Then, shockingly, out of the soft air came a face next to mine, a glossy red shell above, an oversized mouth below, twisted and shouting. I couldn't hear the words, but I felt their heat and moisture. Next, stone, a cold flat fist to the head.

When I came to I was lying in a narrow hospital bed, pale pleated curtains pulled smoothly around me, and my left hand was bandaged and resting in a sling on my chest. My skull felt as though it had been tipped up and used as a whisk, all thoughts and memories folded together, all sense lost. I searched for the assistance button and pressed. Soon a woman appeared, dark skinned and bright eyed. Her hair had been rinsed with purple. I got the impression that her expression of determination had been set in advance, as if she'd already decided I was trouble and would stand no further nonsense from me, thank you very much.

'What happened?' I asked. My mouth was horribly dry. I looked about for water, but saw none.

'You were in a collision.' She spoke with a strong, lilting West Indian accent that made her sound amused.

'You mean with a car? I was driving?'

'No, you were walking.' Now she openly chuckled. 'You walked into the path of a cyclist and hit your head on the kerb. You were lucky you put out your hand to break your fall or you might have broken your jaw.'

'Is my wrist . . .?'

'Broken, yes, you don't remember? You were conscious when you had your x-ray. It's just a minor fracture. It doesn't need to be set in plaster, just strapped. You'll be wanting some more painkillers?'

I shook my head. 'Please, what day is it?'

'Thursday. You came in at about, oh, one o'clock this afternoon.'

But I was remembering on my own now, gasped as the pain suffused my body, not just my arm but the core of me, spreading outwards like poison as each clue clicked frantically into place. 'I need to go!' I cried, trying to swing my legs out of the bed, but they were pinned tightly under the top sheet as though the bed had been made with me in it. I began plucking at the sheet with my good hand. 'Help me get this off!'

The nurse moved towards me. 'I don't think so. We'd rather you stayed—'

'I have to go!' I kicked wildly under the bedclothes, still unable to free myself.

'Hang on now, Mrs Easton, the consultant needs to sign you off . . .'

I stared at her and stopped. 'How do you know my name?'

'You told us. Kate Easton, that is right, isn't it?'

I looked down. 'Yes.'

'Anyway, Mrs Easton, I'm not allowed to discharge you this evening. You may need a scan in the morning.' She stood like a sentry as she consulted her notes, her body blocking my path. I resumed my struggle with the sheets.

'I'll have to come back for that, I have children, they need me!'

'Don't you worry about that. We've been in touch with your

friend . . . Abigail, is it? She was the first number on your phone. That's right, she said she'd pick your son up from school and then come straight here. Perhaps she can help you with overnight arrangements?'

'Abi?' Thank God not Alistair, her alphabetical neighbour. 'I need to speak to her straight away. Where's my bag, it's got my phone?'

'You didn't have a bag with you, as far as I'm aware. We have your phone, though. Funny, they survive these things better than we do.' She chuckled once more.

'Give me it,' I shrieked. 'I need it now! It's an emergency!'

She silenced me with another scolding look. 'Please do not raise your voice with me. And mobiles are not allowed inside the building, I'm afraid. But I can bring you the payphone when it's free. It's in use at the moment.'

I glared at her. 'I can't wait! I need to call my daughter's school. Why are you being so horrible?'

At that she merely raised her eyebrows. 'It's after six, I don't suppose there'll be anyone there. Please be patient, I'm sure your friend will be here soon.'

I couldn't argue any further. She was like a boxer punching me down with every new challenge. I would wait for her to leave me and then I'd make my escape without her permission. In fact, she'd hardly been gone when I saw another staff member leading Abi and Matthew to me, Abi walking closely behind Matt and guiding him by his shoulders as they glanced from bed to bed. She was in her work clothes, he in sports sweats, his usual array of school bags swinging against his legs.

'There you are!' Abi's voice was artificially bright for Matthew's benefit, but her eyes registered alarm at the sight of me bandaged and bruised. 'He was in the middle of football club, so I thought I should let him finish since they said you were sleeping.'

Matthew sprang forwards. 'Mum, look at your arm!'

199

'Careful,' Abi said to him as he began prodding me, 'It'll still be very poorly. So what happened, Kate?'

'I bumped into a bike,' I said, 'near the flat. I didn't see it coming.' I turned to Abi. 'Abi, I need your help before—'

'Did it *really* hurt?' Matt demanded, interrupting. 'I've never broken anything.'

I tried to hide my despair. 'Not at the time. I can't really remember. It's sore now, though.' 'Sore', 'poorly', 'bumped', such soothing nursery words, when what I really felt was crucified, utterly crucified.

Abi didn't seem to notice my agitation, but began smoothing the disarrayed sheets around my legs. 'No offence to Davis, darling, but these cyclists are complete menaces. I think we should get rid of the racks in the garden in an effort to discourage the practice. Bring back trams, that's what I say!'

Matt, taking her at her word, was anxious. 'Will I not be allowed a bike for Christmas, then? Dad said if I came top in maths . . .'

I looked desperately at her. 'Abi,' I tried again, my voice starting to crack, 'I need to talk to you on your own for a minute.'

'Sure.' She looked at me strangely.

'Can you ask someone to mind Matt? Or there may be a children's play area or something . . .'

'That's for babies,' Matt objected. 'I saw it on the way.'

'Come with me,' Abi said, cheerfully. 'Let's see what we can find down this way . . .'

To my relief she returned alone and sat on the edge of the bed, her face quite white. 'God, Kate, they haven't found something, have they? I mean, other than the wrist?'

'No, no, nothing like that. Oh, Abi . . .' I choked back a sob. 'I don't know where to begin, it's horrible, horrible . . .'

She took my uninjured hand and squeezed. 'Hey, what is? What's happened? Tell me quickly, before that little devil of yours finds his way back.'

'They've gone,' I gasped, 'both of them, I need to stop them.'

'Who's gone?'

'Roxy and Davis.'

'Roxy and Davis? What do you mean?'

I cleared my throat, swallowed a ball of mucus. 'I found out and I told him. I shouldn't have rung him, he'll have gone to her school, taken her away.'

'Taken her away?'

'They're together, Abi!' I cried. 'They're having an affair!'

Her pale face flushed scarlet. 'You're not serious? Oh my God.'

There was a ghastly silence. 'She may have tried to phone, but I don't know where they've put my mobile. You can't use them inside, I need to get out of here and find her, but they say I have to stay.' I turned my hand in hers and gripped, increasing the pressure until she winced. 'I need to see her, Abi!'

She nodded. 'Listen, this isn't a prison, they can't force you to stay. I'll find out exactly what your condition is. But first why don't I nip out and call Roxy from my phone?'

'Yes, good, but she won't be at home. Try her mobile.' I recited the number; it was one of only three I knew by heart, Roxy's, Alistair's, mine. I had not yet memorised Davis's.

'What about him?' Abi asked. I could tell that already she couldn't bring herself to say his name. 'Shall I call him, as well?'

'No, just Roxy. Tell her to come here, wherever she is, to just turn back and get here as soon as she can.'

'Got it.'

The wait was agonising, not least because Matt was soon returned to me, marched back from wherever Abi had put him by the same jailor who had battled me earlier. She reminded me that childcare was not provided on the ward and turned on her heel.

'Mum, I don't need "childcare"!' Matt moved restlessly about

201

the small cubicle, tugging at everything in reach. Then he remembered he had learned a new trick of vibrating his body that he very much wanted to demonstrate to me. 'It's a kind of body-popping. If I do it for too long my eyes will jump out on gooey stalks. Watch.'

'OK. Wow.' I didn't know how much longer I could keep from screaming. When would Abi be back? Had she been able to reach Roxy? Roxy wouldn't recognise her number when it came up on her phone; was that a good thing or bad?

Clearly disappointed with my reaction, Matt ended his performance. 'It's not like the hospital where Elizabeth was born,' he remarked.

'No, that was a special maternity one. I must have come into A&E. Accident and emergency.'

'I *know*.' He peered again at my bandaged arm. 'When will you be able to arm wrestle again?'

'I'm not sure.' I felt a rush of shame at my offhand treatment of him. 'But I could maybe try with my right hand?'

'Now?'

'In the morning, darling. I'm a little tired.'

He shrugged. 'I'd easily beat you, anyway.'

I tried to listen to an account of football practice, but had already lapsed into jittery wordlessness by the time Abi reappeared. Her mobile was concealed like a playing card in the palm of her hand.

'Did you speak to her?'

'No, I just got her voicemail. But I left a message saying to check in as soon as possible, that you've had an accident. I left my number since she obviously can't call yours.'

'No, no, this is terrible, we have to speak to her directly. *He* might pick up her messages . . .' Groaning, I began to kick at the sheets again, eyes searching for my clothes.

Abi placed herself between me and Matthew's interested face. 'Kate, you need to stay in bed.' She lowered her voice. 'They collared me just now and said you could haemorrhage if you leave without having this scan. I think you should do what they say. Let me go to the flat. I've got spare keys. If she's there, I'll keep her under house arrest, trust me.'

'What about Matt?'

'He'll come with me.' Turning, she slapped a hand on Matt's shoulder. 'I'll get him fed and watered. Why don't I stay over? That's the best idea, isn't it, then I'll be there in case . . .' She hesitated. 'Or should I call Alistair?'

'No,' I said, quickly, 'not Alistair.'

'Are you sure?'

'Yes. *Please*, promise me you won't phone him. I'll ring in the morning, just as soon as I'm better.' I turned to Matt. 'Is that OK, sweetie? You'll be with Abi tonight, but either Dad or I will be back tomorrow.'

Matt narrowed his eyes, sensing an opportunity for personal gain. 'What will she make for dinner?'

'Whatever you like. Show her what's in the freezer, OK? Pizza or something.'

'And ice cream?'

'Definitely, however many scoops you want.'

I hugged him, overwhelmed with gratitude that he was still – just – on the side of childhood that allowed him to miss the adult subtexts in favour of his stomach. He was entirely innocent of the true nature of this accident and I had to keep it that way. Whatever happened, I had to protect him from the truth.

Abi kissed me on the cheek. 'I'll get a message to you as soon as I can. The best thing you can do is rest. OK?'

As they left I let my head fall into the pillows, pounding the fist of my uninjured hand on the mattress as I clenched my eyes shut, half mad with fear and misery.

Whether or not she'd tried to leave one with the hospital staff, Abi's message did not reach me until I got back to Francombe

Gardens the following morning and recharged my mobile phone, dead after a night in the nurses' care. Her account held no surprises: Roxy had been gone when she'd got there, they both had. Abi had tried her phone repeatedly, eventually leaving a second message that pleaded with her to check in with one of us as a matter of emergency. This Roxy had not done. I tried not to wonder how serious my injuries would have to have been for her to have turned around and come back.

I picked up the rest of my messages. One from Tash; one from the network; one from Ruben's mother about a birthday trip to the cinema. I checked the landline: nothing. Then I rang Roxy's mobile number at least a dozen times, alternating between my mobile and the landline, but each time received the same network message that the phone had been turned off.

I found her note on the corkboard. Abi had missed it in the chaotic layers of school newsletters and correspondence.

Dear Mum,
I have gone away with Davis. This is what we both want, so please do not try to find us. I will contact you again when the time is right.
   I'm sorry about school and everything. I will contact Dad separately to explain.
   Love, Roxy x

There were clothes missing from both their wardrobes, and bits and pieces strewn about, just as you'd expect when someone had left in a tremendous hurry. They couldn't have known about my accident at that point, must have thought they had only minutes to elude me and any back-up forces I might have mustered at short notice. I didn't need to look to know that passports and driving licences would be gone too, or that in Davis's living room the notebook would no longer be on the coffee table where I'd left it.

But I didn't care about the notebook. I didn't need his fragments now. They told me only the story so far, not what happened next.

Abi had taken care of everything. She had dropped Matthew at school before going to the office, arranged for Evert's mother to pick him up later, and had even left me a note about homework. She promised to leave work as early as she could in the evening to come back and be with me. 'Call Alistair', she'd written at the end of her note, and underlined it with a thick, curved stroke. She would ring me soon, I knew, to check that I'd obeyed. I could only assume that Roxy had not yet got around to contacting her father herself, as her note had promised. Had she done so, the phone would be ringing itself out of its cradle by now, my mobile jumping from my pocket. Wild horses wouldn't keep him from getting here and demanding to know how I had allowed this grotesque situation to occur.

I closed my eyes. It was a good question.

Alone for the first time, I succumbed to numbness. The colossal weight of my concern for Roxy's safety fought for headspace with my devastation at Davis's betrayal – the end of my marriage already! Was this some sort of record? My survival instinct was to anaesthetise myself to all of it until only the physical pain remained – for that, at least, I had drugs. In the kitchen I got myself a glass of water and swallowed the painkillers I'd been given at the hospital. The label on the box had my name printed on it: Mrs K. Easton. I must have been semi-conscious when I'd given it, but I'd still been able to deny I'd become a Calder. Well, that was one dilemma I would no longer have to resolve, wasn't it?

I sat waiting for the pills to kick in, staring at the printout on the corkboard:

What can I do at age seventeen?
• You can leave home without your parents' consent

205

It might have been highlighted in fluorescent yellow, fitted with flashing light and siren, the way my eye kept going back to it.

Only when the phone rang did I spring to life, snatching up the receiver, desperate for her voice. But it didn't come. First, the school-uniform supplier: an item Matt needed for PE had finally come in, did I want to collect it or should they send it by post? I couldn't hang up fast enough. Next, Tash.

'Hi, Mum!'

'Roxy,' I breathed, misunderstanding. 'Is that you?'

'No, silly, it's me, Tash! Welcome back!'

'Oh, Tash.'

'You don't sound very cheery! How was it, then, the honeymoon? And keep it clean, there are probably children listening!'

'Yes, it was OK. Thank you.'

'Just "OK"?' she exclaimed. 'That doesn't sound very promising. Wasn't it *wickedly* good? Well, maybe I won't bother ever getting married myself after all!'

Her blithe, carefree voice was unbearable. 'Tash, this isn't a great time, to be honest. Can I phone you back?'

'Sure. I'm in London actually, staying with my friend Fiona in Stoke Newington. I'll give you her number, hang on . . .'

Obediently I scratched the numbers onto the notepad in front of me, but they were nothing more than abstract shapes, made no sense to me.

'Are you OK, Kate? You sound a bit weird.'

'I'm fine, honestly. I'll call you back.'

Ethan phoned soon after, concerned that I had not turned up for a meeting that morning, but I was able to fob him off with the story of my accident.

'Kate, that's awful! Don't worry about us, just take all the time you need to recover. You will call if there's anything I can do, won't you?'

Erase the last six months from history, I thought. Return my daughter to me and take us back to April, to the morning of the viewings, to the day Roxy had sunbathed with Marianne while I made Davis coffee in the kitchen and invited him into my life – into *our* lives. Make me look him in the eye and tell him that the flat had already been taken. Make it the first and last time I laid eyes on him.

'How is the other guy doing?' Ethan asked.

'What?' I thought for a second he meant Davis, but of course he meant the cyclist. 'Oh, fine, I think. He came off his bike, but there were no bones broken. I think he just went home. It wasn't really anyone's fault.'

'Hmm. Sounds as if it's worked out as well as it could have done, to be honest. I had someone come in while you were away who wanted to sue a pedestrian who'd stepped into a cycle lane. He ended up knackering his front wheel to avoid hitting him. He kept saying, "But it was my right of way." I had to say to him, "Look, mate, pedestrians always have the right of way. There's never a situation where you're *allowed* to mow them down!"'

I forced out the chuckle that was expected of me and managed to end the conversation there.

Finally, as the afternoon light warned me that Matthew would soon be home, I made a call of my own, to the local police. I knew the answers even before I asked the questions. There was no crime to report. Not only was Roxy with a trusted family member ('trusted' – that in itself was enough to make me gag, but how on earth to explain why I had married him less than two weeks ago if he were not to be trusted?), but she had also left me a note informing me of her absence in perfectly unambiguous terms. As for her studies, however ill-advised the world might think it, a student of her age was free to leave school without anyone's permission. By police standards she was safe and accounted for. There was no way this could be considered a missing-person case.

'I have reason to believe they are having a personal relationship.' It was odd, I'd expected to choke on the words as I had

207

with Abi, but I just sounded mechanical, like a poor recording of a human voice.

I could sense professional sympathy from the other end of the line, but the message remained the same. 'Again, I'm afraid that doesn't constitute criminal behaviour.'

'You mean there's absolutely nothing you can do about this?'

'I'm sorry, Mrs Easton. I've noted your concerns. Do keep us informed if you want to, but at this stage, there isn't anything specific to investigate. I suggest you continue trying to contact your daughter and your husband by phone and try to resolve this situation between you. The fact that she left a note is a positive sign. It means she will probably get in touch again soon. She knows you'll be worried. Check your email regularly. She may not want to speak to you straight away, given the circumstances, but may try to communicate another way.'

I put the phone down as someone might who'd been listening in on an extension to a conversation between two strangers.

'Kate? What are you doing sitting in the dark?'

Abi strode into the room and snapped on the lights. 'Have you heard from her? What does Alistair say? Is Matt already in bed?' She peered at my face. 'You look absolutely freezing. Oh my goodness, you're in shock. I'll make some tea.'

Though the light was bright, her figure was blurred as it moved about the kitchen, and all the sounds she made – cupboards opening, mugs clinking, water splashing – were at such a low frequency I could hardly distinguish one from the other.

She pressed a red-hot mug into my right hand and sat opposite me at the table. 'OK, have you done *anything* since you got back this morning?'

I shook my head. With the exception of those few hours when Matthew had come home and needed tending to, I'd hardly moved from my kitchen chair. 'I mean yes, I rang the police.'

'Good. What did they say?'

'They can't help. He's done nothing wrong.'

'Bullshit. Well, fuck them. Kate, I know this is hard, but you have to get to work. You know the rules about runaways: the first twenty-four hours are the most crucial. Or is it the first forty-eight?'

I looked blankly at her.

'You should be doing something constructive! Come on, I'll help you. Where's that address book I used earlier to find Matthew's friend? . . . Ah, here. Right, this is what we do first: ring everyone Davis knows and ask if he's been in touch, either yesterday or today. Don't say why. Actually, maybe it's just as well you're a zombie, you won't break down on the phone.'

The book contained only a handful of names, those who'd been invited to the wedding and whose details had therefore been recorded, and we got through the list quickly. All accepted our apologies for the lateness of the call, but none had heard from Davis – not since the 'happy' day, one friend added.

'What about that other guy you told me about?' Abi said, flicking through the pages. 'The one in York?'

'Graham?'

'Yeah, why isn't he in here?'

I struggled to remember. 'We didn't send a written invitation. Davis invited him in person.'

'What's his surname? We'll Google him.'

But I didn't know.

'Well, we're going to have to track him down somehow.' She looked at her watch. 'Tomorrow. For now, I suggest we go back to the beginning and search Roxy's room for clues: ticket receipts or travel itineraries or whatever. And the same with Davis's.'

I looked helplessly at her. 'I can't.'

'Stop this, Kate. You can. Come on, get up and move.'

I followed her into Roxy's room, where a tangle of clothes remained on the bed. At the sight of them I connected once more with the crisis, only for a moment, but long enough to picture my daughter rummaging through her wardrobe, stuffing whatever she could drag out into her big canvas holdall as Davis rushed her from the door. 'This wasn't planned, Abi. I don't think there'll be anything to help us. I'm fairly certain they just panicked and took off without knowing where they were going.'

Abi nodded, encouraged by the contribution. I saw that she had taken possession of Roxy's note and was shaking her head at its contents. 'Well, this doesn't suggest she's planning to return to school, does it? No chance of them trying to brazen this out. We need to get into her laptop, they had to have had somewhere in mind and I bet they used to email each other. Did he use email while you were away?'

'There was a computer at the hotel, but I don't remember seeing him use it.'

'OK, I'll check the laptop, you look in all the hiding places for the more traditional stuff. Diaries, photographs, love letters, that's the kind of thing we need . . .'

As she fiddled with Roxy's computer, I began pulling out books from the shelves and forming little piles on the floor, just as I'd done with Davis's yesterday when I'd found the notebook and set this catastrophe in motion. Unsurprisingly, there was nothing.

Abi beckoned me over. 'Here we go: "New messages".'

'How did you get into her account? I have to put in a password for mine.'

'It's set up to open automatically for hers. But look, there's nothing in her inbox or her "sent" folder. She must have moved or deleted her messages before she left, or maybe she's accessed it from somewhere else. What a shame we weren't able to check straight away.'

I nodded mutely.

'Anyway, I bet she's got some other account only she knows about.' She swivelled in the desk chair with sudden inspiration.

'Would that awful friend know anything, d'you think? Maybe hers is the email we should be breaking into.'

My eye drifted to a framed photograph of Roxy, Marianne and two other cast members from *Bugsy Malone*. 'Possibly. I'm going to have to contact her, aren't I?'

'I'm afraid so.' She reached for my hand. 'You poor, poor thing, this must be awful for you. Look, why don't you go and have a quick check next door and I'll finish in here. Look through his mail, anything that might help.'

Davis's flat was just as I'd left it that morning when I'd come back from the hospital and after a half-hour of desultory lifting and replacing, I returned to the main flat with just one discovery: an address for the storage units Davis used down in south London, presumably not far from the Battersea flat he used to share with his first wife. A statement of account had been sitting in a pile of opened mail on his desk.

'That's good,' Abi said. 'We might be able to find this Graham's contact details in an old file or something. We'll go down there tomorrow and have a good hunt.'

The idea of travelling across the city to face another roomful of Davis's possessions was completely overwhelming. 'I don't think I'm up to it, Abi.'

'You will be in the morning, you just need a bit of sleep. And anyway you *have* to. You'll need something to present to Alistair when you finally speak to him.'

She moved into my eye line and held my gaze firmly. Even through the fog of the day's shock and confusion I sensed a deal in the air. 'What about Matt?' I asked. 'It's Saturday tomorrow, he won't be at school.'

'That's a point. You go on your own then, and I'll stay and look after him. We got on pretty well last night.' She laughed drily. 'Hey, maybe I'm a natural caregiver, after all.'

211

Chapter 18

I slept fitfully, falling into proper sleep only at the dawn of Saturday morning and woken painfully soon after by the squeal of the intercom. Someone was pressing the button continuously, making it into one long hysterical siren. My first thought was Roxy, back home, keys lost, and I was instantly frantic, out of bed and rushing to pick up.

'Rox, is that—'

'Kate? It's Alistair. Buzz me in, will you?'

He must have taken the stairs three at a time he appeared so quickly, striding into the hallway just as Matthew's bedroom door opened and a pair of sleepy eyes peered out.

'Daddy! Why are you here?'

But Alistair hardly seemed to register the greeting – or presence – of his son. Without saying a word to either of us he thrust a sheet of paper at me and stood scowling in the shadows. 'How do you explain this?'

'What is it?' Matt was at my side and I put a hand to his pillow-tousled hair. 'Darling, go back to bed for a bit, it's still early. Daddy and I just need to talk on our own for a minute.'

'I'll take him.' The three of us looked up as Abi emerged from the living room, knotting the belt of an old dressing gown of mine at her waist. She gave Alistair a small smile. 'Hello, Alistair.'

212

'What's she doing here?' he asked, rudely. The two of them had met several times, including at the wedding, but I could see that this morning his anger left no room for common courtesy.

'She stayed over last night,' I said, as sharply as I could without alerting Matt to any intrigue. 'We were up late and I get the feeling you might know why. Come into the kitchen, OK, and we'll talk?'

One hand already shepherding Matthew towards his bedroom doorway, Abi sent me a meaningful look. 'How are you this morning?'

'Better,' I said, firmly.

'Sure?'

'Yes.'

'Good. Right, come on then, Matt, show me that computer game we were talking about the other night. Will you teach me how to do it?'

'Thank you, Abi.' I pulled on a robe of my own and I led Alistair down the hallway to the kitchen. Clicking the door shut behind us, I looked at the printout he'd given me. It was an email from Roxy, sent from an account I didn't recognise. I read the words with dread:

```
Dear Dad,
You probably know by now I have left home.
Please do not try to come after me. I'm
really sorry but I won't be doing my A-levels
or going through with uni applications this
year. Please respect my freedom of choice.
I just wanted you to know that I am safe
and happy and will be back in touch soon.
   Love, Roxy
```

There was no mention of Davis; *he* was for me to explain.

Alistair glared at me. '"Freedom of choice"? What the fuck is that supposed to mean? Where is she, Kate?'

'You'd better sit down.' Already I felt my legs start to give way and I clutched at the worktop. I'd meant what I'd said to Abi, I *did* feel better, the shock that had so debilitated me yesterday had lifted, but into the emptiness poured pain, true, liquid pain, coursing through me in an unstoppable tide. 'Why don't I make us some tea?'

Alistair planted himself on one of the kitchen chairs, but kept his upper body poised slightly forward, ready to spring up and pounce at the slightest provocation. 'I don't want tea, I want to know what's going on. Have you two had some kind of row? She was absolutely fine while you were away.'

I turned from the kettle and faced him. His whole face and neck were flushed, the nerve endings as livid as his mood. 'I don't know how to say this, Alistair, but she seems to have run away with Davis.'

He stared. '*Davis*? As in your new husband Davis?'

'Yes.' I could hardly bear to watch as he made the split-second connections, incredulity breaking across his face.

'You're not telling me the bloke's been molesting my daughter?'

I battled to keep my voice steady. '*Our* daughter, and not "molesting", no. But they do appear to be having some sort of relationship. I found bits of a diary—'

He cut in, 'Well, if that's all. I wouldn't believe a word of a teenager's diary. Pure fantasy.'

'*His* diary, not hers. And since they've disappeared together, I think we do have to believe it.'

He frowned. 'Show me this diary.'

'I can't, he took it with him. But it seemed to suggest they think they're . . .' I hesitated. '. . . that they're in love.'

Alistair snorted. 'Don't be ridiculous! If they're so "in love" then what the fuck was that little celebration out there two weeks ago?' He motioned to the window and I followed his gaze to the walled garden where Davis and I had so recently

214

stood, fingers threaded tightly together as we greeted our guests as a newly married couple. How proud I had felt, how thrilled to show the world that things had worked out for me, after all. Alistair's mouth twisted unpleasantly. 'This is beyond a joke. How many members of my family is he sleeping with exactly?'

I didn't answer. Never in all my life had I felt such anguish, such humiliation. Only now did I know that losing Alistair had been easy – easy compared to losing Roxy. Given the choice, I would have welcomed his desertion. But I *had* to be strong, I *had* to stand my ground. 'Listen, I'm as appalled by this as you are. More, I would imagine – he was my husband. I had absolutely no idea this was going on, and if I had then obviously I would never have allowed him anywhere near the house, let alone married him.'

Alistair regarded me without mercy. Then his mouth opened and I thought he was going to yell at me, but what came out could only be described as a strangled roar, directed not so much at me as at the whole world. 'This is sick, Kate, sick!'

'Shush, please . . .' I nodded towards the door. 'Matthew doesn't know anything about this. He thinks Davis is away for work and Roxy is at Marianne's.'

'Well, make sure you keep it that way, OK? Hang on a minute . . .' His face changed once more and he rose from his seat. I realised he had noticed my bandaged wrist. 'What happened here? It wasn't that bastard, was it?' He rested my hand in his cupped palm as one might an injured bird, and despite myself tears welled at the gentleness of his touch.

'I had an accident in the street. A cyclist ran into me and I wasn't looking. It was my fault, nothing to do with all of this.' My mind started to race. That was when they ran, though, wasn't it? When I was in A&E. Had I been looking where I was going, the collision would never have happened and I would have reached her school in time, or at least been back in time to confront them as they tried to leave. Maybe I could have reasoned with Davis at that point, got rid of him before he had time to dream up this crazy vanishing act … I grabbed for some kitchen roll to mop my eyes. 'Whatever Davis is, he is not violent. I honestly don't think she's in any danger. She wanted to go. She left me a note, as well, I'll show you.'

I retrieved Roxy's note from the drawer where I'd buried it late last night out of Matthew's sight and passed it to Alistair. 'Look.'

He scanned the message. 'Unless he *made* her write it. Have you considered that? And he could easily have typed that email to me.'

I shook my head. 'I don't think so. She jumped at the chance to go. And it makes sense, it explains a lot of other stuff.'

In an instant his compassion for my injury was replaced with pure suspicion. 'What stuff? You mean you suspected this and didn't do anything about it?'

I took a sideways step away from him. 'No, of course I didn't suspect it. I just mean her behaviour over the last few months has been strange. She hasn't been herself. She's been moody, preoccupied, more than the usual teenage stuff, and now we know why.'

'Yes, we do. She's been being harassed by a pervert *you* brought into this house.'

Still leaning against the cupboards for support, I took a deep breath. 'No, Alistair, I know you think this is all my fault, but I won't have it. You've played your part, too, you know.'

'*What*?' he spat. 'Are you totally insane?'

We looked grimly at each other. There was a brief, frightening moment when it could all have tumbled out – Lord knew I had rarely been less in control – when the questions that lashed inside my skull almost found voice: Would Roxy have done this if her father had not left her when she was a child? Or if he had displayed just a little more respect and sympathy for her mother over the years? Would she have needed Davis if her father had not begun a second family? Would she have met him? 'It's true,' I said coolly. 'You were the one who insisted on a lodger, remember? And you also went behind my back about continuing the French sessions at the beginning of term. That must have been when they started to get closer.'

'That's crap,' Alistair snapped, but I could tell by the way he stood blinking, arms lifeless by his sides in a rare posture of surrender, that I'd disarmed him.

'Look,' I said, seizing the initiative, 'this is neither of our faults. We mustn't waste time arguing. Roxy has gone, and we have to work together to get her back.'

He nodded. Arms active again, he handed the note back to me and reached into his pocket for his phone. 'I'll need to talk to Victoria, see what we can do.'

There was involuntary fear for a moment as I thought he was saying he couldn't confide in me, he couldn't work with me, but then I realised he meant he needed Victoria's legal expertise. 'You think we could get Roxy back through the courts?' I asked, hopefully.

'I have no idea. That's what we need to look into.'

'The police seemed to suggest otherwise.'

He jerked up from his phone, glowering afresh. 'You've already spoken to the police?'

'Yes, yesterday, as soon as I got back from the hospital.'

His face flushed deep with new fury and he snapped the phone shut. 'When exactly did they take off, Kate?'

'Thursday afternoon, I think.'

'Thursday? You think? That's two days ago! Why the hell didn't you tell me straight away?'

I matched his scowl. 'Because I've been in hospital having head scans! Will you please stop swearing at me!' I paused. However cruel he was being, I knew I owed him a fuller explanation than the one I was giving. I remembered how I had prayed in hospital that I might somehow have misunderstood the situation, that it might be a delusion brought on by my injuries. And only last night, after that midnight ransacking of their rooms, I had gone to bed fantasising that when I woke up I would find that none of this had really happened and they were both exactly where they should be. 'The thing is, I suppose I hoped she might come back. After a night or two away, I thought she might change her mind. Just now, when the buzzer went, I thought you were her.'

But Alistair was not persuaded by my show of vulnerability. 'So you thought you'd be able to just brush it under the carpet and not tell anyone? Let that bastard come back and start all over again?'

The edge of the worktop felt sharp against my spine and I realised I was still using it to keep myself upright. I took a step forward, my legs strong now. 'No, that's not what I thought at all. I just hoped that if Roxy came back this weekend then she could at least go to school as usual on Monday, get on with her life, while we sort out,' I bit at my lower lip before expelling the word, '*him.*'

Again Alistair and I stared at each other, searching the other's face for the compromise that in a decade we'd never quite been able to achieve. 'She still might, Alistair, it's only Saturday morning. She hasn't been gone for long. She might be coming to her senses as we speak!'

His face was expressionless as he clicked open his phone again. 'I think I'd better call my wife.'

It was a Saturday, but for the first time in living memory Matthew had no morning sports practice or fixture to go to, no play date or birthday party scheduled for the afternoon. Thank God, then, for Abi. With minimal input from Alistair and me, she supervised his breakfast, got him to wash and dress, and announced that she was taking him to her place to play chess with Seb. Meanwhile, Victoria drove over for an emergency conference. I dreaded seeing her, especially when I remembered my manner towards her at the wedding, those feelings of gloating at my being, after so long, the queen bee once more; she must have picked up on that, even in her state of new baby exhaustion. Now, if she wanted to, *she* could gloat, a gloat to end all gloats. Well, I would just have to take whatever she decided to dish up. Her help in this could be crucial.

She arrived looking both tired and purposeful, her arm hooking the car seat that contained a sleeping Elizabeth.

'Oh, she's gorgeous,' I said, unable to stop myself reaching out to touch the little girl's tiny cheek. Babies were like newly opened flowers, impossible not to want to run your thumb across the surface of their precious new petals. Roxy had had such beautiful, translucent skin . . . but I couldn't allow myself to think of Roxy like that, I couldn't allow myself to glimpse the possibility that I might never see my baby again.

Victoria found a quiet corner for Elizabeth, retucked the blanket with great care, and then took a place at the kitchen table next to her husband. When she finally looked at me it was with genuine compassion and my face flooded with shame and relief.

'What do you think?' I asked, pouring her a mug of tea. She, at least, was willing to accept refreshment. 'Is there anything we can do?'

She took a sharp breath. 'Well, it's a slightly grey area, the age of seventeen. The age of consent is sixteen, of course, which suggests that Roxy is an adult in the eyes of the law, has been for eighteen months, but there are still things she isn't permitted to do as well, and that suggests she's not entirely responsible for herself, like drink alcohol, or get married without your consent.'

'Hmm.' I was grateful that neither of them pointed out that Roxy could not marry her lover even if she cared to, since he was already married to me.

'I think what they've done is extremely unsavoury,' Victoria went on, 'especially on his part. But it's not criminal. We should consult a family specialist just to be sure, but to be honest I don't think there's anything we can do from a legal standpoint.'

'I think that's a good thing,' Alistair said, unexpectedly. He'd certainly calmed down since the arrival of his wife and baby daughter. Every so often his eyes strayed to Elizabeth, curled like a little shrimp in her upholstered seat, eyelids sealed, and his whole face softened. I could only guess at his thoughts, his silent avowal to protect this one better than he – we – had the first.

Victoria nodded. 'I have to agree. The last thing we want is the press crawling all over it, making it into some kind of wild-child Lolita scenario. But there's absolutely nothing to stop us tracking her down ourselves and persuading her to come back. And she might get in touch again herself soon.' She turned to me. 'I'm sure Alistair told you he replied to her email right away.'

'No, we didn't get that far.' I looked at Alistair. 'What did you say, exactly?'

His raised his eyebrows. 'Obviously I demanded in no uncertain terms to know where the hell she is.'

'I don't think she's going to tell us that.'

'I don't think you have any idea what she's going to do.'

'I thought we agreed we wouldn't argue?'

Victoria ignored this exchange. 'Can you think of anywhere they might have gone, Kate? Did Davis keep a flat from before you met?'

I shook my head. 'No, otherwise he would have lived in it and not rented mine.' Though I sounded confident, I was not. For all I knew, Davis could have ten flats. I didn't know the first thing about him, that much was becoming obvious to all of us. 'His closest friend lives in York and I'm trying to get hold of him in case they might have gone there.'

'That sounds promising, doesn't it, Al?'

But the lift I felt at the sight of their optimistic nods vanished just as swiftly as the details returned to me: Graham had two children of his own, didn't he? I couldn't remember their names, but they were young, school age; a holiday had been planned for half term. A family home was hardly the natural sanctuary for a middle-aged man and his teenage lover, was it? Even if this Graham could be swayed to sympathy, his wife surely would not.

'Or might they have gone abroad, do you think?' Victoria asked. 'I was thinking that on the way over. Get themselves a bit further out of reach? Davis presumably knows Germany pretty well, for instance?'

'I don't know.' There was no point arguing that he wasn't well off enough to have taken Roxy too far or for too long, because he could have all manner of secret funds that I knew nothing about. We had not discussed in any depth how our separate finances might work in the marriage, or been organised enough to open a joint bank account. 'I suppose the police could find out easily enough if they've been through the airports, but they say there's nothing to investigate at—'

Alistair cut in again, something he never did with Victoria, I noticed. 'The police won't tell us anything, but a private investigator could.'

'Do you think that's necessary?' Victoria said, frowning. 'It would be very expensive.'

'I don't see an alternative, darling. How else are we going to find her?'

'There must be something we can try before it comes to that.'

'I'll find them,' I said, anxious to wrest back some control of this situation. I was the one who knew Roxy best, after all; there might be clues that only I could recognise. Besides, I was the one who'd been betrayed, whose life was damaged beyond recognition, who had the fundamental motivation not just to find Roxy, but also to try to understand. Abi was right: now that the shock

221

had passed, I knew I would not rest until I'd found them. 'I'll track down Graham, and there are a few of Roxy's friends I can question as well.'

Marianne Suter was at the top of the list, of course, though I very much doubted her willingness to help. Then there was Jacob, the new third, but I suspected I'd only be able to reach him through Marianne, which made him an equally unlikely informant. Who else? I could only assume that Damien knew nothing of this, that that reconciliation Roxy had mentioned had been a fabrication intended to throw me off the scent (and conceived, I now saw with sickening clarity, during that last 'chat' with Davis). Otherwise, Roxy had hardly mentioned her friends in the last few months, and it seemed to me now that this was consistent with the keeping of a terrible secret (not that Marianne or Jacob would consider it terrible, I imagined, only brilliantly scandalous). No, she'd kept a closed circle throughout, had probably tightened it further once term started, not wanting any rumours to reach her teachers' ears.

Victoria was nodding her encouragement. 'Yes, Marianne's your best bet, isn't she? And whatever happened to that girl Rox always used to be with? Susannah, was it? And the dark-haired one, Toni?'

I was a little startled to hear her correctly name old friends of Roxy's. It had always suited me to believe that her attitude to her stepchildren was a reluctant, deliberately distant one, that she was as keen for them to grow up and leave her alone as I was to keep them. 'She doesn't seem to see either of them much any more,' I murmured.

'What about *his* friends?' Alistair said, impatiently. 'Other than this Graham character who Kate hasn't actually met and who probably doesn't exist?' He raised his eyebrows at me. 'Or are they all still in school uniform, as well?'

'Not funny,' I snapped.

'Alistair,' Victoria said, warningly. 'That won't help.' The two of them looked at each other and I felt as though their support for me hung in the balance. Extraordinarily, Victoria seemed my safest bet.

'Give me a day or two,' I said, appealing to her directly. 'Please. I'll do everything I can. Someone must have some idea where they've gone. And I still think she might come back of her own accord.'

'If she isn't back by Monday, we'll need to talk to the school,' Alistair said. 'Fob them off with some family emergency. I don't want them deferring the Cambridge application or anything rash like that. You'd better let me handle it, Kate, if they start asking any awkward questions.' The implication that something so important was not to be trusted to a shambles like me did not pass me by, but I thought it best to quit while I was ahead.

On their way out, Victoria lingered on her own for a moment as Alistair carried the baby down to the car. 'Kate, I know this is the last thing you want to think about right now, but you might want to consider getting an annulment.'

'An annulment?' I parroted the word; it tasted like death.

'Yes. I'm not sure you'll even have grounds, not in this country, but it's still worth talking to a specialist about it. These are unusual circumstances and you've been married for such a short time.' She paused, sparing me the exact count (I knew it, of course: two full weeks, almost to the hour). 'You need to consider what assets you brought to the marriage, as well, the flat and so on. You'll want to keep your family home, whatever happens.'

I nodded mutely. I didn't care what I'd brought to the marriage. I would have handed Davis the deeds to the flat in a heartbeat if I thought I could get Roxy back in exchange.

She touched my elbow. 'Would you like me to recommend someone? I can make a few calls on Monday.'

'Thank you.' Even in my distress I was able to recognise how impressive she must be at work, discreet and thorough, utterly reliable. There was something else, too, something had shifted between us, something that quite overtook the fact that she was the woman who had caused my first marriage to end and I the ex-wife who never quite went away. It could only be the fact that she was now a mother herself. She was imagining how she would feel if it were a seventeen-year-old Elizabeth who had taken off with a man like Davis. She knew – almost – how I felt.

'Thank you, Victoria,' I repeated.

Chapter 19

The storage company in Battersea that Davis had used since the end of his first marriage was thankfully not one of the high-tech ones with CCTV surveillance and security codes, but a low-budget affair involving a man with a bunch of keys and a long row of lock-ups under a railway bridge. At least it was open on Sundays; I didn't think I could have borne a twenty-four-hour delay.

This time I needed no urging from Abi to make the expedition, and convinced her that I could handle the task alone, despite my strapped hand, while she occupied Matthew at Francombe Gardens. Though I had no paperwork or official reference, procedures at the lock-up were relaxed enough for my marriage certificate to be accepted without question and Davis's unit to be opened at once for my inspection. I told the man on duty that I was looking for a missing share certificate and that my husband thought he might have tucked it inside a book.

'Sooner you than me,' he said, as he opened the door to reveal a floor-to-ceiling jigsaw of boxes of various sizes. Most of the outer layer had 'Books' scrawled in black pen on their sides. Noticing my injury, he lugged the top boxes into the alley for me so that I had easy access to every last one, and brought a stool for me to sit on as I worked. I was determined to be thorough – I'd found the fragments hidden among his books, after all. Books were Davis's safe. One after the next I lifted out each volume, cradling it on my lap and using my good hand to flick through the pages for a hidden scrap of paper or phone number scribbled in a margin, any forgotten clue that might get me to Graham or beyond.

Hours passed. It was slow, repetitive work and my neck, back and arms ached badly by the time I came to a box marked 'Miscellaneous'. It was lighter than the previous ones – finally something other than language dictionaries! – and I took the lid off with a gush of fresh hope. Inside was a jumble of objects: a desk lamp coated in dust, a pot of pens and paper clips, an old phone set, some cassette tapes and CDs, a Rolodex of blank cards. Wedged at the bottom, however, was something more promising: a lever arch file so crammed with documents it didn't close properly. I set everything else aside, took a deep breath, and began reading. There was paperwork for a flat rental in Kew fifteen years ago (judging by the dates, this was the last place Davis had lived before he married and moved in with Camilla); a collection of documents from university days, including notification of his First; letters of recommendation for early teaching jobs in the 1980s (these I examined with particular regret, for I'd never asked for any myself when he started coaching Roxy, preferring instead to hail him as the new, multilingual Messiah). Then, almost four hours after I'd arrived, I came to something that might constitute a lead: a bundle of letters to Davis from the firm of solicitors that had handled his divorce from Camilla. If I could just find Camilla's current contact details then I could ask her for Graham's number in York, perhaps discover if there were any other old confidantes I might not know of, too.

I was in luck. Her address appeared on a photocopied document near the top, a management statement of some sort for a flat not far away, near Battersea Park. (Presumably it had been the marital home and Davis had chosen this facility for its convenient proximity.) Skimming the contents of the rest of the

226

correspondence, I saw that their divorce had been swift and undefended. Just as he had told me, he had been the petitioner, his wife's adultery the reason, and a financial agreement had been reached without the need for court proceedings. Though I had only one side of the exchange – and incomplete at that – it was clear that Davis had rejected a number of monetary offers from Camilla's camp until the final deal was struck:

Mr Calder,
We are advised that the respondent has now agreed to your sole request as regards marital assets, and the process of transfer to your name of the deeds to the holiday residence will proceed forthwith.
    We will be in touch again when we are in possession of the aforementioned deeds and other documents . . .

My pulse quickened. I stared at the printed words before me until they no longer made sense to my brain. There was no documentation attached, and a quick scan of the remaining correspondence yielded nothing at all from after this date. Davis must have kept anything further – including the deeds – in his possession. I returned to the original letter and read it once more, still not quite able to believe my eyes. 'Holiday residence': not once in the course of our relationship had Davis made the slightest whisper of its existence.

The girl who answered my ring was evidently hosting some sort of Sunday lunch and told me with merriment that Camilla had not lived in the flat for over three years. I was not, however, the first to have made this mistake, and she had a forwarding address to hand, apparently willing to issue it to all who called – and even give directions. 'Just off Albert Bridge Road, a blue house near the corner, you can't miss it.'
    It was closer to the park than the flat and a considerable

227

upgrade for Camilla, judging by the four smartly painted storeys that rose above a pristine front garden of box hedging and mosaic tiling. The door was answered by a housekeeper or domestic help of some sort, who scurried off to fetch the lady of the house. There were suitcases in the hallway, expensive designer ones piled like children's building blocks in order of size, and I had a sense that my luck had changed. I'd caught the first Mrs Calder just in time.

'Hello, yes, can I help?' The voice was aristocratic and breathy, but when I looked up I saw that her smile was guarded. She was in her early thirties, about my height, though considerably thinner, and had a fresh-faced prettiness that was slightly at odds with the very fashionable beaded top and stiff, dark jeans she wore. Her mid-brown hair, clasped in two loose ponytails below the ears, contained several hundred pounds' worth of golden highlights.

'Are you Camilla . . .?' I realised I didn't know her maiden name, or whether she'd reverted to it after her divorce. 'Formerly Camilla Calder?'

The smile disappeared altogether now and the voice hardened. 'That's right. And you are?'

'I'm so sorry to bother you like this, especially at the weekend, but I'm Davis's wife. His second wife.' My smile faded as she fixed me with a gaze of unsettling intensity. 'My name is Kate. I wondered if I could have a word with you about him.'

She made no move to invite me in, just went on staring. 'Davis married *you*?' There was nothing sneering in her tone, however, only intense puzzlement.

'Yes,' I said, pleasantly. 'You seem surprised.'

My response appeared to jolt her to life and she stepped aside to usher me in. 'Of course, I'm sorry, that must have sounded terrible. Please come in – Kate, did you say? Would you like a coffee or something?'

After my hours in the lock-up I'd lost track of the time and

228

saw that it was now close to four o'clock. I was hungry and thirsty. I eyed the suitcases again and wondered where she was headed. She looked exactly the type to disappear to Marrakech or St Tropez for months on end. Perhaps that was why she was surprised by me; perhaps I looked too unglamorous, not worldly enough to have caught Davis's eye. 'Er, yes, thank you. Coffee would be great.'

She led me down a long red runner into a breakfast room that overlooked the garden. Through an open door to the left of the hallway I caught sight of a well-dressed man in his sixties, patting at the pockets of a blazer as he checked his appearance in a mirror, obviously about to depart. I realised the farewell I'd interrupted was not Camilla's but a guest's, and I began to apologise. 'Should I come back another time?'

'No, no, it's fine.' She settled me into a seat at the dining table, adding, 'Will you excuse me a moment? I must just say goodbye to Daddy.'

She left the room and a moment later her voice carried down the hallway towards me. 'Oh, just an old friend of Annie's who's dropped by for a natter, you don't know her.' Then came the sounds of goodbye kisses and the front door shutting, followed by Camilla's footsteps hastening back towards the kitchen.

'Right, coffee, let me get Magda on to it.'

When she finally took a seat opposite me at the table, my face must have betrayed that I'd heard her lying to her father, for she said at once, 'I thought it better not to introduce you. I didn't want to subject you to some sort of . . .' She searched for the right term and finding it, smiled grimly, '. . . attack by association, shall we say.'

'Ah,' I said, understanding. 'My husband is not popular with your family, then?'

'That's one way of putting it.'

'My husband': my words seemed to settle in the air between us. I would need to stop thinking of him as that, and the sooner the better. Swallowing the lump in my throat, I saw that Camilla was still regarding me with consternation, as though there had to be some mistake to this, if she could only work out what it was.

'Ah, good.' She smiled as Magda, the girl who'd answered the door, brought us mugs of coffee and placed a plate of biscuits in the centre of the polished oak table. It felt like an official border between us. I reached for a biscuit, buying myself a last moment or two, and looked about. Propped against the wall behind Camilla was an enormous canvas of a vase of roses, one of about twenty paintings and framed prints that decorated the room. I remembered Davis's superior comments about her artistic tastes, but there were nothing but beautiful works in evidence here. In fact, it was one of the loveliest rooms I'd ever seen, with curved table tops and antique dressers laden with photographs and jugs of flowers, a pair of armchairs stacked with embroidered cushions and facing each other across a richly coloured kilim. Exactly the kind of feminine sanctuary you'd create if you'd escaped from relationship traumas. The thought jarred: that wasn't quite right, though, was it?

'So, how can I help you?' Camilla asked, before I could develop the query any further.

My quest for Graham's address forgotten for now, I made the spontaneous decision simply to tell the truth. I explained in the simplest possible terms that Davis had disappeared with my daughter. 'I haven't heard from them since they left on Thursday.'

The brightness left her eyes. 'That's terrible. I'm so sorry. How old is she?'

'Seventeen.'

'Seventeen,' she repeated. 'My God, hardly even grown-up.'

'I know.' I felt confident of my first impression of the woman before me. She was privileged, certainly, a daddy's girl, perhaps, but she clearly had a heart. She wasn't going to be able to help, but her sympathy would be unconditional. So sure was I of this judgment that I was quite taken aback by what she said next.

'Well, I suppose since it's you who's come to me, we can be totally open about this.' She looked at me expectantly, apparently awaiting permission to proceed.

'Of course,' I agreed. 'I'd like to be open.'

She sighed, obviously relieved. 'That's why I was so shocked when I saw you. I mean, you're obviously not old or anything . . .'

'Me?' I was bewildered by her comment. 'I'm thirty-nine.'

She nodded. 'Exactly.'

'I'm sorry, I'm not sure I understand what that's got to do with anything.'

But she didn't seem to hear me, continuing her own thread. 'I got too old for him, as well, you know, and I was still in my twenties. Crazy!' She leaned towards me with deep, empathetic eyes. 'The fact is that Davis is attracted to younger women, always was, always will be.'

'Younger women? What do you mean?' I blinked as adrenaline spurted into my bloodstream. Surely she couldn't be suggesting that something like this had happened before, that the disaster I was dealing with had, in fact, been inevitable?

'I feel for you,' she went on, 'I really do. You're well and truly caught up in it. I mean, if it weren't your daughter, you could just walk away and try to forget you ever met him. Like I did.'

She rocked back in her seat. For a moment she looked quite distraught, as though any walking away of her own had been done just hours ago, not years, but I was much too confused by what she'd said to be able to address her sudden distress.

'What do you mean, "Walk away"?' I thought of the solicitor's letters I'd held in my hands just an hour or so ago. 'I thought it was Davis who filed for divorce? He told me it was you who met someone else. He wasn't involved with anyone . . .'

She nodded, composing herself. 'I did begin a new relationship before we split up, that's true. But he'd been playing around with students for a long time before that.'

I felt a surge of revulsion in my stomach. 'Students? You mean more than one? How many, exactly?'

'I don't know, to be honest. But none that lasted. He certainly didn't run away with any of them, nothing like this.'

We stared at each other. Between the pain I'd stirred in her and my own growing horror, I wasn't sure who was expected to comfort whom, or whether either of us was even capable of it at this point.

'My therapist explained it to me once,' she said, quietly. 'She said he must have had a defining love for someone of that age the same ended in some kind of trauma, probably when he was that age himself. Seventeen or eighteen. It's a kind of arrested development thing.' She paused, took a biscuit from the plate, put it down again without taking a bite. 'But I don't know if I believe that. It sounds too much like an excuse. Personally, I think it's more of a power thing. You know, the greater the age gap, the more control he has. He gets older, but the girls never do.'

I was about to retch, had to swallow the reflex, painfully, audibly, to stop myself. As I looked at Camilla and the glorious colour that framed her, all I could think about were the times, so many times, that I'd angled for snippets of Davis's innermost desires, pressed him to confess to me, imagined those desires for myself, believed that they concerned me!

'Was he ever in trouble?' My voice was hardly more than a whisper. 'I mean, has anyone ever complained to the authorities about him?'

The question brought a spark of anger to her eyes. 'You mean the parents? I don't think they ever knew. It wasn't as if he was silly enough to get anyone pregnant. I can only assume that most of the time he insisted on absolute secrecy. He was married, after all.'

'What about the girls, didn't they report him?'

She snorted. 'As far as I could work out, the only time they complained was when he ended it. I remember the phone calls, all the wrong numbers, how keen he was to get a mobile before the rest of us had one. He always covered up, of course, claimed they were just giving him a hard time about exam results. That should have been a clue in itself – he *always* got them their grades, always got whatever university it was their parents were so desperate to get them into.'

I blinked away the sudden image of myself and Alistair, discussing Roxy's education like a pair of government ministers, scheming to get her to her work placement, forcing her future upon her. 'So you never met them when they came to the house for lessons?'

She shook her head. 'He never taught at home, at least not in the evenings when I was there. But one of them did turn up at the flat once in the summer after A-levels and I could just tell there was something going on. For starters, her sessions had ended by that point, she was just waiting for her results. And she was all dressed up in the middle of the day, like she was going to a big party. But it wasn't even that, actually, it was more . . . she was just so defiant in the way she looked at me, almost contemptuous, as if I didn't matter. It was frightening, really.'

I thought of Marianne, and, less eagerly, of Roxy, the way they'd treated Abi that time and plenty of others besides, including me. Camilla's description could fit either of them.

'You know, if it's any consolation, these girls really don't think of themselves as victims. They see themselves as seductresses, like having an affair with a teacher is something they want to tick off their list, no different from a gap year or something. I don't know your daughter, obviously, but I'd guess she's probably enjoying the drama, sees it as a bit of excitement, like she's in a movie or something.'

I nodded, understanding her better than I ever thought I would. There was no doubt in my mind that she was telling me the truth. I thought again of the divorce papers I'd seen. 'I don't understand, though. If all this was going on, why didn't you divorce him sooner? Why wait for him to set things in motion?'

She smiled, sadly. 'I did throw him out, which you could say got the ball rolling, I suppose. But he was cleverer than me. My affair was easier to prove, he had a co-respondent's identity and I didn't. And anyway, even if I did have names and addresses, I wasn't about to hunt down a young girl and ruin her life.'

I nodded, feeling admiration for her as well as sympathy. I didn't think I would have been a tenth as forgiving of Davis's teenagers were my own not directly involved in this nightmare. I would have judged them equally culpable. But Camilla was remembering herself at that age; she hadn't been much older than Roxy when Davis had selected her, she knew she couldn't have been equally culpable

'He ended up holding all the cards,' she said, sadly. 'And he knew it was always going to be easier to get what he wanted from me if he was the one to start proceedings.'

Seeing my opening, I tried to pull myself together and remember that I'd come here for specific information. And I had to get it, however badly I felt for having ruined her day. 'That's the reason I'm here, actually. That holiday place of yours he won in the divorce. I'm starting to think that might be where they are now.'

A cast of bitterness settled in her eyes and I had a feeling this might turn out to be as far as we would go in this conversation. 'There's only one way to find out, I suppose. Go there.'

I pulled a face. 'The thing is, I don't actually know where "there" is.'

She gaped at me. 'You mean he never told you where his own house was?'

'No.' Something occurred to me then, something that could explain why Davis had never mentioned the property to me. 'Oh, but he might have sold it, mightn't he?' And even before she shook her head, I loathed myself for thinking of excuses for him.

'No,' she said, emphatically. 'He would never sell it. It was his obsession.'

I nodded. 'I remember him saying he spent time with your family in Paris, I wondered if it might be there?'

'No, not Paris. On the coast. Ile de Ré.'

'Ile de Ré?' The name sounded familiar but I couldn't quite place it. Camilla's eye drifted to a painting behind me and I turned to look. It was in brightly coloured pastels, boats in a harbour, with words in French scrawled across the top.

'It was my grandmother's house. We used to go there every August when I was little. When she died she left it to me. Davis loved it as much as we all did. We spent our honeymoon there. I never would have agreed to let it go, but he didn't want anything else, even though he could have had so much more. And I just wanted the whole thing to be over . . .' She broke off, corrected her posture, took a series of deep, controlled breaths as though in meditation. 'But there we are. I made a mistake and there's nothing I can do about it.'

'I'm so sorry,' I said, 'I feel terrible bringing all of this up.'

She smiled. 'No, it's fine. It's not your fault. I was taken in just the same as you. I just hope you're right about them being in France. Let me write down the address for you.' She reached for pen and paper. 'Fifteen rue de Loix, Saint-Martin-de-Ré. He's disconnected the old phone line, that I do know, but I'll write my number here, in case you have any problems finding the house.'

'Thank you, I really appreciate it.'

She showed me to the door. 'We had a conversation, you know, at the end. He tried to explain how he felt in his own pathetic way.'

'Oh yes?'

'He said that he would know when he found her. They were his words: "I'll just know her when I find her and nothing else will matter." Not what a wife wants to hear, but then, well, I guess you know that.'

We looked sadly at one another. 'Right, well, just let me know if there's anything else I can tell you.'

'Oh!' In the nick of time I remembered. 'There was something else. I wanted to ask you about Graham.'

'Graham?'

'The friend in York. I thought he might know something about all of this, Davis might even have gone there. I don't suppose you still have an up-to-date number for him, do you?'

She looked at me in bewilderment, a little as she had an hour or so ago when we'd first faced each other on the doorstep. 'I do, yes, but I don't think there's much point dragging him into this. He and Davis haven't spoken for years, not since before the divorce.'

The two men must have kept in touch separately, then, I thought, presumably to spare Camilla's feelings. That was difficult. 'OK, well if you wouldn't mind letting me have the number anyway? Just the last one you have? I don't want to leave any stone unturned at this stage.'

'I don't know, Kate. It's a bit awkward with Graham.' Her shoulders drooped; she seemed suddenly exhausted by me. 'Look, leave me your number. Let me call him first and find out if he's willing to speak to you. If he is, I'll give him your details.'

It was a frustrating proviso, not to mention risky – what if Davis and Roxy were with him after all and overheard any of her phone call, or if Graham went straight to them with news of the enquiry? – but given how generous she had been, how lucky I was to have this new French lead, I had no choice but to agree. 'All right, but could you do it today, maybe? I know it's a lot to ask, but it would really help me out.'

She nodded. 'I'll have to wait till he wakes up, obviously. It's the middle of the night in Singapore.'

I started. '*Singapore?*'

'Yes, he moved out there in the spring.'

'But . . .' I swallowed. 'I thought he was still in York. Davis saw him about a month ago, the last weekend in September, I

236

think it was. He went up to visit him in York to tell him about the wedding.'

Camilla frowned. 'I don't think so, Kate. Graham left the UK in March and as far as I know he hasn't been back to Britain since. And there's no way he would want to go to Davis's wedding, you'll have to take my word for that.'

'Right.' I tried to get this straight. Graham didn't live in York, he lived in the Far East. Where, then, had Davis gone that weekend in September? Obviously not Singapore. Did he have a second friend up in York, someone he'd met through Graham, perhaps? My knees buckled a split second before my brain supplied the answers and I reached for the door to steady myself: oh my God, how grotesquely obvious it was! The weekend when Davis had supposedly been in York, just weeks – days – before he married me, Roxy had been away, too, on the Saturday, at Marianne's house. I remembered it clearly because Matt had had a sleepover at Ruben's house, a last-minute invitation, and I had enjoyed an evening in on my own, wallowing in the wonderfulness of my new life, thinking how I should relish the solitude while I still had the chance. They must have been together. Had it been . . . had it been, their *first time*?

'Kate? Are you all right? Do you want to come back in?' Camilla peered with concern at my face and I realised my mouth was trembling. With a terrific effort I managed to control the spasms.

'I'm fine, thank you. Forget about Graham, you don't need to phone him. They're obviously not with him if he's in Singapore.'

'OK, if you're sure.'

'I am. Goodbye. And thank you again for everything.'

'Bye, Kate. And good luck.'

Sucking painfully at the cool, still air, I managed somehow to stumble the short distance to Albert Bridge Road, where, ignoring the glances of passers-by, I bent double as if to vomit on to the pavement. Across the street was an entrance to Battersea Park – I could see an empty bench just inside the gates – and I stepped mindlessly into the traffic towards it. The instant blare of a car horn made me jump violently off the ground before freezing where I landed. The driver gestured angrily to me to get out of the way.

'Sorry, sorry!' I made a second dash for the park gates and reached the empty seat. I slumped into it, crying out the words: 'How could you do this, Davis, how could you do it? She is my *daughter*!' But my throat was dry, the words virtually soundless.

My brain sorted images at frightening speed, a twenty-second summary of the events of the last month. He'd been different when he'd come back from Graham's, more relaxed, readier for what lay ahead. Happier. As for Roxy, I couldn't remember anything about her return from Marianne's, so caught up had I been in Davis's arrival home, in my magical new romance, in myself. Where had he taken her that weekend? To the secret house in France, or somewhere closer to home? *Had* it been their first night together? Had that been her first night with any lover? Or was I still light years from the truth?

Unable to bear the mental image of the two of them together a second longer, my mind's eye alighted automatically on Marianne. She was smiling at me, that sly, knowing, adult smile of hers, and my chest heaved with fresh fury as if she really were standing in front of me. If she had been used as an alibi, then she most certainly must have known what she was covering up, the worst kind of deceit, the most sordid of betrayals. I wanted to shake it out of her, get her to admit that she had willingly colluded in this, that she was as immoral as Davis himself. My arms flailed violently as I imagined falling on her, attacking her, and I heard myself cry out again, full-voiced this time, to no one, to all of them. Then I closed my eyes, brought my arms to my sides, concentrated on breathing. I was losing my mind. Marianne was not to blame for this. She was not the adult here. This was Davis's doing, Davis's and mine.

238

'I made a mistake,' Camilla had said, 'and there's nothing I can do about it.' But hers had been understandable, forgivable; she'd been young, no wiser than Roxy was now. But I was almost four decades old, I should have known better. Completely overwhelmed by the enormity of my own wrong decisions – and by the brutality of Davis's – I finally gave in to the sobs that had threatened since the moment I'd woken that morning and discovered I could feel again. The defeat was so crushing, so complete, I could have slithered to the ground and curled into a ball. At that moment in Battersea Park I could willingly have died.

'Excuse me? Are you OK?' I looked up to see a woman's face angled in concern towards mine. She was about my age, though considerably better turned out. One elegant, leather-encased hand clutched the glove belonging to the other, as though she'd removed it in readiness, offering me her bare fingers as one might an animal in distress.

'I'm fine,' I said, sniffing. 'I've just had some bad news.'

'I've got a tissue you can have.' She handed it to me and hovered for a second, facing that hazardous dilemma of whether or not to stay and hear out the details of a stranger's heartache. The next moment she was moving reluctantly away.

Raising the tissue to my face I saw that my hands were balled into angry fists, sending whooshes of pain up my injured arm. I had to redirect this anguish, I had to keep moving, keep searching. What was I doing, allowing myself to fall to pieces again? I'd almost been run over a second time – and then what? There'd be no one for Roxy to return to, no one for Matt.

Look forward, I repeated to myself, that's what I told clients all the time when they came in stricken with life's injustices. Do something constructive, breathe, act, move! It was the only way to cope with trauma, with grief.

At home, even before I got out the atlas to look, I remembered that Ile de Ré was one of the islands off the coast of La Rochelle.

I'd noticed it on the plane as we came in to land, a long, flat stretch of field and forest trimmed with sandy beaches. Later in the week, when Davis had suggested a day trip, I'd mentioned it again, but he'd dismissed it – just a beach place, he'd said, nothing to do at this time of year. Instead he'd booked tickets for the crossing to another island, Ile d'Aix, where Napoleon had spent his last days in France before surrendering to the British.

I'd been happy to agree.

Chapter 20

Of course everything that had happened in the past six months had new resonance now, not just the missing weekend in September, everything. Every glance Davis had cast in Roxy's direction, every comment he'd made to her and she to him. And every conversation between us, too, like the one we'd had about starting a family. It was soon after he had proposed to me and our relationship had developed so quickly we'd hardly thought to discuss such defining matters in any formal kind of a way (unlike Alistair and Victoria and their mutually satisfactory pre-nup. Well, I could sneer no longer at their unromantic clauses; they, after all, were still together).

The subject had come up only by accident. I was remarking at the sheer pace of the summer's events, marvelling at the way life could suddenly accelerate and overtake you, delivering everything to you in one go.

'There are years when everything happens, and it always seems to be summer, too, have you noticed? I remember the year I graduated from college, moved to London, married Alistair and become pregnant with Roxy, all in the space of three months. Five years' worth of life in one summer!'

Davis smiled indulgently, as he often did when I became animated in this way. 'In for a penny, as they say . . .'

I didn't add that the next of my hotspots had been the one that contained a roll-call of events oddly symmetrical with the earlier one, except this time I'd moved house, had a baby and lost my husband.

Often people I counselled at work would present me with a timeline of disasters in which a domino effect was all too clear to see: the bank error led to the credit-rating problem led to the house repossession led to the marriage breakdown led to the alcohol dependency led to the loss of access to the children, right up to the moment when they came to be sitting in front of me with a cup of tea and a box of tissues.

The thought sobered me somewhat. 'Anyway,' I said to Davis, 'this is obviously one of those years. When I think how much has happened in such a short time, it takes my breath away. What next, I wonder?'

That was when I noticed the look of apprehension on his face, as though he'd only just grasped what I was saying. 'You're not thinking of getting pregnant this time around as well, are you?'

'God, no!' Then, realising how uncompromising that sounded, I tried to backtrack. 'I mean, that's not what *you* want, is it?'

He gave one of his wry chuckles. 'To be honest, Kate, I have no aspirations in that department and it's a relief to hear you say the same.' He paused. 'I suppose I've always thought my teaching was my way of doing my bit. I really don't feel the need to have children of my own.'

'Well, I think that's very noble,' I said to him. 'After all, there is a population crisis in the world.'

How could I have been so smug, so pleased with myself, so deaf to the clues? 'Doing my bit'! If only the words had been transferred to the printed page, set in italics as a warning. *Clear and present danger, Kate, do something!*

But, even then, would I have allowed myself to notice?

*

The next day was Monday, four days since they'd left. I woke with red, inflamed eyes and an ache in the left side of my ribcage that, impossible though I knew it to be, seemed to pulse in time with the contractions of my heart.

'Why is your face all weird?' Matthew asked at breakfast.

'It's swollen up a bit after the accident,' I said. 'But it's fine, don't worry.' He was still young enough to take me at my word and not worry.

His next question was more problematic. 'Why isn't Roxy back?'

'She's still staying at Marianne's,' I said.

He frowned up at me across the kitchen table. Fridays and Saturdays were one thing, but for Roxy to have stayed out on a Sunday night there had to be a special reason. 'Why?'

I delivered my prepared lines. 'Because they need to spend some time together. They're working on an important school project.'

'Another play? Can I go?'

'I'm not sure what it is.' I stood up. 'More toast?'

He wiped crumbs from his mouth. 'I'm full. When will she be back?'

I sat back down. 'Soon, I promise.'

'The same time as Davis?'

'Possibly. I'll try to speak to her today and find out. No need to worry, though, sweetheart, and no need to mention it to anyone at school, OK?'

I was determined to follow Roxy's example and close ranks. Alistair, Victoria, Abi and Camilla: that was as far as this scandal would go – for now. Others in my life, my parents (thankfully now on holiday on the other side of the world and spared any part of this horror), my colleagues, all could be kept out of this in the short term.

I watched as Matthew lifted his chin, as he always did when an idea struck. 'You know what, Mum? If I had my own mobile I could phone Roxy myself.'

'That's true. But you don't. Now, ready for school? Where are your shoes? Did you clean them yesterday?' I beamed at him, cheered despite myself by how easily he had dropped the interrogation in favour of this ongoing campaign of his for a mobile phone; that meant he hadn't yet picked up on the seriousness of the situation. I knew I couldn't keep him in the dark for long. He was nine, almost ten, and no fool. In any case, as far as my new marriage was concerned, there was little need to hide from him the fact that it had ended. Nothing was going to change that; it was over between Davis and me, there was no way back. I would tell him soon, not the full story, but a simplified version of it, before he overheard something he shouldn't.

Once he was safely at school, I could be more open in my operations. I had set up HQ in the front flat, moving Roxy's laptop from her desk to Davis's. Only after Alistair and Victoria had left on Saturday had I noticed that his computer was gone, which at least explained Roxy's promptness in clearing out her email. It also meant I couldn't look up contacts for any of the schools or private homes in which he'd taught. We'd never had a separate landline installed in the front flat; all of his business had been done by email or on his mobile. I wondered if he intended letting his clients know of his absence, whether he even knew how long it would last. He'd always been so dedicated to his work, it seemed quite out of character for him to abandon his business in this way, to leave the likes of Jasmina without his regular support. But then I could no longer claim to know his character, could I? And Jasmina may not even exist for all I knew; she might simply have been a story to impress me, or, more likely, to encourage me to grant my own daughter greater independence – independence that had served Davis so well.

'Forget him,' Abi had said last night, when I'd returned from Battersea in obvious disarray. She'd taken one look at me and gathered me into a hug. 'I know it's impossible, but you have to do it. You have to focus, for Roxy's sake.' She lowered her voice and motioned to the living room, where Matthew sat watching his cartoons. 'And for his, as well. He needs his sister back.'

Looking at her kind, eager face, gratitude ripped through me. 'I know,' I said. 'I won't let him get away with it. I won't have this family broken up again.'

But now Abi was at work and I was on my own again, my conviction wavered. I was stationed at Davis's desk, settled in his chair, how could I not imagine him sitting in this spot day after day, sending emails, making notes, checking something online? How could I not imagine his reaction every time there was a knock at his door, his posture stiffening, hope suspended as he waited to discover which of us it was?

Abi was right. If I did not focus, I would not survive this, it was as simple as that. I looked at my list. My first job was to ring Alistair to report the previous day's findings.

'Get over to France right away,' he instructed. 'They're obviously there. We'll take Matt.'

'But how will you manage the school run?'

'I'll drop him in the mornings on my way to the office and Vic can pick him up in the afternoons, no problem. Just let me know his after-school schedule and I'll make sure she's there at the right time.'

'That would be great,' I said, not quite quick enough to suppress my insecurity at the thought of Matthew spending additional time with Victoria. It was an old fear of mine, and a defining one: that Alistair might decide he wanted to take Matthew away from me. And how easy it would now be to demonstrate that I was subject to the kind of errors of judgment that put minors at risk! I imagined the authorities labelling Davis a paedophile, interrogating my son to find out what he might have seen.

I rubbed at my sore eyes. I was at it again already. I had to keep this sort of terror at bay, just as I had to my broken heart. Nothing else mattered except locating Roxy and bringing her home. 'Thank you,' I said to Alistair. 'I'm just about to look up flights right this minute.'

'Good. And what about the mate in York? Did you get his details? I can always whizz up there myself one evening while you're away. Call it a two-pronged attack, eh, a double raid.'

'Oh, that came to nothing,' I said, hastily. 'He's moved away, apparently. They're definitely not with him.'

'France it is then. Right, let's check in again later, shall we?'

'Yes, no, hang on a minute.' There was a pause while I considered once more the dilemma I'd faced since leaving Battersea yesterday. I had still not quite resolved it in a long night of tossing and turning, but now I saw I had no choice. I couldn't keep secrets on Davis's behalf; he was the enemy now, and he didn't deserve a shred of my loyalty. 'There's something else.'

'What?' Alistair's tone sharpened. 'Come on, you need to tell me everything, Kate.' He stopped short of adding an 'or else', but I knew the alternative. He would take the investigation away from me, hire some horrible detective and consign me to a period of helpless dread. 'It's just that Camilla said Davis has a bit of a history of this sort of thing. He's had relationships with students before.'

'*What*? The fucking pervert!'

'And I was wondering if it might be worth checking if he has any kind of . . .' – the words faded in my windpipe – '. . . criminal record. If he has, then maybe the police will take the situation a bit more seriously and help us get her back sooner. A lawyer would know how to find out.'

I waited for the explosion, but for once it didn't come. 'Fine, I'll ask Victoria.' Evidently I was not the only one curbing my instincts. 'I'll call you back.'

While I waited, I rang Roxy's school on the other line and told the office she would be off sick for a few days and that I would be sure to keep them up to date on her recovery. Mrs Prentice was surprisingly unquestioning. There had been two incidents lately of sixth formers ending up in hospital after parties and getting their stomachs pumped; perhaps she suspected that this might also be the cause of Roxy's sudden malady. Well, it was certainly less sensational than the truth.

I'd just hung up when the phone rang. Alistair already, far too promptly for me to have prepared myself for the worst. 'I spoke to Victoria and she says the Criminal Records Bureau has a disclosure service that gives access to the police national computer and other organisations. It's for employers to check whether someone applying for a job with their company has any kind of record.'

'And has he?' My chest rose, braced for the blow.

'We don't know for sure,' Alistair said. 'You need the consent of the person you're screening to be able to run it. But Victoria says there's very little chance he's ever even been reprimanded.'

'Really? Why?'

'Well, if he's worked for any kind of school or educational institution over the past few years, they would have insisted on a check. Individual parents might ask for that, too. We're interviewing nannies at the moment and the police check comes as standard. So I think we can assume he's clean.'

'OK.' All of a sudden I was breathless; the force of my own relief had come as a shock to me.

'That doesn't mean Roxy should be anywhere near him, though,' Alistair added. 'We've got to find her, Kate. I don't care what we have to do to get rid of him, I just want her back.'

'Agreed,' I said. 'I'm going to Marianne's this evening to see if I can get anything out of her.'

'Why wait? Go and grab her at school now and then you can get straight off to France.'

'No, I don't want to cause a scene at the school. Better to get her at home, I thought, when her mother's in. I'll go to France tomorrow, after I've dropped Matt at school.'

'Good thinking. Well, make sure you don't give anything

away when you do. We don't want that little slut tipping him off. He's probably got her under his spell, as well.'

I winced. 'Alistair, please, she's not a "slut".' If she were, then I couldn't imagine what labels might reasonably be applied to our own daughter.

'Just play dumb, OK?' There was an unmistakable hint in his tone that he trusted I wouldn't find this too hard to do. But I knew from long experience with Alistair that I needed to choose my fights – and this was not one of them.

Marianne lived in a smarter-than-average terraced house by a greener-than-usual north London park. The shutters were still open and lights blazed within from a pair of spherical glass chandeliers. I was grateful I'd had the day to prepare myself for the confrontation: now that I was certain she had known of those early, treacherous developments between Roxy and Davis, I didn't think I would have been able to conceal my antipathy towards her without several hours' rehearsal. Even now I couldn't be sure of my performance.

In any case, first I had to get through her mother. I had never met Naomi Suter and was not at all surprised that my first impression of her was of a potentially tricky woman. She was, after all, Marianne's mother. She had a strong, broad face, her features a little sharper than Marianne's, a little more predatory, but still very attractively arranged. I had not phoned in advance and she invited me in with the polite caution of someone called to a business meeting without having been forwarded the agenda; she didn't like not knowing what was expected of her. I was instantly doubtful that I would win her support, as I had Victoria's and Camilla's, on sororial sympathy alone.

She ushered me into a glamorous open-plan living room in which a large gilt-framed mirror over the fireplace reflected the light from the nearby chandelier, sending it dazzling in all directions. Naomi's well-kept figure trailed a scent of rich, sweet rose and I became aware that I smelled a little of stale sweat. On the dining table at the far end of the room a laptop was open next to a pile of files, crowned, somewhat unsteadily, by a large glass of white wine. Naomi picked it up and held it with both hands against her chest as though cuddling a guinea pig.

'Can I get you one?'

'No, thank you. I'm taking painkillers for my wrist.'

'Yes, I noticed the strap. What have you done to it?'

'I was knocked over by a cyclist.'

'Oh, yes, nasty.' She spoke as though such incidents were routine and this was not the first of its kind she'd heard of today. 'Well, if you're sure about the vino. I used to have a no-drinking-on-Mondays rule.' She laughed. 'That was before I realised Monday was the day you need it the most.'

She seated me by her side on a pale sofa under the window. 'So, is this about the girls? Roxy's not coming over tonight, is she? I thought Marianne was meeting her at the club, or wherever it is they're filming.' She sighed. 'I assume yours is as hazy with the details as mine?'

'Hazier, I would guess.' I didn't know whether to be relieved or frustrated that she obviously had no idea what was going on. 'Roxy's left home,' I said, baldly, 'with my husband, Davis.'

'You mean . . .?' She gasped, getting it straight away. 'My God, how dreadful. I assume you've called the police?'

'Yes, but they're not prepared to investigate it.' I explained briefly the legal position.

'But what about other agencies, the child-protection people?' Her thoughts, like Victoria's, were instantly constructive and I cringed at the memory of my own initial paralysis (and I the one who worked as a professional advice-giver!). 'You might find that some of them will treat the age thing differently.'

'Possibly.' But the look that passed between us only confirmed that no one, however well meaning, could seriously believe that a seventeen-year-old girl in twenty-first-century London was a child, least of all either of the two specimens *we* had raised.

'We decided that it might be easier and more discreet to track her down ourselves. Roxy's father is keen to keep this quiet so as not to affect her studies. We haven't told the school yet, so I hope you'll keep this confidential.'

'Of course, goes without saying.' Naomi rolled her eyes. 'We're not exactly bosom buddies anyway. They were a pain in the arse over Marianne taking time off to shoot that commercial last year.'

I nodded diplomatically. At the time I had thought it extraordinary that any mother with an academically bright daughter would prioritise the filming of a cosmetics commercial over schoolwork, but now I would have given my eye teeth to be in a position where that constituted my worst error of judgment.

She cocked her head to the ceiling, presumably indicating Marianne's bedroom above. 'Well, I suppose you're wondering if my darling angel knows anything about this little adventure?'

I nodded. 'Anything that might help me find Roxy. She may not even realise she knows something.' I thought it best not to expect Naomi to share my view that her daughter had been party to every last detail of Roxy's deceit.

'I'll call her down. You're lucky to catch her, actually, she must be running late.' Naomi sprang up and called up the stairs in a brisk, no-nonsense way, as though bringing a dog to heel. A minute later Marianne strolled into the room with such a conspicuous lack of surprise it was clear to me that she had been anticipating this visit. The geometric patterned mini-dress and heavy eye make up she wore were for the camera's benefit, however, not mine. Unwittingly proving her mother's and my exchange two minutes ago, she looked at least twenty-five.

'Hi, Mrs Calder.' She was probably the only person in my brief marriage, bar those at the guesthouse in La Rochelle, to have called me by Davis's name and it infuriated me that she had, knowing as she did that the union had already been blown apart. Part of her innocent act, presumably, or more likely simple malice. Alistair had been right: I couldn't let on that I knew about the French house. This girl knew exactly which side she was on.

Neither she nor Naomi made any move to take a seat, so I stood up to join them. 'Hello, Marianne. I'm sure you can guess why I'm here.'

She widened her eyes, huge with smoky eyeshadow. 'Actually, no. Are you guys going out? I didn't realise you were chums.'

'Kate is here because Roxy has disappeared,' Naomi said, sourly. She cracked her wineglass down on a nearby surface and Marianne winced theatrically at the sound. 'We "guys" are not going anywhere, and nor are you unless you tell us what's going on.'

'Hmm, yeah, she wasn't in school today . . .' Marianne wrinkled her brow as though the thought had only just struck her, but her lack of concern was completely wrong. This was equally obvious to Naomi, whose face darkened like the sky before a thunderstorm. 'Let's not pretend you don't know anything about this. If you didn't, you'd be as distraught as Kate is. Have you spoken to Roxy today? Have you spoken to her at all since . . .' She swung around to me. 'When was it, Kate?'

'Thursday,' I said. 'They went missing on Thursday.' I hoped the word 'missing' might frighten the girl, but Marianne merely made a little moue at me and shrugged in exactly the way Roxy did when she found herself momentarily outsmarted. Win some, lose some, that was their position. I was alarmed by how badly I wanted to hurt her, to see her fall apart and cry.

'Marianne!' Naomi's fury was rather less contained than mine. 'Do you realise this is extremely serious? If you know something, you *must* tell us. Otherwise you could be charged with obstructing the course of justice.'

At this Marianne tilted back her sweet, heart-shaped face and tinkled with laughter. 'Oh, don't be so ridiculous, Naomi.'

I had known that she called her mother by her Christian name – more than once it had been cited by Roxy as evidence that their rapport was stronger than our own – but it was still a surprise to hear it and, more than that, it had the effect of making my heart sink deep into its cavity. With that one word any sense of authority Naomi might have over her daughter was eliminated, any sense that there was anything familial to bind them at all. Marianne might have been a flatmate sticking her head around the door to say goodbye.

Naomi reached for her glass again and took a large mouthful. I wished now I'd taken her up on her offer. 'Look, Marianne, this isn't a game. Roxy is in big trouble.'

'I don't see why,' Marianne said, frowning. 'I mean, she hasn't done anything illegal, has she?'

Naomi pounced, almost spitting. 'So you do know what she's done then?'

The pout returned. 'I didn't say that. You're twisting my words.'

'Where are they, for Christ's sake? We're talking about an abduction here, not some weekend away! Have you seen them since last Thursday? Answer the question!'

'Please stop barking at me, Naomi,' Marianne said, coolly. She regarded her mother with actorly relish. 'Honestly, you're acting like I'm in the dock.'

'As far as I'm concerned you *are* in the dock. Now, where the hell are they?'

'If you insist on speaking to me in this accusing manner then, you know what? I choose to exercise my right to remain silent.'

'Well, how very convenient. I would never have guessed.'

I suppressed a sigh. There was a honed quality to this exchange, a sense of competitive debate. (Even their perfumes competed for dominance, Naomi's that cloying rose, Marianne's

252

something muskier, more male.) I guessed that Naomi was as angry with Marianne for having left her out of the loop as she was for her daughter's part in any wrongdoing. Marianne's performance, meanwhile, was quite chilling. To think that I'd felt guilty for my original wariness of her, that I'd worked hard to suppress my negative instincts, when all along she'd been laughing at me – and encouraging Roxy to do the same. That look that had passed between us at the wedding, when she'd been holding court with Jacob, it must have been Davis they'd been discussing, Davis who had made her boyfriend seem suddenly so unsatisfactory. 'Ask Roxy,' she'd said to Jacob. Ask Roxy!

'How long have they been having a relationship?' I asked, my voice clenched. 'Just tell me that, Marianne.' Responding to the change in tone, mother and daughter looked at me with matching expressions of pity. (Naomi's, at least, contained genuine care.)

'I have no idea, I'm afraid,' Marianne said, agreeably. 'I honestly didn't know they were. We really don't tell each other everything, you know. We are independent beings, believe it or not.'

At this point Naomi lost her cool completely, slammed her palm down on her own thigh and began shouting angrily. 'Oh, don't give us that! I want you to get on your phone and call her right now! Do you hear me?'

Marianne stood firm. 'I tried her earlier, she isn't answering.'

'Then try again. Right now, go on, do it! Otherwise you can wave tonight's outing goodbye. And everything else for the rest of this week.'

'There's really no point, Naomi, believe me.'

'I don't believe you, that's the problem.' Naomi reached out her hands as if to frisk her daughter, but Marianne stepped nimbly out of reach. 'Where's your mobile? Here, give me it to me and *I'll* call.'

To my great surprise Marianne willingly produced her phone,

even holding it up to us so we could witness her selection – 'Rox Mob' – before she hit 'Call'. Naomi immediately snatched it from her and handed it to me, just in time for me to hear the words I'd heard a hundred times over the last few days: 'Your call has been forwarded to the network's voicemail service . . .'

'It's still off,' I said.

Marianne took back the phone. Her fingers, when they touched mine, were smooth and cool. 'See? I'm not a liar.'

'You've obviously put in a false number,' Naomi glowered.

Marianne sighed. 'Believe what you like, I really don't care, but that *is* her number. Check it again if you like.'

But I didn't need to see the digits to believe her. All this told me was that mine were not the only calls Roxy was leaving unanswered – she was possibly avoiding all contact for the time being to allow for just this sort of scenario. She probably had a new phone, anyway, a pre-paid thing we'd never be able to trace. Unless . . . My mind sparked suddenly. Unless the France lead was correct and she was simply unable to pick up calls there. Her bills went through my household accounts and she did not, to my knowledge, have international roaming services on her phone.

'Have you spoken to her at all on this number since last week?' I demanded. 'It's important, Marianne.'

'I've said already, no. Would you like it in writing?'

'Yes, we would!' Naomi snapped. 'What about email and Facebook and all that other stuff? Have you looked this evening?'

'No, I've been busy getting ready!' Marianne was tired of us now, checking her watch with restless eyes. It was a man's heavy model with a large face and wide leather strap that made her wrist look fragile, like a child's. 'Look, I'm going to be late if I don't leave in the next two minutes. They'll have closed the doors.'

I'd had enough of this. I could no longer bear to look at the girl. 'It's OK,' I said, reaching for my bag and turning to Naomi. 'I'm leaving. I think I know where they are, anyway. I suppose I was just hoping Marianne might confirm it, but clearly that's not going to happen. Well, thank you anyway.'

'Oh, really? So where d'you think they are?' Naomi asked on cue. Marianne, though now dismissed, also waited for my answer, and just a little too alertly, if my antennae were still working.

I kept my tone as natural I as could. 'York. I think they might be with a friend of Davis's who lives there. You won't know him, Marianne, he didn't come to the wedding. I haven't met him myself, actually, but I know they're very close. I'm heading up there first thing tomorrow, so hopefully I'll be able to bring her straight back and all of this will be over.'

'That's great, why didn't you say earlier?' Naomi turned on Marianne afresh. 'Does that sound right? Have you heard anything about this?'

Marianne shrugged. 'Possibly.'

'What do you mean, "possibly"? I won't have you sending Kate off on some wild goose chase.'

'I'm not sending her anywhere,' Marianne protested. 'For God's sake, can I *please* go?'

'Just remember, I'm on your back,' her mother called after her.

'Yeah, yeah. Enjoy the view.'

Naomi saw me to the door. 'Kate, I'm sorry about this, I really am, she's not normally so obnoxious. Honestly, I could strangle her.'

'No,' I said. 'Please don't worry. I'm used to it. She's been more helpful than she realises.'

She peered at me with open curiosity. 'Really? How so?'

I wavered for a moment, tempted to tell her about the French house, then I decided against it. This was clearly not going to be the end of the matter between the two of them and any information I gave Naomi in confidence would almost certainly be blurted out in a future row, just as it would were the situation reversed and it was I who'd been asked to confront Roxy. Their dynamic wasn't so different from ours, after all, laughable that I'd ever imagined it might be. The only difference was that Marianne was still here. 'I just mean that if she *is* in touch with Roxy, if she *has* spoken to her these last few days, then that means wherever Roxy is, she's obviously not in any danger. She's safe.'

Naomi nodded, 'Yes, that's the main thing, isn't it?' And she patted my arm in reassurance, not noticing it was the bandaged one. It was all I could do not to cry out in pain.

Back home I checked on Matt, in Abi's care for the last time before he was handed over to Alistair tomorrow. He was in his bedroom, but not yet sleeping, and I spent a few precious minutes with him before taking Abi into the front flat to update her on my visit to the Suters. Roxy's laptop was still switched on from my research into flights that afternoon, and a downloaded map of the town of Saint-Martin-de-Ré sat on the desk next to my passport and driver's licence.

'I'm a bit worried about you going to France on your own,' Abi said, perched behind the desk chair on the back of Davis's sofa. 'I wish I could come, but it's the worst possible time for me at work. I'd probably be sacked if I tried to take any more time off.'

'Don't be silly,' I cried, 'you've done more than enough. Honestly, you've been an amazing help. And I'll be fine on my own. All I need to do is hire a car and get to the house. If they're not there, I'll just drive around until I find them. And when I do . . .' With a tremendous effort I blocked the thought of a face-to-face encounter with Davis, of him standing in front of me (smiling? Sneering? Pitying me?). I shuffled my documents on the desk and reached clumsily for the computer mouse to print out my booking details. I was still getting used to doing everything with one hand, but so long as I did things one at a time – all those boxes at the storage unit! – I could still do them at near to normal speed. Aware suddenly of Abi having fallen silent behind me, I looked around. She was staring at my bandaged hand, mouth slightly agape. I stared too, my thought processes just a couple of seconds behind hers.

'There's no way you can drive in France,' she said in a horrified whisper.

I felt my breath catch in my throat. 'I know. Not for weeks, the consultant said.' Only this evening I'd taken taxis to and from Marianne's house, and yet somehow I had pictured myself in France fully functioning, my left hand gripping the steering wheel as my right worked the gears. 'OK, well I'll just have to hope they've got buses.'

'But Kate, you need a way of getting—' Abi halted mid-sentence. 'I don't think you should go on your own, seriously. You need someone with you in case things get difficult. You're not up to it physically.'

'I have to go,' I said, shaking my head. 'I have no choice. I'll be all right.'

'Tell me again why Alistair can't go with you?'

'There's no way. He's got a big presentation on Tuesday, and Elizabeth isn't well, apparently. Plus he'll have Matt staying with him from tomorrow. One of us needs to be here, we can't both disappear.'

She considered this. 'Isn't there someone else? Someone who could take time off at short notice, who you trust?'

I paused. On the desk in front of me the laptop made a sudden whirring sound and the screensaver came on, pink and purple butterflies fluttering about, and my heart clenched at the sight of so sweet and childish a choice. Roxy's choice. Clicking the mouse I saw confirmation of my flight selection for the following morning and felt a fresh explosion of disbelief. In all those years of my avowed independence, when I'd reminded myself like a mantra of the worst that could happen if I fell in love again, I had never pictured an outcome like this, never.

'I suppose there is someone,' I said to Abi, slowly.

'Fabulous. Who?'

I struggled to my feet. 'Give me a minute, I think I might still have the number next door.'

Chapter 21

Why was it that so many memories of Roxy involved the seaside? In my daydreams, the place where I retreated from this nightmare, it was always on the sands that she danced, her long legs sugared with pale grains, her eyes intent on some challenge or game. Without a sibling for so many years, she played quite happily alone. There was a dead jellyfish in Spain she kept prodding with a stick, going back to it over and over like a ghoul to the wreckage of a plane crash; a sand island on a Dorset cove that she named Mermaid Island, rescuing her toys from it one by one as the tide washed in. Always I would picture her at the age of six or seven ('What can I do at age seven?' Love my mummy . . .), her ice-cream-pink jeans wet to the knees and her hair glued to her cheeks with dried sea water. Matthew, I tended to picture against backdrops of grass and brick, the playground at Francombe Gardens, my parents' lawn, the sports pitch at school, but Roxy, no less an urban child, was ever associated in my mind with sand and sea.

When she was about four, before she'd even started school, Alistair woke up one sunny Friday morning in July and said he wasn't going into work. He was going to call in sick and we were going to pack a weekend bag and go to the seaside.

'Am I coming too?' Roxy asked in that heartbreaking way

small children do, as though we'd ever think to leave them behind.

'We're all coming,' I said, cuddling her. 'It will be just the three of us.'

We drove south out of the city, checked into a B&B in Rye and headed straight for Camber Sands. Roxy was in heaven, dazzled by the endlessness of the beach, determined to investigate every last pool and channel and abandoned sandcastle.

I was weary from the drive and so Alistair took her off to explore while I napped under the umbrella. Perhaps it was one of the countless times that I thought I might be pregnant, in which case, a phantom weariness. When I woke to a spangle of yellow, I'd forgotten where I was, but the pinch of anxiety was soon gone when I saw the two of them in the distance. Roxy was on Alistair's shoulders and he was propelling her forwards into an elaborate twisting dismount. The splash of the water around their legs was a silent explosion of liquid silver. I imagined him exclaiming like a sports commentator and her calling out, 'Again, again!', regressing a couple of years as she did when she was excited and couldn't wait for more.

My friends, at least those I still had from my pre-Roxy days, thought I was insane to have had a child so young, to be married so young, to be somewhere like the English seaside in my mid-twenties while they did what I 'should' have been doing: island-hopping in Thailand, clubbing in Ibiza, hiking the Great Wall of China. Happily, that was not what I thought. As I watched my husband and daughter playing together, straining to catch the notes of their laughter on the breeze, I thought to myself, 'How did I get to be here? How did I get to be so lucky?'

Soon she was haring back to base, Alistair following behind and calling that he was going to the shop along the beach to get us ice creams, and Roxy came to lie next to me, pressing against me like a damp kitten. 'Are you asleep, Mum? Shall I tell you a bedtime story?'

'Oh, yes please, Rox.'

'You have to close your eyes.' She pressed my eyelids shut with her fingers, cold from the water. 'Once upon a time there was a seagull who thought that the sky was falling down . . .'

'Like Chicken Licken?'

'Yes, except he was wrong. His friend told him the sky wasn't falling down. Actually . . .' ('Actually' was her most-used word of the moment) '. . . *actually*, the sky was floating away.' She paused dramatically.

I opened my eyes and squinted at her flushed face. 'Floating away? You mean carried on the wind?'

'Yes. The first seagull hadn't seen it properly because you're not allowed to stare at the sky in case the sun hurts your eyes. But the second seagull knew the truth.'

'I see. So when the sky floated away, what was left?'

'Not the seagulls. They were blown away too. Just us would be left. No one else. Just Mum, Dad and Roxy.'

'OK, *voilà*, this is it!' Tash let out a long, theatrical sigh as she took the curving slope of the road bridge, driving at a cautious pace as she familiarised herself with the left-hand drive of the hire car. 'The Ile de Ré! Well, it's pretty easy to get to, considering how keen he was to keep it a secret, eh? Sly bastard.'

There was a beach right at the foot of the bridge and her eyes narrowed in fierce scrutiny, as though Davis and Roxy might be standing right there, faces turned to the incoming traffic, the very first people we saw. But the sands were empty, for we were at the end of October now, the weather overcast and the ocean the colour of clay. As we drove on, through the first villages and into flat, wooded terrain, it seemed to me that even the autumn fields and wooded areas had lost their richness to the clouds, one melancholy mix of brown and green after another, and the little white cottages designed to gleam in the sun looked instead drab, drained of colour.

'Thank you for coming, Tash.' I'd already thanked my sister several times since we'd met at the airport that morning. She'd been at the check-in desk before me, bag labelled, biker's bandana tied around her head as though pitching up for some epic road trip. She imagined the wind in her hair, the sun on her face, some cinematic game of cat and mouse. She'd read, she said, that the Ile de Ré was a glamorous playground that attracted the Paris A-list. Still, her powers of mobilisation were astounding, I was grateful for that, as was the quickness of her brain as she grasped and logged every detail of my tragedy. (Her gasps and curses enlivened a good hour of queuing for many dozens of other travellers, too.) Once briefed, she spent the whole flight in intense speculation: how quickly would we find them, how hard would it be to extricate Roxy from him, how long could Alistair – and the school – be held off before we admitted defeat?

'Hey, no problem,' she said now, braking at a red light and giving me an earnest sideways smile. 'Of course I came. Just wait till I get my hands on that arsehole. Unbelievable what he's done to you, Kate. Unbelievable. The police might not be interested, but I am.'

I was not at all sure this was going to work out. It wasn't that I doubted her enthusiasm or the genuineness of her disgust, it was just that Tash way she seemed to be revelling in it all, as if her dramatisation of the situation was more compelling than the reality. As we waited for our luggage at La Rochelle she'd collected up tourist brochures with the zeal of Nancy Drew, offering observations about the people around us as though they were somehow under suspicion. It was exactly like watching an actress immerse herself in a new detective role. Alistair had predicted as much when I'd updated him that morning ('She's the last thing you need, Kate, she won't take it seriously enough. You'll be better off on your own'), but I'd given his views short shrift. I *did* need someone, not only for the mechanical tasks, but for the physical presence, for the other voice. The fact was, Tash was my only choice.

'Anyway,' she added, 'anyone would have stepped up. You're a woman in need. This is a serious emergency.'

Well, it was an odd place to come for an emergency. It felt almost comical that we'd entered so tranquil and innocent a place in order to hunt down a criminal (or whatever it was that Davis was). Judging by those we passed, the Ile de Ré was where people cycled about in twos and threes, long golden baguettes sticking out of their baskets, where they stopped by the roadside to feed handfuls of grass to donkeys or to look through binoculars at the waterfowl. It was very small – just eighteen miles long, according to the map and skinny enough in parts for the ocean to be visible on both sides – and within a few minutes we had already reached Saint Martin.

'Isn't it lovely?' Tash exclaimed, and even as my body was beset with fresh nerves, my eyes could see that it was lovely, built within thick defensive walls and retaining an air of gracious self-protection, of look-but-don't-touch beauty. At the town gates stood a large, handsome chateau, clearly now used as some sort of institution, possibly a prison. I felt convulsions in my stomach.

We were able to find rue de Loix quite easily. It was a cobbled road between the harbour and the main square, densely lined with horse chestnut trees that had begun their picturesque seasonal shedding. Number fifteen was shielded from public view by a tall, painted gate set within a pale stone wall. To the right a set of shutters, apparently belonging to the property, were tightly closed.

'This is it,' Tash said, killing the engine. 'Hopefully we'll be in and out before they know what's hit 'em.'

'Yes.' Was this it? Would we merely have to get out of the car and ring the doorbell to have Roxy returned to us, like parents collecting their infant from a childminder? I thought not. It was as unlikely as the gendarmerie escorting Davis to an underground cell, never to be seen again. Tash's bravado was touching, but it was Alistair I needed now, I realised. I should have insisted he came. Looking at that painted gate, I missed him acutely, like the knife wounds of our early separation; I needed his strength for the scene that was to come.

'Are we getting out?' Tash asked.

'Of course we are,' I said. But, stepping into the street and glancing about, I felt pain of a different sort: fear that we'd made a terrible mistake, that they were not here after all. For Davis's were not the only shutters drawn, they *all* were; the street might have been evacuated. The quiet was overwhelming, even the shuffling of our shoes and the scratch of dry leaves stirred by the breeze seemed to be swallowed by it, instantly erased. A single bicycle propped against a garage door a dozen doors down was the only sign that anyone had recently set foot here – and even that might simply have been abandoned.

I reached forward and pressed the buzzer.

'It might have broken,' Tash said after a minute or so. 'I can't hear it ringing inside, can you?' But the equipment looked recently installed to me, and quite high tech.

We waited a full five minutes before Tash suggested she give me a leg up so I could look over the top of the gate. I was able to keep my balance long enough to see that it was a much grander property than I had expected. The shutters opening on to the street belonged not to the house, but to some sort of annexe, which ran the length of a pale cobbled path towards a broad two-storey villa with a pitched roof and central, glass-fronted entrance. On a small tree-lined terrace a pair of deckchairs flapped in the breeze, a scattering of fallen leaves having collected on each seat, and just inside the gate a set of wrought-iron bicycle racks stood empty. From what I could make out through the glass doors of the main house, there was a third, smaller building beyond, alongside which the cobbled path continued into a rear garden. The whole place looked deserted, every door and shutter locked.

I slumped back to the pavement, gripping Tash's arm to stop myself from falling. 'It looks shut up for winter. They're definitely not here.'

'They're not *in*,' she corrected me. 'They might just be out for the day. This is a fantastic place to hide out if you ask me. It's a ghost town! Come on, let's try the neighbours.' Undeterred, she was off rapping on doors and peering through letterboxes. One house, a tiny cottage that opened onto the pavement, had a disproportionately ornate door knocker carved in the shape of a woodpecker, and it was this that roused the only neighbour in residence.

'*Bonjour, madame. Parlez-vous anglais?*'

'*Oui.*' She was elderly but straight-backed, snugly wrapped in a wool jacket, and listened to Tash's schoolgirl French with an expression of wariness.

'*Nous cherchons une Anglaise – elle s'appelle* Roxy Easton.' Tash brandished the recent photo of Roxy I'd brought with me, taken after the school play, and the sight of it made me lurch, as though the exposure of my private family world had only now fully begun.

Not wanting to crowd the woman, and no match even for Tash's French, I continued along the picturesque little street past gleaming pastel doors and clumps of the last hollyhocks of the season. I couldn't help thinking of the city across the water, hardly more than a half-hour drive away. Despite its name, La Rochelle was an adult, masculine sort of place, the choice of the historian, not the romantic. Davis had taken me there to look at castle walls and anchors and lighthouses, even though he had a house nearby in one of the most beautiful villages I'd ever set foot in. And it had been nothing to do with delicacy, with sparing me the ignominy of being honeymooned in a house he'd won from his first wife in their divorce. No, he'd deliberately kept me from here – kept me from knowing of its existence – because he'd been saving it, saving it for someone else.

'I'll know her when I find her,' he'd told Camilla. 'And then nothing else will matter.' No one else will matter. Despite Abi's warnings that I should block him from my mind, I felt a fresh swell of rage and humiliation. There had never been any question in his mind that I might have been that one. He'd never viewed his marriage to me as anything but an emergency measure – 'the only way to avoid banishment from you for ever'. And how easy I'd been to hoodwink! As malleable as any of his teenage lovers. I remembered those doubts that had surfaced that morning on our honeymoon, proper fight-or-flight doubts, and yet I'd been ready to dismiss them at the first assurance, the first sweet nothing ('I really do love you, of course I do'). I was disgusted with myself for that. Yes, I had made the biggest error of judgment of my life in falling in love with Davis Calder and, whatever the police said, I had exposed my daughter to risk. It was simply not feasible that she had had equal weight in this decision to disappear. Believed herself to be madly in love, yes, that made sense, but running away? She must have been pressured by him, caught up in the panic and emergency of the moment, fearing my anger, fearing losing him if she didn't go along with his plan.

The faint tapping of the woodpecker in its cradle brought me back to the present. Tash was striding towards me, long hair swinging below the bandana, eyes optimistic. 'She said she's not sure if the owner is around, but she agreed he was Monsieur Calder, so it's obviously the right place. It was rented out during the summer, apparently, to a family from Paris. She hasn't seen a girl.'

'Has she seen him? Recently, since the summer rental?'

'She said maybe she thought she heard someone arrive last week, but she couldn't be sure. She was very discreet, but I read between the lines. They're here. Come on, let's look in all the parked cars. We might see one of their coats or an English news-paper or something.'

'Good idea.' I had to admit that I was less hopeful than Tash about this first eyewitness of ours. If Davis and Roxy were here, then how could a neighbour possibly not have seen them? They could hardly have been lost in the teeming mobs. Our sweep of the street's parked cars proved similarly fruitless. In any case, I didn't think they would have hired a car; it would be too easy a way for us to trace them.

'Let's go down to the harbour,' I said, remembering the crowds at the quayside in La Rochelle. 'That's probably where people congregate.'

It was just a couple of gently sloping streets away, a picture-postcard scene of cobbled quayside and bobbing boats, but I had eyes only for the faces. There were plenty of them, too, mostly well-heeled tourists in good coats and expensive sunglasses, though the latter could hardly have been needed in this weather, and many leading pedigree dogs back and forth on an elegant afternoon stroll. Others sat at terrace cafés and ate crêpes, or picked through the goods laid out on shop forecourts – mostly distressed pails and other nautical-looking items. There were very few children of school age, only the occasional toddler or baby, and although a carousel stood open for business, it was empty of customers. I wondered what time it would start to get dark.

'We need to find somewhere to stay,' I said to Tash. 'Somewhere near here.' But the hotels overlooking the water were expensive, so we left the car in the public car park and wan-dered inland through the alleys and lanes, the first lined with shops, those after residential. While Tash admired the quaintness of the architecture, I continued to watch for human life, my heart in my mouth every time I saw a new figure emerge from a door-way or approach from a side street. But every time it would collapse back into its cavity, shrunken with disappointment, as my lips were left to mumble greetings to strangers.

'Here's a place,' Tash said, 'Maison Saint Martin, let's try here.'

Though the exterior of this one was simple, inside it was cosy and welcoming. The landlady had no other customers and upgraded us at once to the best room in the house, an extravaganza of wrought iron and white linen, a roll-top bath with a wooden shelf of lavender toiletries. It was some sort of honeymoon suite with a view over the terracotta rooftops towards the abbey.

'This is amazing,' Tash said, excitedly. 'Look at the lovely trees! This place must be so beautiful in summer. Look at that old well, and it's all cobbledy everywhere. Are those hollyhocks? Mum's got those, hasn't she, in our front garden?' She settled herself on the big white double bed, feet tucked beneath her, and began poring over the map of the island we'd just acquired from our landlady.

'Any ideas?' I asked. 'They might be hiding out in another part of the island for now.'

'Maybe. Looking at this, there are quite a few little villages, more than you'd think.' She sighed. 'It's a real shame you can't cycle with your wrist, because I think we'd be able to find them more easily if we were on bikes. It's all cycle lanes here.' Her confidence that success was simply a question of adopting the right mode of transport cheered me a little.

'You think they're out cycling?' Again, an image from my honeymoon broke through my defences: Davis and I wheeling about on bright yellow bicycles, resting with a beer, drinking in the leisurely rhythm of provincial France after a hectic summer in London. Cycling had felt fantastic, another form of freedom for me, and we'd even talked about getting me a bike of my own when we got back home.

'What else is there to do here?' Tash asked. 'It's pretty dead. Surely someone like Roxy would be bored as hell here?'

'If she is actually here,' I pointed out, but even as I spoke my brain seized a detail only now crystallising in my memory: that pathway to Davis's front door, the two deckchairs on a terrace shaded by trees, there'd been piles of leaves on the deckchairs, but not on the paving stones themselves. It was autumn, leaves must be falling continuously, which meant the path had to have been recently swept. Someone must be about, at the very least a rental agent or a gardener, someone who might be willing to point us in the right direction. I decided to wait till our next visit to the house before sharing my theory with Tash. Managing her excitement was going to be crucial to my energy levels over the next few days.

'Hey, do you think Davis has enrolled her in school?' she asked, still examining the map. 'The secondary school is on the mainland. We could go there tomorrow and demand to see the register.'

I shook my head. 'It's only been a week or so, I doubt they've even considered it. And not having to go to school is probably a very appealing part of this as far as Roxy is concerned. Besides, I don't imagine either of them would want to draw attention to the fact that she's a schoolgirl, do you?' An undertow of exhaustion tugged at my lower body, almost physically rocking me. I would go and fetch my painkillers from my bag in a minute, when I could get my legs to work again.

I gripped the arm of the chair with fresh frustration. 'I wish she could have confided in you, Tash, when you were talking together that time, do you remember? If I hadn't been listening at the door, she might have said something, anything that set the alarm bells ringing.'

Tash frowned. 'You mean you think they were already involved, way back then?'

'Probably not, but it would have been in motion, you know, the initial attraction.' Just as my own had been, distracting me from the parallel rumbles, from the rumbles that would grow and grow until they erupted to life and devastated everything in their path. 'I can't imagine what's been going through her head these last few months, and I didn't have a clue!'

'Don't blame yourself,' Tash said, soothingly. 'It's Davis who's divided you like that.' She searched for the phrase. 'Divide and conquer, that's what he's done.'

I tried, but failed, to smile. 'Roxy and I were divided before he came along. That's how he was able to conquer in the first place.'

Chapter 22

We must have searched ten different villages the next day, each a variation of the last with its narrow streets of fishermen's cottages and holiday villas, the main square arrangement of wooden bicycle racks and carousel, the corner bistros and their competing chalkboard menus of *moules et frîtes*. There were several holiday complexes and campsites, too, and at every new community we would pull up at its edge and watch for several minutes before crawling up and down the streets, Tash's foot perpetually poised over the brake. Then we'd be off again, across the flat fields towards the next church spire, the next depleted village. As we worked our way up the island, the air seemed to grow heavier; now there were oyster beds and salt pans and beaches dragged with seaweed, a silver landscape that had lost its shine with the sun.

Though we'd begun the day with optimism, by early afternoon I could feel gloom settling inside the car as Tash understood that this was not going to be nearly as easy as she'd thought. In spite of our thoroughness, we'd drawn only blank after blank. Even the vehicles that passed the other way seemed slant-faced and inscrutable, like they were hiding something, protecting someone.

'They've *got* to be back in Saint Martin,' she said, as we

departed the site of a beach café boarded up for winter and agreed to head back. 'If he's got a place there and it's available and doesn't cost any money, then why abandon it for somewhere even more remote? Somewhere you can't even get a pint of milk?'

'I don't know, but the fact is they're not at the house.' We had tried the buzzer at rue de Loix repeatedly that morning before setting out in the car and, once again, there had been no sign of life from within.

'It doesn't make sense,' Tash said, eyes on the road but picturing, as I was, that forbidding white gate and smooth stone wall. Beyond her I could see a pair of magpies chasing one another across a field and I imagined pointing them out to Matthew. 'Why aren't they there?' she cried, crossly.

I had considered little else for the last twenty-four hours. 'Maybe they *were* there, before yesterday, but moved on because they know we've arrived.'

Tash glanced across at me, uncomprehending. 'How could they know?'

'Well, they might have seen us, it could be as simple as that. We've been hanging about the house openly enough. And for all we know there might be a security camera or something at the gate.'

'I don't remember seeing one.'

Nor did I. 'Or they might have been tipped off.'

'Who by? The only people who know we're here are Alistair and Victoria and Abi.'

'And Camilla,' I pointed out.

'Yeah, but she's on our side, right?' It was both comforting and exasperating to me that Tash viewed the situation in purely black-and-white terms. Davis was wholly evil, I unimpeachably good – as, by extension, was Alistair – and she, of course, was the classic avenging angel. The difficulty was Roxy. What was her classification?

'And if you were right about that cow from school,' she went

272

on, remembering Marianne, 'she'll have told them what you said about going to York and they'll assume you're looking there. If anything, you'd think they could relax a bit.'

I nodded, remembering also the terrace that had been neatly cleared of fallen leaves. 'You're right. I think they are here, or at least are planning to be here soon. Wherever they are, they'll be lying low, not wanting to draw attention to themselves. You know, not answering the phone or the doorbell.'

'That's what I would do,' Tash agreed. 'At least for the first few days.'

My fingers reached for my mobile phone in my jeans pocket, though it had not rung. 'I wish she'd get in touch. I just want to hear her voice, even on a voicemail, to just hear her say she's all right.' Every half hour I checked my phone, just in case I'd missed its ring in the noise of the car engine or during one of our many unproductive quizzings of locals, but so far neither Roxy's name nor any unidentified number ever appeared on the screen. There'd been no email, either, though we'd already checked twice at an internet café near the B&B.

The road back to Saint Martin was clear; Tash changed gears and increased her speed. 'Did you do anything like this when you were her age? I mean, I can't remember any big dramas, but I guess I would have been too young to have had much of a clue what you were up to.'

I smiled thinly. 'At seventeen? I had boyfriends, sure, but it never occurred to me to leave home with any of them. That was only something people did who hated their parents.' I paused, not caring to develop that line of thought. 'And leaving the country? I don't think I even knew where my passport was. Mum kept them all together somewhere safe.'

Tash nodded. 'In the desk drawer with the lock, the one with all the bank books and bills and stuff. I used to have to report to Dad there every Saturday morning to get my pocket money.'

It was comforting to remember an old family ritual. 'Did

273

you?' I asked, wondering where this conversation was headed. Tash's teenage years had coincided with my own as a young mother and so reports of her rites-of-passage crises would likely have washed over me.

She sent me a wicked little smile. 'Yeah. I mean I didn't run away from home, but I had an affair with a teacher when I was in the sixth form.'

'What?' I laughed in disbelief. 'Are you serious? Who?'

'Oh, no one who taught you. One of our history teachers, Mr Hodgson. Russell Hodgson, but I quite liked calling him Mr Hodgson, or "Sir" for a joke.'

I remembered suddenly how Roxy had sometimes called Davis Mr Calder, using a teasing, Marianne tone of voice, and that he'd liked to call her Roxana, her full name. All of that must have been before anything physical had happened between them. And that mysterious cooling that had come later, that must have been when caution had set in, when the subterfuge was properly underway, when something real had begun.

'How old was this Mr Hodgson?' I asked Tash.

'Oh, just early twenties, not old like . . .' She broke off, checked unnecessarily over her left shoulder for cyclists that were not there, and added, 'He wasn't long out of teacher training, actually. I'm not sure he could decide which camp he was in.'

She outlined the chronology of their affair with utter dispassion, as though reciting the steps of a chemistry experiment. 'He was always in the pub with us, more like a friend than a teacher. I wasn't the only one, either. Lucy slept with him as well, and he definitely liked Sinead.'

'He had all of you on the go at the same time?' I said, appalled.

'No, don't be silly, it wasn't that dramatic! But he always had someone on the back burner, a new admirer.'

'Dramatic', that was the word she chose, exactly as Camilla had. 'Your daughter is probably enjoying the drama, sees it as a bit of excitement.' Just something they tick off their lists, like a

Duke of Edinburgh award or a gap year. Perhaps I should have talked to Tash before now; perhaps her adolescent relish of life's dramatics was exactly what I needed here, after all.

'Was he married?'

'No. He had a girlfriend, though. Another teacher, but working out of town. They didn't seem to see each other that much. I remember we used to talk about her constantly. We were obsessed. We used to fantasise about spying on her.'

Hard though I tried, I couldn't stop tears of horror rising in my eyes as I imagined Roxy and Marianne discussing Roxy's situation in just such a way, discussing me. Had my daughter viewed me as a rival, then? Had she made a fiction of me, desensitised herself to my feelings, or did all teenage daughters dismiss their mother's feelings as a matter of course, thinking us too old to have 'real' emotions? Perhaps her own had been so well managed by Davis that she'd believed herself to be the one betrayed in the first place? That breakdown she'd had, that weekend of inconsolable crying, it *had* been in response to my getting engaged, but for completely different reasons from any I'd originally imagined. If only I had forced the confession before it was too late. Instead, what? I'd let Davis talk to her, work his famous miracles . . .

I blinked my eyes dry. 'Did Mum ever find out?' I asked.

For the first time fear flickered in Tash's face. 'Of course not. I would have murdered him and hidden the body to avoid that.'

We both fell silent thinking about what she'd just said. 'That's what's so weird about this,' she said, finally. 'Roxy running away, leaving a note for you. It's like she wanted to get it out into the open, she wanted you to know. Maybe she's hoping you've come after her, whatever her letter actually said.'

I wished I could agree. 'It was more impulsive than that, Tash. They thought they had no choice. They knew I'd found the notebook and it would be the end of everything. If I hadn't found out, God knows how long they would have continued in secret.'

Yet another 'if' I couldn't bear to develop: if I hadn't let on, if I hadn't been so stupid as to phone Davis and leave that hysterical message, if I'd waited and recruited Alistair and Victoria, or anyone for that matter, how different the outcome might have been. 'They probably thought I'd get a restraining order on him or something.'

'Then why bother with the note?'

'Without it the police might have been more interested.' I paused. 'No, they had to go to be together. They think they're the original star-crossed lovers.'

'Don't we all at that age?'

'At her age, maybe,' I said sharply. 'At the age you were when you fell for your Russell guy. But there's a big difference between that and a forty-four-year-old adult.'

'Yes, of course. Sorry.' She looked at me with a concertedly sobered expression. We had reached Saint Martin and we did not speak again until she had pulled into the car park, casting an eye to the skies – dark clouds had stacked threateningly overhead. 'What shall we do now? I'm not sure I fancy getting on a bike in this weather, and I can't believe anyone else would, either.'

We had agreed that if our initial forays by road were unsuccessful, the next step would be to split up, Tash hiring a bike and searching the cycle lanes and I doing whatever else I could by foot. But I had to agree with her that in this weather most people would surely prefer to stay indoors than risk a drenching – especially those already confined for reasons of their own.

'We'll stay put for now,' I said, decisively. 'Come on, let's check out the market. If they are here, they've got to eat.'

The grand indoor food market was situated on the waterfront and drew hundreds of people from the town and beyond, more than I had imagined actually living here out of season. Once we were inside, it seemed like the most obvious place to look on the whole island, where we should have been stationed all day; I felt certain we would have caught them, or at least one of them, as they slipped unsuspectingly between the aisles of lobsters and quiches and jars of preserved fruits to pay for their bread and milk and other basics. But now, in the few remaining hours of business, there was no one. Or, more accurately, everyone but them: Davis's woodpecker neighbour, our own landlady, several locals to whom we had only that morning shown Roxy's photograph and who had passed it back to us with identically assured '*Non*'s, who may have been acquainted with Davis and passed on the news that two strangers were in town looking for a missing girl . . . How naïve we'd been to believe that the only people aware of our arrival were safely back in London!

Refusing to succumb to panic or disappointment, we waited for the market doors to close and positioned ourselves instead at a café table with a clear view of the entrance to the town supermarket. Tash reminded me that *we* needed to eat, too, and just as we were ordering coffee and sandwiches, my phone finally rang. It was Alistair.

'She's sent another email. It's to both of us.'

My heartbeat tripled its usual volume. 'What does it say?'

'Nothing much, just that she's fine. It's literally a line, I'll read it out: "Dear Mum and Dad, Just to let you know I am OK. Please don't worry, love Roxy". Please don't worry! We'll bear that in mind, shall we?' Though he chuckled, I had a clear picture of his grim expression. 'Anyway, presumably Marianne has reported your little visit and this is the result.'

'Yes, sounds like it. I don't suppose she answered your question about where she is, did she?'

'Sadly not. But I think we knew that was a shot in the dark.'

Over the top of her coffee cup Tash raised her brows at me, eyes hopeful. I shook my head. 'Are you going to email back?' I asked Alistair.

'Yep, of course. I thought about saying something about you being in York, what d'you think? Just in case Marianne didn't mention that bit clearly enough. We want to really lull them into a false sense of security, don't we?'

I considered this. 'No, I wouldn't, Alistair, they'll know it's a bluff. Don't forget they're one step ahead of us, not the other way around.'

'True. I take it no progress, then?'

'Not yet, but I'm hopeful. The house looks empty, but we've only been here a day, it's impossible to say for sure. And maybe sending the email will make them drop their guard a bit. Anyway, Tash and I are splitting up tomorrow to cover more ground.'

Again Alistair's hollow chuckle filled my ear. 'I can't believe you've got *her* there with you. Not exactly the blind leading the blind, but you know what I mean, eh?'

I glanced at my sister, her eyes now trained unblinkingly on the door of the supermarket. At about midday, somewhere on the blustery northern tip of the island, she had replaced the bandana with a warm woollen hat. 'I don't, actually,' I said, curtly. 'She's being extremely helpful. But if you'd like to come over and take her place, then please just say the word.'

'All right, calm down, I'm only joking.'

'Good. Because this is not easy, I can tell you.'

'Hey, they'll turn up,' he said confidently. 'Runaways always do. Look at Bonnie and Clyde.'

Now it was my turn for a humourless laugh. 'I'd like to avoid a shoot-out if I possibly can.'

Alistair being Alistair didn't miss a beat. 'Let's just hope they feel the same.'

We were wrong about them letting down their guard – or any other of our theories, for that matter – for the rest of that day and two further days passed in fruitless search. Though Tash and I staked out rue de Loix for hours at a time, the house remained quite undisturbed, the shutters never opened and the bell not once answered. Several times we re-enacted that precarious balancing act as I peered over the wall and called out Roxy's name, over and over like someone crying for a missing cat. But she never came.

Return flights, optimistically scheduled for Thursday, were missed. Tash had no employer to inform, but I sent a brief email to Ethan pleading as reason for my absence my ongoing recuperation after the accident. He'd give me the benefit of the doubt, I knew he would, but if I was completely honest his response was not going to make any difference to my actions: I was here now, and here I would be until I was satisfied Roxy was not.

'Today's the day, I reckon,' Tash said on Friday, our third full day on the island, and her words had the ring of a catchphrase to them.

'I certainly hope so!' I was determined to match her show of positive thinking with one of my own. Without it, this whole expedition would founder in a matter of minutes. I helped her adjust the seat of her rented bicycle and tighten the straps of her backpack in preparation for the afternoon's explorations. Her route along the busiest cycle paths between Saint Martin and the village of La Flotte in one direction and Loix in the other would be largely identical to the previous day's. For all her extracurricular gusto, Roxy was not sporty and it seemed unlikely to me that she would be willing to cycle any greater distances than these, if any at all.

'Remember, if you see anything at all, even if you're not sure, just phone me and I'll jump in a taxi. Though not if you're following them, you don't want to lose them. Is your phone switched on? Did you remember to recharge it?'

'Yes, Mum, stop fussing!' The old affectation of hers slipped out before Tash could stop it and she gave me a rueful look. I pretended not to have noticed, just continued issuing her with final instructions even as she pedalled off, but, as her gliding figure got smaller and smaller, finally vanishing altogether, I felt all my vulnerabilities resurface. The truth was her words *had* released a switch: consumed every waking moment by Roxy and yet spending so much time with Tash, there had begun to be moments when the two would blur, when I felt I *was* her mother, that we were trapped in some surreal, warped universe where Tash had somehow replaced Roxy. A place where Roxy no longer existed.

For the last day or two after waving Tash off, I had found myself drawn to the beach. (Odd how quickly a routine had emerged generally, a structure to our days: the first visit to the gate as soon as breakfast was done; the morning consultation with Alistair; the once-over of quayside cafés and food market; the constant email runs and remote checks on my landline message service at home; and, finally, the evening catch-up with Alistair – I had not spoken to him this often when we were married!)

Saint Martin had its own beach, a small sandy stretch on the far side of the castle grounds, beyond which a second community had sprouted. It was a pleasant new town of landscaped roads and red-roofed summer houses, most of which were shut up by now for the winter. Tash and I had patrolled the streets in the car on the first day and noticed nothing remarkable enough for us to repeat the journey.

For pedestrians there was a second approach, a short, windswept route past the town park and along the sea walls, and it was this that I took today. The town was a little busier than usual, weekenders having arrived early for their break, but even so there was no one on the path behind me and only a cluster of cyclists ahead. The only sounds were the work of the wind and the seagulls. What was it Tash had said when we'd first arrived? Surely someone like Roxy would be bored as hell here? But I was starting to see that it wasn't as simple as that. Who was Roxy, after all, if not a girl who loved the sea? Well, here it protected her and freed her at once, freed her from the relentless study programme, the frenzy of parental expectations, and, most importantly, from the barriers between her and the man she thought she loved. Yes, I imagined she could be happy somewhere like this.

I settled on a wooden bench on the bank of grass at the near side of the beach and drank from my water bottle. Though dry, it was a violent, blustery day, the water foaming brown at the shoreline and the only swimmer an excitable dog. Twenty metres out a bathing platform bobbed on the waves. There was so much yellow-white cloud, it was like being at the bottom of a bowl of whipped egg.

To my right stood a row of beach huts, all painted white, and I counted them with the precision of a ritual, one, two, three . . . fourteen, fifteen, sixteen. Ahead, an old wooden deck lay beached on the sands, its wood warped and peeling, the kind of place a younger Roxy would have commandeered for a princess's ship or a magic raft. I repeated the line of her email over and over: (I am OK . . . don't worry . . .) That was something, wasn't it? There were parents out there with children who were properly missing, not just absent without leave like ours, but snatched or lost or worse, much worse. Those parents would swap places with me in a heartbeat.

As usual, I scanned all around me for human life: a couple eating a picnic on the grass, their bicycles laid flat behind them – they were serious cyclists, judging by all the kit spread out around them; a family of four building a sandcastle, arms and legs ambitiously bare, and a toddler stumbling towards the water in sandalled feet – British, I decided, determined to have their seaside holiday whatever the weather; a couple walking together at the water's edge, exactly the same height and trudging through the wet sand so perfectly in rhythm they might have been tied together for a three-legged race (they, at least, were wrapped up warm, understood that the season was over, must be French); three or four men with fishing equipment, probably locals; a young man and two women in wetsuits, just in from windsurfing, faces pink and raw; and, finally, a couple of teenage girls in candy-coloured fleeces; too young to be Roxy and, in any case, they chattered in fast, native French. I wondered idly why they weren't in school, what *their* mothers had said to their headmistresses.

At that moment the sun slid behind thinner cloud, brightening the scene by several tones. I closed my eyes and held my face up to the sky, praying for illumination of a different kind. Now my mind sifted only the sounds: the water, the cries of the wind-surfers, shrill from exhilaration or cold, the belch of a canned drink being opened, the crunch of a car door. I opened my eyes. For the first time I noticed the black rags of seaweed on the sand. The little toddler was collecting it up in long trails and placing it inside the moat of the castle his parents had built. Every time he added another handful he would exclaim with new satisfaction. I thought of Matthew, what he might be doing right now, sitting in his classroom with his workbook open in front of him, eyes on the whiteboard, or perhaps drifting to the window for a view of his beloved sports field.

That was another part of the routine here, my evening con-versation with my son, and in many ways it was the hardest job of the day. For each time I heard his voice all my feelings about the Roxy situation would become complicated further by elation, guilt, and – more often than not – self-pity. My poor little boy, the one who'd done nothing wrong in this but somehow seemed to be losing out, and it was all my fault!

'So everything's all right?' I'd asked last night. 'You're absolutely sure?' There'd been some sort of misunderstanding in the morning involving Elizabeth's new nanny and the wrong school bag, a piece of homework that would now be noted as late. It was incidental but, magnified by distance, became loaded with significance.

'Ye-es, Mu-um.' Were they new, those humouring, drawn-out vowels, or was I imagining them?

'I'll be back just as soon as I can, definitely by the end of the weekend.'

'Oh-kay.'

'I love you, sweetie.'

'Ye-es, Mu-um.'

'You must be missing him,' Alistair said, unusually eager to resume our own conversation after Matt had said his goodbyes.

I was off guard and spoke more freely than I intended to. 'Of course I'm missing him! I feel like I haven't been there at all for him lately, and I haven't, have I? I mean, he was away for ages with you in South Africa, then I had all the wedding preparations and the trip to France' – I could no longer bear to call it a honeymoon – 'and now I'm away again. And we still haven't told him why his sister's suddenly disappeared . . .'

'Hey, come on,' he said, as sympathetically as I'd heard him since this crisis had begun. 'It feels worse than it is. He's honestly OK. There's loads going on here, Elizabeth is a great distraction.'

'But I've been away four nights already. He must think I've abandoned him!'

'Not at all. You know how loyal kids are. If only adults were so accepting.'

He was thinking about work, undoubtedly, but his remark provoked emotions in me that were overwhelming for different reasons altogether: all those nights that he had spent apart from the children – my run of four was nothing compared to his years of Saturdays only – and how many of those had I begrudged? Not once had I given him a moment's sympathy, thinking only that he'd deserved it because he'd chosen to leave. 'You've made your bed,' I'd said to him once when he complained that pick-up arrangements didn't suit him, and I'd thought it a thousand times since.

If only adults were so accepting. It was impossible now even to hear the word 'adult' without thinking instantly of Roxy and of the question that had yet to be resolved during all of this. Was she an adult, entitled to make her decisions for herself? I didn't think so, and nor did Alistair, but I was slowly coming to accept that we might be the only ones.

All at once I started, like the jolt back to consciousness you get just as you lose yourself to sleep, and stared at the beach scene in front of me: something was missing. Not the family, not the windsurfers – the couple with the hoods! My pulse raced and I waited a second or two for my brain to catch up. The man had been on the shore side, his boots splashing in and out of the water, which had lost him inches to his companion, but on flat ground he'd be taller, several inches taller; he'd worn a waterproof jacket, not the mustard yellow I was familiar with, but who was to say he didn't have a second one here, a whole collection of them.

I sprang to my feet, began dashing down the bank and onto the wet sand, towards the point at which I'd last seen them walking. Heads turned at the suddenness and speed of my chase; still in the water, the dog held its head clear and barked. The beach was divided into two by a tide-breaker of rocks and, reaching the end of the second section, I saw there was no pathway beyond, only a rocky stretch that quickly became impassable. Unless they had climbed up the rocks and into the grounds of one of the villas that lined the seafront, they could only have done as I did now: double back and follow the causeway up past the café and into the car park. On the flat, I spun from side to side: nothing. How could this be? Had they seen me and fled? It seemed doubtful, for they'd had their backs to me and been walking away, strolling, not retreating. In any case, I'd been sitting for some time daydreaming – it could have been several minutes – and they'd had plenty of time simply to idle off at their leisure, by car, cycle, foot. I squinted up the road that led inland, but there was no sign of either pedestrians or cyclists. The route towards the sea walls was also deserted, but it curved soon after behind a wall of shrubbery and it was impossible to judge beyond that point.

I had to make a decision: road or path. I chose the path, but was at once hindered by a long convoy of cyclists coming towards me, some riding two abreast, forcing me to stand aside and let them pass. It seemed to go on for ever, the tring-tring of the bells, the polite *bonne-journée*s, the calls from one to the other as they spotted the beach. Finally free to pass, I broke into a jog and by the time I reached the park, coming to a halt by the children's swings, I had a stitch in my chest and had to double over to gulp for air. I grabbed my phone to call Tash. It clicked on to her voicemail, but seconds later she called back.

'Sorry, I had to pull over, it's pretty busy along here today. Nothing so far, though.'

I broke in, breathless. 'You might as well come back. They're here in Saint Martin. I think I just saw them.'

She gasped. 'What? Where?'

'On the beach.'

'No way! Did they see you?'

'No, I'm pretty sure they didn't. They were just walking along normally. But I lost them, I didn't realise who they were until they'd gone.'

There was a pause. 'You actually saw their faces, did you?'

'No, but I just know it was them, there was something so familiar about them. You know when you just have a really strong instinct? They're here, Tash, and they don't know we are!'

She gave a little whoop of triumph. 'Then you were right, Kate. It's only a matter of time now!'

I heard her exhale then, not one of her theatrical gasps and groans, but the sound of true, heartfelt relief. However she'd begun this adventure, she was connected to it now, connected to me. I felt a smile stretch my cheeks, until then stiff from the cold (or from pure wretchedness, I didn't know which): I'd found Roxy, and I was no longer alone.

Chapter 23

Now that the seal was broken, my vision sharpened and suddenly I knew I would be able to find her, to pick her out of the same crowds she'd moved through unnoticed just the day before. I told myself it was a mother's instinct, a sixth sense that until now had been prevented by shock from functioning properly.

As if to confirm the epiphany, the next morning the sun came out, properly out. Vivid blue tore through the grey and before we knew it we were pooled in blazing light. With it the doors and shutters of Saint Martin opened, voices rang out and people congregated more heavily than usual at the harbour-side. They sat at café tables in neat rows, facing the water with identical expressions of pleasure like spectators at a regatta.

As Tash and I took our usual seats at the café by the gates of the *marché*, she peeled off her jacket and exclaimed her thanks to the sky. '*Le soleil*! That's more like it! Well, today's the day, don't you think? Let's give it an hour here and then go down to the beach. I just know they're going to be there again, especially now the weather's better. Let's find a waiter.'

Even though I'd already completed early morning stake-outs of the beach and the house, neither with success, I remained buoyed by yesterday's breakthrough. The sight of my sister, beaming her support in the full blaze of autumn sun, made me certain she was right and, something more than that – that this wouldn't be unfolding the way it was without her, that she was the lucky charm, the energy source, that had made it happen. 'Tash?'

'Yeah?' Her glance moved beyond me as she sought the waiter's eye.

'I just wanted to say how much I—' But I broke off with an abruptness that caused me to freeze in my seat and Tash to abandon her mission and spin around in hers to share my line of vision. My heartbeat was suddenly the smack of a drum and I pressed a hand to my chest in an effort to subdue it. It was her. Roxy. And this time there was no doubt about it. She was standing directly across the water on the inner islet of the harbour, hands resting on the handlebars of a bike. She wore jeans and a jacket I didn't recognise – khaki, army style, with a belt tied tightly at the waist – and sunglasses, also unfamiliar. Her hair hung loose down her back, billowing a little in the breeze. She looked quite French, right down to the *élan* with which she wheeled the bicycle over the cobbles, stopping to wedge her handbag into the basket and adjust her sunglasses. She was like a starlet from an old Truffaut movie.

'She's over there,' I hissed. 'Look! In the green jacket.'

Tash shaded her eyes with her palm and squinted. 'Oh my God, yes. She looks so different, I don't know if I would have recog—'

'I know.' I interrupted her, leaping to my feet. Without moving my eyes from the figure across the water, I put my arm up to wave.

'Don't do that,' Tash said, gripping my arm.

'What?'

'Better to follow her to wherever she's going, don't you think? Like we said we would? Find out where she's staying. If we go up to her now, she might give us the slip and we're back to square one.'

'OK.' She was right, of course – my daughter had crossed the Channel to avoid me and now she and Davis weren't even taking the risk of staying in his own house. She certainly wasn't going to greet me with a kiss and start discussing the weather. The question was, could we keep pace with her on her bike, whether she knew we were following or not? What if she'd come from further afield than Saint Martin? If so, we'd lose her the minute she picked up speed on the cycle paths out of town. But there was no time to go back to the hotel and pick up Tash's bike; for now, we were on foot. 'Come on, we need to hurry.'

'Wait,' Tash said. 'Let her come over the bridge before we move.'

Roxy was on the bike now, crossing the bridge in a matter of seconds and bearing left, away from us. I allowed an agonising ten seconds to pass and then hastened after her, Tash at my heel. At the corner of the steep rue du Baron de Chantal we held back. It was a stiff climb for someone unused to cycling and she was riding more slowly than we'd expected, standing up from the saddle to press harder on the pedals. At the top she turned right, once more on the flat, and we had to sprint at full pelt to reach the junction in time to see her turn again – into rue de Loix.

'So they *are* there,' Tash whispered. 'I don't get it. We must have tried that gate a hundred times, so how come we've missed them? Did they just arrive this morning?'

'That's what we need to find out.'

As Roxy coasted away from us, her carefree joy was plain to see and I felt my heart clutch. If the circumstances were different the lump in my throat would be from pure delight. Instead, it was an intense ball of emotions and none of them delight: relief, hope, anger and, strongest of all, fear, plain fear.

Hanging back at the corner of rue de Loix, we watched as she slipped from the bike and held out some sort of magnetic device to the white gate. It began to swing slowly open, very slowly, and she had to wait for a few moments before she was able to push her bike over the threshold. Meanwhile Tash and I wordlessly repositioned ourselves just across the road from the gate; we had a clear view of Roxy as she manoeuvred the bike towards the rack and, having slotted the front wheel into place, squatted to the gravel to attach the lock. Clearly the gate was operated by motion sensors, because it remained tantalisingly open as long as she moved about within range.

I turned to Tash. 'I'm going in before it closes.'

She picked up at once on the singular. 'I'll stay here, shall I?'

'I think that's best.' I gulped the words, breathing rapidly.

'Of course.' She grabbed my hand and squeezed it between hers, as though passing all her strength to me. 'Good luck.'

Roxy was on her feet again, standing on the far side of the bicycle rack with her shoulders turned away from the gate and towards the house. The gate had begun to close as I slipped in behind her but, picking up on my movement, it stopped and began once more to ease open. She didn't notice at first, was too busy rummaging in her bag for something, keys presumably, and there was a perverse moment when I was conscious that I could still change my mind, I could dart out of sight and stay hidden, discover what was going on without the two of them even knowing I was there. Perhaps it was natural, after days of futile pursuit, that subterfuge should be my first instinct.

I adjusted my feet with an unexpectedly loud crunch and she looked up at exactly the same moment as I opened my mouth to speak: 'Roxy!'

Her hands froze in front of her and the only motion was the flood of colour to her face. 'Oh God, what . . .?' Then she began backing away from me, up the stone path, which put paid to my desire to gather her up in a hug and lead her away before she could think to object.

'Wait!' I hurried after her, drew up by her side at the door, careful to keep my voice calm. 'Please don't run away.'

She waited, the rapidity of her breathing visible through her jacket.

'Is Davis here?'

She bit her lower lip, shook her head.

'Are you sure?'

A nod.

'Good.' The relief was acute. As I'd reminded myself a hundred times a day, the removal of Roxy from Davis's grip was my primary goal here and every nerve in my body told me that this would be better done without him present. That he had enormous influence over Roxy was no longer in dispute; whether he still had any over me was not something I dared put to the test – not until I'd won my daughter back.

'Can we go in then and talk? Please.'

She nodded again. Head bowed and still utterly mute, she unlocked the front door, revealing a wide, stone-flagged hallway with a large oak dresser and umbrella stand. Leading off to the right was a kitchen, and to the left what looked like a sitting room. Roxy, however, bypassed both of these, proceeding instead through a second door and out again into the open air. I was confused by the route, but there was not the time to question it before we'd passed another outbuilding, a refurbished barn of some sort, and halted at a secluded terrace at its rear. Here a second set of deckchairs flanked a low wooden table.

She gestured for me to sit down. 'I'll make some tea.' Her voice was quite emotionless; there was no sign now of the youthful *joie de vivre* we'd spied as she cruised along the streets, and it broke my heart that it was the sight of me that had caused it to vanish.

'Tea would be great, thank you.' Shaking, I stayed on my feet and watched her head back to the main house (was he in there, after all? Had she gone to fetch him? Or to warn him to stay out of sight?), but seeing her at the kitchen window filling a kettle from the tap, true to her word, I turned back and ventured a few steps further into the garden. It was larger than our walled space at Francombe Gardens, formally laid out with close-cut hedging and apple trees trained low to the ground. Some sort of purple flower blazed as though in full spring bloom.

Minutes passed. Just as I was beginning to fear she had bolted after all, she returned, carrying a tray of tea things. She had already poured the tea into little china cups and saucers, once the property of Camilla's family, perhaps, for they didn't strike me as Davis's taste (though, of course, I could no longer claim to know what that might be). I supposed he must have won the house lock, stock and barrel. Roxy passed me a cup, her hand evidently steadier than mine, for it was only when I'd taken possession of it that it began to clatter in its saucer and the liquid spill over the brim. I could hardly believe this was happening, only now realising that there'd been a reserve of doubt within me right until this moment, doubt – or hope, the two were indistinguishable – that she and Davis were together, after all.

We sat in the deckchairs, neither of us the slightest bit relaxed, despite the style of seating. 'Did Marianne tell you I was here?' she asked, finally. She'd dispensed with her own saucer and cradled the cup from underneath like a mug. The familiarity of the mannerism made my insides lurch.

I shook my head. 'No, no one did.'

'Then how did you—?'

'It doesn't really matter, Roxy, does it?' I looked at her then, hardly daring imagine the emotions that poured from my eyes to hers, or whether she would even allow herself to access them. It was possible that she was blind to me now, just as she'd seemed for so long deaf. 'The important thing is we found you.'

Her chin jutted stiffly forward. '"We"? Is Dad here as well, then?' Her obvious fear of her father took me aback.

'No, he's in London, with your brother. We couldn't both abandon everything to chase you across the world.' I'd told myself to avoid accusations but already I couldn't resist the urge to make her acknowledge her guilt.

'It's only France,' she said in retort, then, more hesitantly, 'How *is* Matt?'

'A little bewildered, as you can imagine. Looking forward to seeing you again.'

She went silent then, looked beyond me to the garden, and I took the opportunity to study her appearance more closely. Now I could see what was different: her hair had been cut into a fringe, which fell, blunt and natural, into her eyes, an alteration that made her appear considerably older. It was as if she had shed the self-consciousness of the teenager and grown into herself. It was as though I hadn't seen her for several years.

I was relieved, of course, to find her safe and well, here of her own free will and not by some kidnapping that had been dressed up as love, but what I had not expected was to find her quite *so* well. It wasn't just that new haircut, it was the fact that she was glowing almost, as bright and alive as that purple flower behind her. She had the bloom of . . . of what? A new bride? Was this it, then? The transition, the evidence of deflowering I'd always imagined I'd be able to detect on sight.

She caught my eye and blinked heavily, as though weighed down by her own eyelashes – the liner was winged at the outer corners of her eyes and her brows thickened with pencil, another change of style – and to my surprise I felt sudden raw fury. I didn't need a mirror to know that I looked dreadful, drawn and lined, grey with worry. *My* transition at Davis's hands had been from youth to middle age. And all the time that I'd been close to collapse with sheer misery, my every waking moment spent searching and searching, dreading and dreading, she'd been sitting about perfecting the right image for a runaway heroine, the right eye make-up. I pictured the two of them watching old movies together, Davis making a masterclass of it, Roxy wondering if she'd rather be Jean Seberg or Brigitte Bardot.

'How could you do this, Roxy?' I cried, before I could stop myself. 'How could you? I just don't understand.'

292

'What?' But her eyes were suddenly less certain. She looked over my shoulder again as though praying to be rescued.

I waited for eye contact before I answered. 'Do I have to spell it out for you? I don't understand how any daughter could start a relationship with her mother's fiancée, her new husband. It's horrible, dishonourable, incredible!' The last word set off an echo, Alistair's reaction to my news of my relationship with Davis, 'It's incredible,' he'd said. 'Do you even know what kind of a person he is?'

She stared for several seconds. I guessed she was going to resort to the silent treatment again, but when she spoke it was in a calm, reasonable tone, as though she'd expected to be asked to explain herself and now that the moment had arrived, she was damned if she wasn't going to be perfectly equal to the task. 'I knew you'd think that, but it's not how it was. We knew how we felt about each other before you got engaged, even before I went to South Africa.'

My intake of breath was audible to both of us. 'You mean you'd already slept with him before you went on holiday?' This was something I had not dared believe, that Davis had seduced her before he had me.

'No.' Her voice was already terser. 'Of course I hadn't. It was only when he told me what had happened, that he'd proposed to you by mistake . . . That was when we told each other how we really felt. But it was too late by then for him to get out of it.'

My head was giddy with the callousness of her language. 'By mistake', 'too late', 'get out of it' and that self-confident stream of 'we's! My only cause for hope was that she had still not used Davis's name explicitly, not once, surely an acknowledgement of her wrongdoing? But, catching the alert look in her eyes, I saw that it was more likely owing to the fear that his name might provoke me to greater anger. For what was becoming clear was that my suspicion had been correct: she believed I had stolen the man she loved and not the other way around. It took every last ounce of creativity to approach this from her position, but I had no choice but to try, for she was seventeen and there was no question of her approaching it from mine.

'Why was it too late?' I asked, levelly. 'If what you say is true, then he should have just broken off our engagement. He should have admitted he'd changed his mind.'

She shook her head. 'He felt he couldn't. You were already telling people, planning the day. It would have been humiliating for you to have had to cancel . . .'

'Humiliating?' I was agape at her sheer gall. 'And this isn't? Come on, Roxy, this is far, far worse. Surely you can see that?' But it was hardly worth arguing. I knew that whatever she said, Davis's actions had had nothing to do with some warped respect for my pride. He had feared banishment, it was as simple as that. Reneging on his proposal would have drawn the same response from me as had his original withdrawal. I loved him; I'd already told him I couldn't bear to be near him unless he felt the same. 'But what about when I spoke to you, Roxy, you, not him. After we got engaged, I told you I would only go ahead with the wedding if I had your blessing. Why didn't you say something then? Why didn't you tell me you were unhappy about it? You wouldn't even have needed to explain why.'

She shot me a scornful look. 'Of course I would. You would never have changed your mind if I'd just said I didn't like the idea. You would have demanded an explanation. And then you would have gone ahead with it whether I liked it or not.'

Her words had the sting of truth to them and I felt my control slip away as my questions spilled out. 'But how could you let me be so happy about something that you knew wasn't what I thought it was? Didn't that mean anything to you? And how can you trust this man when you've seen how he's treated your own mother? Don't you think he'll do the same to you?'

Now the look she gave me was half sullen, half contemptuous, identical to the one Marianne had used to defend herself against *her* mother's tirade. Clearly I would get no answers to my questions, but it didn't matter, because I could guess them well enough. Roxy had no fears for her own future because Davis's love for her was real, not faked, as it had been for me. As for having seen my happiness, all she'd seen was an old fool determined to embarrass herself, whose feelings could not be taken seriously. Or perhaps, like Davis, she had understood that my feelings were real, but had taken the view that my short-term pain was a small price to pay for their being together, that anything was better than being denied their time, *anything*.

My tea was cooling. I'd lost track of how long I'd been there. 'What made you come back?' I asked.

She frowned. 'What d'you mean?'

I indicated the main house. 'You haven't been here all this week.' But as I spoke I saw that the terrace we were sitting on could be accessed by a set of French windows from the nearby barn. The interior was obscured by dark, floor-length curtains, but between the drapes a length of lamplight was visible. What was more, the shutters on the window to the right were hooked back to the stone walls, allowing the occupants a view of the garden without themselves being visible from the terrace. It was the perfect hideaway. Roxy may have gone into the main house to use the kitchen, but she and Davis were not living there, they were living here. They had been on the premises all along; pure bad luck had made us miss every one of their comings and goings.

'You mean you've been here all week?' Roxy asked, 'in Saint Martin?'

'For almost five days. No one's answered the bell the whole time. I thought the house was shut up for winter.'

She stared, digesting the information. She was so cool, far more composed than I was. 'Oh, yes, it is, except for the kitchen. It's way too expensive to run, we'll have to rent it out again in the spring. You can't hear the buzzer all the way back here. I guess we need to fix it so you can.' The authority in her voice both incensed and frightened me. To speak to me as though she and Davis were the established pair, sharing domestic decision-making, fixing doorbells together – had she forgotten that the man of her cosy plural was my husband? And to hear her refer to the future with such certainty, as though long-term plans were already under discussion, underway; it was terrifying.

'I called your name, Roxy, I was shouting, really loudly. Anyone could have heard.'

She pushed out her lower lip and shrugged one shoulder. '*I* didn't.'

Too busy doing her make-up, too busy lying in bed with him, listening to all those secrets he'd never wanted to share with me, but no doubt poured out endlessly to her. Too busy revelling in her glamorous new sexuality.

Totally off balance now, I allowed my fury to sway my fear. 'Where is he? My darling, devoted husband. When is he due back?'

She pulled up her knees to her chest and folded her arms around them, as though sensing that the fight was really about to begin. 'It doesn't matter, Mum. He doesn't want to see you.'

It was the first time in this encounter that she'd spoken my name and the word released the final coil within me. To her horror – and my own – I lunged across and grabbed her shoulder with my right hand, shaking her backwards and forwards so that her chin bumped violently against her knees and causing my injured left hand to be crushed against my own body. Pain surged upwards from my wrist and into my shoulder as she struggled to uncurl herself and get to her feet.

'Get off me! God, do you really think attacking me is going to make me change my mind?'

'I'm sorry.' I fell back into my seat, desperate and appalled. I didn't know what I had done or what I was capable of, what else the scene might tear from me. As the silence lengthened, I sensed that my only remaining option was to plead.

'Come home, Roxy, *please* come home. Come back and talk about this. Go back to school, do your A-levels. You'll be eighteen in February, decide then. It's only a few months, it will go by so quickly, and then you'll be free to do whatever you like.'

Through all of this she just shook her head calmly and deliberately – I might have thought tauntingly if I hadn't seen the tremble of her mouth. She was battling to compose herself just as I was. She was vulnerable. I rushed on. 'You don't know what you're doing, darling, you're throwing away opportunities that will be impossible to get back. I know how it feels at this age, everything's distorted because you're still growing up and doing things for the first time, things that seem huge when—'

She broke in then, and as soon as she spoke I realised that her wobble had been not from vulnerability but from anger. 'It's just a number, Mum! For God's sake, don't you get it? It doesn't matter whether I'm seventeen or eighteen or thirty-five, I know how I feel. There's nothing "distorted" about it. It's huge because it just is! I love him and he loves me and that's all there is to it!'

She was breathing heavily, the rise and fall of her chest almost perfectly synchronised with mine. I clamped my lips together to stop myself from contradicting her further, matching her own teenage clichés with parental ones of my own – You don't love him, You don't know what love is, You'll look back on this and wonder how you could have taken it all so seriously – and sooner than you think! But it will still be too late . . . I sucked in an extra mouthful of air and said, 'OK, I accept that's how you feel. But even so, sometimes you have to walk away from someone you love, Roxy.'

'Why?'

I gazed sadly at her. 'Because of the impact it has on other people.'

She glared back at me and I saw in her eyes not, as I had expected, the confidence that we argued now as equals but, far worse, the arrogance that she had left me behind, that there was nothing I could tell her that she hadn't now learned for herself. That there was a final theory about these actions of hers in respect to me and that it was both the most likely and the most ghastly: she simply hadn't thought about my feelings at all. Or at least hadn't thought enough about them. And that was the difference, wasn't it, between a girl and a woman, a child and a grown-up? One understands that others feel as intensely as she does, that everyone's experience is, at least to herself, equally as crucial, equally as pivotal; but the other has not yet stepped away from herself to know that.

She lifted her chin with cool finality. 'So, did *you* walk away from the first man you loved?'

Alistair, her father. I had been barely eighteen, a year older than she was now, but younger than her in so many ways, a teenager of a different time. 'No, I didn't.'

As I looked down, she held her head even higher. 'Well, there you go.'

And go I did, minutes later, back down the cobbled path, without my daughter, without knowing if I would ever be permitted to return.

Chapter 24

There was nothing left for it but to tell Alistair that I'd failed. His reaction was entirely predictable – and understandable: he swore energetically, cleared his schedule with immediate effect, and flew to La Rochelle. After my confrontation with Roxy, I worried that she might anticipate as much and bolt a second time (her panic at the suggestion that her father was already here had been virtually her only betrayal of weakness in our entire conversation), but I told myself that she couldn't possibly expect him to materialise the very same day, a Sunday no less. It felt so remote down here, light years from La Rochelle, much less London. The bridge to the mainland, when it came into view, looked sketched in pen and ink on a paper sky, not built for real in concrete and steel.

For me, his arrival couldn't come fast enough. The adrenaline that I'd relied on to sustain me until now had drained from my system in the few minutes it took me to walk away from Roxy at rue de Loix to Tash at our guesthouse. Details of the encounter emerged only in a tearful, incoherent tangle, but my sister got the gist.

'You mustn't give up,' she said, her own eyes wet with distress. 'You've just opened negotiations, that's all.'

'No,' I said. 'There's no deal here, not with her.'

'But how can you say that? You might really have rattled her.'

I shook my head so vigorously that tears slid outwards towards my ears. 'I know her. That's the thing, Tash, the thing I've been forgetting: I know her. I've had seventeen years to see how bits of me and bits of Alistair have come together and fused into this—' I broke off, sobbing, unable to find the words, and Tash sat gazing helplessly at me.

'Please don't be upset, I know it's awful, but let's see what Alistair says. He might have a new idea. You should try and sleep, Kate. You're completely done in.'

As I collapsed into bed, her voice turned into my mother's, strong, exasperated, but oddly admiring, as well; she was talking about Roxy – or was it me? A remark overheard twenty years ago? – 'She knows her own mind, that girl. I'll say that for her, she knows her own mind.' Those bits of us that had made Roxy, those bits of my own parents that had made me, they were the worst bits and the best bits all mixed up, because only the strongest survived. She knows her own mind . . .

I drifted off.

I slept all afternoon, a deep, sticky sleep, and had to be shaken awake to come and greet Alistair downstairs.

'Hi girls . . .' As Tash and I hurried down the stairs, he looked up from the check-in desk and calmly held up a palm in greeting. Though I'd seen him only days earlier, his physical likeness to Matthew struck me suddenly in a completely new way, like a premonition of the future, of a time when our son would be grown up, too. Standing there, tall and broad shouldered in the cottage proportions of the guesthouse hallway, his eye contact so true and sincere, he seemed all at once the embodiment of strength and goodness. Heroic, almost. As we embraced, I felt a sudden gush of emotion as I remembered exactly how it had been when we were together and happy, walking along the high street on a sunny Saturday, swinging Roxy between us, never imagining we'd end up in a situation like this.

He kissed Tash and treated her to a considerably more respectful look than he had the last time they'd met. That was a relief; I didn't think I had the energy to police his discourtesies. 'Not a bad trip, is it? I stepped off the plane, what? Forty-five minutes ago.' He wore jeans, a green wool sweater and raincoat, and appeared to have travelled with only an airport shopping bag for luggage. How confident he was that this would be nothing more than a flying visit, that he'd breeze in and accomplish in a morning what I had not managed in almost a week. He probably hadn't even brought spare socks. 'I literally ran out the door,' he said, seeing me eye the carrier bag. 'Passport, wallet, phone. Oh, and my legendary powers of persuasion, obviously.'

'Was Victoria OK about you leaving so suddenly?'

'Sure, fine. She was half expecting it.'

'And Matt?'

'Oh, he's used to me rushing about for work.'

Was he? Even at weekends? I didn't know that. I'd always imagined their time together to be spent in mutual and spellbound devotion. 'Well, I'm really glad you're here,' I said. 'We thought we'd update you over dinner, if that's all right? Decide what to do next.'

'Sounds good, I'm starving.'

It was odd, to say the least, to be strolling down to the waterfront in this configuration, Alistair, Tash and me, I in the middle drawing strength from each of them, wondering if I'd be able to keep myself upright without them. As I watched them examine menus and debate which restaurant to try, I felt buried alive by the avalanche of events of the last few weeks, events that had obliterated almost everything I thought I knew for sure: Roxy, the loyal daughter, Tash the hopeless-case sister, Alistair the enemy, Davis the hero. Now it was all out of kilter, no one recognisable any longer, and the outcome . . . well, if Alistair did not succeed where I had failed, then no one would.

In the bistro, I felt my spirit slowly dribble back. The music and warmth were comforting, as was the carafe of wine full to the neck and the warm, meaty smells drifting from the kitchen – *grandmère* cuisine, they called it here. I'd known just one of my own grandmothers, my father's mother, who had died when Roxy was a baby. I remembered we had been summoned to her bedside in the nursing home so that she could meet her great-granddaughter and the thinnest of tears had appeared in her weak old eyes at the sight of a new generation. She'd been so sucked of life she couldn't even cry a full tear! Thank God, she – and my own parents for that matter – had no idea what was currently unfolding in a little seaside village in western France.

'Right.' Alistair was businesslike, phone on the table, fingertips rapping, ready for his briefing. 'Tell me what's happened then, right from the start.'

It took two courses and a second carafe of wine to do so. Had Tash and I been reporting to a line manager in the office, we could only have been proud of our thoroughness, but the result remained the same, however admirable our attention to detail: Roxy was not at the table with us, this was not a farewell supper before we returned her to her home in the morning.

'I think we have to assume they'll move on if we keep harassing them,' I said. 'This isn't the sort of place where trouble just blends in.'

'If you ask me, we need to remember who's harassing who here,' Alistair said, grimly. 'This man has taken advantage of a minor. If anyone is trouble, it's him, and I intend to make that very clear to him.'

'I know, but even so, let's try to keep it as civilised as possible when we go along tomorrow. He may not even be there.'

Alistair interrupted me, eyes incredulous. 'Tomorrow? What are you talking about?' Diners at the next table looked up at the sound of his raised voice and I prepared myself for a scene, but Alistair merely gestured to a waiter for the bill. 'I'm going along there now. If we're all finished, that is. Tash?'

Tash glanced reluctantly at her empty coffee cup. 'Kate's right, Alistair, we should wait till morning.'

'Why? It's late, we'll catch them off guard. And if, as you say, they won't answer the bell, well, it's got to be easier to climb over the wall in the dark without being seen than in daylight, hasn't it?'

I tried to describe the fortress-like set-up at the house, the fact that to reach Roxy he'd need not only to vault over an eight-foot wall but also somehow get through a series of locked doors, but he just cut me off again. 'I don't care, Kate. I haven't come all this way to get a good night's sleep.' The bill settled, he leapt up, face flushed with wine. 'Come on! Show me the way.'

He was out of the door before I could reply. Tash and I exchanged a look before following and I could see what she was thinking: we didn't have much choice. It wasn't as if we could lead him in the wrong direction either, because we'd pointed out the intersection that led to Davis's house on the way down to dinner less than three hours ago. All the way up rue du Baron de Chantal I continued to remonstrate with him, but it was hardly worth expending the energy. I knew my ex-husband. He was fired up by the wine – and Dutch courage in a man who had never lacked drive was a potent proposition. He was unstoppable.

'This is the street,' I said, automatically whispering, though we were still some way from the gate.

'It's so quiet,' Tash muttered. 'It doesn't normally feel this creepy.'

She was right. It was dark, cold and utterly silent. I started to reply that we didn't normally skulk about so late at night, but was distracted by Alistair's urgent hiss: 'I thought you said they were holed up out of sight? Isn't that the fucker right there, by the white gate?'

Tash and I gaped in disbelief. Miraculously, after days of failed surveillance, we had caught Davis in the very act of leaving his house. Though it was cold, he hadn't put on a jacket or coat, was obviously slipping out for supplies of some sort. I felt bile rise from my stomach and fill my throat. The sight of him, the shadows of his cheekbones, the rumpled curly hair, the easy stroll of his legs, it was terrifyingly immediate. It was almost as though I could smell him and taste him as well, feel his skin under my fingers.

'Stay quiet,' I croaked in Alistair's direction. 'We don't want him to see us.' I assumed we would follow Davis wherever he was going, as Tash and I had Roxy earlier in the day, corner him indoors if we could, but Alistair clearly had other ideas and, ignoring me completely, yelled out into the silence: 'Hey, mate! Over here!'

Davis faltered mid-step. Then, after a short moment and without even looking up in our direction, he turned on his heel and began striding back towards the gate.

'D'you think he saw who it was?' Tash whispered to me.

'Of course he did,' I said, numbly. 'We need to get in before the gate closes.'

But things were happening so quickly, my sentence was redundant before I could finish it. Alistair had marched across the road and pushed Davis front-first against the wall by the gate, exactly as might a police officer who was apprehending a suspect, and there was the sound of scuffling and huffing as Davis managed to twist himself around and face his assailant directly.

Tash and I stood rooted to the spot. 'Quick!' she said, reacting first. 'We've got to stop him before he does something stupid.' She meant Alistair, I realised; bewilderingly, he was the dangerous element in this situation, not Davis. She stepped into the road, coming to a halt by the car nearest Davis's gate, just feet short of the men's grappling figures, at which point she turned back to look to me for guidance. It was hard to give, however, because I could scarcely keep up with my own reactions, much less intervene directly in the action. I felt nausea and confusion, but also the beginnings of a dark kind of excitement. Wasn't this what I'd wanted, subconsciously, why I'd encouraged Alistair to come, at least partly? To physically attack the man who had betrayed me?

'Where is she?' Alistair demanded in a horrible murderous voice. 'Open the fucking gate and bring her out!' Now I saw that Davis was as much restraining Alistair as he was submitting to an assault; they were locked together like wrestlers in a pre-agreed sequence of moves. Until Alistair broke free, shaking Davis off and slamming his own body against the gate, trying to force it open like a ram, hammering with his fists.

'Kate, we've got to stop this!' Tash mouthed – but I could only lip-read her words through the pounding of flesh on wood.

'Keep the noise down,' Davis said from the shadows beyond, and I felt a shiver on my skin at the sound of his voice, his breathing laboured after their tussle, but his voice otherwise tight with its customary control. 'She's not in there, anyway. You're wasting your time.'

'Don't give me that,' Alistair snarled. 'Got her locked in the basement, have you?' (More likely Davis had arranged with Roxy that she should lock herself in, were just this scenario to occur.) 'Where's the key, eh? This is kidnapping!'

'Kidnapping? I'd advise you not to bandy these sorts of terms about here, Mr Easton. It could be viewed as slander. And the same goes for your wife.' With this Davis flicked one hand in my and Tash's direction, the first indication that he was aware of our presence.

Alistair abandoned his pounding and turned angrily on him. '*My* wife? If you're talking about Kate, then I think you've forgotten whose wife she is, mate. You don't have much respect for your wedding vows, do you?'

Davis sneered. 'About the same amount as you, I imagine. It's not as if I'm the first to have left her, is it? At least I'm not deserting a whole family.'

At this Tash sought my hand with hers, gripped it tight. We might have been struck by the grim comedy of two husbands fighting over who didn't want me the most if the action hadn't started up again immediately. Alistair had lunged once more at Davis and they brawled together from side to side, their bodies moving in and out of the beam of a security light. As Alistair got the better of Davis, I heard the thwack of Davis's upper body as it met the stone wall behind him. This was getting dangerous; at least the timber of the gate had some give in it, but great blocks of stone were a different matter.

'This is not good,' Tash gasped, 'the police are going to come. We've got to do something!'

Still I didn't act, still a part of me wanted to see how far Alistair would take this. Then, at last, I stepped forward. 'Stop!' I shrieked. 'Please stop!'

At once Alistair eased off his shoving, though he still held Davis in his grip, their faces inches apart. His voice, when it came, was hoarse. 'Listen, Calder, this is the deal. I will come back here tomorrow morning at eight o'clock and if she is not here I will smash down that door and kill you, do you understand?'

'Don't be a fool,' Davis said. 'No one's going to kill anyone.'

'I think you might be underestimating me.'

'And you are threatening me, something that both the police and your daughter will be interested to hear, I'm sure.'

At this, Davis's first direct reference to Roxy, Alistair's fury rose afresh. 'You will not get away with this, you fucking paedophile.'

'I've already asked you once to watch what you say—'

'I'll say what I fucking like, you animal.'

'Alistair, stop this!' I cried out a second time. 'You're making things much, much worse!' This time neither of them reacted, they just continued their gruesome face-off, both panting, until a sudden show of strength on Davis's part caused Alistair to step heavily backwards towards the kerb. I thought he would call an end to it then, but instead he sprang forward and hit Davis, not the crunching sound I might have imagined, but a small, flat noise, like someone dropping an apple onto the concrete path. Davis cringed back against the wall, clutching his face, directly under the beam of the security light. There did not appear to be any blood.

'I mean what I say,' Alistair said. 'I want her back tomorrow morning.'

Davis muttered something in response, inaudible to me but within range of Alistair, who promptly took several steps backwards as if to judge the best distance and angle for a new assault. Thinking he was going to kick Davis, I rushed forward to pull him away, causing both of us to stumble slightly. I was aware of Tash hiding her face in her hands, as though wary of catching a blow herself.

'You're lucky I know when to stop,' Alistair spat in Davis's direction as I continued to pull him away. 'Come on, Kate, let's get out of here.'

Tash scampered after us like a terrified child, sobbing quietly, and I felt appalled at being responsible for having subjected her to this drama. Not only that, I had willed it to continue! What a poor protector I had proved to be, on every level imaginable.

About to turn into the main street, I alone cast a look back towards the white gate. Davis was standing in profile, the fingers of one hand nursing his left cheekbone. Not once in the entire episode had he looked in my direction.

At the guesthouse Tash excused herself and went straight up to bed. I could tell she left us on our own as much out of lingering shock as any sense of discretion. The sitting room was empty. I was fairly sure we were the only guests in residence and that the landlady lived off site – just as well, if Alistair was going to start shouting again. I watched as he pounced on the honesty bar and selected a bottle of brandy and two glasses. Then he slid open the glass door that led to the courtyard and stepped outside. Clearly I was intended to follow him.

It was a small cobbled space, no bigger than a boxing ring, with high, pale walls, a plastic garden table and chairs and a yellow parasol strapped shut for winter. Fairy lights glittered in a potted fern in one corner. More useful, it seemed to me, was the antique lifebelt nailed to the wall. I was ready to cling to it then and there and never let go.

Alistair splashed liquid into the glasses and we sat for a couple of minutes drinking in silence.

'This isn't the way to do it,' I said, eventually. 'If they weren't scared off before, they will be now.'

He gave a half smile. 'I didn't see you objecting back there.'

'Then maybe you weren't listening,' I said. Our eyes met. I wasn't fooling anyone. 'Or maybe I should have been firmer. Anyway, it's not about what *I* want to see happen to him.'

'He's lucky I didn't put him in hospital,' Alistair said, speaking into the cavity of his glass. 'That's what I'd like to see happen to him.'

I sighed. 'And then what? Go to prison while Roxy sits at his bedside playing Florence Nightingale?'

He ceded the point with a nod.

'We don't want her on the run, Alistair.' I left unspoken the thoughts that had licked the edges of my anxiety ever since this crisis began, thoughts to do with my working knowledge of the homeless, all those statistics about disease, drugs, mental health, life expectancy. Occasional encounters at the Advice Centre had left me in no doubt that most of these poor souls had actively chosen the dangers of sleeping rough over reconciliation with family, many having left home in the first place for reasons hardly more serious than Roxy's (and sometimes considerably less). 'Better we know where she is, with a roof over her head, decent food—'

Alistair cut in, 'Better she's back where she belongs.'

'Not like this, though. Beating Davis up won't make her come home.'

'Nor will negotiation, apparently.' He drank deeply from his glass before adding another large measure. Seeing I'd hardly touched mine, he brought the bottle to the table with a heavy thud, but I was too exhausted to recoil.

'Not with her, no,' I said. 'But I haven't had the chance to speak to *him* yet.'

'You mean you actually want to talk to the arsehole?'

I nodded. It would not be over until I had, I knew that now. And I would get my chance, Davis couldn't deny me forever. But Alistair could not be there when I did: this was between Davis and me. 'To be honest, Alistair, I think we might have to leave it, at least for a while. Come back when the dust has settled.' I wasn't sure how and when that might occur, but years of experience of other people's disasters told me it would. 'We have to get life back to normal for Matt.'

At the mention of his son's name, Alistair gave a long, tortured groan and it seemed to me that all of my own destroyed emotions were also contained in its sound. I looked at him with more tenderness than I had in a long, long time. All those years of thinking as one, of loving as one, they didn't just go away, and right now we were the only people in the world who understood exactly how the other was hurting.

'Poor little sod,' he said, 'just sitting there without a clue.'

'Fast asleep, I hope.' I tried to smile. 'It's late, you know.' I hated the idea of my little boy sleeping with neither of us near him. It was Monday tomorrow and I would not be there to start the school week with him as I always did. We *had* to bring this pursuit to an end. 'Look, I think we know they're not going to be at the gate at eight a.m. Why don't we go home, lick our wounds, and come back in a few weeks?'

Alistair nodded, silent for a while, apparently scrutinising the brandy bottle. I could sense him willing the brandy to do its work and obliterate the evening's events.

I took a gulp of my own. 'I'll try one more time to get to him, and then that will have to be it for now. I'm not sure he'll meet me, though, not this time. As you saw, he didn't even acknowledge me just now.'

The soft-hearted look Alistair settled on me was unexpectedly touching. 'I can't believe what he's done to you. It really is despicable.'

'He won't win,' I said, evenly. 'He'll lose. It just might not happen straight away.'

He raised his eyebrows. 'You're very philosophical about this all of a sudden.'

'I just don't think we can force things. Speaking to Roxy this morning made me see that. As far as she's concerned, this is the great love affair of her life. She has to realise for herself that it's not.'

Alistair gazed at me. 'You know, Kate, when I . . .' And he groaned again, as though tormenting himself with some unbearable truth. 'When I left, it was a very different situation, you know?'

I nodded. 'Of course it was. He's a sociopath, you were just . . .' I paused. Even after nine years I struggled to define what it was that had caused Alistair's desertion. 'You were just a man.'

He laughed at that, not entirely with displeasure, and once more we stared at each other. Then, at the same moment, we both noticed that I was shivering badly. 'You're freezing,' he said, and dragged his chair around the table to meet mine and put his arm around me. Without thinking, I rested my head in the curve between his shoulder and his ear. It wasn't just his warmth that was comforting, it was the familiarity of that curve. In happier times I'd slept every night with my face nuzzled into his neck. I looked up to smile in apology, but I'd barely had time to turn up the corners of my lips when he moved his face closer to mine and kissed me.

I broke away. 'What are you doing?'

'I don't know,' he murmured.

'This isn't the solution, Alistair.'

'Of course it isn't, it isn't meant to be.'

'Don't, then. Please.'

'I didn't mean to – I just . . .'

As we whispered our lines, our lips were somehow moving closer together again, until finally they were about an inch apart and he was tilting his face to kiss me again. And there was a split second when I was tempted, so eager for human comfort it didn't matter who was offering it, all the details of the whys and wherefores blurred in any case from my having drunk far more alcohol than I'd planned to. And then there was the pressure of the pain in his eyes, and I saw I'd been wrong, his hurt *was* different from mine. I was acclimatised, resigned to Roxy's loss, not only by the events of the last week, but also by those of the last few months, but he had not really known until this evening how hopeless our quest actually was. What he was experiencing was the rawness of those first moments of understanding.

He pressed his lips against mine a second time, murmuring into my mouth, 'Please, can't we . . .'

'No, Alistair!' I scraped the chair away from his, so that now we had each moved a quarter-circle around the table. This struck me as farcical, like we were pieces in some sort of human-sized board game. 'Come on, let's go back in before we both get hypothermia.'

We locked up behind us, rinsed out the glasses and recorked the brandy, and made our way up the stairs. As we parted at our doors I was possessed suddenly by an echo of the recent past, of Davis and me standing outside our front doors at Francombe Gardens, our keys poised at our respective locks, turning away from one another to push the door inwards at exactly the same moment.

'Are we all right?' Alistair asked, mistaking my haunted expression for disapproval of him.

'Of course we are.' It took some effort to stop myself from

311

reaching to take his hand in mine, he looked so boyish and forlorn, just as Matthew did when he'd done wrong. Unsteady on his feet, he leaned to kiss my cheek.

'See you tomorrow, Alistair.'

'*A demain*, you mean?' he grinned. 'Sounds better in French, I always think. Like only good things will happen.'

'*A demain*.' I smiled back. And for a second there, the words did sound more hopeful.

Like the cleverest of the three little pigs, Alistair was at the meeting point well in advance of the assigned time. The only problem was this was his assignation, not the wolf's, and none of us was the least bit surprised when Davis did not materialise to deliver Roxy to her father, bag in hand, ready to roll. After an hour of pestering and the emergence of a couple of neighbours to complain, I managed to persuade Alistair to fly back to London.

'You go with him,' I said to Tash, when we were alone, partly because I wanted someone to escort him to safety, but also because it was time for her to go, too. She needed to return the hire car, which we had not used for days, and, more importantly, to reclaim her own identity before she was subsumed altogether in mine. Helping her pack, I gave her my house keys and told her to make herself at home in the flat.

'Thank you, Tash, for everything.'

She looked surprised. 'I wanted to come. And it's not like I had anything else to do.'

'Well, even so, I won't forget this.'

'I think it might be better if you did.' She smiled, only half joking.

'Maybe. But I mean it, honestly. I feel like, well, thank you isn't enough. I think I owe you an apology, as well, a big one.'

Her eyes widened. 'Don't be crazy. You didn't do anything, it was Alistair.' She thought I was talking about last night's horror movie.

312

'I don't mean that, I mean, well, for the way I've always been.'
She coloured. 'I don't understand? What?'

'Oh, just everything. Not helping you out as much as I could, leaving you to Mum and Dad.' Not taking her seriously, that was what I really meant, or more to the point, taking myself so seriously that it had left little room for anyone else, even my own sister.

Tash looked at me, clear-eyed and smiling. 'You do blame yourself a lot, you know. It's not your fault I've been useless in the past. Anyway, I think maybe I've liked all of that, especially with Mum and Dad. It's been nice to stay a student for so long, to not have to worry about who's paying the bills. But maybe I'm ready to spread my wings a bit.' She laughed. 'Sounds pathetic coming from a twenty-seven-year-old, doesn't it? But I suppose we all grow up at our own pace.'

We gazed at each other. Figures of speech, well-worn phrases, they all had such heightened meaning now and judging by the way Tash's eyes strayed instinctively to the window I was not the only one to be reminded, once more, of Roxy. Was she thinking the same as me, that just as there were late developers there were early ones, too? At dinner last night I'd been ninety per cent reconciled to the fact that when I returned to London I would not be bringing my daughter with me; now I was ninety-nine.

I picked up Tash's bag. 'Let's go down. Alistair will be waiting. Sorry to send you off with him, I guess you're going to get an earful on the journey home.'

'He has every right to feel angry. You both do.' She buttoned up her jacket. 'So you're definitely not coming with us?'

'No. I'll stay for the rest of the day and if I still haven't managed to see Davis, I'll come home. There's a flight at nine tonight, I'll get that if there's a seat and I'll be home by midnight. I can't leave Matthew any longer, not for anyone.'

Not even for Roxy.

Downstairs, standing in front of the old stone fireplace, Alistair was already tapping at his BlackBerry, tending to the

Monday morning needs of his staff. 'Rupert? You wanted me? How did the conference call go? Good. Is Ellen in this morning? When does she leave for Budapest?' For each ten-second interval that contained his colleague's queries, Alistair responded with an instant decision. Just yes or no. Did we do it better, once we were parents, making decisions, fighting fires, or did we just do it more recklessly?

'Whenever you're ready, Alistair,' Tash said, when he was off the phone. 'I'll wait in the car.'

We watched her walk out into the sunshine. It was another gloriously bright day. 'Sorry,' Alistair said, turning to give me an awkward squeeze goodbye. 'I haven't exactly helped, have I?'

'It doesn't matter. It's an impossible situation.' We looked at each other then, his face a collage of sheepishness and remorse and fear and exhaustion. I imagined mine was not so dissimilar a composition, though I'd begun avoiding catching my reflection in mirrors if I could help it.

'Sorry,' he said again. 'I mean it, Kate.' And I had a sense that he was thinking not only of last night's events, but of others, too, in the past.

It seemed that this was a morning for apologies long overdue.

After they'd gone I waited by the gate at rue Loix. I couldn't think of anywhere else to go. Though I'd already been there earlier that morning with Alistair, I still approached more cautiously than usual, half expecting to find evidence of violence – scuff marks, drops of blood, a scrap of torn clothing – but it was the same as always. The same glossy, impermeable gate, the same centuries-old stone. I wondered which others, if any, had come to this house over the years with broken hearts, broken lives. I couldn't believe that Alistair and I were the first.

At first I didn't even press the buzzer, just imagined her on the other side, imagined her walking down that pretty cobbled path and turning a key in the lock of that elegant glass door. It was like an image from a fairytale, *Hansel and Gretel* or *Little Red Riding Hood*, an innocent entering the lair of a beast. And yet she'd been ready to go, I saw that now. Another year under my rule – under anyone's rule – had been an unbearable prospect to her. Even without Davis's catastrophic seduction, it would have been a miracle if I'd been able to keep her at home, to stop her from escaping at least some of the time to Marianne's or her father's, or to the home of a different lover altogether. (To think I used to ponder my ideal boyfriend for her, someone she could grow up with, learn alongside, to think that Damien had fallen short, at least in Alistair's eyes – 'harmless', he had called him! Well, anyone would be preferable to the one she had chosen.)

I reached for the buzzer and held it down until my fingertips went white. I knew they couldn't – or wouldn't – hear it. Hard to believe the thing was still functioning, anyway, after so much abuse. Finally, I gave up, slumped to the ground and closed my eyes.

Time drifted by, I wasn't sure how long, but my ears suddenly caught the sound of a door opening, followed by footsteps on the stone flags, faint, soft-soled, unhurried. And then they stopped. I stiffened. The gate didn't open, which meant that whoever it was had come to a halt just short of the sensors. Still hunched on the ground in the corner of the gateway, I snaked my hand up the wall and reached once more for the buzzer.

A voice called out: 'Who's there?' It was Roxy.

Heart soaring, I scrambled to my feet and put my mouth to the crack where the gate met the frame. 'Roxy, it's me, let me in!'

There was a pause. 'Is Dad there?'

'No, he's gone.'

'I don't believe you.'

'He has, I promise you. He's flying back to London right now.' I began pumping my good fist against the gate, shouting for her to open it, until she cried out, 'Oh, stop it, for God's sake, this is pathetic! I'll open up!'

The gate began its interminably slow opening, revealing a sliver of her at a time, like some sort of guessing game. She stood there in a short pink jersey dress, bare legs and muddy wellington boots, holding in her hands a collection of tiny apples, as though she'd been interrupted picking them. 'I *thought* I heard something. Have you been here all this time?' She hesitated. 'Since eight o'clock?'

'He told you then? That we were here last night? That your father arranged to take you back this morning?'

Her mouth remained impassive, but her eyes glittered with objection. 'You can't "arrange" to take a human being, Mum. I'm not some kind of parcel.' She chuckled scornfully. 'What were you going to do with me, anyway? Tape me up and stow me in the boot? Who was going to sign for me in London? My brother?'

I didn't answer. I was back where I always was with Roxy, caught out by my inadequate language skills, juggled about by hers until I was too dizzy to remember my original point. Well, no more. 'Where is my husband?' I demanded. 'I think he needs to come and speak to his wife.'

She blanched, not expecting that bald reassertion of my technical status in all of this, of my stake in Davis, and when her eyes met mine again they were suddenly unseeing. 'I'm afraid he's recovering after last night's assault.'

'You know why Dad got angry,' I said, sharply. 'The same reason I'm still here, camped out on your doorstep like some kind of . . .' I searched for the right word, one that might elude her instant damnation, '. . . protester. We want to take you home, where you belong.' I stepped forward, over the threshold, appealing to her with my eyes and my hands, but she remained throughout a bloodless statue in front of me.

'It's not gonna happen, Mum. Don't you get it? I say where I belong, not you. Please just leave me alone.'

We stared at one another. I blinked back the beginnings of

tears. 'I will go, but not until I've seen him, not until I've heard what he's got to say.'

She sighed. 'He's not here.'

'I don't believe you.' I echoed her earlier line, but she didn't falter.

'I swear to you, he isn't here. He's gone to visit a friend on another part of the island and he won't be back till tonight.'

'Then why didn't you go with him?'

'I just wanted to be on my own for a bit.'

I searched for eye contact, but received the same soulless look. However scrambled my instincts about her had become, I felt sure she was telling the truth about Davis. He wasn't here. I wasn't going to be allowed to see him. My eyes dropped to her bare legs, white-cold, and for a moment I forgot myself. 'Aren't you freezing, darling? Do you have a coat with you? I can give you mine.'

But she didn't answer the question. 'Please, Mum, stop all this. It's doing my head in.'

I gazed sadly at her. 'Just come out for a coffee with me, or a walk or something, so we can talk?'

'I don't think so.'

I had told myself not to argue with her, not to leave things on a note I couldn't live with. 'OK, I'll go. But pass on a message for him, will you? Just—' My voice started to crack. 'Just tell him he's a coward. Tell him I deserve better than this, he knows I do. *You* know I do.'

'Mum . . .' And, finally, there was something in her eyes, something real and vulnerable, something for me; pity that I'd been reduced to this broken, begging state, or maybe just simple sorrow at the separation that lay ahead of us. If not remorse, at least there was that.

Chapter 25

There'd been a phase when Roxy was thirteen or fourteen when she'd become interested in family photographs and wanted to document her childhood for herself. She compiled the best of my stocks in an album and framed her favourites for her bedroom wall. One of these had been taken that day at Camber Sands and I remembered quite clearly Alistair waylaying another day-tripper and asking him to snap the three of us together. I picked Roxy up, hooked her long legs over my right hip, adoring the feeling of her clinging to me, feeling the beat of her heart through her ribcage. She was at the age of becoming self-conscious about photographs, often pulling a silly face or sticking her tongue out, but this time she just pressed her cheek flat against mine and turned to the camera with the sweetest of smiles. I was glad the memory was as special to her as it was to me, for, as it turned out, Alistair's glorious, spontaneous abandonment of work that day in favour of spiriting his family to the seaside was never repeated.

There was a tin of shells, as well, among them her famous 'Russian' shells, as she called them (though they were found not in Russia but in Cornwall). They were fan-shaped shells, painstakingly selected for their perfectly decreasing sizes, so that she could nest them one inside the next just like a *matryoshka* she'd seen in the toy shop. They were a rare souvenir, the Russian shells, for Roxy had never been a collector, not like Matthew, who had several years' worth of pebbles and pine cones under his bed. When he was small he'd ask to go out gathering 'interesting things' and we'd go into the garden or to the park in search of them. He'd show me a fallen petal or an abandoned lolly stick and ask, 'Is *this* interesting?' And woe betide I slipped anything into the bin, for he had a stocktaker's thoroughness and would spot a missing item in a flash.

No, Roxy was not a collector; she never saved anything for best. That wasn't to say that as she grew up she didn't become as materialistic as the next teenager, for she was, in fact, quite intense in her acquisitions, coveting a certain item with a passion and campaigning for it with skill and patience. Her persistence would have been admirable had it not been for the indecent speed with which she'd grow careless of her prize. She'd use it up without giving it a moment's thought, she'd treat it as everyday.

Then, just as quickly, she'd forget she ever had it.

Later, with several hours still remaining before I needed to leave for the evening flight, I paced the cobbled streets of Saint Martin, thinking of Roxy in her fortress just a street or two away. That was what this place had become to me, a succession of protective layers between my daughter and me, just like those little Russian shells of hers. Individually the layers might be broken, but as one they held firm.

I climbed to the top of the old clock tower, from which there was a fine view of the burnished terracotta roofs below, the cobweb of streets sloping down to the harbour, the grey line of ocean all around – even a small corner of Davis's garden could be seen from here. There were lookouts at every turn in Saint Martin, it was a town that had been built with surveillance in mind – laughable when you considered how easily Davis had stayed out of sight. Without Alistair's hot-blooded leadership Tash and I might never have found him at all.

I wandered down to the harbour. It was Monday, but notice-ably more bustling than last week – a French holiday, perhaps. The carousel was in motion, lights twinkling and music playing as half-a-dozen children sat astride the ponies and other crea-tures. Parents, some with cameras, occupied the semi-circle of chairs that had been set out on the cobbles, and I slipped into an empty one at its edge, watching as the attendant stepped onto the moving ride and began collecting up the tokens. I wondered how it must feel to do his job, riding around and around and never going anywhere, every day like the one before.

The music changed. 'Somewhere Over the Rainbow'. One small girl who'd been laughing a minute ago had grown bored and was resting her head on the neck of her pony, looking out at the audience, waiting for the ride to end. She had hair a little like Roxy's had been at that age, dark and gleaming, the colour of the midnight sky, and almost limp with softness. To touch it in weather like this would be like handling lengths of cool embroi-dery silk. Davis, no doubt, had a lover's simile of his own for just that sensation.

The ride stopped. The girl clambered down and joined her parents. She was slighter than Roxy, not much like her at all, now I looked at her properly.

I moved on. Across the way there was an art gallery open and I passed almost an hour looking at the exhibition there, square paintings with dark brown colour applied with a knife, like pieces of bread laid flat and spread with treacle. Incomprehensible. I imagined Davis and Roxy standing in front of the same pictures, making up stories for each other, finding meaning in them simply for having looked at them together. And I understood then that I could make no headway here, I was not going to be able to see Davis, I could only follow Alistair and Tash back to London and try to make some sense of all of this from home, devise a new strategy that might have a greater chance of success.

Resolved to return to the B&B and pack my belongings, I

hesitated at the sight of the island bus pulling up opposite the gallery. The village names of its route rolled in lights above the windscreen and I stopped to read them. Some were so familiar now – Le Bois-Plage-en-Ré, La Couarde-sur-Mer, Loix, Ars-en-Ré, Saint-Clément-des-Baleines, Les Portes-en-Ré – it was as though I'd been here for months. As the rotation completed a second time, I felt my eyebrows draw together: that second-to-last name rang a bell for a reason of its own, one I couldn't quite grasp. I waited for the names to display a third time – Loix, Ars-en-Ré, Saint-Clément-des-Baleines – and this time I had it: Phare des Baleines, the lighthouse in the picture above Davis's mantelpiece. What had he said when he'd seen me looking at it? So many steps to the top, that was right, and . . . a friend of his who lived 'right near there'.

As I stared, the bus doors closed with a brisk hydraulic puff and through the windscreen I could see the driver preparing to pull out. 'Wait! Wait!' I cried in English, though he couldn't hear me anyway, and sprinted forward into his path. He'd opened the door again before I could begin to plead and, blessing the old-fashioned manners of the rural French, I paid my fare and got on. As we glided out of Saint Martin, I studied the timetable left on the seat by a previous traveller. The village of Saint-Clément-des-Baleines was at the far end of the island; Tash and I must have driven through it on our tour of the first day, though we hadn't gone to the lighthouse itself, I would certainly have remembered that. Nor had we lingered in a second settlement close to it, a place called Le Gillieux.

I could hardly contain myself as the bus made its genteel progress through the villages, only occasionally taking aboard a new passenger as it trundled past the farmland and vineyards and salt marshes, the miles and miles of cycle paths, the gentle, flat vistas broken only by the odd church spire or windmill. At Le Gillieux, I was the only one to get off and I waved the driver goodbye with an earnestness that surprised me as much as it did him, as though I never expected to see human life again.

'Are you here?' I whispered to myself. 'Are you? I have a feeling you are.' But the only souls in sight were heading the way I'd come, two cyclists, lean and bare legged, and they didn't even look up from the road to acknowledge me. I took a short stroll in the opposite direction to the edge of the village, the rear of the bus still visible on the road ahead, and looked about. There were more of those low, single-storey white houses I was used to after a week on the island, some built in picturesque lines around freshly ploughed fields. On the surface of the road the tyre marks left by a tractor looked like the footprints of a giant bird. A kilometre or so away stood the lighthouse itself, tall and solid against a cold, marbled sky. Even at a distance it had a kind of pull to it, as though it might once have lured those on ground to the water as powerfully as it guided sailors to the shore.

I returned to the bus stop on the main square and studied the village plan displayed there. There was still plenty of time before I needed to worry about returning to Saint Martin, time to circuit every street, scour the shops and restaurants (if there were any), peer in windows and sneak into gardens where I dared. He could be in any one of those whitewashed houses – or none.

My eye was caught suddenly by something reflected in the display glass, not so much movement as a sudden suspension of it, and I spun around, all senses on high alert. A figure on the far side of the square had frozen mid-step, a figure in a grey tweed blazer, of Davis's height, Davis's build – the distance between us was just too great for me to be sure whether or not our eyes had connected. Evidently he had been breaking open a pack of cigarettes and the cellophane fluttered in his fingers. I remembered that the bus had passed a *tabac* a little further down the road, he must have just bought them there and was now on his way back to his friend's (all those hours at the *marché* in Saint Martin, but the *tabac* was where we should have been all along!). My eyes moved involuntarily to the main road, as if for the *tabac* sign, to confirm I'd really seen it, and in the second it took me to realise my mistake and look back to him, he had gone.

'Davis!' I yelled, shattering the silence. 'Where did you go? Where are you?' I hurried to the spot where he'd stood just seconds before and whirled about in disbelief, searching for a clue, a trace of scent. The ribbon of cellophane from the cigarettes had settled in the road by the kerb and I was tempted to pick it up, to touch it, the only tangible evidence that he had been here. How could he simply have vanished? Narrow alleys ran down the sides of several nearby houses and I checked each one for an escape route, but there was not a whisper of recent disturbance, no swinging gate or dislodged shrubbery. I hurried back to the main street and scanned first the road south that the cyclists had taken and then the one north to the lighthouse. And there he was, the coward, already some way off, running at a canter. Hurtling flat out, I couldn't quite close the gap between us – clearly he was much fitter than I was – but I did at least keep him in sight, grateful now for the endless flatness of this place as I tailed him past the entrance to a theme park, down a stretch of long, pale road and into a car park. Only then did he come to a halt and look over his shoulder. Instinctively I slowed up, too and, seeing me so close behind, he accelerated. He was heading straight for the lighthouse, the end of the road, the end of the island.

'Davis! Stop!' Stumbling and panting, I set off after him once more, past cars and cafés and souvenir shops, barely clearing the outdoor displays of caramels and soaps and wooden seagulls and stuffed donkeys, until I saw him enter the broad, low building from which the lighthouse rose. I was exhausted now, my early pace impossible to sustain, and by the time I reached the entrance myself, I had lost sight of him. It didn't matter, however, because I knew now what he was doing. He was heading for the top. Why else lead me all the way here if not for the drama of the ascent?

Evidently tickets had to be bought at the cash desk of the gift shop and there was quite a queue of tourists buying their postcards and trinkets, fussing over credit cards and unfamiliar currency. By the time I had my ticket I had lost a further five minutes at least. If my instinct was wrong, if this had been simply an elaborate way of giving me the slip, then he'd be halfway back to the village by now. I'd see him perhaps from the top, out of reach once and for all. I imagined him lighting a cigarette and sniggering at my amateurishness, rehearsing the witticisms he would use when recalling the drama later for Roxy. Drama: always it came back to that word.

I thanked the cashier and took the final doors to the interior of the great tower itself. I recognised it at once from Davis's picture, the smooth curved stonework, the elegant spiral of the staircase, the way it curled in and out of shadow until all that was left was a shell-coloured circle at its centre. Of Davis there was no trace, however, and I continued craning upwards for some time, dizzying myself with the perspective, not knowing whether to begin the climb or to wait for some sort of sign. Then I saw something pale and ball-shaped on the rail about a third of the way up, a hand wrapped around the banister, the forearm masked by the spindle, just as in the photograph itself.

'Davis! Is that you?' My voice echoed around the hollowed-out stone, all the more sinister for the silence with which it was met. I stepped onto the staircase and began climbing. 'Say something, for God's sake!'

The hand withdrew. Now I could hear the faint rhythmic smack of his soles above my head between the heavier sound of my own step below. He was on the move again. The rail was on the left, which meant I couldn't clutch it properly with my injured hand, a considerable discomfort, as I saw at every window how the ground was withdrawing further and further from me. Below, the circle of black and white marble at the foot of the stairs shrank first to the size of a darts board, then to a playing counter. I was giddily, unnaturally high. At last the stone gave way to a narrower spiral of green-painted iron and, transferring my grip from warm wood to cool metal, I felt my fingers tremble. My lungs burned from the climb and my heartbeat filled my ears, brutally loud, as though somehow amplified by the acoustics outside my body.

'Davis? Answer me!' But still there was no reply. He wanted to drive me mad, that much was clear, to exhaust me and to wind me up in one, to give himself the advantage when we came finally face to face. And though I'd chased him down with every last breath of my body, a part of me did wish that the steps would never end, but would go on and on and on until the ground had faded and all that was left was sky.

I emerged into an empty, wood-panelled room where the lighthouse keepers must once have slept, judging by the enclosed wooden bed that served now as a resting place for out-of-puff tourists. It was the only feature between two tall windows, one of which looked out to sea, the other to land, and at both swarms of black flies clamoured to get in. In different circumstances I would have felt safe here, protected by the stone and wood. I glanced to the ceiling. It was too thick for me to be able to hear anything from the observation deck above, but he was up there, he had to be, there was no possible alternative. In front of me a third, narrower spiral awaited and I approached with jellied legs. I had him now – or he had me.

I heard his voice before I saw his face. 'Hello, Kate. So you've found me after all.'

Instinctively I stopped, looked slowly up to where he stood in the doorway, outlined against a rectangle of white sky. He leaned slightly to one side, his right hand out of view, and for a melodramatic moment I imagined him with some implement in it, ready to beat me back, finish me off. But instead he held out his left hand towards me. 'Can I help? I see you've injured yourself.'

'No thank you,' I said, curtly. 'I don't need your gallantry.'

'Ah, I see. Fine.'

He stepped aside. Without his assistance I struggled to steady myself at the top and to adjust to the cold breath of the wind. I couldn't bring myself to look at his face, not yet, but concentrated instead on the space around us. The deck was just wide enough for two adults to pass and a circular grey stone balustrade, about rib-height for me, was all that separated us from a fifty-metre drop to the ground. To my left and over Davis's shoulder, the wooded coastline curved out of sight, while to my right I could see the long golden ribbon of a sandy beach. Above our heads, out of reach, sat the great old light itself.

Davis waited as I returned my attention to him, scrutinising his face without quite meeting his eye. I'd forgotten, in the darkness of my new disgust for him, how extremely beautiful he was, those features arranged to perfection below a youthful head of curls teased now from his face by the breeze. There was a red mark on his left cheekbone – presumably where Alistair had struck him – but this seemed to enhance the elegance of his bone structure rather than to blemish it. I felt a twinge in my abdomen, residual acknowledgement of the desire I'd felt for him; my brain knew the truth, my heart too, but my body still lagged a little behind.

'So, here we are.' He spoke perfectly agreeably, as though this were the conclusion of some amusing parlour game. 'You always were fascinated by this lighthouse, weren't you? I'd forgotten that.'

You've forgotten me, I thought, and how easily, too, how remorselessly. He didn't seem the slightest bit unnerved by my silence, as I had been by his, or anxious, as I was, about our position halfway to the clouds. He didn't breathe heavily or look uncertainly about – he even had one hand in his pocket. (The other, the one he'd offered me just now, the one that had held mine as we'd exchanged wedding vows, played idly with the hair at his neck.) I stared, astounded by his coolness. But, then, when had I ever actually seen him lose it? Even last night, under attack, he'd been in complete control of everything he'd said, a self-possession that could only have intensified Alistair's fury. No, there had been only two losses of balance that I could recall: once when he'd been overwhelmed by wedding plans (or so I'd thought – I realised now that there had been deeper torments at work), the other when he'd come to my door and pleaded with me to marry him . . .

'Breathtaking, isn't it?' He took his hand out of his pocket and patted the stone wall, a familiar, teacherly gesture. I had been right about his reason for bringing me here: as settings for show-downs went, this was both improbable and perfect (no wonder he had been so contemptuous of Alistair's crude ambush under a streetlamp). In a movie only one of us would take the stairs back down, the other would crash over the side. 'A real work of art, don't you think?' he said.

'Yes.'

'Is Alistair still in Saint Martin?' There was a trace of wariness to his tone now.

'No,' I said shortly, 'he's gone back to London. So there was no need for you to rush up here to hide.'

'I wasn't hiding. This is a longstanding arrangement with a friend.'

I wondered if he were being deliberately ambiguous; 'up here' could mean the lighthouse, the 'friend' me. I decided not to give him the satisfaction. 'Not that longstanding, surely?' I snapped. 'Or were you already planning this before I found out, before we even got married? Did you write to your little chum and say, "See you at the end of October, my marriage should be over by then"?'

He ignored my sarcasm, maintaining his own infuriating top note of politeness in his reply. 'Well, I'm pleased your ex-husband has gone home, anyway. He was lucky not to get himself arrested last night.'

I snorted. Ambiguous though I felt about Alistair's attack, I still believed there was only one man in this miserable situation who was lucky to have eluded arrest.

A sudden gust ruffled Davis's hair and, as if reminded by it of a more pressing matter, he asked, suddenly, 'How did you know we were here, in Ile de Ré?'

'It's not important,' I said, dismissively. I didn't want to mention Camilla's part in my investigations. I imagined her a thousand miles away, shuddering at the sound of him speaking her name. In time, would my own revulsion run as deep? Perhaps it already did.

'I'm sorry Kate. I didn't mean to hurt you.' He sought my gaze with an expression of humility that I would, only weeks earlier, have happily mistaken for the real thing. At first I was disarmed by so instant an apology, but then I remembered that when you didn't mean it, 'sorry' could be issued as cheaply as breath itself.

'I don't care about me.' I kept my voice flat and steady, using it to plug the emotion that welled beneath. 'I'm here for Roxy.'

Davis bit down on his lower lip. 'I realise that. You must have been worried about her.'

I glared at him and he took a step back as though my loathing had produced a physical force. I followed, taking myself out of reach of the door and the staircase down, the shore now on my right and the flat of the island to my left. 'Worried? *Worried*? Surely a man of your great learning can come up with a better word than that to describe how a mother feels when her daughter has been abducted!'

His eyes narrowed a fraction, but he didn't say anything, taking me at my word perhaps and sifting words, trying them in different languages. I sensed the storyteller in him thrilling to this exchange (it would appear, no doubt, in those pathetic 'fragments' of his), and when he finally spoke it seemed to me that it was with increased relish. 'We both know it's not an "abduction", Kate.'

'That's what it is to me. Along with other things . . .' I'd intended leaving it at that, but I couldn't stop from spitting out the words: 'Like betrayal, for instance. Marital infidelity. Total and utter disrespect for a human being you're supposed to care for. But let's stick to the abduction, shall we?'

He nodded, the faint exaggeration of the motion conveying to me that he was merely humouring me, congratulating himself on possessing the skills required to manage a hysteric like me. That was his gift, I realised, he directed you and never the other way around, he cast you in the role of his pleasing. First I'd been the downtrodden mother in need of rescue ('rescue', he'd even used that term once), the woman who'd vowed never to love again; then I'd been the lover, the convert, the person he'd drawn out of me to my own shock and delight; now, however, I was the unwanted wife whose emotions had run away with her, who'd become difficult.

'I do care for you,' he said, 'but I don't expect you to believe that. I'm not stupid, I know how it must seem.'

'You can't possibly know,' I said, stonily, 'or you wouldn't have done it. Unless you're a sadist and you get pleasure from treating someone like this.'

He gave a long sigh. 'No, I get no pleasure from it. And I can't defend myself, I know that. I should never have let it reach this point.' Hope flared; then died as quickly. He meant us, of course, not Roxy and him.

The wind picked up again and I supported myself on the rail as I tried to rein in my thoughts. I needed to get this back to the subject of Roxy and not be lured into a consolatory conversation about his treatment of me. 'Let me tell you something you should never have done, Davis: remove a child from her home, from her school. You're a teacher, for God's sake, you know how crucial her education is.'

He frowned at my use of the word 'child', but otherwise remained impassive. 'It's not ideal, I agree, but it couldn't be helped.'

329

'Of course it could!' I lashed back. 'Every day she's losing ground. We need to get her back to her school straight away, forget all this nonsense ever happened!'

At that he threw up his hands – again a mannerism employed for his own enjoyment rather than a spontaneous reaction – as though in recognition of the crux of this confrontation. 'Oh, Kate, that is your great failing, you know. You think everything can be controlled by common sense. And only your own definition of it will do, your own judgmental take on things. But there's nothing "nonsensical" about what has happened, I promise you.'

How I loathed the self-importance of his tone, almost as much as I feared the meaning of his words (my tendency to be judgmental continued to be my weakness, even after years of working in the job I did). 'What do you mean?'

'I mean it's inevitable. Pre-destined.'

'It's doomed,' I corrected him. 'At least for her, it is. This will ruin her life, Davis, can't you see that?'

We stared at each other. The wind had subsided enough for us to be able hear the sound of the tide; I didn't know whether it was coming towards us or shrinking away from us – either way, it seemed to me that it moved in rhythm with him, not me.

'Give her up,' I said simply.

He looked at me, eyes giving but mouth stubborn. 'I can't.'

'She is still a girl.'

He shook his head. 'She is a young adult. And she has a wisdom far greater than ours.'

'Oh, don't talk bull!' My anger was dangerously close to the surface now, I stepped towards him so that he was forced against the balustrade and our bodies were a hair's breadth apart. I smelled the cigarettes on his breath, the scent of his skin and hair, and I had an image of us writhing together in the August heat, behind us drawn blinds glowing with daylight. 'I know this person, remember? A lot better than you do. And I can tell you that she is not wise and she is not an adult. Do you know all the

330

things she's not allowed to do? By law.' My mind searched that list at home, the last page in the printout and the longest. 'What can I do at age eighteen?' 'She can't vote, she can't make a will, she can't buy a drink in a pub, for Christ's sake!'

Still his absurdly genial expression remained. 'It's different in France.'

'No it's not! It's not different anywhere where there are civilised people! A child is defined by most authorities as someone under the age of eighteen.'

He moved away from the edge, once more plum in the centre of the walkway, hand back in pocket. 'You can spout the statistics at me until you're blue in the face, but I really don't think UNICEF is going to be interested in this particular case, do you? Roxy has willingly left you. Accept that. You've seen her here, tell me she is not happy!'

I shook my head. 'She's not happy, she's deluded. She's a deluded schoolgirl and she should be in class!'

He raised his eyebrows a fraction, considering whether or not to lecture me on the semantics of it, deciding against it. 'Her education can be continued in another form, Kate. She will be a success in life because of who she is, not because of which university she goes to. I've explained that to you before, at least I thought I had. Get this into proportion, please.'

I hated him then, a hot, physical hate with a violence of its own. I wanted to push him over that famous weathered stone and watch him split on the cobbles below. And had I done it, I would have felt no remorse, I was absolutely sure of that. 'She's my daughter, Davis, I gave birth to her. Don't tell me to get it into proportion.'

'Well, if you can't, I'm afraid this conversation is over. I'm going back down.' He turned away from me and began moving around the deck, taking the long way around to the door to avoid having to get past me, to risk making physical contact with me.

331

'This conversation is not over!' I cried, crashing after him, through the door, down the steps, grabbing for his shoulder to stop him from continuing any further. We came to a clumsy halt in the wooden room and the sudden calm and warmth of the enclosed space made our proximity more intimate, more frightening.

He glared at me with real exasperation, having at last abandoned that insufferable mannered graciousness. 'What, Kate? I'm getting sick of this. What is it you want me to say? Something other than sorry, obviously. Just tell me and I'll say it and then we can go our separate ways.'

I closed my eyes. Now that I had his true attention I could no longer stop the yearning from surfacing, the yearning for his admission that there had been something genuine between us, that I hadn't fabricated those weeks in summer or imagined the closeness of our conversations, our dinners, our love.

'Just tell me why you married me, why . . .' I corrected myself before he could reply. 'No, don't answer that. I know why. But why did you even start a relationship with me when you knew you were attracted to someone else? Why would you do that? I mean, regardless of who she was? I just don't understand it.'

He looked longingly at the doorway and then reluctantly back at me. 'I *was* attracted to you, Kate, but not in the way you wanted, not with the same intensity. I had thought . . . and when I realised . . .' For the first time he struggled to find the words, and for the first time I found I could fill the gaps quite ably on my own. He had thought Roxy would never be interested in him, that was what he was trying to say, he had decided that an older, more grateful model was the closest he would get to being with her. But then he discovered that she *was* attracted to him, and more than that, she actually shared his rapture. Their problem was that, by then, I was rapt too.

I took a small step towards him. 'When exactly did things start with her? Just tell me that.'

He blinked. 'It hardly matters now.'

'It does matter! I know you spent a night together just before the wedding, when you were supposed to be with your great friend Graham. How could you have even entertained the idea of being with both of us at once? You must have slept with us within days of each other, hours! It's grotesque!'

His obvious surprise was swiftly replaced by another doleful look towards the doorway. I imagined him wishing Roxy there, standing there smiling at him, his sweet reward for all my sourness. 'I really don't think it's helpful to go into that.'

'Well I do!' I cried. 'I think it's very helpful if I'm going to get an iota of understanding of the mind of a complete—' I broke off. There was no one word I could summon that properly classified him. 'Pervert' Alistair called him, Tash 'bastard'. 'Someone so completely warped.'

He pressed his lips together, cocked his head: the condescension was back. 'Kate, you're getting hysterical. Why don't we go back down to the village, find a quiet bar somewhere and talk this through. Get your feet back on the ground, eh?' Without waiting for my agreement he moved towards the doorway but I was already there, blocking his exit and screeching, 'No! Don't you dare run away from this! You will not go until *I* am ready!'

We were both shocked by how weirdly shrill and animal my cry sounded. He made no further attempt to descend, but instead crossed the room and took a seat on the wooden bed. I made a last, painful effort to remain calm. 'Let me take her back, Davis. She'll finish school, she'll have her eighteenth birthday, and if she still wants to be with you after that then it will be her choice. I promise you her life will be her own. I will bow out. But let her finish her childhood with me.'

He shook his head. 'You're living in some sort of nineteen-fifties' fantasy, Kate. Girls like Roxy finished their childhood a long time ago. Whatever you like to believe, I was not her first "delusion", as you put it.'

I gasped. The upward flicker of his eyebrows, the way he tasted the words made it obvious what he meant. Right here, standing in front of me, he was thinking about how it felt to have sex with my daughter. I imagined him getting aroused even by this conversation, waiting for me to leave and summoning her to him. I wanted to be sick.

I stood over him, his head within my reach. 'You animal. You must know a girl of her age doesn't have the experience to make a judgment about any of this. She thinks it's romantic, she has no idea of the repercussions. But you are much, much older, Davis. Twenty-seven years older. You know exactly what the repercussions will be. You have to be evil to do this.'

He got to his feet again, lips twitching. 'Evil? I think that's a little gothic, darling. I can see you're more inspired than I thought by our nineteenth-century backdrop.'

I pushed him then, hand flat and forceful against his chest, and he stumbled slightly against the wood. 'Oh, fuck you! I couldn't care less about the bloody lighthouse! If you weren't such a coward we'd be having this conversation in London. In *my* house, the one that *you* have poisoned for me forever!'

He turned back to face me, blinking that long, weary blink of his, and in that moment I knew that as long as I lived I would never again hate someone with the same completeness as this. Just as he had stirred deeper desires in me, he now provoked darker loathing. 'And if you don't co-operate, you know Alistair will be back out here to make you. If she won't come of her own accord, he'll bring her back by force.'

'In which case it will be he who is breaking the law, won't it? And next time we won't hesitate to call the authorities, that I can promise you.'

We, the same appalling plural Roxy had taunted me with, just two letters and yet what a breach they opened up between us. I fought off the beginnings of tears, heard the choking in my voice as I made my final pleas. 'Do you want her to be estranged from her parents? Do you? And her brother, as well? For how long? How can that possibly benefit her?'

We both started at the echoed sound of shouts from below, the slap of steps, the reality of someone – two people or more – coming up towards us to enjoy the view. I couldn't bear to face their triumphant faces, to submit to the inevitable request to take a photograph of them. As I stood staring at Davis, no longer beseeching, no longer accusing, simply appalled that this man was in my life, in our lives, I calculated that I had about twenty seconds before we were no longer alone.

'Imagine she was your daughter, Davis, your flesh and blood. How would you feel?'

But he seemed to sense that my arguments – and my energies – were finally exhausted, that I was no longer expecting an answer. 'What can I say, Kate? It's her choice, not yours.'

I shook my head and turned to leave, flinging my last words over my shoulder without caring whether or not they reached them. 'No, Davis, it's yours.'

Chapter 26

I lost Matthew once. We were at the London Aquarium on the South Bank, he, Roxy and I. He was three, Roxy by then eleven. One minute the world was as it should have been, the two of them sitting at the foot of the main tank watching for the sharks to come close, their faces lit silver-blue as though by the moon; the next, it was tipped, suspended in a kind of blind hell before it tumbled from its axis altogether.

I had felt my nose running – I always seemed to have a cold in those days – and looked down for a moment to hunt in my bag for a tissue. When I looked up again there was still a young boy in the spot next to Roxy, but he was older, dark-haired, someone else's . . .

'Roxy! Roxy!' I reached through the ranks of tourists and grabbed for her shoulder. 'Where's Matthew?'

She frowned up at me and looked about, her eye resting on her new neighbour, taking in the family members beyond him, the adults to whom he must be attached. Then she came scrambling out through the crush and stood next to me, face lifted to mine for guidance.

'I thought he was with you,' she said.

'I thought he was with *you*. He was a second ago!'

Somewhere behind the growing panic I acknowledged the

336

wrongness of my treating her as my equal like this, as someone equally responsible, equally culpable. A co-parent. It was not fair, she was still a child herself. I should be reassuring her, but instead I wanted to rely on her, blame her.

'Oh my God, oh my God, where is he, Roxy? Anything could happen to him.' There'd been stories in the press recently of a gang snatching children from supermarkets, shopping malls, tourist attractions. In one case involving a three-year-old boy, by the time the abductors had emerged with their victim from the fire exit, they'd shaved his head and reclothed him from head to toe. I looked wildly about. How big was this place? It was impossible to tell, for in every direction there were staff doors and fire exits and routes through to further exhibits. A half-lit subterranean labyrinth, this couldn't be worse! We'd need to seal the whole place as soon as was humanly possible.

'I need to get the manager,' I cried, frantic.

Roxy's eyes were wide with confusion. 'Mum, should we look around for him ourselves first? He might still be—'

'You stay here,' I ordered, hardly hearing her, 'in case he wanders back, and I'll get help. He can't have gone far.'

But it was a Saturday, the city's schoolchildren had just broken up for half term, and the place was at full capacity. As I darted from zone to zone screaming his name, I could hardly be heard above the clamour.

Finally, sobbing, I found an assistant and managed to convey the basic facts.

'I'll get my manager,' she said, 'and we'll organise a search. Do you want to come with me?'

'I have to get Roxy, my daughter. I left her by the main tank, the one with the sharks, oh, I don't know which way it is now.'

'I'll take you there, don't worry. Follow me.'

But now Roxy wasn't where I'd left her, either. She must have decided to go off looking, after all. A single day-lit image flashed in the darkness: me, walking alone by the Thames, my children lost.

The girl squeezed my arm. 'We'll find them, don't worry. They can't both have disappeared. I'll take you upstairs to the meeting point and we'll get something out on the PA system.'

Then, it couldn't have been five minutes since this whole nightmare began, there came an announcement from somewhere above our heads: 'Could Roxy please come to the lobby area to meet her brother Matthew.'

It was repeated a second time and the girl turned to me hopefully. 'Is that them, do you think?'

'It must be.' Relaxing a fraction, I looked at her properly. She was young, no older than a sixth former. It seemed hardly any time since I'd been that age and yet how sorry I'd come to feel for myself about how my life had turned out. Well, never again! If the children were safe, that was all I cared about, all I wanted from life. As we hurried along the tunnels that took us back to the ground floor, my mind clasped the thought like a precious stone in a fist.

They were standing together by the customer services desk. Roxy had Matt's hand tightly in hers.

'He was with the stingrays,' a member of staff explained. This one was older and male and my helper automatically surrendered authority to him. 'He wasn't upset or anything, but it was obvious he wasn't with anyone. Luckily, he remembered his sister's name.'

Matthew often called out for Roxy instead of me – when he fell down in the garden or wanted a drink of water in the night, the times when only Mummy was supposed to do. She'd give him the cuddle he needed and mop his tears. I wondered if it was to do with all that hands-on help she'd given when he was a baby. He trusted her as completely as he did me.

'I thought I ought to come,' Roxy said to me anxiously, 'when I heard my name.'

I hardly heard her, gripping Matthew until he cried out in protest. 'You silly boy, you could have fallen in the water! You

338

must never wander away like that again, do you understand? This is very serious. We could have lost you!'

Roxy just stood silently by.

'Well done, Rox,' I said, reaching for her hand. 'You were brilliant, darling. Come here.' And I hugged her to me, too.

On the bus home she and I were both still a little shocked. I kept Matt on my knee, repeating in my head the words the man had said, 'It was obvious he wasn't with anyone,' as my cheeks flamed with shame. I watched Roxy in the seat across the aisle, her lovely profile, the upturned nose and low, solemn brow. I'd never lost her, never, but then at Matthew's age she would have been my only charge and on a trip like this, Alistair would have been there, too, two adults for one child, not one for two, as it was now. She would never have been out of sight, not for a second.

Everything was different after Ile de Ré. Not in the seismic, overwhelming way it would have been had she died – and for that I still remembered daily to thank the heavens – but in small ways, in every small way, in everything I said and did and thought and believed. Life just had a kind of Roxy Easton echo to it. Typing up case notes at work, for instance, I would have to stop my fingers from working of their own accord and making official the details of her disappearance, like one of those heartbreaking posters you saw on the bus. Name: Roxana Easton. Last seen: Thursday 25 October 2007. Age at time of disappearance: seventeen years, eight months. A photograph of how she looked then, or might reasonably look now. An artist's impression.

There had been contact in the five months since she'd gone, but precious little. I received a reply to about every twenty or so of the emails I sent, a page of news from me drawing a line from her. Nothing more than an acknowledgement of receipt really, a way of telling us she was still alive. I couldn't be sure that she even read my bulletins, and there were times when I felt as though I were writing a diary for a child of the future, someone who'd not yet been born and with whom my own life would not quite overlap.

There were phone calls, too, three or four, none revealing much, but each picked over and over afterwards for that vital sign that she might have changed her mind, changed her heart.

'Do you think you might come back?' I dared ask, just once.

The reply was scolding. 'Oh, don't start that again or I'll just hang up. You know the answer.'

'I just mean for a visit, to see Matt and your father and me. A weekend? An afternoon? We could send you the plane ticket.'

A short silence, and then, 'I don't think that's a good idea, do you?' But it didn't matter what I thought, she wasn't going to wait to hear, anyway.

She did not phone her father. In the beginning, within days of our return from France in early November, Alistair had had his solicitor send Davis a stern letter, frightening on the surface, but nothing more than bluff and bluster, and it went duly unacknowledged. School fees were paid for the spring term and her place held open, though we learned that Roxy had written to the head herself and told her she was never coming back. That re-ignited Alistair's fury, just as she must have known it would, but it was gradually overcome by the day-to-day demands of his work, his second wife, his second daughter – his second chance. As far as Roxy was concerned, I had recently come to believe that he was as close as he was ever going to get to peaceful resignation.

'She still might come back,' I told him. 'She definitely will, eventually.'

'Eventually,' he repeated. 'The question is, will we want her after all this?' And he was half-serious, as well. 'She's ripped this family apart.'

Well, she wouldn't be the first, I started to think, but I tended not to follow that line these days. I no longer had any desire to

340

cause Alistair pain, to pay him back. He had been paid back. Later, he rang me to say that he hadn't meant what he'd said, of course he hadn't. I told him that it went without saying.

Elizabeth's first Christmas came and went, a special occasion no matter what. Matthew and I visited on Christmas Eve to deliver her present and I signed the gift tag from the three of us, Kate, Roxy and Matthew. Tash was sweet: when she produced her presents she brought one out for Roxy, too, just slid it under the tree without saying anything, just in case.

In late February, Roxy's eighteenth birthday arrived. Matthew and I sent cards to the house in Ile de Ré, but we never knew if they'd been received, never heard how she'd chosen to spend her day, the day that finally released her technically to her own devices. By then, Matthew had stopped asking daily if she was coming home – or at least had stopped asking *me*. I suspected that he went to Tash instead to spare my feelings. He was too young to be worrying about sparing his mother's feelings, but there it was. And, if I was honest, Roxy had had a similar experience at that age, watching her mother struggle with the aftermath of another terrible abandonment, go through the motions, do all she could to protect herself from further exposure to life's risks. It was not the best example to set, not much better than Alistair's explosions, but I didn't know how else to behave.

Davis and I were still not divorced. Though he had inarguably committed adultery, I could not bring myself to name my own daughter in my petition. Camilla pointed out that, in time, I would be able to cite desertion, much less bloodthirsty. If nothing else, that was closer to how I actually felt. Whenever I met someone I hadn't seen for a while and was asked how married life was treating me, I just said very calmly that it hadn't worked out. Usually, people were sensible enough to leave it at that.

341

Chapter 27

The letter came first. The envelope bore a Parisian postmark and contained a single sheet of paper, the tissue-thin airmail kind I hadn't seen for years. The handwriting was unmistakably hers, but it looked considered, as though she'd taken a deep breath before picking up her pen. I couldn't wait to get upstairs, but tore it open in the lobby, standing by my pigeonhole in the same spot where once I'd lingered to chat with Davis, allowed myself to be intrigued by him, to want him.

It was a masterpiece of simplicity:

Dear Mum,

I hope you are well and that Matt is getting on all right at school.

I am not in Ile de Ré any more, I am not with Davis. We split up a while ago. Nothing serious happened, it just wasn't working out.

I know how it sounds, like I'm just walking away from something that caused so much fuss and expecting everyone to forget what I did to you. The only way I can justify it is to say that it didn't seem possible to me that you two could be together, not properly, even after you got married, not when he felt the way he did about me. It couldn't be real. I had a lot in my head and it felt really brilliant to be able to clear it. He really helped me do that. He was the only one who knew how.

I've been in Paris for a while. Don't worry, I have somewhere to stay and I have a job. Davis gave me some money as well. Whatever you think, he does care about me and he wanted to make sure I was safe.

He asked me to tell you he is sorry, even though he said you wouldn't accept an apology from either of us. That was something we disagreed about. I told him I knew you better. That's why I'm writing now. I wanted to know if you would be able to forgive me and let me come back? I'd really like to.

I'll wait to hear from you.
Love, Roxy

P.S. I've changed my mobile and email. The address to write to is below. Don't come, it's not where I am staying.

'"Nothing serious happened,"' Abi repeated, drily, when I showed her. 'Well, that's a joke. Why d'you think she's changed all her contacts? It sounds very cloak and dagger, doesn't it?'

'Presumably to shake him off,' I said. 'You don't think she's in danger, do you? Should I go to Paris and try to find her?'

Abi sent me a look that managed to be both tender and forbidding in equal measure. 'Absolutely not. Look where that got you last time. Besides, she sounds perfectly safe to me. And if she's taken money from him, they can't have fallen out that badly.' I watched as she read the letter a second time; I'd memorised it by now and could follow her progress phrase by phrase without needing to look at the paper. 'I hate to say it, Kate, but

I think it took a lot of courage to write this. She's surprised me. I don't think I could have said sorry like this at her age.'

I considered. I didn't think I'd had anything to apologise for at that age, at least not that I had noticed. 'She's grown up a bit, I suppose.'

Abi raised her eyebrows. 'Shame it had to be at your expense, eh?'

I thought about Naomi and Marianne, about the stories of stomach pumps that the school office tried so hard to stop from spreading. I thought about Alistair's digital diary with its rows of appointment slots and how a teenager had been prepared to carve up her day into the twelve sixty-minute slices of a corporate lawyer. I thought of the note I had sent within an hour of receiving her letter, just one line: *Of course I forgive you*. Posting it, I hadn't dared succumb to the elation that hovered around me like mist; by now I knew better than to make assumptions, to mistake the mist for stone.

'I think it's always at the mother's expense,' I said, 'one way or another.'

I was alone in the office when the message came. It was a Friday in early May, about a month after I'd received the letter. Part of my new role as supervisor was to be available to the volunteers for advice and support when Ethan was not, and any free time I had I spent assisting with our helpline. It was coming to the end of my shift and I'd just finished with a phone enquiry when I checked my mobile as I always did for any calls concerning Matthew. His routine was established now: on days when he had no sports practice he was enrolled in an after-school club, after which he would walk home with his friend Evert and stay with him until I picked him up at six.

There were three missed calls, about an hour apart and all from an unspecified private number. That was unusual, unusual enough to stir the beginnings of hope and panic, especially when

I saw the alert 'New voicemail' that followed. I felt myself tremble as I selected 'Listen'. I even found myself closing my eyes as if to protect myself from the words: 'Mum, it's me. I got your note. I'm coming back. My flight is first thing in the morning, Saturday morning, that is.' Pause. 'Could you meet me at Heathrow, maybe, at about seven-thirty?' Pause. 'Actually, don't worry if you don't get this, it's a bit last minute and you probably won't be up that early. I'll just make my own way home.'

They were the words I'd longed for continuously since she'd left but never quite expected to hear, not even since the arrival of the letter. I played it once more. It was still there, still the same. The third time I allowed myself to believe it.

Home. She would make her own way home!

Even in my joy, though, I remembered the necessary cautions. I wouldn't say anything to Matt (it would hardly be the first time I'd kept news from him) – it might raise hopes that might yet be dashed, or, worse, jinx the homecoming in some way. Alistair, too, could wait until she was actually here. He'd been sceptical about the letter, suggested it was nothing more than a prelude to some extravagant demand for money. He was pleased she was out of Davis's clutches, of course, but her long absence, her devastation of his dreams for her, so carefully constructed and so easily disregarded . . . no, that would take a little more forgiving.

Tash was out, as she was most nights, making a mockery of my original fears that she'd get under our feet if she moved in. I waited up for her and told her I had a last-minute work arrangement, a visit to a client's house very early the next morning to help prepare him for a visit from a social worker. This was not something I ever had to do, and nor did local social workers tend to make weekend visits, but Tash was tired and didn't spot the clues. She offered to see to Matthew before I could even ask.

The Tube journey to Heathrow was lost forever; I might have been transported by magic carpet for all I knew. I was the prisoner who'd been pardoned, the cripple whose paralysis had been miraculously lifted, the little girl who'd been waiting for Christmas all her life and finally been told it was here. And all the while I still dreaded, not a trick exactly, but rather that the truth was not quite to be trusted, not until I saw her, not until she was next to me and I could see that her eyes matched her words.

At the terminal, pitched among the thousands of others who were departing, arriving, separating, reuniting, I felt fear of a new kind. What would happen if I missed her, if she looked completely different or I glanced away at the wrong moment? Would she do as she'd suggested and find her own way to the flat, or would my opportunity be gone forever? Without a phone number to reply to, I had been unable to let her know that I'd got her voicemail and intended to be there to meet her. Might my lack of a reply have caused her to change her mind, to doubt me after all? Studying the arrivals screen I realised I didn't even know where she was coming from. Paris, presumably, but most of the early arrivals were long-haul flights from India and the Far East, followed by one from Madrid, another from Frankfurt . . . the list went on, minute by minute, covering two monitors, until there it was: 07.15 Paris. It had not yet landed.

I stationed myself with the blank-eyed taxi drivers and gulp-throated loved ones in the roped-off area by the arrivals doors. I bought a large coffee I didn't drink and a thick magazine I didn't read, though one was soon chewed at the lid and the other frayed at the edges. My head nodded up and down like a puppet's every time the automatic doors whisked open to sweep forward the next knot of travellers and trolleys. All I could do was wait and remember to breathe in and out. I was reminded of those long hours in Saint Martin spent sitting and watching, bones getting cold as the light faded, eyes trying not to blink.

And then there she was, sooner than I expected, mercifully alone.

'Mum!'

'Oh! Roxy!'

She hurried over without a moment's hesitation. 'You're here, I'm so glad!' Her face was anxious and she was beginning to cry, but not the tears of a survivor of trauma or a victim of crime, more the brief bubbling over of a child exhausted by a long journey and longing to be tucked up to sleep.

I helped guide her around the barrier of other greeters and spent a minute just looking at her. I stopped short of putting a finger to my lips, but I would have done had she tried to interrupt my study. Her hair was shorter, at her neck, the fringe tacked off her forehead with a series of grips, and her straight, serious brows and flecked eyes were completely free of make-up. She wore a thick winter coat and carried a single canvas holdall, resting now on the floor at her feet.

Then I stepped forward and took her in my arms. She smelled of alien brands of shampoo and chewing gum, but she *felt* exactly the same. 'Of course I'm here,' I said, fiercely, 'I've always been here, every moment.'

Her nose snuffled into my hair. 'I'm so glad,' she said again. 'Were you on the Paris flight?'

She nodded. 'The train was booked up. I couldn't get a seat.'

We stepped apart. It occurred to me at that moment that I'd never seen them together, Roxy and Davis, not since before they'd left. It would help, I knew, in forgetting that they ever had been. 'I didn't bring the car,' I said, 'I thought we'd take a taxi home.'

She looked at my left hand, which still gripped the unread magazine. 'But your arm is better?'

'Yes, it wasn't as serious as it looked. I just never got back into the habit of driving. I guess I've lost my nerve.' I went to take her bag, but she insisted on carrying it herself. Her fist gripped the handles, the long sleeves of her coat falling down to her knuckles, and for some reason I thought of the charm bracelet. It had become for me a talisman of her relationship with Davis, even though I'd never proved – never asked, in fact – that it was he who had given it to her. I had resolved never to do so.

We walked towards the exit doors, neither of us speaking. I sensed that she was as determined as I was to avoid any kind of hysterical scene. At least I'd told myself I was determined, just as I'd told myself that I should learn from what had happened in France and give her time, not bombard her (and scare her off) with the force of my relief, my censure, my curiosity. But now that she was here all my questions stacked up in my throat, choking me, telling me that my time to learn the truth was limited and should be seized here and now. 'What happened?' I asked, simply. 'Why did you leave him?'

Though she didn't break her step, I felt her hesitate. 'It just . . . it just all got a bit intense.' She caught herself, slid me a sideways look. She realised how it must have sounded, like she was expecting to pass herself off as a daughter returning late from a party, or from a weekend away with friends. 'I think . . .' She paused again, settling on her phrasing. '. . . I think the excitement was all at the beginning.'

I nodded. 'Is he still there, in Saint Martin? Did he try to come after you?'

She didn't answer, knew that she didn't need to, I supposed. Of course he'd gone after her. His own flight from me, from his home town and his established life, had been done with breathtaking ease, but it had not been done lightly. He'd understood the magnitude of the desertion. And now that he, in turn, had been deserted, he would have done exactly as I had: followed her, begged her, scanned those implacable eyes for flickers of lost loyalty. And he'd appreciate the symmetry of the story, too, that much I felt quite confident in assuming. The question was whether he would consider it complete.

I began again. 'He hasn't been causing any trouble, has he?'

Again she risked a sidelong look – to see, perhaps, if I was going to acknowledge the absurd understatement of my question – before she answered. 'He was upset, yes. But I changed my number, moved around a bit. He got the message. I mean, you can't force someone—' Again she broke off, leaving me to fill in the rest: you can't force someone to want you, to love you, to stay with you.

'Mum?'

'Yes.'

'Would it be OK if we don't talk about it? Not yet, anyway? I'm just so tired.'

'Of course.' She would never want to talk about it, I knew that, and not only because guilty confessions were painful to make, but also because she was bored with it, it was as simple as that. She was eighteen and her life was ahead of her, not behind.

'Did you tell Dad I'm back? And Matt?'

'Not yet.' Again, I sensed her reading my thoughts: I wanted to judge for myself first; I didn't want to give them joy and then take it away again, to deepen the shadow over another day; I wanted to be certain of you.

Outside she began to move towards to the yellow lights of the taxi rank, but I caught her arm and held her still. To our right I was aware of our reflection in the glass wall of the terminal building, the two dark heads, the two sets of serious eyes. 'Are you sure coming back is what you want, Roxy?'

She made no attempt to remove either her arm or her gaze. 'I'm sure.'

In the taxi, she relaxed, leaned back into her corner and looked out of the window. She stretched her legs and crossed her feet; they were in the same boots she'd worn when she left. I couldn't stop staring at her face, had to cover my mouth with my hand to stop myself repeating her name aloud over and over. I couldn't get over the physical reality of her being here, sitting with me in a taxi, sharing space, travelling to the same place together. The girl who began it all and almost ended it all and who never stopped filling every bit of me in between.

It was going to be a clear day. The sun hadn't been up for long and as it rose over the city ahead of us it was still pale enough for us to be able to look directly at it. Roxy's eyes reflected its flame, moving now and then as they tracked its position in the sky.

I looked too, remembering a childhood game she'd liked to play in the car when she was very little. Alistair would be driving, she in the back with her retinue of toys. They called it Catch the Sun. You could only play it early in the morning, like this, or near sunset, when the sun was low enough to be chased through the windscreen.

'Look at that big ball behind the trees,' she'd said that first time, not recognising it for its colour, darker and redder than she'd seen it before.

We'd laughed at her innocent wonder. 'Where's it gone? Oh, no, Rox, it's going to come and bounce on top of the car!'

Then, on endless occasions afterwards, 'We've lost it again! Someone else has caught it!'

'No, there it is!'

'I saw it first!'

'*I* did!'

One time, Alistair veered completely from the planned route, chasing it over the western horizon as the squeals from the back seat got more and more excited. I think she really thought we'd catch it, just scoop it from the sky with our hands and carry it away with us. Maybe Alistair did, too, just for a moment, powered by the confidence his daughter had in him that he could do anything she asked.

A sign for central London came into view and the cab switched lanes. The sun was now directly visible over the driver's left shoulder.

'Look Rox,' I said, breaking the silence. 'The sun. This time we really might catch it.'

She didn't say anything, she didn't even nod, but I knew from the light in her eyes that she'd heard me.

Coming in 2011

THE HOMEBREAKER

Louise Candlish

He saved one life – but left another in ruins

On a perfect summer's day in Paris, tourists on a boat trip on the
Seine watch in horror as drama unfolds. A small boy has fallen
overboard and disappeared below the surface of the water, while on
deck his mother stands frozen to the spot, unable to act. As the 'Man
Overboard' cry goes up another passenger leaps into the river and
risks his own life to make an extraordinary rescue. The child is
returned unharmed to his mother and the hero reunited with his
wife – his wife of only a few days, for the couple are
in Paris on their honeymoon.

It should be a happy ending for all concerned – except no one is
able to let go of the episode. Soon, both families have been turned
upside down by an unbreakable new bond, a bond that transforms
one woman's life beyond her dreams just as it devastates another's.
Then, as things finally look like they're settling, a third woman
enters the frame. She was also on the boat that day in June,
and she remembers events quite differently . . .

'Utterly compelling. We love, love, love Louise Candlish's writing'
Heat

978-0-7515-4355-1

Out now

OTHER PEOPLE'S SECRETS

Louise Candlish

Everybody wants the truth . . . until they find it

Ginny and Adam Trustlove arrive on holiday in Italy torn apart by
personal tragedy. Two weeks in a boathouse on the edge of peaceful
Lake Orta is exactly what they need to restore their faith in
life – and each other.

Twenty-four hours later, the silence is broken. The Sale family have
arrived at the main villa: wealthy, high-flying Marty, his beautiful
wife Bea, and their privileged, confident offspring. It doesn't take
long for Ginny and Adam to be drawn in, especially when the
teenage Pippi introduces a new friend into the circle. For there is
something about Zach that has everyone instantly beguiled, something that loosens old secrets – and creates shocking new ones.

And, yet, not one of them suspects that his arrival in their lives
might be anything other than accidental . . .

'A brilliantly told, emotionally charged tale'
Dorothy Koomson

978-0-7515-4354-4

Out now

BEFORE WE SAY GOODBYE

Louise Candlish

'What would you risk for a second chance at happiness?'

The day Maggie Lane dies, she leaves her daughter Olivia
a piece of dangerous information: the address of Olivia's first love,
Richie Briscoe. Olivia has not seen Richie for over twenty years,
not since his desertion of her as a teenager almost destroyed her
for good. She cannot understand why her mother's last act
should be to stir up an old drama like him.

Convinced that the message conceals hidden secrets, Olivia sets off
for the idyllic seaside village where Richie now lives with his
young daughter Wren. Soon she is falling for him all over again,
and finds in little Wren the daughter she never had.

But there is a problem. For Olivia already has a family – a husband
and two sons. Where does this second chance
at happiness put them?

'It shouldn't be long before Louise Candlish's page-turning,
thought-provoking reads make her a household name'
Glamour

978-0-7515-4038-3

Other bestselling titles available by mail